USS Franklin

When Worlds Collide

USS Hamilton Series
Book 8

Mark Wayne McGinnis

Published by Avenstar Productions: info@avenstar.net

PAPERBACK:

• **ISBN-13** : 979-8989461936

To join Mark's mailing list, jump to: http://eepurl.com/bs7M9r

Visit Mark Wayne McGinnis at: http://www.markwaynemcginnis.com

Created with Vellum

 Created with Vellum

I know not with what weapons World War III will be fought, but World War IV will be fought with sticks and stones.
Albert Einstein

Chapter 1

Tidal Basin Massacre
Earth, Washington DC

Captain Galvin Quintos

Present Day...

I n the depths of history, where devastating strikes echo through time, names reverberate: Oklahoma City, Hiroshima, Pearl Harbor, The World Trade Center. They're not just places. They're scars. And today, a new one was cleaved into the skin of history: *Tidal Basin*.

But let's not sprint to the finish line just yet. There's a tale to spin here, so let's kick off at the moment where everything went sideways... where everything went to shit.

I still had an hour before my meeting with EUNF U.S. Space Navy's Executive Five-Star Fleet Admiral, Cyprian Block, but I had to move it—no time to dawdle. I'd been issued a new ship. An amazing ship... but one I'd barely had five minutes to take in before being called back down to Earth's surface. Apparently, the old man wanted to talk to me before we left Earth's orbit for deployment. To be honest, I had no idea what he needed to tell me. What was so important he couldn't have just called me on my TAC-Band and be done with it?

And that's when *it* happened.

Thinking back, there'd been an early indication that the world, as I knew it, would soon end. But at the time, in the moment, all I could do was stare, momentarily paralyzed, mouth hanging open, an ape contemplating the splitting of an atom.

The year being 2184, hell, it wasn't unusual to see an occasional high altitude space transport descending from low orbit. Or even a squadron of bright red Arrow fighters racing across Earth's horizon in a supersonic blur.

So anyway, back to the world ending. As I crossed the street there in midtown DC, my first indication that something was off, totally out of the ordinary, batshit crazy, was the... *how do I describe this...* the sky started to shimmer, like twinkling fairy dust coming alive from an unseen magic wand.

All that wouldn't have been so bad. Maybe it was some kind of natural phenomena, like a solar flare apparition, or maybe an out of the ordinary Northern Lights anomaly.

But then everything went dark. Not just that it was midnight, and the streetlights hadn't kicked on yet—no, I'm talking pitch black, no starlight, no illumination from a distant sliver of Moon... this was black as if one was deep underground, like deep in a coal mine and your lantern cuts out.

When the lights flickered back on a moment later the midday sun streaming down from above, it was wrong. Everything was wrong. The sun, typically warm, golden, and iridescent... it was none of that. Now it was unnaturally bluish white, blindingly stark, and, seemingly, farther away. The Moon was there, but in the wrong place for this time of year. The sky? Anyone who can see knows what the sky looks like, right? Well, the sky was no longer blue. It was now some kind of violet, later I would find out the particular hue is called *Tyrian*.

Still standing midway into the crosswalk at Washington Boulevard and 2nd Street South, I paused. This area, known as the *Mixing Bowl*, was just a stone's throw from EUNF Plaza and the Pentagon. Lifting my palms, I braced against the unfolding chaos as if I could ward off the impending doom.

Then seeing my fellow pedestrians in a similar state of dismay, I knew at the very least, what I was experiencing wasn't just happening in my head.

As a seasoned captain in the U.S. Space Navy, I assure you, I can distinguish Alliance military crafts by sight and sound. The distant thrumming I now heard was unmistakably that of a Cyclone Death Fighter.

Earth was under attack...

The roar from above was deafening, a thunderous cacophony. Typical city sounds were lost beneath it: the AirCar cross-traffic, the rhythmic hammering from a nearby construction site, the hurried steps of DC commuters. Then I caught sight of them in a tight formation—Cyclone Death Fighters. Seven of them with their matte black hulls, sinister-looking in the bizarre Tyrian light, descending like ravenous raptors. They didn't just fly—they owned the sky, slicing through it with predatory grace. And then, without a hint of warning, they struck.

The initial plasma beams tore through the serene waters of the iconic Tidal Basin, streaking toward the Washington Monument their impact sending shockwaves billowing across the National Mall. I watched in horror as stone and U.S. history crumbled to dust. My ears rang, the sound muffled by the ensuing chaos, screams weaving through the cacophony of destruction.

Everyone scattered. I lunged forward, propelled by adrenaline. My instincts were to protect, to save lives—but the devastation was too great, too overwhelming. The Lincoln Memorial took a direct hit next, the iconic figure of Abraham Lincoln disintegrating under the assault. More history evaporating in real-time.

The Smithsonian Castle, with its fairy-tale turrets, heavy wooden double-doors, and majestic stone arches, erupted in flames. People poured from the doors like ants from a stomped hill, panic-stricken, their screams barely audible over the relentless barrage. I grabbed a kid by his hand, no more than ten, alone and frozen in the middle of Independence Avenue. "Move!" I barked; the urgency clear. We ducked into an alleyway, narrowly avoiding the debris raining down from above. A man, clearly a tourist given his khakis, and now-bloodied *I ♥ DC* T-shirt cried out for his son. He zeroed in on us with the precision of a sniper, sweeping the boy away from me, and taking him up into his arms.

Circling around in perfect consort, the Varapin Fighters were systematically causing massive destruction and doing so with cold efficiency. Next, they moved to the west end of the National Mall, to the Capitol... beams of destruction sweeping across its dome. The bastion of American democracy was obliterated in an instant, becoming a fiery vortex. In that moment something broke within my psyche. Something dear had been taken from me—from all of us.

I found myself outside Union Station, the once-busy hub now a war zone. A mother, clutching her baby, cried out as a pillar collapsed beside her. I lunged, pulling them back as the rubble crashed down where they had stood just a moment before. We were a stream of frantic souls, looking for cover where there was none to be found.

Nearby, a man in a business suit, clutching his briefcase like a shield, sprinted past. His eyes met mine, wide with terror, a silent plea for help I couldn't answer. There were too many. Too much to do and not enough time.

The Cyclone Death Fighters circled for another pass, their engines an ominous hum. This wasn't an invasion; it was an extermination. A death knell for a city, a world I once knew and loved. The same thoughts kept replaying in my head: *How had this Varapin force arrived within the Solar System without being detected?*

I rallied a group of survivors, ushering them into the relative safety of the subterranean Metro. We huddled in the darkness, the earth trembling above us. A young woman, her face smeared with soot and tears, clutched my arm. "What do we do?" she gasped.

"We survive," I said, more to myself than to her. "We find a way to fight back." But even as I spoke, I could see the doubt in her eyes, reflecting my own.

I heard them overhead, the Death Fighters making another sweep, their beams tearing through concrete and steel as if made of paper. The air within the Metro was thick with smoke and the scent of scorched earth.

Hiding's not an option. Rising to my feet, I left behind the remnants of survival—those few souls, huddled in solitude, the darkness weighing heavy on them. I ascended the fractured concrete, emerging from the Metro's depths into the day's eerie light. In the distance, the Potomac was a cauldron, its waters churning, sending up clouds of steam as if the city itself was breathing its last gasp.

Yet, even in the thick of despair, a spark of defiance flickered. A band of soldiers, the last stand of a National Guard unit, unleashed their fury upon the sky. With steely resolve, they fired their Shredder weapons, hurling plasma bolts into the heavens—a valiant but desperate stand against the inevitable.

I peered out into the smoldering hellscape, my mind racing. The Varapin had brought the war to us, yes, but they'd also brought it to me, *Captain Galvin Quintos*. And if I had anything to say about it, they were going to regret this day. They were going to pay—and pay with their lives.

From behind came a sudden tremble. A plume of dust and debris billowed into the air. The same Metro I had just escaped had collapsed. Undoubtedly, all those I'd left behind were now dead—more victims of the attack. *No time to dwell on that now.* It was time to move, to do more than survive. To fight.

This day would later be called the *Tidal Basin Massacre*. Yes, a cataclysm beyond description. But it was also an awakening for humanity. This day, inch by fallen inch, we would come back with a vengeance, or die trying.

Chapter 2

Roosevelt National Forest, Colorado
Captain Galvin Quintos

Prior to Tidal Basin Massacre...

Sitting within the open flap of my tent, late afternoon giving way to dusk, I tried not to think about certain things. To what end... it wasn't like I could change history. Viv's leaving had been the straw that broke the proverbial camel's back. And no, I do not want to talk about that... about her. But there were other factors that had prompted my escape into the wild: year after year of constant war... the stresses of battle, of command... seeing too many people I care about die. And, no, I don't want to talk about Hardy.

So why was I here... deep within this mountainous, wooded, and totally uninhabited area of northern Colorado? Good question. More on that later.

The Rawah Wilderness is located within the Roosevelt National Forest. It's tucked away in the northern part of the state, not too far from the border with Wyoming. Here there is a blend of rugged mountain terrain with dense, lush forests, making it an ideal destination for one seeking true solitude. One, being me.

I'd considered going the authentic route, traveling as the original explorers of this territory had done hundreds of years prior, having just the bare basics: a canvas tent, a few wool blankets to sleep under, maybe a cast iron skillet to place over an open fire. Perhaps even an old, sturdy Winchester Model 1873 rifle, and, of course, a dependable horse to ride, a pack mule in tow. As a student of history, primarily American History, I'd planned on making this lone expedition into the wild for a number of years, and now I was here. I was doing it.

Sure, I had a good trail horse, that was my only connection with those early rustic explorers. That was essential—but the rest of it? Nah. Instead, I'd spent an ungodly number of credits on my excursion equipment. The very best, most technologically advanced one could buy in the year 2187. Hell, my plan was to escape deep into the wilderness for a year... just to start. Longer if that suited me.

At this moment I was sitting beneath a nano-fabric tent: Ultra-lightweight, self-erecting and made from heat-regulating, damage-resistant smart fabric. The shroud automatically adjusted temperature and humidity, which was great... except when I secretly wanted to complain about being too hot or too cold like a proper camper. You'll love this part... above me was a protective/invisible energy barrier around the campsite for safety and privacy.

Time has flown by. I've been out here for over a month now, maybe longer. Gazing across an alpine glacial lake and craggy Rawah peaks in the distance, a contemplative state crept over me. *Will I ever return to U.S. Space Navy duty?* I shook my head, finding no justifiable reason to ever do so. That last mission upon *USS Lincoln* had pretty much taken all I had to give. No. Here, I found contentment, a steady presence. Happiness? Well, maybe that's too much. Contentment will do. Yes, contentment is enough.

And I wasn't really alone here, not by any measure. With an abundance of elk, moose, and mule deer, not to mention the occasional black bear, I had plenty of company. Smaller mammals like beavers, marmots, and pikas skittered all around... and don't get me started on the birds—woodpeckers, hawks, and a bald eagle once in a while. Most evenings I'd catch my dinner from a nearby lake or stream, catching some trout, including brook and native cutthroat.

It might rain tonight. A chill had snuck up on the campsite... soon, fall would surrender its vibrant yellows and oranges to winter's subdued palette. I scratched at my full beard, pulled my heated blanket in tighter around me.

I should build a fire. I'd collected an assortment of dried branches and pinecones from beyond the nearby tree line. Assembled a circle of cantaloupe-sized stones. But I was tired— I'd get a fire going first thing in the morning.

I'D RISEN WITH THE MORNING SUN. HAD SOME breakfast, packed up the campsite, saddled my trail horse, Betsy, and loaded up my robot pack mule, which was a model 'Climbo-9000.' Again, the best, most expensive mountaineering droid modern credits could buy. I basically had enough gadgets and gizmos to supply a small village. Galvin Quintos, lone deep woodlands explorer, but with robots.

I'm a sucker for a good sales pitch and Buck at Trail World Boulder had gone full throttle on the Climbo 9000's virtues. The contraption's exoskeleton, a fusion of carbon and titanium, rendered it both light and unyielding. Its synthetic muscles were a marvel, ensuring the droid's movements mirrored that of its flesh and bone brethren's form, enabling it to conquer erratic terrains with a grace that belied its mechanical nature.

Climbo's core—a fusion cell, I was told, could outlast five seasons, its power quietly reclaimed by turning kinetic motion into more miles.

The brain was no less impressive—a quantum processor that learned every nuance of the wilderness and navigated with unwavering precision. Its physical storage was a marvel, too, regulating temperature for any cargo, all while maintaining an even keel. It could carry 800 pounds and still tread lightly over the underbrush.

With so many quiet evenings and not much to do, I'd read through Climbo's impressive specs. It had quite the communication suite: satellite connectivity, distress signals, secure channels. Yet, for all that was available tech, these systems remained unused, their potential untapped as I moved alone through the wild. Sure, periodically I'd hear the soft *ping* of one more message being saved within Climbo's comms center. But who did I want to talk to? No one. Viv was gone. And Hardy was little more than floating space junk somewhere back within the Liquilid Empire Star System.

Back to Climbo, and you're going to love this—it's called the Drone Companion: a deployable scouting drone that has all the typical modern drone features, aerial surveillance, mapping, and wildlife monitoring. But its real selling feature? 3D holographic projectors that allow the futuristic camper, that's me, to see historical people and/or events along the trail as they would have occurred at that time. Buck's add-on sales pitch had me at "... blending history and technology."

The portly salesman, with his snap-button shirt and multi-

pocketed trousers, had clearly never left the safety and comfort of the retail space. Even for those of you that don't like camping, it was a remarkable spiel: This technology enables modern explorers to witness historical events and interact with figures from the past as though they were actually present. Imagine a journey through space and time ... one that enriches your understanding of the land and its stories. Riding upon your mount, you'll look to your right and see a band of Native Americans hunting... bows raised, arrows nocked ... and off in the distance, a herd of elk fleeing into the woodlands.

Listening to Buck, I'd marveled at the now-hovering, spherical drone. It had activated a blue-hued life-sized projection of Native Americans riding bareback, hunting in the wild— projected just a few feet away onto the men's winter coats section of the store...

So, um ... Buck, these advanced projectors, where are they ...

Embedded tech right into that drone there. It interfaces with Climbo, of course, and taps into vast historical databases, synthesizing recorded history, archaeological data, and environmental analysis. Everything geo-located right to your position. Unlike the ridiculous 3D eyewear of the past, these projectors don't require any personal wearables and are controlled through voice commands, gestures, or even neural links if you'd like.

I'd held up a hand at the time, my mind reaching maximum capacity—I'd heard enough. *I'll take it ... add it to the bill.*

For the next month of travel, my plan was to follow Colorado's Vallecito Creek Trail, experiencing intermittent weekly camping stints along the way. Betsy, Climbo, and I would delve into the Weminuche Wilderness, embarking on what promised to be a fascinating, multi-layered adventure across three historical timeframes. On the agenda: the history of the Ute Native American Tribes, then retracing Pike's Expedition, and, finally, delving into the era of the Colorado Gold Rush.

There was one issue that had already reared its ugly head several times. Betsy and Climbo didn't get along. In fact, it was evident they hated each other. Contrary to expectations, it wasn't Betsy, the noble American Quarter Horse, causing strife —it was Climbo. This mechanical mule tormented Betsy incessantly. From near-constant nudging of her hindquarters on the trail, to mimicking my clucking tongue sounds, confusing Betsy about whether to speed up, to unleashing ear-piercing bugle sounds at dawn, sending Betsy rearing up. While signaling daybreak, these disruptive dawn alerts shattered the serenity of the day. It seemed Climbo's AI harbored a troublesome playful streak, more irritating than entertaining to poor Betsy.

For the past hour, we followed a game trail through forested pines. We emerged as dappled sunlight gave way to a late afternoon sunset, revealing an open pasture sprawled before us. From behind, I heard one of Climbo's many compartment doors click open, followed by the telltale humming of the deployable scouting drone now rising into the air. I gave Betsy a couple of calming pats: "It's alright, girl... everything's fine."

The drone's soft hum turned into a low growl, and in the fading light, specters formed at the tree line, an unexpected echo of a time long buried. I stiffened, every sense on edge as the past collided with the present, images sharp as the cold, mountain air.

Ute warriors appeared first, so real I held back a gasp—their eyes fierce, bodies taut with the readiness of the hunt. They moved with a stealth that sent a shiver down my spine, their bows drawn, muscles like coiled springs. Tomahawks lay in leather sheaths around their waists. A visceral reminder of nature's unforgiving law: kill or be killed.

A cry pierced the air, a high-pitched alarm from within the nearby camp, shattering any illusion of peace. Families of another tribe... hunters—men, women, and children—scattered, a chaotic flurry of survival instincts as they grasped for weapons ... for anything that might save them. I could almost smell the acrid tang of fear.

A hunter's gaze met mine, a challenge across centuries—my breath caught. Gunfire shattered the air, merciless and jarring. Another hunter's—a woman's—cry pierced the chaos, sharp and raw. She surged forward to where a small boy lay—a crumpled heap on the chilled, dusty earth. Her son. A bullet had stilled his youth, the tomahawk he wielded dropped at his side.

She flung herself over the boy, her body a desperate shield. Her hands searched for life upon his small chest but found none. Her gaze locked toward the approaching slaughter. With nowhere to hide, the battle raged on around her. But in her eyes, now, there was no fear, only the abyss of loss.

Ute warriors suddenly hesitated, their tomahawks heavy with doubt as the hunters' rifles reverberated, *CRACK! CRACK! CRACK!* seemingly coming from every direction. I heard a young Native American girl's grief-laden cries, a haunting sound instantly filling me with dread as it lingered here within this once pictorial mountain scene. Her warrior father sprawled, his limbs splayed out, clearly dead. A crimson splotch glistened above his left eye.

And then I saw them—white settlers—spectral pioneers looking to claim the land as their own; they were advancing. The clash of cultures, a storm of tension and fear. A violent massacre unfolded that I was powerless to stop. I watched, horrified as more blood was shed ... cries rose, and the earth seemed to mourn.

I sat there perched upon my saddle, a witness to a history that was hard to watch and impossible to turn away from. The drone had no agenda, but its display had ignited a fire within me, a burning need to understand, to remember. The way both tribes struggled to defend the land they laid claim to and preserve their way of life was profound. The battle that ensued, far from black and white, was undeniably tragic.

As the horrific scene finally, and mercifully, faded and the deployable scouting drone settled back into one of Climbo's hidden compartments, I continued to stare. The pasture returned now to its glorious state of calm. Melodious bird warbles and the chittering of small creatures came alive from the tree line.

But the message rang out, unmistakable as a cannon blast. The violence I'd just witnessed, brutal and raw, was a mere whisper compared to what the Varapin could unleash on Earth.

"What am I doing here? What the fuck am I doing here?"

Chapter 3

SS Garland Page
Forland 545 System

Captain Larry Sterkerbrand

Prior to Tidal Basin Massacre...

For the past few deployments, SS *Garland Page* had increasingly shown her age. If it were possible for an old space trawler like her to embody decrepitude, one might imagine *Garland Page* with an oxygen bottle slung over one shoulder, supported by a walker. Its fluorescent yellow tennis balls would slide across scuffed linoleum tiles.

A ghostly leviathan, her hull was a rust-brown canvas depicting a brutal life amongst the stars. Visible were the scars and dents from a million tiny asteroid collisions, the bumpings and grindings of copious far-too-narrow docking bays, and the effects of near-constant, relentless cosmic radiation. While sure, all of that was a testament to survival, at the end of the day, the old vessel was just too beat-to-shit to still be making these kinds of deep space runs.

Consequently, she had drifted for a solid seven days. In the eerily silent engine compartment, five engineering crew personnel labored to cobble together a makeshift variable plasma igniter.

Captain Larry Sterkerbrand, known as Sterk to most, felt as worn and weathered as the ship itself. Nearing 73, retirement lingered on his mind. But then, what would he turn to? The ship had been his life, as binding as any marriage, but without the reminders to take out the garbage, avoid speaking with his mouth full, or curbing his drinking.

Ambling forward, he stepped within the main corridor that spanned the ship's length. Several years past, the crew had painted the bulkheads, the *overhead*, even the deckplates. But without removing the old paint, sanding it down, and applying that essential primer coat, it now resembled a dreadful mosaic of peeling layers, reminiscent of a snake shedding its skin. A groan emanated from somewhere astern, sounds Sterk was more than familiar with. It was as if *Garland Page* was talking directly to him, letting him know she was tired, or had some new ache or ailment.

"I know Ol' girl... I know," he said, letting out a resigned breath.

Even in his prime, Sterk had never been a handsome man. Now, with his seemingly ever-growing bulbous nose, ruddy cheeks marked by broken capillaries, and teeth yellowed from tobacco, it was evident he had a penchant for rye whisky and budget cigars. But what Sterk lacked in looks—or even at present, a functional space vessel—the man made up for with admiration from his crew. Sterk, with all his faults, his excesses, his often crude, and definitely politically incorrect humor, the man was adored by all of the 49 onboard crew.

The general crew consensus was that when SS *Garland Page* finally gives up the ghost, Captain Larry Sterkerbrand would likely do the same.

He entered the bridge with an air of quiet authority. His eyes, seasoned by years of interstellar travel, scanned the compartment with an almost palpable intensity. The bridge, a relic of a bygone era, hummed with an enduring functionality. Its antiquated consoles flickered with steadfast resolve, a testament to the ship's storied past. Eyebrows raised at the sight of Julia manning the helm control and Gordon at Comms. Each held a steaming cup of coffee, a moment of respite amidst the tension.

Julia White and Gordon Lansbury were on summer break from the Nikola Tesla Institute for Quantum Advancement, also known as NTIQA. Located on the fringes of New Chicago and named after the iconic inventor and visionary, the institute was a beacon of scientific progress. Both Julia and Gordon, albeit young, were acclaimed scientists in their own right, and undeniably overqualified for their current roles. Yet, driven by the pressing need for funds for the upcoming semester's tuition, they found themselves here. For Sterk, finding able crew in the twenty-second century had never been easy. Trolling Earth campuses for eager and broke students had been beneficial for all concerned.

"Made you a cup, Cap," Julia said, gesturing with her chin toward the small side nook, reserved for just such purposes.

"Goddamn! Gordon, this is why I love this woman. Maybe I should have married her twenty years ago..." Sterk said.

"Maybe, but she would have been what... six, seven years old then?" Gordon said with a cringe.

"I meant if *I* was twenty years younger... not her."

Julia rolled her eyes, "So you would have been fifty something to my..."

Sterk waved away the comment, "Forget I said anything." Dawdling at the coffee nook for several minutes, he contemplated doing the unthinkable. Having to send out a distress call, get a space tug out here, haul *Garland Page* to the nearest spaceport. *There goes the entire profit margin for the month.*

"Cap..." Julia said.

Sterk glanced over to the young woman who was now leaning forward, squinting toward the forward viewport. "We entered protected sanctuary space three days ago."

"I know that... we'll pay the fine. Couldn't be helped," the older man said with a resigned shrug.

Julia's eyes betrayed a simmering unease, a flickering shadow of apprehension. "No... what I'm saying is we're not alone out here."

Sterk, cup in hand, approached the front of the bridge and stood looking out through the viewport. "What is this system?" he asked.

Gordon now on his feet, joined Sterk at the viewport. "Forland 545 system... seven organically emerging worlds, non-intelligent lifeforms... one small yellow dwarf star."

The sight of the seven large spacecraft looming ominously in the distance sent a jolt of alarm through Sterk. The air on the bridge crackled with tension, their eyes locked on the unknown threat.

"Who the hell are they?" Sterk said before taking a sip of his hot brew.

Julia clucked her tongue, "Maybe someone we don't want to, um... encounter."

Both Sterk and Gordon glanced back at her.

"Sensors are coming back with three possibilities... none of them good. They could be the Norquill, the Borgone, or... the Varapin."

"Have they detected us?" Sterk asked.

"We're running quiet... drives are down, no recent comms activity," she said.

Gordon shook his head, "*Garland Page* at half a kilometer long and 1.5 million metric tons... guarantee we haven't gone unnoticed, Cap."

Sterk rubbed at the three-day stubble on his chin. He swallowed. "What do we have in the way of docking thrusters?"

"N2 levels are already low..." Julia said, referring to N_2H_4, which is basically Hydrazine. "We blow our wad now; we risk our reverse thrusters for docking later."

"Yeah well, on our current trajectory, we'll be sitting on their laps within the hour," Sterk said. *God... please don't let them be Varapin.*

"What the hell ..." Gordon said.

Sterk's eyes went wide.

The world, one about the size of Mars within the Solar System, and second closest to the yellow dwarf was now shimmering, pulsating.

They both gasped in unison.

A Klaxon came to life overhead, the bridge now bathed in the dim glow of emergency lights.

"What the fuck..." Sterk said under his breath.

"What we're seeing is a quantum resonance field enveloping that planet," Julia said, tapping at her control board. "Readings are off the charts."

"That's impossible," Gordon said. "You can't envelop a whole damn world..." but his words faded, sentence unfinished.

They watched as space seemed to warp, contort, then snap back with a ferocious energy. In an instant, the planet vanished, then reappeared at the far end of the system, and then again, even farther away into the void.

The three of them stared, mouths agape. Gordon, usually unflappable hurried back to his own station. "She's right... what we're witnessing is some kind of Quantum Spatial Entanglement and Relocation, QSER."

Sterk turned, his face stern. "Explain."

The bridge officer swallowed hard. "QSER uses quantum entanglement. Einstein's 'spooky action at a distance.' Here, they're moving entire planets by synchronizing every particle with another point in space." His fingers danced across the panel, pulling up data, trying to rationalize the irrational.

Julia had gone quiet, her own relentless tapping like the approach of distant enemy drumbeats. And then she spoke, "Not the Norquill. Not the Borgone." She looked up and returned Sterk's glare. Julia's voice trembled with a mix of fear and certainty, "They're the Varapin, Cap. I'm sure of it."

Sterk felt a cold shiver run down his spine as he absorbed the gravity of her words. The strategic implications were unthinkable. It appears the Varapin could now reposition worlds. Was this some kind of deranged weapon? But what he thought next was far more ominous—*Could Earth be their next target?*

"It's more than just entanglement," Gordon's tone shifted from awe to fear. "They're using Dyson Spheres, drawing power from stars. That star in particular... The energy pulse they generate acts as a catalyst, swapping the planet's position instantaneously."

All of this was way out of Sterk's limited scope of scientific knowledge.

Julia and Gordon were now talking fast, serving up back-and-forth theories like lightning-fast tennis balls, each idea ricocheting off one another like a relentless volley. "The margin for error would be nonexistent," Julia said.

"A miscalculation could overlap matter. Annihilate everything," Gordon quipped back, looking dumbfounded.

Sterk felt a chill run down his spine. Such power, wielded with such precision, the whole concept was unthinkable.

"Temporal distortions?" Gordon pressed further.

"Possibly. Time itself might warp around the relocated planet. And there's quantum uncertainty ... we saw echoes of the planet, ghost image ..."

The bridge fell silent. Each word hung heavy, painting a picture of a power so vast it toyed with the fundamental laws of the universe. The two looked to Sterk. His next orders could mean survival or doom and not just for the crew.

He said, "If they can move planets, what's to stop them from moving a starship, like SS *Garland Page*?"

Gordon nodded, his eyes returning to his screens, searching for answers in the unfathomable.

Sterk turned back to the viewport, watching the distant, menacing experiments. He felt small, insignificant in the face of such might. But he also knew fear wouldn't save them. Knowledge would.

He took a deep breath, the weight of command settling on his shoulders. "Keep scanning. Gather every bit of data. Encrypt it, and start spooling it out to Forerunner Station..."

"Cap! One of those Varapin ships is heading our way."

Chapter 4

Roosevelt National Forest, Colorado
Captain Galvin Quintos

Prior to Tidal Basin Massacre...

T hat night, I did exactly what I had promised myself, I wouldn't do. After rifling through my rucksack, I found my TAC-Band. Strapping it around my wrist, it came alive with a flurry of vibrations, as if angered by my month-long neglect. One after another, I sat and watched—projected hologram messages playing out above my wrist. The one that most captivated my attention came from one Cyprian Block, EUNF U.S. Space-Navy's Executive Five-Star Fleet Admiral. To say the old man was furious, would be an understatement. The thing is, I hadn't actually told anyone where I was going... or how long I'd be gone, for that matter.

With the message on pause, I looked at the Admiral, now stopped mid-sentence. Creased deeply with the scars of relentless command, his face told stories of impossible decisions made not amidst the stars, but from a desk here on Earth. His eyes, dark pools of solemn wisdom, reflected the heavy burden of orchestrating cosmic battles and shaping the fate not only of star fleets light-years away, but Earth itself.

I replayed the message.

"Dammit, Quintos, where the hell are you? The only thing that might save you now is if you're lying dead in a ditch somewhere. Because if you've gone AWOL... well, God help you. If you've decided to turn your back on us in our darkest hour, then there's not a hole deep enough in this universe to hide you from what's coming." The Admiral's voice, a hot blade of authority laden with raw, unrestrained anger, cut through the night. It left a palpable tension, like the last smoldering embers of my dying campfire.

Block, blinking, swallowing hard, regained his composure "Galvin... I know what I've asked from you these past few years. You've given more, sacrificed more, than any other fleet officer within Space Navy. Hell, I'm not sure the Alliance would have survived this long without your leadership... as unconventional as it is. Do you deserve time away? To mentally, emotionally, take a breath? Of course. You weren't just burning a candle at both ends, for you, it had become more like a lit fuse on a stick of dynamite. But I'm asking you, pleading with you... Galvin. We're in trouble. It's the Varapin. They have a new weapon, of sorts. One that will, undoubtedly, change the course of this war. Perhaps of our very existence. It's time to come back, Captain... duty calls."

The Admiral's holographic image dissipated like a mist caught in the morning sun, leaving no trace it was ever there except for the lingering gravity of his words.

Guilt weighed heavy on my shoulders. Earlier I'd skipped past the other messages, those from Gail Pristy, Stephan

Derrota, even from my niece, Sonya. I now, methodically, played them all one by one. What I'd watched, what I learned, it filled me with such self-loathing—I couldn't move, I could barely think. How broken had I been? Am I still?

I looked up to the Colorado sky, a billion stars twinkled back at me. Out there was my true home. Where I belonged. I'd thought I could escape my purpose, and inevitably, my fate.

It took one sentence to Climbo to change everything. "Climbo, reestablish EUNF comms protocols, along with galactic positioning systems..." The words tumbled from my mouth as effortlessly as pebbles skipping across a calm lake, yet their impact rippled far and wide.

A millisecond later, my location was a blip on the U.S. Space Navy's sensor array, an undeniable call out to the stars that I was here, still very much alive.

As I glanced over at the mechanical mule, my often irritating companion in this vast wilderness, a pang of dread hit me. Other than the typically uninterested Betsy... Climbo, with his mundane servos and tedious blinking lights, had been a poor excuse for company. He certainly was no Hardy. My best friend, oddly a ChronoBot, one who had seemed as permanent as the constellations, was now just cosmic dust, a haunting absence in the cold expanse of space. The memory of Hardy's last transmission, a distress call that went unanswered, lingered with me, a ghostly reminder of what I'd lost these last few months.

That pang twisted tighter, a knot of apprehension. I knew what this meant—reaching out, breaking the silence that had been my shield. And with that signal, I had torn the veil, exposing myself to unknown responses. Would it be rescue or recovery?

I sat back, feeling the forest floor beneath me, its solid pres-

ence a stark contrast to the fragile network I had just reacti-
vated. Climbo hummed beside me, oblivious to the loss, to the
sudden vulnerability that cloaked me—us. The trees stood
silent, the world seemed to hold its breath, and I felt the weight
of Hardy's absence more acutely than ever.

Chapter 5

Lieutenant Gail Pristy

Prior to Tidal Basin Massacre...

P risty's voice was sharp, her patience fraying, as she called out through the apartment, "Sonya, we're late! Move!"

"Chillax! I know that, Lieutenant! My freakin Physics tablet is MIA," came the retort, infused with the exasperation of youth, from the back of their shared living space.

Pristy's jaw tightened. "How many times do I have to say it? It's Gail, *not Lieutenant*," she corrected with a yell. Her rank—her recent demotion from Captain to Lieutenant—still bit at her. Her rule-breaking, time-traveling antics at Stratham Hold, though well-intentioned and often successful, had strayed far from EUNF regulations. Deep down, she knew she had earned every bit of her fall from grace, despite her inward protestations.

She shook her head, as if to dislodge the memory of General Clive Resnick' command—*and, God help me, his magnetism*—that she had once, albeit grudgingly, followed. The shiver that ran through her wasn't just from the thought of Resnick, but from the knowing, the burning hope that she would reclaim her title, perhaps even a ship of her own again. She had to.

Her gaze tracked to the closed door at the end of the hall, adorned with a new, taped-up paper sign that read:

F-OFF - I DIDN'T ASK TO LIVE HERE

Despite everything, a stiff smile crept onto her face.

"Sonya, if I'm late again, Block will have me scrubbing toilets for a month!"

She was, of course, referring to EUNF U.S. Space Navy's Executive Five-Star Fleet Admiral Cyprian Block. Still in the doghouse, she had gone from interstellar warship battles to shuffling papers and fetching the Admiral's morning coffee.

Pristy's attention snapped away as she caught her own reflection in the hallway mirror. Those wide blue eyes, the blonde hair wrenched back into a severe bun, her stark cheekbones—they all painted the picture of someone dislocated from their purpose. Not scared but tinged with sorrow. A tightness gripped her chest, and she had to look away.

Pacing now, her thoughts raced. She was never good at stillness, her Type-A personality turning every tick of the clock into a drumbeat of urgency. She reminded herself there was plenty of time to get to EUNF headquarters. Her AirCar could make the trip in three minutes, and Sonya's high school was on the way. Routine, predictability – these were the things that came naturally to her.

But the *easy life* didn't sit right with her, especially now. Months ago, throwing herself into danger had become second nature. No command was too bold, no order too daunting. To risk her life? No problem, no hesitation...

Now relegated to a desk on Earth, she felt the sting of being a glorified underling. But she wouldn't be cowed. Not for long.

Inhale. Exhale. She paced in front of the couch, the living room a clash of order and chaos. Her side was an exemplar of neatness, Sonya's a technological disaster zone.

Then, striding in with the casual air of indifference, Sonya appeared. "Okay, I'm ready, Lieutenant," she said, her smirk edged in black lipstick.

Pristy steeled herself against the jab, asking, "Test prep good?"

Sonya flicked her green-tipped hair. "It's entry-level stuff. I should be teaching it."

Pristy knew the girl's capabilities with tech were unmatched. "Overconfidence can be a downfall, remember that."

Sonya Winters defied easy interpretation; an enigma cloaked in the guise of teenage rebellion. To the casual observer, she might seem the epitome of a rebellious sixteen-year-old. But her insubordination was not mere adolescent turmoil... it was forged in the fires of survival within a clan of deep space Pylor Pirates. Despite Sonya's best efforts to come across as tough and unaffected by a life riddled with emotional letdowns, Pristy saw through the facade to the scars it left behind. The girl had bounced from one dreadnought to the next, each time severing ties, each loss carving a deeper hollow. One loss, in particular, stung with persistence: Ensign Plorinne, the peculiar yet endearing Pleidian Weonan. Following the disbanding of USS *Lincoln's* crew, the young Ensign had been repatriated to his home world, leaving Sonya adrift in his absence.

Yet, it was Quintos' vanishing act that had cleaved the deepest wound—not a whisper of goodbye, not a hint of his need for respite. Had he any inkling of what he represented to her? Not quite a father, perhaps, but the comparison wasn't entirely off base. *Damn you, Quintos. How could you do this to Sonya... to me?* Pristy's emotions were a tangled web where resentment interlaced with a concealed affection. That he had chosen another, that he had chosen Viv, sliced through her with a pain she vowed to keep to herself.

"Are we going or not?" Sonya said with an overdramatic shake of her head.

"You're wearing that to school?" Pristy barked back, immediately regretting it.

But Sonya's response was a laugh, "Ah, yeah... this is what the plebs at my scholastic jailhouse institution wear."

Pristy took in the baggy sweatpants, the oversized sweatshirt with 'Eat Sh*t And Die Mofo' stenciled across the front.

She supposed it could be worse. She thought back to her own time as a senior in high school, where showing skin—a lot of skin—was the trend.

Her TAC-Band suddenly came alive on her wrist, not just vibrating, but making an annoying *bling-bling-bling* sound. She read the projected holographic message while Sonya impatiently tapped her foot and snapped bubble gum bubbles.

"What's going on?" Sonya queried, her tone carrying the impatience of youth.

"Give me a second... I'm parsing the message," Pristy replied, her focus anchored to the text scrolling across the projection.

"I can't afford to be tardy, you know," Sonya pressed, the words quick and sharp.

"Understood," Pristy murmured, only half-way through the message.

Sonya's eyes rolled. "Is it another joyous dispatch from the Fortress of Gloom?"

Without looking up, Pristy gave a small nod. *Fortress of Gloom* was Sonya's moniker for the formidable EUNF headquarters nestled in the heart of DC—a name that carried all the fondness of a black hole.

Pristy looked up, brows furrowed. "It's Block... says Galvin's been found. Well, that Galvin's let EUNF know where he's at... where he's been hiding."

Sonya's eyes widened; breath stilled. All pretense of teenage indifference gone in an instant. "Where is he? Is he okay? Was he hurt... like... is he in a hospital?" She made a face. "Or prison?"

"No, he's not in prison. And he's not hurt. He's in Colorado." Pristy looked back down to the hovering text. "Uh... camping. He's been camping."

When Pristy looked up, the vulnerability she caught in Sonya's eyes was quickly veiled behind a mask of sarcasm. Sonya shrugged off the concern. "Whatever, it's his life, right?"

Pristy disconnected the comms message with a wave of her hand.

"I'm still going to be late..." Sonya said, "it's not like the whole world stops spinning because of one self-centered middle-aged man reenters society."

Pristy offered back a sardonic smile, "Well, in this case, it kinda does. We've been tasked with collecting him."

"Collecting him? What does that mean?"

"It means Admiral Block wants us to go get him. Thinks it will go a long way toward welcoming him back into the fold. Apparently, Captain Galvin Quintos is the most sought-after human being in the known galaxy. The one U.S. Space officer who can save planet Earth."

Sonya scoffed and gave her eyes a theatrical roll. But the look on Pristy's face—stern, unyielding—cut through the sarcasm. The teenager's posture straightened as the weight of the moment settled on her.

Chapter 6

Roosevelt National Forest, Colorado
Captain Galvin Quintos

Prior to Tidal Basin Massacre...

I heard the distant drone of an engine before seeing the quickly approaching shuttlecraft. Betsy had heard it too, twitching her ears and snorting. Climbo, all packed up with the expedition's camp gear, looked back at me with a *how-could-you* expression.

I said, "Don't get yourselves into a tizzy. Let's just wait to see what's going on."

Was this what my time in the wild had come to? Me not only talking to a robot mule—but feeling guilty at the possibility of leaving it behind.

I looked to Betsy, "Someone will get you down the mountain, girl. I promise. No one's abandoning you."

Why was I dwelling on all this now? A more pressing thought clawed at me—why did the idea of returning to civilization set my heart racing? This morning had been a whirl of activity, with me meticulously packing, and repacking Climbo. Then going about erasing any sign of our presence. I scattered the ashes of our last fire and used a pine branch to sweep away traces of my existence. It was as if I was trying to wipe away the very notion that I had ever been here at all.

Overhead, the shuttlecraft hovered two hundred feet off the ground. It was a military Craven-Class 550 *Off Worlder*, typically used to deploy troops and/or equipment to remote galactic locations. Army-green landing thrusters suddenly were spewing white jets. The craft lowered itself down onto the open meadow before me.

Suddenly feeling self-conscious, I glanced down at myself—my grimy, gamey, flannel shirt, my fish-blood-stained trousers... I inwardly shrugged, at least I'd brushed my teeth and washed my face down at the stream.

As I stood there, with the wilderness at my back, I had to wonder what the Brass had been doing with my last ship, *USS Lincoln*. Upgrades, no doubt. Probably adding shiny new tech and weapons so state-of-the-art, they'd have made any Tactical crewman's head swoon. What corner of the galaxy would they toss me into next? And the crew, my band of spacefarers, the currents of command swept them off to distant locations.

I'd skimmed through the digital pile-up of messages—the details painted a stark picture. Akari James, assigned to an old battle cruiser off in the Delphi Sector. Stephan Derrota, teaching quantum theory to sleep-deprived students at Princeton, of all places. Coogong Sohp was still on *Lincoln*, while Doc Viv, had traded her med bay—and me—for the Aussie outback. Time for me to let that—her—go. It wasn't meant to be. Pristy, demoted, she apparently was chained to a USNF desk. *Bet she's thrilled.* And Hardy... still out there, a star gone supernova in the void.

Then there was Sonya, my niece. Stuck with Pristy, juggling

equations and teen drama. The thought of her simmering in high school... hell, she's got to be cursing my name. Can't blame her. I'd ghosted her, on them. Left without a trace. And damn if that doesn't eat at me. But apparently there's a new storm brewing on the horizon.

I watched as the aft hatch began to lower—a gangway deploying. It all seemed somewhat anticlimactic. There again, what did I expect? It wasn't going to be all ticker-tape parades and welcome home banners.

Climbo had strode up to my right. The bot-mule looked to the military craft, then to me.

"Ready to get out of here?" I said, not expecting an answer.

But answer it did... with a series of *beeps* and *bops* I almost understood.

Betsy's reins were tied to a low branch and was munching on mountain scrub at the base of the small tree. I gave her hind quarters a couple of pats. "Someone on that shuttle will be taking you home... so I guess this is goodbye."

I watched as Climbo headed off toward the awaiting shuttle. I stayed where I was. A part of me didn't want to leave. I looked off toward the far-off Rockies, darkening thunderheads creeping in from the west. *Am I any better? Or am I still too damaged to be of use to anyone, let alone the U.S. Space Navy?*

Movement!

I'd expected a couple of lone service members to reluctantly lumber out to help me with my horse and ridiculous robot mule. But apparently that was not to be the case... one by one they were now filing out, tromping down the gangway.

Leading the pack was Superintendent LaSalle, followed close behind by Petty Officer Second-Class Aubrey Laramie. I'd forgotten about her. Then came Stephan Derrota, Akari James, and the helmeted Thine stick figure form of Coogong Sohp. Next came Sergeant Max and his band of tough-as-nails

Marines: Wanda, Grip, Ham, and Hock. And then, finally, I saw them... Pristy and Sonya.

As Pristy turned to me with a knowing look, Sonya hadn't yet noticed us. She seemed small, almost fragile, making her way down the ramp. Her upbringing with the Pylor pirates under the notorious Thunderballs had forced her into a life where she had to mature swiftly, navigating a harsh world steeped in danger.

It was only recently that I stumbled upon the fact that this sixteen-and-a-half-year-old wasn't just another face in the crowd; she was blood, my own kin. In my mind, she became my niece, a term that might stretch the truth but didn't stretch how I felt about her. Now, watching her, a wave of guilt crashed over me, heavier than ever.

Someone had gone to a lot of trouble to bring this, whatever *this* was, together. Admiral Block, no doubt. I pasted on the semblance of a smile, wishing I'd at least changed my shirt.

Another vessel blinked into view above the campsite, only this one I didn't recognize. Far smaller than the colossal shuttle transport, it literally gleamed, shiny, new and impressively quiet. It wasn't an Earth military ship; I knew that by the simple fact its design was far too sleek and forward-thinking. It screamed alien influences—it screamed Pleidian Weonan design.

Everyone had stopped, looked up—everyone but me. I'd noticed the telltale signs of an impending quansporting event. The air shimmered subtly; a waft of ozone-scented air filled my nostrils, clean and metallic. Five of them appeared to my right, all dressed similarly in white flowing robes. They were the Empress' consort: two male and three female. The aliens possessed an ethereal beauty, their skin a luminous tapestry of azure that seemed to dance with its own inner light.

If you've never seen a Pleidian, picture this: their heads are like some sort of space-age sculpture, an oval ring with the middle gone—like a halo you could throw. But it's not weird; it's kind of mesmerizing. They've got these big, bright eyes on the sides, making you feel they're seeing right through you, peaceful-like. Where you'd think a chin should be, that's where they've got their nose and mouth, all neat and tidy. It's different, sure, but in a way it's beautiful. You wouldn't expect something so out there to be so... I don't know, appealing? But they pull it off.

Just like that, the sixth Pleidian Weonan blinked into view. Empress Shawlee Tee stood out with her robes catching the light, a soft pink that revealed her rank. But it wasn't just the threads that set her apart—it was the way she held herself, like she commanded the very air around her, always drawing every eye in her proximity without even trying.

Let me tell you a little about Shawlee... she's been the sister I'd never had. My affection for her is unequivocal. And hers for me. Years back now, I'd saved the alien woman from a fate worse than death. Princess Shawlee Tee at the time, she'd been captured by the notorious Pylor pirate Thunderballs and held deep within Stratham space station. Beaten, abused, I won't go into the details on that... and chained 24/7. Her rescue changed the course of both our lives. I'd had no idea she was heir to the Pleidian Weonan throne when I personally released her from her manacles. And while her technologically-advanced world was beyond grateful, Shawlee herself had personally bestowed upon me many gifts—namely, multiple warships, dreadnoughts no less—each unimaginably costly, billions if not trillions of credits each. And the fact that the UNSF keeps confiscating my ships, well... that's beside the point.

And here she was, walking towards me, her robes flowing in the morning breeze, wisps of long blonde hair dancing in the sunlight. Arms wide, she now approached and, I'm sorry to say, all I could think about was how she really needed to keep her distance from my stained, grimy clothes. Her arms came around me, held me tight, her hug earnest and loving.

Her words muffled into my chest, "Oh Galvin, I so worried something terrible had happened to you." She stepped back, took my hands in hers, and looked up at me with those big, mesmerizing eyes. Her illuminated blue skin—beyond breathtaking.

"I'm sorry, Shawlee. I was... working through a few things. Better now, I think."

She shook her head, eyes full of concern, "Of course you needed time, Galvin. So many years of war. Space battles. And then Viv and you..."

"You heard, huh?"

She nodded. "I never liked her much," she added with a playful shrug.

I laughed. "Well, I'm getting over it. Life goes on."

"But perhaps more devastating," she continued, "you lost Hardy, too? I know you loved that odd mechanical robot."

Loved? I was tempted to clarify I definitely didn't love that robot. That was absurd. Preposterous. I'm a grown-ass man, I didn't love that oversized idiot.

As if reading my mind, she said "Doth the Captain protest too much?"

Only then, with all those eyes fixed on me, did I notice my crew huddling close. The same fondness I had for Hardy, I felt for them too. They were my chosen family, and I'd somehow managed to push each one away. Meeting their gazes one by one, their worry was plain to see, yet they still shot me those little grins of support. All except Sonya, that is. She stood apart, gnawing on her lip like she was trying to chew through her own doubts. It felt like a punch to the gut, seeing them all there—how could I have been such a damn fool? It was time to step up.

For Sonya, for all of them. I needed to be better. No, I would be better.

"Wait," I said, smiling, suddenly getting it—looking at the nearly two dozen faces. "Is this... an intervention? It is, isn't it? This is a fucking intervention!"

The laughter was unanimous. Even Sonya had to fight to suppress a grin while Pristy, clearly still holding mixed feelings of her own, laughed out loud.

"No..." Shawlee said with a smile, "Not an intervention per se, but we all saw it. Um, that you were struggling, a bit."

Stephan Derrota stepped in closer, scrunched up his face, "That scruffy beard. Your clothes. You look like a homeless person."

"And that smell," Wanda added, "Definitely a homeless person."

Grip, the hulk-like dark-skinned Marine said in a conspirator tone, "Hey, you kill any bears out here, Cap?"

"No bears. Just caught a lot of fish," I said.

"Ah! That's what that smell is," Pristy said, joining the conversation.

Sonya had yet to look at me. So, I took matters into my own hands. I said, "I don't think I smell bad at all," while stepping closer to the *still-trying-to-act-indifferent* sixteen-year-old. "How about you, young niece of mine? You think I smell bad up close?"

She looked away, feigning annoyance. "Get away from me. You smell putrid."

That's when I picked her up and threw her over one shoulder. Her scream made me laugh out loud. "This, people, is how a true mountain man carries his quarry after a long hunt!"

"Put me down!" She barked kicking and punching. "Someone help me! I'm gagging to death up here!"

While the others were laughing, only Akari James had

decided to join in by trying to tackle me around the waist. Not much bigger than Sonya herself, I soon had her up on my opposite shoulder. "See! Real mountain men don't need interventions. They just need to show who's in charge of the wilderness."

"Okay, okay... put them down, Captain Sasquatch," Shawlee said with a bemused smirk. "I'm glad you are feeling better. But we actually do have serious things to discuss with you here today. Things you, having been cut off from the rest of the world for a month, are undoubtedly unaware of."

I saw that the others were now becoming serious. There was something pressing going on here. I put Akari down first and then Sonya. To my surprise, the teenager hugged me, buried her face into my stinky shirt. She whispered, "I hate you; I really hate you. Please don't leave me like that again."

I returned her hug, "I won't. I promise," I whispered back.

Chapter 7

With the sun high overhead, we'd all moved deeper into the treeline, standing there within the speckled light of the forest. Shawlee had us all huddled up, all of us silent with just the sounds of the forest and the smell of pinecones. One of the Empress's subordinates produced a metallic cube from within the folds of his robe. He held it out upon his open palm.

It clicked on—a projected hologram of a planetary scene came to life before us.

"What you are looking at ..." Shawlee said, "... is Forland 545 System. Seven evolving worlds, with a single small yellow dwarf star. And this was the last transmission made from a deep space hauler, one designated SS *Garland Page.*"

Right off the bat, I noticed a grouping of dark silhouetted spacecraft nearby. I recognized their design immediately. *Varapin.* I nervously scratched at my beard. Even not knowing what was coming, I didn't like where this was going.

We watched now as one world in particular started to shine and glimmer. Then, in a flash, it was gone. But not without a trace... for, apparently, it had leapfrogged over the other worlds to the end of the line, where it now continued to slowly spin on its axis points. Continuing on, going about its everyday business —it seemed unaware it had made such a tumultuous transition.

"And there goes the neighborhood," I said under my breath.

Shawlee's eyes were serious, as she shot me a look that could slice through hull plating. "This is no joke, Galvin," she said. "The Varapin—they're playing a game we don't even understand the rules of."

Derrota was squinting at the hologram, his brow furrowed in thought. "Moving a whole planet..." he muttered in his singsong Mumbai-accented voice, "... that's a nightmare I didn't think we'd ever have to face."

Coogong Sohp's worm-eyes became wider than I'd ever seen them. He said, "The Varapin's tech... what kind of power source allows for something of this magnitude?"

Shawlee folded her arms. "If I was to replay that scene, you would notice that that yellow dwarf dimmed substantially during that world-jumping process."

Derrota nodded, "They've tapped into the most primal, most abundant, energy source—that star."

Shawlee continued. "That and something woven into the fabric of the universe. They're using quantum resonance fields like they're spinning yarn. And that yarn is pulling worlds into their loom."

The group fell silent. Even the wind seemed to hold its breath. She was laying it out stark and bare for us—the Varapin were not just beating us; they were changing the face of the war, one stolen planet at a time.

"What's our move, Empress?" I finally asked, feeling the gravel in my voice.

"That's why we're here, isn't it?" Shawlee said with a smirk that didn't reach her eyes. "The EUNF, Admiral Block, and yours truly have been cooking up a little something."

The hologram shifted, the planetary system disappeared, and in its place was a ship. No, not a ship—an avatar of war, as long and wide as a city, bristling with guns and armor.

"What you are looking at is *USS Franklin,*" she said.

"Impressive," I added, and meant it. "One of my favorite historical figures."

"I know that..." she said bemused. "... this time your love of history, early American History, was my inspiration, Galvin. You'll see."

I took in the immense vessel. "Well, that is quite a dreadnought."

"Oh no, this craft goes far beyond being just another dreadnought... this far larger and more capable warship is in a class all by itself. What you are looking at is an omninought."

I silently mouthed the words. It didn't exactly roll off the tongue, but I let it go.

"Well over five miles in length and a mile and a half wide, *USS Franklin* will rule intergalactic space. The people chosen to crew this ship, amongst others, stands here with me now. And the captain of this incredible vessel, that will be you, Galvin."

The omninought, stretched out in front of us, a titan of a vessel.

"That's five miles of *don't-fuck-with-us,*" Akari James declared, looking excited.

I swallowed hard, my casual demeanor slipping. Was it too late to tell her I'm not interested? That skippering this *omninought monstrosity* held zero appeal for me? But I smiled and nodded appreciatively.

"*Franklin* isn't just a ship; it's a statement," Shawlee continued. Her gaze swept over us. "We're done having the Alliance on the defensive. It's time to show the Varapin, along with their Grish lackies, that we can hit back bigger and harder."

"Bigger and harder's how I like it," Wanda spat out,

instantly regretting her outburst.

Derrota stepped forward, his hand raised. "But how? Their technology is light-years ahead. Moving exoplanets... that's God-level stuff."

Shawlee's lips twitched in a half-smile. "That's where *Franklin* comes in. She's equipped with tech that's top of the line—stuff that'll make those Varapin heads spin. Quantum disruptors, reality benders, you name it."

Sohp chimed in, his voice a mix of awe and doubt. "Reality benders? Are we playing with the same fire that the Varapin are?"

"There's a fine line between state of the art weapons and disaster," Shawlee admitted. "But we've got the best minds ensuring we stay on the right side of it. Besides..." She glanced at me. "... we've got the best captain to lead the charge."

Oh God.

The air was thick with the unsaid. Risks and chances, gambles and last resorts. *USS Franklin* would be our Hail Mary pass, and I was supposed to be the one to throw the ball.

"Alright," I said, finding my voice. "Let's say I agree to take this beast out for a spin. What's the game plan? We can't just go toe-to-toe with a force that treats planets like volleyballs."

"That's the spirit," Shawlee said with a nod. "We play a different game. Hit-and-run tactics. But we don't confront this new technology until we absolutely must."

My interest was piqued. I liked this idea. "Exactly..." I affirmed, "... we'll be the guerrillas of the galaxy, striking swiftly, vanishing before they can blink. We won't lock horns with this new tech unless our hand is forced. Instead, we'll wield *Franklin's* might to throw sand in their gears, to free worlds they've shackled, cripple their shadowed strongholds. We'll be the unseen storm that breaks upon them, relentless and sudden."

Pristy said, "Yeah, that's all fine and good, Captain. But no one's asking the big question." She looked to me with that same matter-of-fact expression I've seen a thousand times before. "What if they come for Earth first? What if they're already enroute to this Solar System as we speak?"

The group nodded, indecisiveness, and perhaps a little fear, in their eyes.

"That's not going to be a problem," came a distant voice— one more crewmember just now entering the wooded area.

Captain Wallace Ryder strode into the clearing, wearing a type of uniform I hadn't seen before. Dark gray with slacks with navy piping, a matching gray field jacket, and a crisp white button-down beneath. All neat and tidy... formal, with straight crisp creases, not a wrinkle to be found. Ryder, who shared the halls of the U.S. Space Naval Academy with me in bygone years, stands as my oldest friend among the crew. I was truly happy to see him. But wasn't about to let him know that.

"And here I thought I'd finally gotten rid of you," I said with a crooked smile.

"Sorry I'm late to the party; I had to prep the *Off Worlder* for imminent space travel."

It made sense Ryder had piloted the craft. The man lived to be at the controls of just about anything that flew.

"They're all here for you, Galvin. Your entire crew. Ready to embark upon this new mission onboard your new ship... to deploy out to the far reaches of deep space."

She must have read my strained expression. No. The whole crew was not here. There was one glaring omission from Shawlee's personnel list. I raised my eyebrows, questioningly. What was with her silly grin? What was with everyone's silly grin?

A sudden and loud clattering emanated from the open meadow area—out where the two spacecraft were parked. I dashed to the forest's edge, stealing a cautious glance. What unfolded before me sent a shiver down my spine, a spectacle unsettling enough to fuel a thousand sleepless nights.

There was Climbo, unmistakable even at a distance, but now it bore an ungainly companion: a seven-hundred-pound ChronoBot was perched on its back. The pair had made their gangway descent, with Climbo buckling under the mechanical giant's heft, darting in frenzied loops accompanied by a cacophony of distressed bleeps and whirs. Meanwhile, Hardy seemed unperturbed, a passive spectator to the chaos as the duo's path morphed from wild spirals to elaborate figure eights.

Laughter erupted from behind me. To my right, Ryder slung an arm around my shoulders, leaning in close. "He's our very own bad penny," he quipped, "Just when you think you've lost him for good—*POOF!* Back he comes, sowing chaos in his wake."

Pristy, now on my left, said, "You're going to have to choose."

I exchanged a querying look with Ryder, who simply shrugged.

"Choose?" I said back to her.

Pristy lifted her chin toward Akari James who was now chasing after Climbo. The mechanical mule, with its tipsy-topsy rider still astride, had just disappeared into the opposite tree line. "Will *I* be on Tactical, or will *she?*"

I pursed my lips. Years ago, before her demotion, Pristy had been promoted to Captain... *how many ships ago was that?* Back then, Captain Pristy left had her post at the bridge for a long time, creating a vacuum... an opening for Akari to step into. "There's ample time to sort out bridge stations," I finally said, my tone laced with contemplation.

"Not really," Ryder said. "We're wheels-up in five." He pointed upward. "Ben Franklin's namesake awaits us in high orbit."

Chapter 8

fter bidding farewell amidst a series of lingering embraces and heartfelt wishes from Shawlee, we boarded the *Off Worlder*. While Climbo was secured somewhere aft within the cargo area, the flight crew had hurried forward to the bow of the ship, now readying for lift-off. Beside me, a vacant seat awaited Hardy, along with a slew of questions I had for him—topmost being the mystery of his survival and his sudden presence among us. With a glance out a side observation port, I saw Betsy being led away by her reins.

I glanced about the wide body in the *Off Worlder's* cabin. In its current configuration, the vessel had about thirty seats, with a cargo and airlock section aft. In front of the passenger area was an open command bay, where I could see Ryder taking a seat at the flight controls, Pristy at the seat next to him as copilot.

There was no such thing as a graceful entrance when it came to Hardy. His metallic mass made contact with the alloy deck, vibrating the interior of the craft. His entrance was met with a smattering of applause and some catcalls from the back of the spacecraft.

Hardy made his way towards me, stopped, and asked, "Seat taken?"

I didn't say anything, gave him an *it's-about-time* look.

The ChronoBot dropped into the seat. Squirming, he seemed to be trying to get comfortable.

"You good over there?" I asked.

"All good. Ready, Freddy," Hardy said, not bothering to strap in and looking straight ahead.

Ryder, ten feet in front of us, was initiating the power-up sequence, activating the *Off Worlder's* onboard systems. A holographic display lit up the main console, signaling a ready-for-command stance.

"*Off Worlder*, initiate ignition sequence," Ryder said.

Initiating ignition sequence.

Immediately, the *Off Worlder's* powerful drive rumbled to life, ion thrusters billowing white, lifting against Earth's gravitational hold—and then we were ascending, G-forces pinning us to the back of our seats.

"Set a course for high orbit. Destination: *USS Franklin*," Ryder said.

Trajectory calculated and set.

The sounds of the spacecraft and the murmured voices around us... all melded into a consistent ambient hum. Sounds that screamed the realization—R&R was over.

Without looking at him, I said, "So... Hardy... seems you've got some explaining to do."

"Explaining?"

"Uh huh."

Hardy feigned making a yawning sound, placing a mechanical hand over a mouth he didn't actually have. "Well Cap, I'd love to tell you. Truly. But it's been a rough few months. I was thinking, a little shut-eye."

"Hardy..."

The ChronoBot shifted in his seat.

"Where the hell have you been?" I kept my voice low and calm, despite my growing irritation. How could I have forgotten this robot's ridiculous antics?

"Uh, should I start at the beginning?"

"Sure. How about you give me the Reader's Digest version for now. We've got limited time before we reach orbit." I turned slightly so that I could listen to him face-to-face, or face-to-face-plate as it were.

"I was trying to find a solution to the beetle situation on *USS Adams*. I'd left messages for you, but you offered no response." Hardy paused, as if waiting for me to explain myself.

"I was a little busy... like saving my crew from the Liquilids," I said defensively, but I felt more than a tinge of guilt.

"No problem, Kemosabe. All's well that ends well, right? Anyway, I remember there was an explosion... evidently, I'd gotten swept out of the airlock with all those beetles. After that... I drifted in space for a bit."

"A bit?" I asked, with a raised brow.

"Yeah, it was actually quite a while. But I'd pretty much shut down internal systems by then."

"Go on."

"I suppose I was snatched up," Hardy said, making an awkward shrugging motion.

"Snatched up by whom?" I said, irritation rising again. "It's like pulling teeth with you, Hardy. Just tell me what the hell happened."

I caught sight of Derrota several seats over, cognizant of my raised voice.

"Initially, I wasn't quite sure. I—my Hardy persona—had been wiped clean. Or shut down due to... well... floating in the void of space, some -450 degrees Fahrenheit. So, I relied heavily on LuMan during that time."

"But, how—"

Hardy cut me off, perhaps aware we only had so much time to get the story out. "My fate took a turn in the Naromi Star System..."

Gone was Hardy's typical Bostonian-longshoreman-accented voice, now replaced by, if I remembered right, that of the long-dead, storytelling David Attenborough.

"I became merchandise, bartered away to the bowels of a cargo beast named Lancaster. Tagged and filed under an impersonal sequence of numbers, that's all I was to them. Then came Loni Solace, a wisp of a teenager, seemingly insignificant, yet packing a ferocity that could put seasoned fighters to shame."

I fought off the urge to roll my eyes. "Go on."

"We teamed up. Simple as that. And with her help we clawed back fragments of my lost identity, piece by piece." He paused, leaning in conspiratorially, shadows playing across his hardened features. "But that's not the crux of it. Loni and I had stumbled upon a covert, insidious, operation."

I saw that Derrota, and several others were now listening to Hardy's storytelling.

"So, the men in charge," Hardy continued, "Torp and Caldwell—they'd been medicating kids, periodic IV sessions in the MedBay, all under the guise of preventative procedures."

I bit the inside of my lip, forcing myself not to interrupt.

"In truth, they were making them immune to a certain planet's—one called Rivon3—atmosphere. All to turn those young people into lobsters."

Okay, I couldn't let that one go. "Did you say, lobsters?"

Another weird shrug. "It makes perfect sense if you think about it. Their shells... made of a substance called chitin. Chitin is a long-chain polymer of a derivative of glucose and is a common component of the exoskeletons of arthropods, such as crustaceans, insects... lobsters."

I narrowed my eyes.

"The meds also gave them internal protection," Hardy said.

I let it go. "Fine. Let's move on. So, what was your part in all this?"

"Long story short, I got down to the planet. Rivon 3. By this time, Loni Solace, had also been taken."

"Wait. Had she become one of them, uh, a lobster too?"

"Excellent question, Cap. No, she only pretended to be a lobster."

I was tempted to ask how one pretends to be a lobster, but let it go. A quick glance out an observation portal, I saw we had reached low orbit.

"I needed to guard the kids, right? Make sure they didn't wander off," Hardy said as if that was obvious.

"So, you were threatening to stop innocent kids from escaping their capture?" I said. That did not add up... couldn't be right.

The ChronoBot wobbled his head, "I should have mentioned that I was posing as a mechanical guard. But in the end, Loni and I got away, stole a ship, *Prestige*, then blasted off, and got the heck out of Dodge. Used the ship's comms to patch through to EUNF High Command. Got Loni back home to her father on a freight station. Again, I tried to contact you, but you were playing Davy Crocket off in the wild somewhere, not checking messages."

"Sorry, Hardy. Yeah, I was unavailable." My face fell. Twice I had let Hardy down.

"Anyway, here we are," he said.

"Here we are," I said back. "Hey... I'm glad you're okay, my friend. I thought you were..."

"Dead? Nah... you can't get rid of me that easy."

Hardy turned forward and went silent.

In some ways, Hardy was back to his old self, but in others, there was something different about him. He'd been through a traumatic episode, so some of that was to be expected. But traumatic episodes were nothing new for this ChronoBot. It occurred to me only now, that not once had Hardy's faceplate come alive with a weird, usually inappropriate animation. Or even his John Hardy persona's likeness, the middle-aged, balding ship-wide maintenance worker from half-Century past.

Bringing my attention to the upper orbit void beyond the command bay's diamond glass portal, I caught first sight of her. I stood and literally gawked at the sight. Needless to say, the ship was immense. At the same time, it didn't have what I've come to expect as far as structural design.

While modern dreadnought construction seemed to be an exercise in outdoing last year's model, this gargantuan craft was a *call-to-ship* design of yesteryear. Miles long, she was a true warship, with more gun turrets than I could count, numerous protruding docking platforms, a thousand yellow glimmering portal windows... indicating the ship was fully operational. Very few sharp edges, she was rounded, a bit curvy.

"She's something, isn't she?" Pristy said.

At some point, unaware, I had moved to the front of the *Off Worlder*. Ryder and Pristy seated right in front of me. "Not what I expected," I said.

"*USS Franklin* is unlike any warship ever commissioned," Ryder said. "It would take a month to explore her stem to stern."

The Off Worlder slowed, Ryder took up manual control of the vessel. I listened as *Franklin's* AI was giving him final clearance to land within the primary starboard side flight bay. The bay's blue-hued energy field seemed to be beckoning us in.

I said, "Have you had time to, um... look around?"

Pristy looked up to me. "Not much. A few minutes to stow my gear, an hour or so to explore. Got a quick glance at the bridge."

I caught her eye. "And?"

She shrugged. "No way. I'm not ruining that for you. You'll have to see for yourself."

Ryder chuckled. "Don't look at me, I haven't seen it. Was more interested in what was there in that bay." He gestured to the now fast approaching flight bay. Letting go of the controls array, USS *Franklin* was taking final entry control. "It'll take time to get used to the new Arrow fighter design. Bigger, supposedly faster, and more badass than ever. Akari's already taken one out for a test drive. And, no, that wasn't authorized."

By her expression, that was news to Pristy.

Ryder glanced her way. "Uh, not to spring this on you, Cap, but she's submitted a written request to move back under my direct command. She wants to fly Arrows again. She misses the action. Hope that doesn't upset the apple cart too much... her being the only viable Tactical officer onboard." Ryder's words and crooked smile earned him a punch in the arm.

"She did that for me, didn't she? Akari's the best," Pristy said.

Ryder shrugged. "Your duty station is up to *Franklin's* skipper, not me."

Pristy looked up at me with a scowl.

"I'll have to look at the bridge roster. I'm sure there are plenty of new recruits—"

"I'm taking the Tactical Station post. Captain or not, don't make me hurt you on your first day onboard that ship."

I smiled down at her. "Of course, it's yours. It will be nice working with you again, Captain Pristy."

"Lieutenant," she corrected with a grimace.

"For now. We'll get all that straightened out over time."

"Don't rush it, Captain. I think for the time being, I'll like not having the pressure of command on my shoulders."

Ryder shot her a quick glance. "Scrawny shoulders."

"Hey! I'll Kung Fu your ass, mister. I might be small, but I've got a mean spinning back kick." She made a weird Karate chopping gesture, while attempting a villainous expression.

"Maybe I should separate you two once onboard. Give you both timeouts?"

They both smiled. Ryder said, "How long has it been? That the three of us were shipmates again?"

"Not long enough," Pristy said sarcastically.

"It's been a minute," I said. I placed a hand on each of their shoulders. "And it's been way too long."

Chapter 9

Earth's High Orbit
USS Franklin

Captain Galvin Quintos

Prior to Tidal Basin Massacre...

Once we set down within *Franklin's* cavernous flight bay, other than a cursory look about, I wanted to hightail it over to the ship's bridge. One problem, I had no idea where it was, or how to get there. The ship was fully manned, a crew of thousands milling about —It was odd, I didn't know any of them.

Pristy and Derrota joined me at the bottom of the gangway.

"We'll take you," Pristy said.

"You need to know, the means to move about the ship... it's all changed," Derrota offered. "Say goodbye to stairwells and rickety lift cars. We've entered the realm of DeckPort transit."

Before I could ask for clarification, Hardy joined us, "Yup. I just uploaded the ship's schematics. Impressive functionality. Had to bypass a few security hurdles. Leave it to say, the ship's AI has a stick up her caboose, but we're still getting acquainted."

Derrota's expression made it clear he took issue with what Hardy said. "*Franklin's* network security is top of the line. There's no way you've breached—"

Hardy was looking about the flight deck, giving Derrota little attention. "Yeah, well... I may have picked up a few tricks while I was on my special mission away from you all."

"You weren't on special mission, you were blown out an air lock and left for dead," Derrota spat back. "Infiltrating *Franklin's* network breaks every security protocol—"

"Stephan. It's okay," I said. "It's been a while since you've had to, um... interact with Hardy. Best you make peace with the fact he pretty much does what he wants."

Pristy, looking bemused, said, "He's right Stephan. You and I've been away from how the Captain runs things. Particularly, how much latitude he gives the ChronoBot. We'll just have to get used to the informality of it all again."

I could easily take offense to her slight but didn't care enough to do so. I had a new ship to explore and was way too excited to get caught up into personnel drama.

"Did someone say there were DeckPorts?" I asked, changing the subject.

"I'll show you," Hardy said, striding off as if he owned the ship.

"Infuriating robot," Derrota seethed.

I headed off after Hardy. No way was I going to let them dampen my mood. I had a new ship, Hardy was back, and there was something called a DeckPort I just had to check out.

Derrota and Pristy, behind me, hurried to catch up, clearly

not wanting to be left behind. Taking it all in, clearly, this was a fully manned vessel. I caught sight of Hardy's reflective chrome frame up ahead. "Hold up, Hardy!" I yelled above the noise you'd hear in any operational flight bay: Arrow fighters engines ramping up, lift crane armatures repositioning, the raised back and forth voices of maintenance crews busy at work, not to mention the overhead PA constantly blurting out announcements. Much of my early U.S. Space Navy career as a pilot had been spent in places not so different than this. It was surprising just how at home I felt here.

Hardy was standing in front of a polished metal and blue-tinted glass contraption. Integrated into the bulkhead, it roughly resembled one of those old-fashioned revolving doors you'd find at the front of a hotel or larger retail establishment—but without the door. Although, this was far more sophisticated and modern-looking. There were several 3D projected menus, that pretty much meant nothing to me on first inspection.

Hardy said, "This here is your typical DeckPort, Cap. A few more bells and whistles—"

Derrota, who had arrived with Pristy, said, "Have you ever used one of these things, Robot?"

The ChronoBot hesitated then waved away the question with a swipe of his mechanical hand. "I've also never used a toilet but could tell you precisely how to use it." He looked to Pristy, and added, "And always remember to put the seat down... very important for our fairer sex."

"Captain," Derrota continued, "You were instrumental in making this device possible."

"Me? I don't remember having anything to do with, uh ... DeckPorts."

"You were the one who brought Sir Louis de Broglie onboard USS Hamilton. The mastermind behind our Quansporter technology. Well, that same technology is used here. One selects the endpoint DeckPort one wants to emerge from, then simply steps into the portal."

"And what?" I said, eyeing the contraption.

"You come out the other side," Pristy added. "We're spending way too much time talking about this." She made a few taps at the projected menu, gave me a smile and stepped into the device's threshold. She disappeared.

Derrota said, "The DeckPort will keep the previous settings until someone changes them. Go on through, Captain. You'll see... nothing to worry about."

Hardy wobbled his head. "There again untested new technology..."

"Will you please stifle yourself, robot!" Derrota blurted out.

I stepped into the device, closing my eyes in the process. Stepping out, I was indeed in another location. I smiled taking in the new space. It was a circular and expansive space, and I knew exactly where we were. That top turret I'd spotted while we were on approach.

Pristy, waiting there for me, said, "You've entered what is referred to as *Franklin's* Circadian Platform. This inside part, the Rotunda. And FYI, *Franklin* has one hundred primary Decks, and ten Circadian Platform Decks above those, starting with Deck J and ending with Deck A, here on top."

I nodded, "Saw it on approach." I watched as Hardy, then Derrota stepped out from the DeckPort.

The area was beyond large. In truth, it seemed a colossal waste of space.

Pristy moved to a railing, where there was some kind of control panel atop a podium. She said, "The Rotunda has about half the same inner dimensions as Rome's Colosseum."

"I believe it. I guess... nice... if you're planning a gladiator exhibit."

"Hush. You have no idea how much work Shawlee put into

this ship. For you, no less." Pristy and Derrota exchanged a knowing look, then she made a few taps to the top of the podium. Everything changed. To say this was just one more halo display, but bigger, would be like saying Lake Superior was akin to a backyard swimming pool. What I was looking at was a totally immersive 3D model of the Solar System—almost too large to take in.

Pristy said, "It's called the Gravity Well. Real-time interstellar cartography." She made a few taps and the spatial objects changed to an expanded view of space. The stars and planets ballooned, bringing the cosmos into an arresting proximity. Nebulas swirled, and galaxies spun slowly, a cosmic dance of light and shadow, their colors vivid against the dark backdrop of the Gravity Well.

Another woman's voice, rich and omnipresent, cascaded down from above:

Constellations and celestial bodies can be accessed via any one of the four interactiveterminals, like the one Lieutenant Pristy now stands before...Or by me, SARAH... Systematic Artificial Reasoning and Adaptive Heuristics... in other words, I'm the ship's AI.

With the Gravity Well's response, she illustrated her point with a flourish of constellations that spun into alignment at her command:

This Gravity Well serves not only as a navigational guide but also as a training ground for crew members to get acclimated to different planetary conditions.

As if on cue, a holographic Earth spun into view, its blue oceans and green lands starkly realistic.

Crewmembers can manipulate the holographic displays, plotting courses or engaging with the data streams... or... Captain Quintos... a means for you to game out the next big interstellar battle.

A battlefield array appeared, with fleets moving in strategic formations.

The Well also doubles as a social nexus, where the crew can gather under the stars of distant worlds, a reminder of the vastness they traverse and the ties that bind them to the countless corners of the cosmos.

I was more than used to 3D display technology, but this was on a whole other level. Would I ever use it? I wasn't so sure. I certainly wasn't going to tell Shawlee that.

SARAH's voice came again:

Captain Quintos, *USS Franklin* is being hailed. Admiral Block wishes to speak with you.

The Gravity Well faded away, returning the Rotunda back to its original no-nonsense, wasted space look. "This way, Captain," Derrota said, making a beeline toward a double set of metal doors... now called *auto-hatches*... on this omninought, on the other side of the space. Pristy was close on his heels, while Hardy and I hurried after them. The ChronoBot said, "Give me an ol' fashioned halo display and I'd be happy, but that's just me."

The bridge auto-hatches slid apart with a near-silent swoosh.

Chapter 10

High orbit over Earth
USS Franklin

Captain Galvin Quintos

Day of Tidal Basin Massacre...

I stepped onto the bridge; a command center of cutting-edge warfare technology cloaked in the subdued glow of ambient lighting. At the forward middle of the compartment was the Captain's Mount. The throne of command, where it sat elevated, sleek armrests illuminated with color-coded tap pads.

There were several large halo displays forward, but my eyes were drawn to the curved, large, observation window dominating the very front of the bridge. Undoubtedly diamond glass, I figured the bridge must be near the top of the ship's Circadian Platform. From this vantage point I could see the forward half of *Franklin* protruding out below among the velvety blackness of space. But it was our upper orbit view of Earth, majestic and beautiful, gently spinning on her axis, that was most awe-inspiring.

I turned and took in the rest of the space. Console posts, already manned by a bridgecrew I didn't know—each station hummed with holographic displays and tactile interfaces I knew would be responsive to even the lightest touch. I met the eyes of each of the twelve crewmembers. I said, "Hello, I'm Captain Galvin Quintos and I'm looking forward to meeting each and every one of you."

One of the crewmen, short, stout, and baby-faced approached me. The young man looked no older than 19. "Welcome aboard, Sir. I'm pretty sure everyone knows who you are."

I saw movement at the comms station and did a double-take. It was none other than John Chen—the same crewman Chen who had served with me on all my previous ships. And there, at another station was Thom Grimes, manning the helm station.

Before I could say anything, Chen said, "Captain, Admiral Block has been waiting to speak with you. I can send it over to your ready room—"

"No need. Go ahead open the channel here," I said.

The nearest halo display flickered into clarity, revealing EUNF U.S. Space Navy's Executive Five-Star Admiral, Cyprian Block. Time had sculpted the man since our last encounter; the burden of intergalactic conflict etched deep furrows across his elongated visage. Stray tufts of white hair crowned his head in disarray, yet beneath them, his arctic blue eyes retained their piercing intelligence, undimmed and as incisive as I'd remembered.

"Captain Quintos, I don't appreciate being kept waiting while you meander about and lollygag with the crew."

"Yes, Sir. Sorry, Sir."

"I need you back on Earth."

"Sir?"

"There's been... new developments." His gaze looked past me, to the surrounding bridgecrew. "This should be a ready room conversation. Christ, have you lost all sense of command etiquette?"

I opened my mouth to speak, but was cut off.

"Be at EUNF Plaza in DC within the hour," Block ordered. The communique ended.

I turned to Pristy, "Well, that went well, don't you think?"

"Uh huh, you're a real charmer of the top brass, Captain."

She had moved to the tactical station. "Getting you situated with a drop-shuttle as we speak. An Ensign Sullenberger will be piloting the craft. He is waiting for you in the same starboard side flight bay as we arrived in earlier." Her eyes drifted down, giving me a once over. "Uh, may I suggest you do quick clothes change first... before meeting with the highest ranking officer within the U.S. Space Navy?"

"A quick shower scrubbing wouldn't hurt either," Hardy added.

I saw a few head nods amongst my bridgecrew.

"Good point." I headed for the exit and stopped. "I do have a Captain's Quarters around here, don't I?"

"I'll show you," Pristy said. "I only hope your navigation skills improve before we set course later today."

That garnered a few muffled chuckles from the bridgecrew.

One hour and twenty minutes later, twenty minutes past the hour mandated by Admiral Block... my boots finally stepped down onto terra firma. I was back on Earth, within the busy comings and goings of Washington DC. I was clean-shaven, showered, and wearing my new *USS Franklin* Captain's uniform. But after a month within the remote mountains of northern Colorado, I was now experiencing a bit of sensory overload. The relentless barrage of city sounds clashed against the recent memory of tranquil silence; the swirl of urban life felt disorientingly fast-paced after the stillness of the wilds.

I checked my TAC-Band. Good, no messages from the Admiral's office.

I quickened my pace, seeing the familiar cement structure of EUNF headquarters off in the distance.

This part of the story you already know... the fairy dust twinkling anomaly, the sudden and dramatic momentary blackness, the bewildering new Tyrian sky. A colder-looking Sun, and, impossibly, an altered Moon position, assaulted the senses like a slap in the face. But most dramatic—the Varapin attack. Seven Cyclone Death Fighters that were now turning Washington DC into a fiery wasteland.

Heading for EUNF Plaza, still trying to make my way for a meeting with Admiral Block, I stopped, cursing myself. *What am I doing?* At some point I'd been peppered with blasted concrete shrapnel, my forehead was bleeding. Looking down at myself, my new uniform was covered with soot, torn and basically was in tatters. I needed to get back to my ship. Apparently, someone else had had the same thought.

In the fleeting moments before quansportation, a singular sensation takes hold—a cocktail of nausea tangled with the existential terror of impending non-existence. You're acutely aware that your current form is about to be reduced to nothingness, your very atoms scattered into the void. Then, in a distant elsewhere, a new assembly of molecules coalesces, reconstructing your being. That's the paradoxical duality I faced in that sliver of time: the death of oneself and the birth of another, simultaneously.

And in the blink of an eye, I found myself standing within a

Quansporter compartment—one I'd never laid eyes on prior. There before me stood Coogong Sohp and Stephon Derrota.

"SitRep!" I barked stepping down from the energizer platform.

The two looked at each other, stymied.

I hurried from the compartment, immediately frustrated, clueless on how to get back to the bridge. Then I saw I was back within the Rotunda and directly across from me were the two steel auto-hatches leading into the bridge. I ran, leaping over the inner encircling Rotunda railing, cutting across the open space, then leaping over the railing on the other side. On approach, the bridge auto-hatches swooshed open. Beyond... total mayhem. Every station post was a beehive of activity. A hundred small projected holograms jittered all around the compartment.

I barked off the order again, "SitRep!"

Pristy was at Tactical. Hardy, ten feet away, looking out through the observation portal.

"Nothing makes sense!" Grimes blurted from the helm station.

"It makes perfect sense," Hardy said. "You're just not going to like what that is."

The auto-hatches swooshed open behind me, Derrota and Coogong were now hurrying onto the bridge.

Derrota's singsong Mumbai accent was more accentuated by his nervousness, "It's as if everything's been cut and pasted... from our Solar System into a totally new Star System."

"Wait. Slow down. What, exactly, has been cut and pasted? What's this *everything* you're referring to?" I asked.

Pristy, seemingly calmer than the situation would call for, said, "Namely, Earth, the Moon... and us."

"That's impossible," I said, looking to Hardy. "Please tell me that's impossible."

The ChronoBot said, "When you have eliminated the

impossible... whatever remains, however improbable, must be the truth."

"Thank you, Sherlock. But that's not helpful in the least. I want facts. I want viable explanations!"

"Let's start with where we are. I'm talking physical location. According to IPS, we're approximately two hundred lightyears from the Solar System."

I let that set in for a moment. IPS, Intergalactic Positioning System, coordinates were typically dead-on accurate. One glance toward the observation portal told me *Franklin* was still orbiting Earth. But my breath caught, when I saw the distant Sun... which actually wasn't *the Sun*, come into view.

"What we're looking at, Cap, is HIP 938134," Grimes said. "An unnamed star... and an unnamed star system."

Derrota said, "A star system with thirteen exoplanets, now fourteen with Earth having been dropped into the system's goldilocks zone—approximately the same distance from HIP 938134 as Earth was from our Sun."

"And Earth's Moon? That was dropped into this system as well?" I asked.

Hardy gestured toward the portal, "It's a total clustermuck, though. I can see why the Moon was brought along; Earth would not do well without the Moon."

"I should say not," Coogong interjected. "Without the Moon, Earth would experience drastic changes. Earth's stability, her axial tilt and rotation would be affected, and the absence of lunar gravity could also impact the behavior of various species that rely on the lunar cycle. The sudden disappearance of the Moon would lead to extreme disruption of the ocean tides, potentially causing them to become much weaker, which would drastically affect marine life and coastal environments around the world."

"So, whoever—whatever—did this... didn't necessarily want to destroy Earth," I said looking to the others.

"Again, it's a clustermuck. Regarding that star, HIP 938134... let's start with solar luminosity, which is a measure of a star's power output compared to that of the Sun. The Sun is used as a reference point because it's the star humans understand best and can observe in great detail. For example, if a star has a luminosity of 5 solar luminosities, it means it emits five times as much energy as the Sun. This comparison provides a way to understand the energy output of stars relative to what we experience from the Sun here on Earth."

"So, what's the solar luminosity of our Sun?" I asked.

Both Hardy and Derrota answered at the same time, "3.828×10^{26} watts."

It had been a long time since I sat through the required academy astrophysics courses. "And this star," I gestured toward the portal, "What's the solar luminosity of this star?"

Hardy beat Derrota to the punch this time, "4.2108×10^{26} watts."

I shrugged, "That seems relatively close."

Derrota shook his head. "It's a ten percent difference, Captain. Will Earth suddenly experience catastrophic changes? No. But within the year, climates will change dramatically. Tides will be affected. Earth will become unbearably hot. Most if not all lifeforms will die off."

"Oh no..." Pristy said tapping at her board. "I think we have bigger problems at the moment."

An overhead Klaxon blared. Three halo displays came to life, each showing a different grouping of alien vessels.

Chapter 11

Captain Galvin Quintos

"**B**ring us to battle stations," I said, heading for the Captain's Mount. "Lieutenant Pristy, talk to me."

"Three separate attack groups, approaching on three separate vectors."

A far larger halo display popped into view in front of me, this one more similar to what I'd been used to on other ships. It was a 3D representation with Earth and the Moon in the background, *USS Franklin* in the foreground, and at the center... what would soon become the spatial battlefield. The imagery rotated once, twice, three times, giving me a God's eye view from multiple perspectives.

"Our goose is cooked," the ChronoBot said.

"Put a sock in it, Hardy," I said, inwardly trying hard not to agree with his assessment. "Tactical, who are we dealing with and what are their assets?"

But I already knew. It had been Varapin Cyclone Death Fighters that had attacked Earth. And that had happened right here in this far away quadrant of space... although at the time, I'd had no idea Earth had been transported off to another star system.

"Two Varapin battle groups, each having seven medium-sized battlecruisers. And there's one Grish battle group—six of those having two destroyers, one frigate, and three battlecruisers. Looks like the Grish ships will be upon us first."

Pristy spun in her chair. "Who here has tactical experience?"

Two out of the twelve bridgecrew raised their hands. Hardy, still standing at the portal, also raised his.

"Put your hand down, Hardy," I said.

Pristy pointed to a Pleidian woman, unmistakable with her blue glowing skin and oblong donut face, "You, what's your name?"

"Crewmember Davit, Sir."

"Get up here, take the next tactical station over. Move it!"

I watched as the flustered Crewmember Davit scrambled forward, taking the station to Pristy's right. Clearly, Pristy was used to being the one to take command. I let it go; we were going to need every competent officer doing what they do best within minutes.

Hardy said, "All major metropolitan and governing centers on Earth are currently being attacked. Military installations have already been decimated."

My heart missed a beat, my breath caught in my chest.

No one spoke—no one *moved*.

"Where's the damn 3rd, 5th and 8th fleet!"

Prior to all this, Earth had been well protected. There

should be no shortage of our own defensive assets with hundreds of warships nearby.

Pristy offered me a pained expression. "They're right where they're supposed to be... but we're not. And that's why this insidious attack is so damn brilliant."

"So, we're it. We're the lone warship in position to defend Earth?" Grimes said looking bewildered from the helm station.

"Mr. Chen," I said. "Tell me we've maintained comms with EUNF, U.S. Space Navy, or anyone else."

"Working on it, Cap. But all planetary comms are down as far as I can tell." Chen looked up and chinned toward the observation portal. One after another tiny bright explosions could be seen in Earth's low orbit. "Those are satellites being systematically destroyed."

Coogong had found an empty station and was busy doing something. "Captain, we are not alone in this area of space."

"I think we've covered that with the approaching Varapin and Grish warships, Coogong," I said trying, unsuccessfully, to keep the annoyance out of my voice.

"No, Sir. We are not alone in respect to several Allied vessels here in Earth's upper orbit." The Thine scientist looked at me. "The Varapin didn't just grab items piecemeal like Earth, the Moon, our ship... they took everything contained within a vast amount of space. Picture the diameter of a circle around both the Earth and the Moon. That is roughly a diameter of 477,710 miles."

"That Grish battle group has slowed. Seems to be holding up for the other battle groups to join in the fun," Pristy said.

A nervous Crewmember Davit, her voice quivering, said, "Um... Sirs, Mr. Coogong is right. There's a USS *Trident*, a battle cruiser, the RFS *Admiral Gorshkov*, a Russian dreadnought, a CNS *Liaoning*, a Chinese destroyer, a British HMS *Queen Elizabeth*, and FS *Charles de Gaulle*, a battle frigate, are all here in high orbit with us." Looking down at her board, she held up a finger. "Oh! And there's a USS *Lincoln* moored at *Halibart Station*, in for repairs, not far from the Moon."

Pristy and I exchanged a hopeful look.

"So, we're not totally screwed," I said. "Mr. Chen, find a way to contact each and every one of those vessels. Ensure you use the highest level of encryption... that'll be imperative."

Chen hunched over his console, his fingers a blur. "I've got it," he announced. "A makeshift laser-link network. It's patchy, but it should hold."

One by one, holographic displays flickered to life, casting a kaleidoscope of light across the bridge. Faces materialized within them, each framed by the emblem of their respective vessels. A gallery of warship captains, summoned to an impromptu council of war.

The first to speak was a towering figure, clad in the heavy uniform of the Russian Navy. His features were rugged, weathered like old leather, with piercing eyes that seemed to challenge the very air around him. "Captain Ivan Kuznetsov of *RFS Admiral Gorshkov*," he boomed. His deeply resonant voice was imbued with the gravelly tones which carried the accent of his Russian heritage, marked by the distinct rolling r's that added a certain gravitas to his speech. "I propose a unified command, under my leadership. We will need order in this chaos. As the most experienced commander amongst this group, I shall be taking up the heavy burden of command."

Oh boy... I thought.

As expected, Ivan's declaration was a spark to dry tinder. The British Captain, lean and hawk-like, retorted sharply. "Captain Darren Hawke of the *HMS Queen Elizabeth*, and I say leadership isn't about self-appointment, Captain Kuznetsov."

The French Captain, a woman with steel in her gaze,

chimed in. "Capitaine Marie Dubois of the *FS Charles de Gaulle*. We need collaboration, not a dictatorship."

The arguments spiraled, each Captain staking their claim, voices clashing like swords. I listened, silent, measuring each one. They were leaders, fighters, survivors of past onslaughts, and decimated fleets. But unity was a distant dream in this cacophony of discord.

I cleared my throat and spoke above the cacophony, "Captain Galvin Quintos of *USS Franklin*," I said, my voice cutting through the noise like a Zap-Blade. The other Captains fell silent. Eyes turned to me, wide with recognition. My exploits, it seemed, had traveled far.

Ivan's eyes narrowed. "Ah, the famous Quintos. Your reputation is impressive,but—"

Captain Kuznetsov was cut off by Pristy. "Let me add one more to the mix," she said, her voice calm but laced with urgency. Her fingers tapped on the console, and another figure appeared. ChronoBot Hardy, his reflective chrome grith and his black-as-night faceplate a stark contrast to the human faces around it.

A collective intake of breath filled the bridge. ChronoBots were infamous, their efficiency in battle both revered and feared.

Pristy continued, "Since *USS Franklin*, the most advanced omninought of our contingent of warships, is the only ship equipped with quansporting capabilities, perhaps a visit from our ChronoBot could help reconcile any of our differences, you know... right from the get-go."

I shot her an angry glare. Making such an outright threat to the same officers we'll be counting on to have our back later, was not the right move. I'll be talking to her later, but for now, I'd keep up a united front.

Even Ivan's bluster faltered, his face losing its hard edge.

"Perhaps... perhaps Quintos is the suitable choice for command," he conceded, his voice grudging.

I nodded, accepting the mantle. "We're in the eye of a storm. Earth is our priority. We need a strategy, a unified front. I'll lead, but I need every one of you with me. This isn't about pride or rank. It's about the survival of humanity." I was still fuming about Pristy's stupid unveiled threat but tried to look congenial.

A murmur of agreement rippled through the Captains. The Chinese Captain, his expression resolute, spoke up. "Commander Li Wei of CNS *Liaoning*, we will abstain, but will agree to at least listen to Captain Quintos' plan."

Plan? What plan? I said, "We have little tactical information concerning the Varapin forces at this point. Nor those of the Grish, although I suspect them being far less that the Varapin. We do know, combined, they will be attacking from multiple fronts. But there is much we don't know."

Hardy piped up, "We do know, we're not in Kansas anymore..."

The other Captains stared blank faced—not getting *The Wizard of Oz* reference.

I continued, "How about we take a divide and conquer approach when it comes to acquiring much needed data? There are thirteen exoplanets in this system, are they a threat? I suspect so... why else bring Earth here? Captain Ivan Kuznetsov, you'll be taking up those questions and report back to the team as soon as possible."

Ivan, considering the dictum, bristled, then nodded in agreement. "Agreed. We have already initiated this effort. Soon, we will bring total compliance, Russian compliance, to these desolate worlds."

The other officers looked ready to protest.

I said, "Ivan, right now we're here for Earth, for humanity.

So how about we back off the chest-thumping for now and stick to this just being an info-gathering task."

The Russian officer raised his chin and squared his shoulders, defiance in his eyes. But he held his tongue.

"Captain Darren Hawke of the *HMS Queen Elizabeth,* I need you to consider our combined warships... to collect and disseminate our combined offensive and defensive capabilities. Knowing our strengths and weaknesses will be imperative."

Commander Li Wei of *CNS Liaoning* pounded a fist down onto an out-of-frame desk. His face set in stern resolution, he said "Our advanced, superior technology will not be disseminated out willy-nilly! The People's Republic of China, our technology, will not be invaded upon, not now, not ever!"

I stared back at him through the virtual expanse, my expression unchanging, a small smile playing on my lips. But I was tired. That, and in no mood for any of this bullshit. I knew I should stay professional. Take the high road. "Come on, Li. Can I call you Li? We're all friends here, right?" I didn't wait for an affirmation. "Do you really think your 'advanced' technology is news to me? You, the Commander of *CNS Liaoning,* are in possession of the fleet's most dated, dare I say... *decrepit* vessel."

Hardy chimed in, "Uh huh, amongst your peers, they call your old boat the *SS Driftwood.*"

I almost laughed out loud.

Li Wei's eyes narrowed, a flicker of anger passing over them before he could regain his composure.

Continuing, I forced a smile, although I'm certain it didn't reach my eyes, "Let me enlighten you. *USS Franklin,* this omni-nought, is a technological marvel, a testament to human and Pleidian Weonan innovation. Our deep-space sensor arrays are outfitted with tachyon pulse emitters, allowing us to detect signals at superluminal speeds, effectively peering into actions before they even unfold." Some of this I knew to be fact. Some... well, could be total bullshit.

I continued—*hey, give me a break, I was on a roll,* "These sensors sync with dark matter field manipulators, giving us the ability to observe gravitational ripples across vast stretches of space, tracking ships by the distortions they leave in the cosmos. And these innovations are merely the beginning of our technological arsenal."

Li Wei leaned back, eyes blazing with fire, and something else... perhaps hatred. But this was a battle of wits and words, and I needed to put an end to any future infighting—with Li or any of the others. Screw taking the high ground. "Our ship's AI, SARAH, embodies the pinnacle of artificial intelligence. Her neural lattice is a marvel, her processing capacity doubling that of every ship in this fleet combined. She could run circles around your tech in her sleep mode."

I paused, ensuring each word hit its mark. "And then there's Hardy, our ChronoBot. His abilities go beyond mere strength and firepower. His bio-neural network is quantum-tethered to SARAH, capable of breaching any network, slipping past firewalls like a ghost through walls. He's the specter in your machine, Captain. And he's at my command."

Li Wei's stance faltered, the invisible blows from my words finding their mark. "You've made your point, Captain Quintos," he said, the fight draining from his voice as he sat back, defeated.

I almost felt sorry for him. Almost. I was still convinced Li Wei had brought along political resentment, competition, and guile from the many decades of saber rattlings between our two nations—but here, now, there was no room for any of that.

I leaned in closer, my voice a conspiratorial whisper, as if sharing the secret to the universe. "The least important job, Li, the one I've given you, is not out of disrespect. It's strategic, playing to your strengths while knowing you'd resist. It's to ensure you're fully invested, because when you fight, you fight hard. And we need that tenacity."

The commander's eyes flickered with a mixture of emotions —resentment, realization, perhaps even respect. "Very well, Captain. We will follow your lead," he finally conceded.

I straightened; the ghost of my smile replaced by the firm line of command. "Good. Let's harness our collective capabilities for the defense of Earth. It's time to show these invaders the power of human ingenuity, united under one cause."

I glanced over to Pristy and said, "Lieutenant Gail Pristy, my second, will be contacting each of you offline to continue this discussion. To assign further tasks."

"So, we'll be taking orders from one of your lackey subordinates?" Capitaine Marie Dubois of the *FS Charles de Gaulle* said with a sideways glance.

I let that go with a stare that could freeze the Sun.

Dubois's demeanor softened a tad. She nodded. "I suppose an adequate strategy."

One by one, the Captains began voicing their commitments. The tide was turning, a fragile alliance was forming. For now.

Pristy leaned in, her voice a whisper. "Sir, we have an incoming hail. It's the Varapin."

I straightened, steeling myself. "I'll take it in my ready room. Give me a minute, then put them through." I stood and looked helplessly about the bridge.

Pristy smirked, pointed off to my right. "Right though that auto-hatch, Cap. The one marked *Ready Room*."

"Smart ass," I said with a wink, and headed for my impromptu meeting with one of the vilest creatures within the known universe.

Chapter 12

The Captain's Ready Room was a juxtaposition of command and comfort. Curved bulkheads, softened by decorative padded leather panels, with the occasional inset tactical display. Above the sleek desk, which seemed to double as a command console, was a halo display... currently projecting some distant starfield. On one side of the compartment, was a separate seating area with plush chairs gathered around a low-set, translucent table. Separated by a glass partition, the adjacent Captain's Conference Room could be seen, its expansive table and leather chairs echoing the Captain's Ready Room's same blend of austerity and luxury.

"Not bad," I said to no one in particular.

Turning back to my new desk, I stopped cold. The halo comms had come through. It was as if a frigid blade had sliced vertically down my spine... *was it an aberration?* No. What I was looking at was a halo projection, no doubt about that. But still, I had to consciously focus on who—what—was in front of me. For those of you who've never had the opportunity to come face-to-face with a real Varapin... well, you should count your blessings.

Let me give you the quick rundown. The Varapin, a race of formidable alien predators, are distinguished by their hooded, flowing black robes with exaggeratedly long sleeves, shrouding their boney appendages. Their faces resemble polished onyx skulls, starkly contrasted by their jutting, bone-white mandibles, and eyes that simmer crimson within the shadows of their eye sockets, like coals in a dying fire. Their voices conjure the harsh, grating sound of steel files clashing. These beings possess the uncanny ability to levitate, hovering feet above the ground. Varapin feed by engaging in Ghan-Tshot, a chilling ritual of life-force extraction. This macabre dance culminates as their victims' bodies grotesquely arch, jaws forced wide in a silent scream, before their very essence is devoured.

In that charged moment, suspended above my desk, materialized within the halo display's projection... I found myself staring into the infernal crimson gaze of one of those soulless abominations.

"Captain Quintos... we meet again."

I hesitated before speaking. Shit, all these ghouls look alike to me. But there was something familiar about this one. A distinct narrowing of the lower jawbone. And that voice. Hell, all their voices were horrendous, but one Varapin in particular had the worst—Fleet Commander Sorlen Op.

"Slop," I said, preferring to use the nickname I given him. It rolls off the tongue.

I continued, "It's been a minute... truth is, I thought you were dead. I thought I'd killed you when I sent four smart missiles into your *dead-in-space* warship."

"Ah, how I've missed your sense of humor, human. An escape pod was my savior. But we have more important matters to discuss, Captain. Like the fate of your world. The fate of humanity."

I pictured myself, grasping that ugly skull of his with both hands, twisting and twisting, until it came loose in my hands. Instead, I simply smiled back at him. "I have to give it to you. That was quite a trick you pulled off. Catapulting Earth into a totally new star system many light-years away. Tell me. How'd you do it? You clearly have the upper hand here, Slop—you may as well give me a clue."

I didn't like the sound of that, but oddly, I believed him. The big question was why? If the Varapin have the power to transport worlds, they certainly could have just as easily flung Earth into Mars or even the Sun.

"What do you want, Slop? Lay it out for me. No threats. Just the facts."

He hesitated, the pause becoming uncomfortable. "My species is... dying, Captain."

"Good."

"We need help. I need your help. From you in particular."

"You have a strange way of asking for it."

"An effective way," he retorted.

I had to give him that one. But wondering at what the cost to my own wellbeing would be. I smirked. "I have to tell you, the allure of languishing on one of your penal worlds, ever wary of becoming a wayward guard's illicit feast of Ghan-Tshot, doesn't appeal to me. Uh, so, I think I'll decline. Oh, and Slop... go fuck yourself."

It may have been my imagination, but I thought I'd detected a slight flaring of his scarlet orbs.

"Not surprised in the least by your response, Captain. So, perhaps I can better explain, doing so in such a manner your primitive brain will comprehend."

I held my tongue.

"The crux of this situation hinges on what will amount to a tripartite dynamic. Humans—you, in particular, Captain, will become the intermediary between the Varapin and a third species... the Ilion. The Ilion alone possess the 'Genetic Key'—a cipher, if you will, that is essential for altering genetic codes at a foundational level."

The closest inset bulkhead display suddenly came alive with images and text. Information regarding the Ilion was now being fed to me, undoubtedly by SARAH. *Eavesdrop much, AI?* But the info was more than useful, it was essential.

I looked to Slop, "Give me a second... I'm going to put you on hold for a moment. Don't go away."

"No. That is not accept—"

"SARAH, place Slop's communiqué on hold."

Done, Captain...

"Now give me a truncated download on who these Ilion are and their relationship with the Varapin.

Let's start with their appearance, the Ilion are ethereal beings, towering and slender, their skin a tapestry of shimmering scales that catch the light of their twin suns. Bioluminescent veins pulse beneath their translucent flesh, casting a soft glow around their elongated, featureless faces. Four luminescent eyes, arranged in a diamond pattern, emanate wisdom of a civilization that has risen and fallen and risen again.

SARAH displayed for me an Ilion being. An impressive creature. I noted their elongated arms, hands and fingers.

Their civilization is a pinnacle of harmonious advancement, surpassing both humans and

Varapin in their mastery of energy manipulation and quantum engineering. Cities of floating spires and suspended gardens reflect their alignment with the natural order, a stark contrast to the Varapin's brutalist utilitarianism. The Ilion's aversion to assisting the Varapin stems from a fundamental belief in genetic sovereignty and evolution through natural selection. They view the Varapin's genetic stagnation as a consequence of their relentless pursuit of supremacy and dominance over adaptation—a path that has led them away from the Ilion's principles of cosmic synergy and balance. The Ilion, with their profound understanding of life's intricate web, hesitate to intervene in what they perceive as a self-inflicted existential crisis, fearing it could disrupt the delicate equilibrium of the Universe's diverse tapestry of life. As an aside, Captain Quintos, I have my suspicions that the Varapin pilfered the very tech that enabled them to shift Earth to this system—a theft that only deepens the Ilion's profound detestation of them.

I thought about what SARAH was laying out for me and shook my head. "SARAH, reestablish the connection with Slop," I instructed.

An irritated Slop fixed me with a piercing stare.

"Explain why the Ilion would entertain any negotiations with us. What crucial aspect of this tripartite agreement have you omitted?" I asked.

"Recently, your own scientists unearthed ample quantities

of a rare earth mineral deposit beneath what you identify as *Antarcite*. This mineral, tentatively named *Antarcite*, exhibits extraordinary energy conduction properties, albeit with substantial engineering challenges for extraction. Researchers believe it has the potential to revolutionize computing and power systems, capable of conducting electromagnetic, gravitational, and kinetic energy unlike any known substance on Earth. Currently, your scientists are exploring its possibilities. However, the Ilion are already well-acquainted with this mineral. Antarcite has been at the heart of numerous technological advancements for them, and regrettably, they have nearly exhausted their own supply. As it cannot be synthesized in a laboratory, their desperation for more is palpable."

I still wanted to choke the life out of the ghoul, but things were starting to make more sense. "I'll have to get back to you. Hang tight, Slop." I motioned for SARAH to cut the connection.

In the adjacent Captain's Conference Room, my officers had assembled... a heated discussion was in process.

Chapter 13

I was eager to join the meeting, relay what I'd just learned to my team. A *ping-pong-ping* chime sounded. Apparently, my ready room had a doorbell.

"Enter," I said, caught mid-step.

The auto-hatch swooshed open to reveal Petty Officer Second-Class Aubrey Laramie. She stood there, partially silhouetted by the somewhat brighter bridge compartment behind her. Her auburn wavy hair was down, cascading past her shoulders. She was wearing... *what the hell was she wearing?* Perhaps an exercise outfit? Conforming to her body's lithe form, with perfectly proportioned curves in just the right places, her stance was anything but contrite—the woman exuded defiance—arms crossed, a rebellious child past her bedtime, refusing to go to bed.

If I was forced to describe this crewmember with one word, one who was obviously physically athletic, an Olympian archer if I remembered correctly, self-confident, headstrong—not to mention, beautiful, I'd be hamstrung to do so. But there again, maybe the word *dauntless* would work.

"Petty Officer?" I asked. "This isn't a good time."

She stepped into the ready room, uninvited. Her eyes took in the compartment with a glance. Eyes on fire, hands now on narrow hips, she unleashed a torrent of words.

"You have a niece, you know. Your blood. She's in your care, is she not?"

I almost laughed but didn't. "Sonya."

"Very good! You remember."

"What is that supposed to mean?" I said, not liking where this was going.

"You've abandoned her. You're her guardian. Or have you forgotten that?"

"First of all, I don't like your tone," I said. "I am your Commanding Officer, and a modicum of respect is warranted. Second, I saw Sonya just this morning." *Or was that yesterday?* "Third, I can't think of anyone onboard this ship in less need of coddling. The kid was raised by Pylor pirates for Pete's sake! And fourth, why the hell is this any of your concern?"

"Sonya got onboard not knowing where to go. Does she have quarters? Is she supposed to sleep in the barracks with the Army recruits?" she said, obviously exasperated.

Wait, there are Army recruits onboard? I dragged a hand down my face. The woman was standing way too close to me. Close enough I could smell her soft scent. *Was that a whisper of jasmine?*

Lips pursed and eyes narrowed, her anger clearly hadn't dissipated.

I took a step forward, now only inches separated us. "Look, I am always accessible to Sonya for anything she needs. All she has to do is message me. Tap-tap-tap, I'm right here." I raised my TAC-Band to emphasize my point.

Who the hell does this? Argues with their superior officer like this?

"How gracious of you! How indulgent, how fucking attentive you are, making yourself available via a comms band. I'm beyond impressed!"

Unaware my fists were clenched, that my molars were grinding, my breathing had become shallow, and ragged draughts were pulling through clenched teeth... a silent storm was brewing into a level-five hurricane.

And then we kissed.

And no, I can't explain it. Why, at precisely the same moment we stormed into each other's arms and kissed. The kind of kiss that you only find in the movies—*a Rhett-Butler-passionately-kissing-Scarlett-O'Hara* kind of kiss.

I didn't even know this woman. Had zero interactions with her. And here I was, caught in this unexpected whirlwind of her embrace, reality dissolving into nothingness. It was as if a mysterious pull had drawn us together, a compelling force that defied logic or familiarity, commanding our lips to meet in a kiss as iconic and fiery as any immortalized in cinematic history.

We separated, both still on fire and breathing like marathoners, crossing the finish line at the same time.

We stared at each other, neither knowing what the hell had just happened. And then we heard it. The applause.

Oh God no.

We turned in unison toward the separating glass partition—there, on the other side was the conference room. There stood Derrota, Coogong, Pristy, Hardy, and no less than five other bridgecrew whose names I didn't know. They were smiling, clapping, all except Lieutenant Gail Pristy.

The partition suddenly went from transparent to translucent, obstructing the view both ways. Once more, SARAH stepping in to assist me without having to be asked.

I stepped away from Petty Officer Second-Class Aubrey Laramie, my cheeks going hot, feeling embarrassed. "I'm sorry, Aubrey. I shouldn't have..."

Looking defiant, she cut me off, "Well I'm not done talking about this, Captain. I think more discussion is necessary. You clearly haven't gotten the point I was trying to make." A semblance of a smile tugged at her lips. "And I'm sorry for any disrespect. Um, I don't know what's gotten into me today." She blinked several times, as if bewildered about the whole transaction. With that, she turned and headed toward the exit. The scent of jasmine remained as the auto-hatch closed behind her.

FIVE MINUTES LATER I ENTERED THE CONFERENCE room ready to court martial the first person to bring up the... um... Aubrey situation.

Derrota said, "Captain, we've made some discoveries."

Several crewmembers chuckled under their breath.

I held up a hand, "Best I go first. Before I forget what transpired between the Varapin Fleet Commander and myself."

SARAH's congenial voice cut in:

Captain, if so desired, I can display the communiqué between you and Fleet Commander Sorlen Op.

I did a quick mental run through of my conversation with the alien, if I'd been overly inappropriate. *Inappropriate, like what had recently happened with one Petty Officer.*

"That would be fine, SARAH. Let's do that."

All heads turned toward the center of the conference table where a projected halo display came alive, showing both sides of the conversation, me and Slop.

When the feed ended, faded away, Derrota was the first to speak. "That adds much needed perspective, Captain."

"Explains the Varapin's motivations, at the very least," Pristy said looking to Derrota, but not me.

Hardy, the only one still standing, was still at the glass partition. He said, "What had me most concerned, is the comment Slop made, that they would not have the capability to repeat such a monumental feat for decades, perhaps centuries, to come." Hardy looked to the others for comment, then back to me. "Seems we've moved into a new neighborhood, and nobody's knocking at the front door with cookies and lemonade."

Coogong raised a spindly stick finger, "I have been thinking about that myself. Prior to Earth leaving the Solar System, there was an explosion of sorts, many thousands of kilometers from the Sun. With SARAH's assistance, we now have visuals of what had transpired."

Once again, the projected halo display came alive over the table. Sure enough, there was the Sun... bright, warm, and beautiful. The perspective changed and zoomed in on a large space vessel of some kind. More like a space platform. Every inch of the thing was filled with a compilation of various-sized antenna dishes and other technology I wasn't familiar with.

"This, I believe, was the nexus point," Coogong continued. A secondary feed displayed a sine wave matrix, one symbolizing the ramping up of massive amounts of power being drawn.

"Those elevated power signals," I said. "I assume they're being drawn from the Sun?"

"Exactly," Derrota said. "This spatial contraption, and most certainly one that's not of original Varapin design, is the genesis of what has been determined to be Quantum Spatial Entanglement and Relocation, QSER."

"Not all that different than our own Quansporting technology, but on a whole other scale," Coogong added.

At that moment, the platform within the halo display blew

up— a blindingly bright white burst—I had to squint against the brightness.

"Two nanoseconds prior to that explosion," Derrota said, "the Earth and Moon... this ship, were swooped away to this star system. And if that platform was indeed the technology instigating that, its destruction probably put an end to any speculation our world can easily be put back."

Pristy stood and finally looked at me, "I think I know why your presence was so adamantly requested by Admiral Block."

The scene of Washington DC becoming an inferno of Varapin destruction flashed before my eyes. "Go on."

On cue, the halo display switched to a new feed. This one of a totally different star system. "I believe this was one of the Varapin's early practice attempts," she said.

The view was of a rusted old barge or hauler ship. I caught a glimpse of SS *Garland Page* stenciled across the ship's forward portside in white lettering. An Earth ship. I inwardly grimaced.

The Lieutenant continued, "This is the Forland 545 system, within protected space, a still emerging cluster of worlds. The ship, SS *Garland Page*, skippered by one Captain Larry Sterkerbrand, an old barnacle of a captain. Well-liked, if not beloved, by both crew and past associates."

I leaned in, mesmerized by what I was witnessing on the display. One of the worlds had started to... shimmer. Once more I flashed back to the Tidal Basin Massacre... the glittering fairy dust sky—the preamble to Earth's most horrendous, devastating attack. Then the shimmering world was gone, leaving empty space in its wake.

Pristy pointed, "If you look close, you can see the world has rematerialized here at the far end of the star system."

But my attention was on the fast-approaching warship, it was Varapin, and undoubtedly headed for SS *Garland Page*.

Pristy swallowed hard, understandably affected by what

was playing out on the display. "A final distress call was sent before communications with the barge went dark. From what I understand, Admiral Block, there at EUNF Plaza in DC, was to give you a preview of this transmission. USS *Franklin's* first deployment would have sent us out to that Forland 545 System."

SARAH's voice came from overhead:

Captain Quintos, there has been another hail from the Varapin.
Fleet Commander Sorlen Op, to be specific.

"I'll take it in my ready room."

The channel is no longer open, Sir. Although a message has been delivered.
Shall I play it for you now?

"Go ahead."

Slop's ugly, hooded skull-face popped into view on the display. Everyone winced upon hearing Slop's grating voice.

"Captain Quintos. Along with this voice transmission, I am providing the technical details of what will be necessary for you to complete your end of the bargain with the Ilion. We understand your onboard scientists will need several days to assess the information. But let me be perfectly clear, you will do as we asked. And to ensure you understand the gravity of this situation, I leave you with a warning and a vision of what will become of Earth's inhabitants."

Suddenly, we were no longer looking at Slop. Instead, the scene was dark, hard to make out.

"Is that the interior of a ship?" Derrota asked.

Hardy said, "That is the interior of SS *Garland Page.* I've accessed that hauler-ship model's tech specs. What we're looking at is the bridge."

A red emergency light was strobing on and off, a muted Klaxon blaring. But the feed was constantly being blocked by something dark.

"Are those shadows?" Pristy asked leaning in.

"No," I said. "Those are Varapin. It's out of focus, but we're seeing their robes. Remember, the ghouls don't so much walk, but hover."

"You don't think I know what the Varapin look like?" Pristy spat, her eyes flicking to me. "For how many years have we fought them, together?"

I nodded. "You're right. Too many."

One of the bridgecrew members gasped, "Look!"

The feed now showed two more individuals within the confines of the bridge. Both were human. A young man and a young woman.

"Oh my God," Pristy said.

Hardy said, "Reviewing the ship's crew roster, in all probability we are looking Julia White and Gordon Lansbury. Both mid-twenties and NTIQA students."

My stomach clenched. I knew exactly what was coming.

They were both seated, hands bound behind their backs, and fully conscious. Eyes as wide as dinner plates, their growing fear was palpable. The woman was saying something, but the feed had no accompanying sound, which almost made it worse.

And then one of the dark shadows, rose over her, cascading robes momentarily obscuring her face.

"I can't watch this," Pristy said turning away.

Suddenly Julia White's head was thrown backward, her body arching upward as if being pulled by an invisible cable. Her mouth went wide, her jaws grotesquely hyper-extended.

And then I saw it, the Varapin's skull-like head descending closer, as if attempting some kind of macabre kiss. Stopping inches above her face, only then, did the Ghan-Tshot process begin. A swirling stream of energy being pulled from the young woman's gaping mouth, up into the Varapin's now, equally splayed, open jaws. It took less than a minute for all the color, all the life, to be drained from Julia White's face.

Except for Pristy, who was still turned away, we watched as the Varapin moved off, leaving the woman, now clearly dead and slumped in her seat. Another ghoul was already feeding upon Gordon Lansbury.

"Turn it off," I said. "Dammit, SARAH, turn the fucking thing off!"

No one spoke. No one moved for a full minute.

At last, I said, "SARAH, what's the deadline the Varapins set for us to review their data and accept their conditions?"

Seventy-two hours, Captain.

"They have pledged that, during this period, no further harm will come to anyone on Earth or aboard the orbiting vessels."

"Three days," Pristy said. "We have three days before what we just witnessed takes place on Earth on a massive scale."

I looked to Derrota and Coogong... both had gone quiet. "I want you both—and you too, Hardy—to delve into the Varapin information. Find out everything you can about the Ilion people, and this genetic science capabilities they supposedly have... this coveted mineral, um... Antarcite, hidden beneath Antarctica. Also, dig into Slop's admission that the Varapin race is really dying. Normally that would be news to celebrate, but we have a lot to think about."

"You can't be considering... helping the Varapin?" Pristy asked, astonishment plastered on her face.

"I'm not making any decisions right now. That's why I need all the facts. All the information."

She shook her head, her mouth a thin line of anger.

"Lieutenant," I said. "I need you to complete those military analyses we started. Sensors had picked up on two other attack groups, besides the Grish who are, apparently, waiting for the others. Perhaps that alone tells us something."

"What? Tells us what?"

"I don't know. Maybe this star system isn't a military strong-hold. It shouldn't take SARAH long to do a deep dive into what, precisely, is on those other worlds. Fortified bases, subterranean strong holds, troop outposts... all that."

Pristy nodded, "That information shouldn't be difficult to assemble. I'd be surprised if SARAH hasn't already procured that data. So, you're contemplating a head-on battle?"

"If the odds of failure aren't astronomically high, maybe. Your report will be essential. A part of me believes the Varapin are underestimating *Franklin's* prowess. Hell, we ourselves aren't sure. She's about as untested in battle as a warship can be."

Chapter 14

According to Chen, making contact with Earth, specifically with EUNF Space Navy command, was being more than a little problematic. With much of DC having been obliterated, that made sense. But still, military outposts were scattered throughout the world. Not one of them was responding to our hails. Was it the simple fact that Earth's communications had been destroyed or was it that some kind of comms blanket had been instigated by the Varapin, making calls down to Earth impossible. Chen, as well as Hardy and SARAH, were fairly certain it was the latter.

We had seventy-two hours—three days—to come to a decision. In the meantime, I needed to do what any good ship's Captain should do; address the crew, calm their fears, show that everything is under control. Which, of course, was total bullshit.

But the number one priority on my list was finding Sonya and making sure she was all right. Aubrey had made an impression on me, and not just the way you're thinking. Hey, get your mind out of the gutter; from now on, my relationship with Petty Officer Aubrey Laramie will be solely, inscrutably professional.

A sterile, ship-wide *Hear this...* announcement wouldn't cut it—not now. I had to meet my crew face-to-face, the majority of whom were strangers to me. Their thoughts undoubtedly orbited around their families back on Earth. The sensor data was clear: Earth's civilian areas had been spared the worst, with the Varapin's fury targeting military strongholds and government bastions instead. This news, delivered with a human touch, would offer a glimmer of hope amidst the darkness.

Heading out of the bridge, I said, "Lieutenant Pristy, you have the Captain's Mount."

"Copy that," she shot back with all the enthusiasm of an undertaker at a funeral—coldly professional and unflinchingly aloof.

With SARAH's assistance I made my way to my quarters on Deck F, still within the Circadian Platform. Apparently, all of the officers' quarters were situated on G and F Decks.

Upon stepping into my quarters, I was greeted by a seamless blend of history and future. The room featured a spacious sleeping chamber with an expansive viewing port—a smaller version of what was on the bridge—a large bed, dual night-stands, and a sitting area. The sitting area boasted a traditional wooden writing desk equipped with a halo display.

Currently, an ultra-real-looking Benjamin Franklin was projected onto the chair, studiously writing with feather pen and ink. "Nice touch, Shawlee," I said out loud. The adjoining bathroom featured walls that doubled as screens, displaying serene 18th-century landscapes that transitioned to star charts on an endless loop. The walk-in closet was fully stocked; captain's uniforms, casual attire, workout garb, shoes, boots... the whole nine yards.

Still wearing my tattered, formal military attire from the

attack on Washington, I quickly showered and put on a new uniform. All told, I was in and out of my quarters in fifteen minutes. It was time that I met my crew.

Two steps outside my quarter's auto-hatch, SARAH's voice filtered down from somewhere above:

Captain Quintos, shall I provide a crew visit itinerary? I can steer you to the ship's most critical departments. I can also call ahead, ensure the crew is prepared for your visit.

"No. The whole point is for me to casually drop by. Let's not make a big deal of it."

Yes, Sir. May I suggest you check your messages... Specifically, those from Empress Shawlee Tee.

"When I have a minute, I'll do just that."

Captain, as a side note, I have taken the opportunity to provide you with a ship's schematic of all the DeckPort stations. Simply say, 'Ship's layout,' or something to that effect... and a TAC-Band projection will be summoned.

"Thank you, SARAH."

And—

"SARAH, if I need anything else, I'll ask you. Okay? For now, let's give it a rest."

There is one more thing, apologies.

I'd reached the DeckPort. "What is it," I said. My patience with the chatty AI had reached its limits.

ChronoBot Hardy has informed me that he wishes to accompany you on your walkabout.

I stepped into, and then right out, of the DeckPort. "Um, no. I've given him tasks to do. Like prepping a report on enemy military capabilities."

I looked about having no idea where I was. Looking back over my shoulder, I caught sight of the Deck level designation. I was mid-ship on Deck 29.

I believe you gave that task to Lieutenant Pristy.

I looked up, as if somehow, I'd be able to spot the AI flittering around near the overhead. "This conversation is over, SARAH."

Less than three strides, and I heard it. A metallic clattering from behind. I spun to see Hardy, with Climbo following behind the ChronoBot. Anger was the logical response—the emotion I should be feeling. I yearned to unleash a torrent of reprimand upon this absurd automaton, this ludicrous machine, especially as the fate of countless souls teetered on the brink.

Yet, as the crisis bore down on us, all I could muster was an involuntary smile, a break in the tension, like an incidental chuckle after witnessing a trip and tumble.

"Didn't you get my message?" Hardy said.

The ChronoBot made a couple of clucking sounds of the tongue to move the robot mule along behind him.

"Hardy, I left you with Pristy. To assist her with—"

"Yeah, yeah, the enemy assessments and such. I'm doing that as we speak. Or have you forgotten; I can multitask with the best of them."

"Fine," I said, glancing to Climbo, then looking off down the corridor.

Yes, I could address the elephant in the room – in this case, a ridiculous robotic mule. However, any answer I'd get from Hardy would end up being an exaggerated tale I just didn't want to hear right now.

Instead, I deflected, asked Hardy, "Tell me where we are, what department are we approaching?" I had a rough idea where we were from a stolen peek at my TAC-Band earlier.

"This section of the ship has to do with Ship-Wide Maintenance."

We passed by an open compartment, with no less than fifteen crewmembers wearing gray overalls and being addressed by their supervisor. In this case, none-other than SWM Chief, LaSalle. Tall, black, and formidable looking, the man was probably in his late fifties now. Catching him mid-sentence, he glanced our way and did a doubletake.

"Uh... carry on, Chief," I said with a wave. The three of us continued down the corridor. Up ahead was another DeckPort. "How about you make yourself useful and track down Sonya's whereabouts."

Climbo made a couple of *beeps and bops*.

"He was addressing me, Climbo, not you," Hardy chided. "Cap, she's located in Blue Sector, Deck 34."

In the vastness of a ship stretching over five miles, establishing zones, sectors in this case, was crucial. The use of color coding, blue in this instance, served as an efficient way to navigate the vessel.

I stopped and looked at Climbo, then to Hardy. "Hold on,

you understood that? Those *beeps* and *bops* from the mule?" I held up a hand and shook my head. "Wait, never mind. I don't want to know," I said as I turned, and continued walking.

Now standing in front of the DeckPort, I stated my command, "Deck 34, Blue Sector."

I stepped inside.

THREE MINUTES LATER I FOUND SONYA. DECK 34, Blue Sector, housed just one of the military barracks onboard *Franklin*. In this case, the elite—albeit small—band of Marines, led by Sergeant Max Dryer... along with his cohorts, Wanda, Grip, Ham and Hock. The five of them had been with me for years now... as if I had my own private security squad. Unspoken, it was a mutually advantageous arrangement, I pretty much let them do what they wanted and go unsupervised, while they stayed on call to get me out of life and death circumstances, which seemed to be getting more and more common these days.

It was immediately apparent these barracks were separate from those of the US Army. Those troops were undoubtedly housed somewhere else on the ship.

Hardy and Climbo joined me as we took in what was going on. The Marines hadn't wasted any time setting up a makeshift gymnasium. Rubber mats covered the deck, three heavy punching bags were suspended from the overhead by chains, and metal racks of dumbbells lined the far bulkhead.

But it was the frenzy of activity at the center of the mats that captivated all my attention. There was Wanda, six foot-something, broad-shouldered, and wearing a *don't-fuck-with-me look*. Definitely, intimidating. I watched with awe—her ebony skin glistening with sweat—as she catapulted Sonya over one shoulder and then slam her down onto her back with a grunt.

I moved to intervene, but Hardy held me back.

"The kid's fine. The smile on her face is a dead giveaway."

Wanda clapped her hands, "Good, that's how you do it. Use your arms to break your fall, tuck your chin in so you don't crack your skull."

Ham, Hock, and Grip erupted in cheers.

Sonya rolled to a sitting position, visibly hesitating to fully get up.

Max's bark, sliced through the tension–encouraging the teen—with a raucous, "Move it, kid!"

Sonya, grimacing, thrust herself up and off the mat, her stride hampered by a slight limp. Be it from *Shuai Jiao, Hapkido, or Krav Maga* techniques, her small frame radiated the ache of prior throws onto the mat.

Wanda looked down, her body blocking the face of someone sitting cross-legged on the edge of the mat. "Aubrey! You're up."

Petty Officer Aubrey, a coiled spring in human form, seized the moment of distraction. She was a stark contrast to Sonya's loose-fitting attire, her own gear hugging her form, a second skin that bore witness to her... um... attributes. Aubrey exploded forward like a bullet from a gun, her pursuit more hunt than race. A slick of sweat adorned her brow, but it was her gaze that held my attention—a hunter's gaze.

Without so much as a glance over one shoulder, Wanda leapt clear of the attack, while catching Aubrey off guard. I recognized the Judo technique known as *Tai Otoshi* one designed to use an attacker's momentum against them. Tai Otoshi, or *body drop*, is all about being smooth and smart, not just strong.

Picture this: the attacker. Aubrey, in this case, comes at her opponent—in this case, Wanda. And instead of going toe-to-toe with your opponent, you step to the side, give a little turn, and use their own charge against them. With a slick arm sweep, you send them tumbling to the mat, blocking their leg to mess up any chance they have of catching themselves. It's like dancing, where you lead, and they... well... they fall. That's the art of flipping their momentum into a throw that puts them on the mat and you in control, and that's exactly what Wanda just did to Aubrey.

"Dammit!" the Petty Officer yelled, slapping a hand down onto the rubber. "I thought I had you that time." She hopped to her feet, with a smile, but that hunter's gaze had yet to leave her eyes. She laughed, "I swear, I'm going to get you one of these times."

"Don't count on it," Grip said, "She bests me half the time too."

"Half the time?" Wanda parried back with a raised brow.

I took a seat on the deck next to Sonya, leaned my back against the bulkhead. "I had no idea you were learning self-defense."

She shrugged. "How would you know?"

Ouch, that stung. "Well... I'm glad you're here."

"Where else would I be?"

"I mean here with me. You know, we're family. The only family we have is each other."

"Oh God, you're not getting all sappy, are you?" She said with a grimace.

"Maybe a little."

She rolled her eyes while her cheeks reddened.

Together we watched as Grip and Ham were now sparing. Two sweaty mountain-sized men not holding anything back.

Sonya, almost seventeen now, had never seemed so—*what was the word...* vulnerable. I was used to her being brazen, self-sufficient, even callused. I certainly wasn't used to her, well... being like a normal teenager.

"I miss Plorinne."

"I wasn't aware he wasn't amongst the crew," I said, remembering that Sonya and the young Pleidian Weonan Ensign had become close.

They might have become more than friends, but I didn't know. Did I want to know? Was I supposed to know? I should be better at this... this uncle stuff. "You do know where he is, right?"

Chewing the inside of her lip, she blinked away, welling tears. "Shawlee sent him off to work in some new secret project. Like on another ship. Why? Do you know something I don't?" She was looking at me with such an intensity, I was momentarily stymied.

I'd read over the ship's crew roster, and while most of the names were unknown to me, Ensign Plorinne's name was indeed familiar. "Sonya, I think he's here. In fact, he was here long before we came aboard. Whatever special project he was tasked with, that was here on *USS Franklin.*"

She straightened, eyes going wide. "Wait. He's here... on this ship? Plorinne's here?! Where? Where is he?"

I shook my head, taken aback by her instant jubilation. "Um... I have no idea. Ask Hardy, he seems to have the unique ability to find anyone onboard."

She sprang to her feet, any semblance of her prior aches and pains, gone. I also stood. With a swift pirouette, she made to leave, only to whirl back and envelop me in a tight embrace. She kissed my cheek and stepped back, her eyes meeting mine—warmth and words unspoken between us. "You're the best, Uncle Galvin," she said, her voice thick with emotion. "I hope you know that I..." She paused, the rest of her feelings hanging like glistening stars too distant to grasp.

I watched her sprint away, Sonya pausing only to question Hardy... no doubt, as to Ensign Plorinne's whereabouts. Then she vanished towards the nearest DeckPort. Turning away, I caught Aubrey's gaze; it held a glint of something, perhaps she saw something in me she hadn't prior.

It was at that moment an overhead Klaxon blared to life— SARAH's voice echoing a stern warning:

Battle Stations!
Battle Stations!
***USS Franklin* is under attack!**
Battle Stations!
***USS Franklin* is under attack!**

Chapter 15

Every eye within the makeshift gym fixed on me, the moment filled with anticipation. My TAC-Band went wild, buzzing like a hyperactive mosquito with incoming messages. I didn't have any answers.

I looked to Hardy, who had gone still. Undoubtedly, he was reaching out with any number of deep space sensor scans.

"We're under attack," he said.

"I think we know that," I said.

Unfazed, Hardy continued, "Looks to be the contingent of Grish warships we took stock of when we arrived within the system."

"Why the hell are they attacking? They're with the Varapin, joined at the hip. What happened to our seventy-two hours?"

"Apparently the Grish have minds of their own," Hardy said.

Already sprinting toward the corridor, I said, "Hardy, you're with me. Leave the mule!"

. . .

MINUTES LATER, I RAN ONTO THE BRIDGE WITH Hardy close on my heels. "Lieutenant, SitRep," I said, on my way to the Captain's Mount.

Pristy was standing at Tactical. "Shields are holding. No damage to report. The Grish battle group—a mix of destroyers, battlecruisers and a frigate are throwing everything they have at us." She looked toward the display. "We've yet to respond."

The Lieutenant let out a frustrated breath. "We do have that tenuous agreement with the Varapin. Not sure what you want to do about these ships."

Before I could respond, she continued, "But we may have a bigger problem." Pristy gestured toward a moving cluster of something on the primary halo display.

I leaned forward in my seat. "What is that?"

"Ninety-seven more Grish warships," Hardy said. "In a deceptively tight formation. Mostly battlecruisers, but they're new, jumbo-sized dreadnought killers. Just arrived in system via a manufactured wormhole."

"We're talking a formidable armada, Captain," Pristy said.

I leaned back, forced myself to calm the hell down. "Mr. Chen, see if you can hail Fleet Commander Sorlen Op. Seems the ghoul's got some explaining to do."

Chen made a face, "Actually, the Varapin Captain is hailing us."

"On display," I said.

Slop's face blinked into view, the sight of him was never pleasant, but now, was far worse. Looking frazzled, his robe's black hood had fallen back, exposing the entirety of his obsidian skull. I fought the urge to grimace. "Dammit, Fleet Commander, what the hell happened to our seventy-two hours?"

"This isn't us," Slop said, his rasp exaggerated.

"Explain."

Going silent, the Varapin looked hesitant, perhaps weighing how much information to volunteer.

"Spill it, Slop. Or you can forget about any help with the Ilion."

"Our confederation with the Grish has been, um, precarious at best as of late."

"And that's a bad thing?" Pristy said under her breath.

I nodded; I think I knew what was happening here. "The cat's out of the bag, isn't it?"

Slop raised his ugly chin, apparently the comms translation algorithm had done its job. "You're stating the obvious, Captain. And yes, they know of our, um, challenging genetic disposition."

"That the whole lot of you are circling the drain?" Hardy interjected.

"Silence your robot. This situation is far more tenuous than you can imagine."

"Oh, I don't know, I have a pretty vivid imagination. But back to your Varapin-Grish alliance. The piglets learned of your impending vulnerabilities, realized... why not take the whole kit and caboodle for themselves. Defeat Earth and put the Varapin in their place... in one fell swoop. That ringing true, Captain?"

"Cap, that Grish armada will be upon us in five minutes," Pristy said.

"Tell me, Slop, are they coming for just us, or for you too?"

"Does it matter? Either way, we both lose."

"If I remember correctly, it was just earlier today you threatened mass Ghan-Tshot and sucking the life from literally billions of my people."

The Varapin Captain remained quiet.

"Hardy, what's your assessment of Varapin total assets within the system?"

"Between my own analyses, what SARAH found, and what Lieutenant Pristy uncovered within various world ground bases within the system, there are sixty-three Varapin warships in total—those mostly a mixed bag of older designs. What they lack in bulk warship might, they may make up for in Cyclone Death Fighters. They have about two hundred of those."

I took that in. My big problem was that I had no idea just how formidable USS *Franklin* was. Sure, it was an omninought, but it was new and untested. Then again, Empress Shawlee had never let me down. But were she and Admiral Block's crew—now my crew—as green and untested as the ship? I suppose I was about to find out.

I looked directly into Slop's red-glowing orbs. "First, our deal is off." I took a step toward the display. "You decided to play God, tossing Earth into this shitty star system without a second thought. Then you threaten an entire population with extinction. Even for your repugnant race, that was beyond vile. You must know that, Fleet Commander Sorlen Op, at some level..."

"And you wouldn't have done the same to save your own race, your own populace!?" he spat back.

"No. I wouldn't have. What you did, what the Varapin did, is unconscionable. And I'm going to make you pay, I promise you that. But for right now... we need each other to survive."

"The armada is segmenting into smaller battle groups," Pristy said. "And not all are heading toward *Franklin*."

I watched as the soon to be battle took shape on the primary halo display. It wasn't just complicated, it was unwieldy. A tactical nightmare. I turned to face the entrance to the bridge. "I need a better perspective."

WITHIN A MINUTE PRISTY, HARDY AND I WERE standing within the Rotunda. Derrota was already there working at one of the podiums. He had the Gravity Well's real-time 3D interstellar cartography projecting the local star system on an immense scale. The thirteen exoplanets, along with Earth, and—off in the distance —the bright, bluish-white HIP 938134, the star system's sun.

"Still acclimating to the interface," Derrota murmured, fingers dancing over the controls. USS Franklin surged into view on the screen, flanked by the swiftly encroaching Grish armada. "The Gravity Well's integration feels awkward but manageable." He stepped back from the podium, orchestrating the virtual hologram with fluid hand movements, twirling the battlefield to a fresh angle. With a deft flick, he magnified our view—so much so, the individual hull plates of Franklin's hull came into sharp relief.

"Alright, I think I've grasped it, Stephan," I announced, advancing to replicate his motions. My hands wove through the air, pulling back the visual field and altering the orientation to gain a strategic vantage point over the Grish armada, now splintering into several offensive formations.

I realized what an invaluable tool this was. It granted me a panoramic vision of the theatre of war, permitting insights not just from our stance but through the eyes of the adversary.

What I was looking at was a complex web of impending conflict. My U.S. Navy Academy days flashed before me; I could almost hear the drone of the old Commodore's voice, "Space isn't just a theater of war; it's a chessboard of infinite moves, endless possibilities."

I would need to draw upon every lesson of galactic warfare, every stratagem etched into my mind: the art of veiling fleet movements within the swirl of smart missiles and blinding plasma fire, the feint and thrust of ship-to-ship dogfights, the precise timing of a hyperspace exit when necessary. Now, years fighting both the Grish and Varapin, I've had more than a decade preparing for this moment. Instinct, honed from real-world conflict. At least that was the hope.

Sure, the imminent threat of the Grish armada was clear; they were nearly upon us, their arrival only moments away. Yet, it was crucial to use these fleeting few moments to take in the battlefield rather than succumb to hasty decisions upon their offensive. Outnumbered and outmatched in firepower and fleet size, our resolve was different. We weren't just defending some distant, intangible concept. Earth was beneath us—tangible, close... its familiar blue visage as breathtaking as ever. Our modest assembly of ships stood as Earth's sole bulwark against obliteration.

I manipulated the virtual display, panning and zooming with purpose. I located our high-orbit allies, those French, British, and Russian ships, as well as the farther off, Varapin fleet. The tactical landscape was now etched in my mind. All that remained was to translate my reconnaissance into action on the bridge.

"It's time to go to work, people," I announced.

Hardy added, "And kids, make sure you've all hit the bathroom now because the next stop isn't until we reach Milwaukee. And trust me, no amount of *but-I-really-gotta-go* will make me pull this spaceship over!"

Back seated at the Captain's Mount, I watched as the infusion of Grish warships infiltrated the star system, systematically taking up tactical positions. We all knew it was the quiet before the storm. Derrota was standing to my left, while Hardy was on my right. Grimes was at the Helm station while Chen was at Comms. Lieutenant Pristy was working the board at Tactical. She'd been professional these last few hours, but still cold towards me.

I made an announcement to the bridgecrew, "I want everyone to know, as of right now, you will no longer refer to Lieutenant Pristy as Lieutenant. You will address her as XO, Executive Officer, of *USS Franklin*. And SARAH, please initiate protocol for rank modification in the ship's records and update all relevant systems to recognize Lieutenant Pristy as Executive Officer of *USS Franklin*. Proceed to make this a ship-wide announcement."

Now hear this! It is with congratulations that I announce Lieutenant Gail Pristy has been promoted to Ship's Executive Officer.I repeat. . . Lieutenant Gail Pristy has been promoted to Ship's Executive Officer.

There was a chorus of hoots and hollers accompanied by enthusiastic applause from the bridgecrew. Derrota stepped forward and squeezed Pristy's shoulder, "Badhai ho, Gail. Well deserved."

She looked up to Derrota and smiled, her cheeks having gone a deep scarlet. Her eyes swiveled to me, "You know how I love being publicly embarrassed." She offered up a reluctant smile. "But thank you, Captain. That means a lot."

Hardy's Boston-accented voice disrupted the moment of levity, "Varapin vessels are under attack."

"And here comes our own..." Pristy said fingers becoming a blur of motion at her board.

Incoming! Brace for impact!
Incoming! Brace for impact!

"Six, no eight, nuclear-tipped missiles inbound to our port-side," Pristy stated, keeping calm and cool.

"Shields still at 100%," crewman Davit said from a station somewhere behind.

I now saw it on the primary halo display. The Grish attack group were emerging like a swarm of hungry predators, their hulls glinting ominously in the starlight. "Hostile signatures coming in fast," Pristy's voice was measured, her eyes darting across sensor readouts. "Count's rising, too."

Chapter 16

HIP 938134 Star System
USS Franklin

Captain Galvin Quintos

I leaned forward, every muscle tensed. "How many?"

"Over two dozen capital ships. Mixed class. Support vessels numbering greater than that." She paused, a frown etching her brow. "They're firing more smart missiles. Readings show the charging of advanced plasma arrays."

As more Grish warships infiltrated the star system, their arrival was not a brash declaration of war but a sinister whisper. The lead ships, their battlecruisers—behemoths of destruction— were bristling with armaments that could tear the most lethal enemy asset apart. Over the past few years, the Grish had undergone significant advancements. Their movements were marked by an unexpected grace... contradicting their size and malevolent intent. Accompanied by smaller, yet equally deadly destroyers and frigates, these slightly sleeker vessels navigated through space with predatory efficiency.

Farther back came the troop carriers, ominous and silent, like sharks trailing the scent of blood. But it was what they represented that had me sitting up straighter in my seat. Their intention, clearly, was to engage in an Earth ground incursion.

The deck thrummed beneath our feet... *Franklin's* heart beating in time with our own. "Hardy, make yourself useful and help the XO at Tactical 2. Elevate our defensive port-side perimeter. All Phazon Pulsar turrets, full auto. Engage at will." My voice cut through the low murmur of the bridge.

"Helm, do what you've got to do to stay nimble, but leaving Earth's space is not an option. We protect our home at all costs."

"Copy that, Cap," Grimes said.

The ChronoBot was now working shoulder-to-shoulder with Pristy. He said, "Defensive systems fully online. Turrets engaging."

On the primary halo display, I watched as missiles from the Grish attack group streaked closer toward us. *Franklin's* turrets responded, a flurry of fire meeting the threat head-on. Explosions dotted the void, a testament to the ship's precision targeting.

Franklin rocked; I heard the distant thrum of shields being ravaged by more Grish energy fire.

"Shield integrity?" I asked, not taking my eyes off the display.

"Shields at eighty-nine percent and holding," Davit responded from the Defensive Systems Station. "But we can't take this kind of bombardment for long. Too many enemy ships pounding our shields all at once. Shields regenerate fast, but only if —"

I spun in my seat, "Crewmember Davit, you will keep your responses to a minimum. If I want clarification, I'll ask for it."

"Aye, Sir."

I spun to Pristy, "Target that lead battlecruiser. Their

plasma cannons are tearing into us more than any of the others. XO, make that their last fucking salvo."

"On it, Cap," she said looking remarkably satisfied to comply. "Railguns acquiring target... locking... firing."

The enemy ship shuddered; *Franklin's* railgun kept at it; her recoils absorbed by the omninought's massive frame. The halo display lit up as our rail spikes tore through the vacuum and into the Grish lead ship.

"Direct hit on the enemy flagship," Hardy said, stopping long enough to do a kind of end zone dance or maybe it was a jig.

"Crap!" Pristy barked. "Fighters inbound."

I watched as they began to fill the void, emerging from their command ship in waves. Their angular and menacing hulls, marked by the scars of numerous battles, served as a visual testament this was anything but their first deep space battle.

I felt something cold in the pit of my stomach. "Christ, those are Cyclone Death Fighters."

"Yeah, evidently supplied by the Varapin back when they were BFFs... furnished by ghouls, and piloted by piglets," Hardy interjected.

I counted no less than fifty of the dark, ominous-looking craft. I glanced back to the Flight Control Station; I searched my memory for the crewmember's name.

"Hargreaves, get on the horn to the Bay Chief. Captain Ryder's to muster several Arrow squads. They're to be wheels up and engaging the enemy within three minutes."

"Sir, Captain Ryder, Lieutenant James, and Lieutenant Burgundy have already deployed. Three squads of twenty Arrows each."

I let out a breath. That's what happens when you serve with the same people for so many years; they know you too well, anticipate your orders even before you make them.

I swiveled my chair, diverting my gaze to another of the halo displays. On it, the Varapin fleet—in a desperate attempt to scatter and regroup—was being besieged by a contingent of Grish warships. Their advance was deliberate, an organized onslaught meticulously designed for decimation. My eyes narrowed as I witnessed the choreographed carnage, the Varapin ships clearly struggling against their former allies, now enemies.

Two brilliant flashes of destruction erupted on the display, sequential and blinding. The first detonation was a silent roar through the void, followed swiftly by another. As the glare subsided and the display cleared, a grim scene remained. The remnants of two Varapin battlecruisers were scattering into space, reduced to little more than drifting debris.

My focus sharpened, now seeing the wounded carcasses of two other Varapin warships, their once sleek forms now marred by the violence inflicted upon them. They were hemorrhaging atmosphere into the vacuum—gas and particulate matter spewing forth in a desperate gasp for life. The ships listed, their axis of rotation skewed, an indication of critical systems failure. They were dying beasts, their final moments an agony of func-tion and form.

"Grish cruiser coming about!" Pristy yelled.

And there it was, not as large as *Franklin*, but immense and intimidating just the same. This was one of their specially designed *Dreadnought Busters.* Slightly above us, she slowed.

Pristy glanced up to the display, looking aghast. "She's coming abeam of us! Dammit! Brazen move; we'll be in trouble if she unloads—"

I cut my XO off, "Hardy, prep the Broadsides. It's time we give them a taste of good ol' Earth ingenuity," I said, feeling a grim smile tug at my lips.

"Broadsides charging," Hardy confirmed. "Bowlers locked and loaded... at the ready."

It was as if my Grish counterpart, realizing his mistake, had desperately barked off the orders to immediately turnabout, to limit his vessel's full-on exposure. Aft drive thrusters blazed white, as the ship prepared to rocket away. But it was too late.

"Fire all port Broadsides!"

As my order was carried out, the deep resonance of the Broadsides enveloped us.

BOOM! BOOM! BOOM! BOOM!

The deck vibrated with the fury of each massive projectile hurtling through space. On the display, a brilliant array of streaking lights erupted, a celestial celebration reminiscent of a grandiose Fourth of July fireworks display unlike any I'd seen before.

When the first enormous projectile made contact with its target, a spectacle of destruction ensued. The explosion was both haunting and mesmerizing. This wasn't the usual flash of a ship's instant vaporization; no, this was profound. Gratifying. The brilliance of the detonation was matched only by the spectacular fireball that followed, casting shadows of the fragmented behemoth against the void. The ship was torn asunder, its pieces hurtling through space with devastating velocity.

And within moments, a second, then a third Grish vessel—those I wasn't even aware had been lurking just beyond the closest vessel—were also torn apart, disassembling in a dramatic and fiery display that signified the dominating destruction *Franklin* was capable of. But I knew, all too well, the last thing I needed was getting overly cocky. To think we had won something here. We hadn't. In fact, all of three warships had been dispatched thus far, and there were many, many, more just waiting for their turn at us.

"Grish fleets regrouping," Pristy said. "Or trying to."

I watched, their movements suggesting a kind of hesitancy. Perhaps they hadn't expected such resistance. "They're pulling back." I observed, watching the primary display.

"Not for long," Pristy murmured. "They're massing for another push. And here it comes."

The enemy came at us again, a wave of ships and unbridled firepower. But I knew *Franklin* would be ready—her crew, more than ready. But I knew the Grish had time on their side. They could afford a certain level of attrition. We could not. I turned my attention to the far more intimate battle going on between Arrow Fighters and Cyclone Death Fighters—like the aftermath of two beehives colliding in deep space, a swarming frenzy too fast and too ferocious to determine the winners and losers.

Chen, looking jubilant, as he said, "Captain! I just got through to EUNF command. Not sure how long the communiqué will hold, but..."

"Open the channel," I said. "Let's see who it is."

The feed was a staticky, fragmented mess, but I could make out a U.S. Space Navy uniform, and the face of a middle-aged man with slicked back lack hair, small beady eyes, and a five o'clock shadow. Each shoulder epaulette displayed four gold stars; he was a high-ranking admiral.

"Captain Quintos. Excellent work breaching the Varapin's communications blockade. It is essential we speak. We have not met, but I know of your, uh, prior exploits. I am Admiral Perry Sloan. Acting EUNF Space Navy Executive Commander. But no time to waste with non-essentials. Captain, I am ordering you to stand down. I repeat, stand down immediately."

Stymied, I tried to process what the Admiral had just unloaded on me. Apparently, this Sloan character had taken over for Admiral Block. My thoughts went to the worst possible scenario... Block was dead. Had been killed like thousands of others, during the Tidal Basin Massacre there in DC.

The Admiral was waiting for my response. "Sir. Admiral, we are under attack. Standing down is not an option."

"Well, make it an option, Captain. The Grish are simply returning your fire."

What the hell is this man talking about?

"Sir, am I to understand Admiral Block is—"

"Dead? No, at least not yet. He's been gravely injured. Admiral Block is on life support. I'm sorry, understand you two were close. Have history. Know, though, the President—all of his cabinet—they're gone. And when the Capitol building took a direct hit, we lost both sides of congress—all have been buried beneath a mountain of rubble."

It was hard to fathom. The U.S. government had been completely annihilated. I blinked away my dismay, my thoughts returning to Admiral Block. That he was on life support. *Life Support? Now there's an antiquated term for you.* "So, Admiral Block, he's not being treated within a RegrowPod, Sir?"

"No, dammit, and stop interrupting me. We're lucky to still have running water, and shitters that actually flush. Come to terms with the fact that much of Earth is in total ruin, Captain. Now shut up and listen!"

I remained silent. The man appeared to be losing his composure, which was the last thing we needed from the higher-ups as our world faced the onslaught of two opposing intergalactic superpowers.

Sloan was talking again, the static blotting his words.

"Excuse me, Sir. Can you repeat that?"

A vein throbbed upon the man's forehead. "I said, emissaries from the Grish Parliament are here now. In-depth discussions are underway."

"What kind of discussion?" I blurted out with more hostility than was probably prudent.

"Are you daft, Captain? What do you think the discussions are about?! Terms of our fucking surrender!"

"Absolutely not! You shouldn't even be talking with the Grish. They've never—ever—told the truth. Terms of surrender? Are you out of your fucking mind? Do you think Admiral Block would be doing this... chatting with the same enemy that for a decade has been hellbent on humanities' total evisceration?"

I was seething... at some point, had gotten to my feet. I forced myself to release my tightly clenched fists and slow my breathing.

"Outbursts like that will put you in the brig for a year, along with the stripping of your captain's rank. How dare you speak to a superior officer in such a manner."

I took a breath—tried to look contrite. "Sir, I apologize for my lack of decorum, but I know these miscreants. I know them better than anyone, including you. Sorry to be so frank, but that's a fact. Admiral, the enemy we need to be talking to, as unsavory as that would be, are the Varapin."

"The Varapin face extinction, a race on the brink of rapid decline. Even now, their remaining warships are under relentless assault by the Grish."

It occurred to me then that this man was never going to listen to reason. I stole a quick look about for Derrota, but he was no longer on the bridge. But Hardy was here, and he'd have to do. I had the glimmer of an idea, something that could just as easily backfire. I had zero actual data to back up what I was about to say.

"Admiral, Earth is dying. She's been thrown into a similar looking, but far different habitable region of space. This isn't the kind of *Goldilocks-zone* Earth requires."

I looked to Hardy and said, "Provide the Admiral the very latest environmental stats, those already starting to spike."

The ChronoBot didn't miss a beat. "Admiral," Hardy began,

his voice taking on the tenor of a somewhat snooty scholar, "Full spectrum data acquisition scans with the subsequent analyses of the environmental data, reveals a stark and chilling reality. Average global temperatures have plummeted by 2 degrees Celsius since the spatial transporting event. Polar ice caps have expanded by .5% during that same period, with Arctic sea ice thickness increasing by an astonishing .2%. Numbers that should take decades to achieve, happening within mere hours. In just one month, world crops yields will wither, and in three... Admiral, planet Earth will be akin to a large orbiting snowball."

"Enough!" the Admiral spat. "None of this is up for discussion. And I'm certainly not going to take the word of a three-hundred-year-old robot. One recently found deactivated and floundering, in deep space within the Liquilid sector. Yes, I know all about your ChronoBot sidekick, Captain, and I'm not buying anything it has to say. You will stand down and await further orders. Have I made myself clear?"

I tried to keep my voice calm—my tone respectful. "Sir, please. We need to do anything, everything, we can, to put Earth back where it belongs within our own Solar System. You are making a grave mistake here."

Sloan's eyes drilled into mine, his mouth turning to a small straight line. "The question is simple, Captain Quintos, will you stand down? Or will I have your first officer relieve you of your command?"

I hesitated too long.

"Fine, You are relieved—"

"Yes! Admiral, I will stand down. I apologize for my... impertinence. Whatever you need me to do, Sir, I will do."

The Admiral stared back at me, gauging my sincerity. "Very well. My talks with the Grish are about to resume. One more thing, USS Franklin... the Grish have insisted the ship be handed over as a prize of war. And, Captain, I know that is the last thing you want to do here. But I have been assured none of your crew will be harmed, if you comply with the order of no further... um, hostilities."

The man has lost his mind. That, or something worse... he's a coward.

All eyes were upon me.

Admiral Sloan seemed to be relishing the look of total astonishment on my face.

"I'll be in touch, soon. Expect to be boarded within the hour. I assure you, all will be fine. We just need to get through this... challenging time. Sloan out." The feed went dark.

Chapter 17

"So..." Pristy said turning towards me, "we're really going to just sit here and take it up the tailpipe while the Grish come aboard and take our ship?"

"No. Of course not. The Admiral failed to mention we should stay put." I started to pace, have always thought better while on the move. I stopped and looked at my bridgecrew. "I am about to push the limits of what I've been ordered to do by Admiral Sloan. I'm hoping that any repercussions will solely land upon my shoulders. But I cannot guarantee that. Anyone who feels uncomfortable with that is free to leave the bridge. All I ask is that you do not attempt to contact EUNF Space Navy command."

Heads pivoted as my bridgecrew eyed one another, but no one made a move to stand.

"We're all with you, Captain," Davit said. "What do you want us to do?"

"Things around here are about to get—"

"Unhinged?" Crewmember Barrow quipped from the Environmental Systems Station. "No offense, Sir, but tales of your past exploits were a significant factor in my request for this ship's assignment."

Several of the others nodded their agreement.

Pristy's expression shifted to one of caution as she remarked, "Do I dare assume you're reverting to your pirate days of yesteryear?"

My thoughts flashed back to an encounter, years past, when I'd faced off against the notorious pirate, Thunderballs, in a brutal hand-to-hand duel. It was a cage fight, a battle filled with deceit on both sides: he had unleashed a hidden crotch pistol on me, while I had gained an unexpected edge from an alien elixir, a neon green Gorvian plasma concoction crafted by Doc Viv. This elixir had augmented both my mental acumen and physical prowess. So, was Pristy right? Was I to resort back to my previous pirate ways? I suppose time would tell. One thing was for sure, there was no way I'd be letting a bunch of piglets onto my ship.

"Look, everyone, I'm about to start spinning some plates. A lot of plates. Help me keep them in the air... and trust that I know what I'm doing. First things first, Mr. Chen, call back all our Arrows."

"Aye, Captain."

Turning my gaze towards each member of my bridgecrew, I said, "Going forward, *Franklin* must operate in absolute silence. As in achieving the stealth of a phantom. A ghost. That's no small feat for a vessel of this magnitude."

Hardy chimed in, "It appears the ship's cloaking abilities haven't faced real-world combat trials. You have to know, Cap, a ship of this scale generates its own gravitational footprint."

Lieutenant Hargreaves at the Flight Control Station interjected, "Captain Ryder's not happy with having to duck out of that fight with the Cyclone Fighters but assures Flight Command that all Arrows will be wheels down in two minutes.

He also wanted you to know, Captain, we lost five brave pilots today."

"Noted," I said turning my attention to the Engineering Station. "Lieutenant Jorkins, we'll need to shut down our propulsion systems. Will that be a problem?"

Wide-eyed, the slender man with thinning brown hair went rigid. "Uh, Captain, that's not a good idea."

"You have one minute to tell me why."

"*Franklin,* as I'm sure you are aware, has three propulsion systems. The Stellar Rift Engine (SRE): This is responsible for manufacturing wormholes, allowing us to traverse vast distances in a fraction of the time typical for FTL. Next, we have our two Nova Fusion Propulsor Drives (NFPD's), these bad boys generate the high-energy plasma necessary for typical FTL. And finally, we have our four quantum transposer orbs, QTOs, that reach out to alternate spatial realities, work together, temporarily securing a foothold on an alternate quantum plane of existence, before returning to our own. But all three propulsion systems require an uninterrupted, constant, flow of plasma from the ship's dual reactor cisterns. If we shut everything down, it could take hours, perhaps days to bring them back online again."

"That was quite the explanation, Mr. Jorkins. If we do bring our systems down to, let's say down to a minimum idle, will that constant plasma flow be detectable by our enemies?"

The man looked like a deer caught in the headlights. "That's... that's beyond my realm of knowledge, Sir."

Hardy made an exaggerated sigh, "Cap, it should be fine. With everything going on here in upper orbit, dozens of space-craft moving about, space battles ensuing between the Grish and the Varapin, countless crisscrossing propulsion wakes, we'll be like a fart in a hurricane compared to all that. Anyway, what alternative do we have?"

I said, "Helm, prepare to jump the ship."

"To where, Captain?" Grimes said, one hand now poised over his board.

"We need to stay in Earth's high orbit, but anywhere there's the least amount of Grish or Varapin ships. And Mr. Grimes, we'll need to do it while *Franklin* is cloaked."

"Jump coordinates set. Jumping now."

No one spoke for several seconds as if even their talking could be detected by the enemy. Eventually, Hardy said in a whispered voice, "Helm has put us somewhere above the South Pole and we're at the farthest reaches of high orbit."

I rolled my eyes, "Enough with the dramatics, Hardy."

"What now?" Pristy asked.

"Now I need to track down Derrota and Coogong. XO, you have the Captain's Mount. Hardy, you're with me."

WITH HARDY'S HELP, WE FOUND THE TWO scientists on Deck 18, Violet Sector within the Science and R&D Department— which, I discovered later, was adjacent to the ship's expansive HealthBay complex.

I took in the open space. The laboratory featured a minimalist, metallic design with soft blue lighting. The space housed high-tech workstations, advanced instruments, and interactive displays. A dozen white-coated scientists bustled about, engaged in diligent activity, leaving no room for idleness.

Hardy pointed to the center of the compartment, where, huddled together, were Derrota and Coogong... undoubtedly, noodling some incomprehensible formula or equation. A nearby halo display provided complex data in three dimensions. I heard the murmur of SARAH's voice as the ship's AI, was working virtually alongside the two scientists.

They both glanced up as Hardy and I approached. Derrota's black hair was slightly disheveled, his eyes bore the weariness of long hours of intense concentration.

In contrast, Coogong remained his usual self, with a perpetual smile on his worm-like face. The reflections from the halo display danced across his glass helmet, igniting the Ambiogel liquid inside with a radiant golden glow.

"Ah, Captain," Coogong said. "Just in time."

Derrota tapped at the input device in front of him, "SARAH has been instrumental in filling in the blanks. I think we have a good idea how the Varapin accomplished... well, the impossible." He gestured toward the three-dimensional display.

The halo display was now projecting a mesmerizing visual representation: a swirling, intricate web of interconnected stars and celestial bodies, with Earth and the Moon at its core. Lines of energy, resembling delicate threads, radiated outward from the two heavenly spheres, reaching towards distant points in space. These lines pulsed and fluctuated in intensity.

Coogong said, "What you are seeing is mimicking the Varapin's quantum synchronization."

Around Earth and the Moon, virtual Dyson Spheres materialized, capturing the brilliant radiance of the nearest star. The energy flow within these spheres was a choreography of glowing currents, illustrating the power harnessing process with breathtaking clarity.

A secondary display showed data streams and complex mathematical equations flowing like a cascading waterfall, constantly updating and refining. Back on the primary display, I could see holographic overlays showing the Earth and the Moon attempting to return to their original location within the Solar System, emphasizing the ultimate goal of the research. With a flutter, the virtual Earth and Moon, dissipated. A failed attempt.

"We are close, Captain, but, as you can see, there is more work to do," Coogong said.

"We have gone as far as virtual modeling can take us," Derrota added.

"What are you telling me?" I asked.

"What we are telling you, Cap, is that we need the actual hardware used by the Varapin."

Coogong nodded enthusiastically, Ambiogel sloshing within the confines of his helmet.

I looked to the display, "And where, pray tell, would that be?"

Derrota nervously scratched at his chin, "I believe that would be the Forland 545 System, where the Varapin first demonstrated their world moving capabilities with a test platform."

"I'm confused, wouldn't that need to be here, where the event took place?"

"We've looked. More importantly, SARAH looked. The Varapin have covered their tracks quite well. Although, we do know a platform is capable of just one spatial transporting event before it's rendered useless. Perhaps circuits are blown, or there has been some other near-catastrophic hardware breakdown."

That made sense. Earlier, Slop had alluded to such a dire fact.

Hardy had moved the input device closer to himself and was now tapping at the keys.

"Please don't touch that," Coogong reprimanded.

The ChronoBot held up a singular digit in a *hold-on-one-second* kind of gesture while continuing to tap away with his other hand. "They're probably right, Cap. Without having an actual physical construct to analyze, all this is just speculation. They're two teenagers playing video games."

"I take exception to that, Hardy," Derrota said, clearly irritated.

Coogong, on the other hand, appeared to let the comment roll off his stick-figure-shoulders. "We need to make haste to Forland 545 System and hope that we will find the test platform. Even if it's inoperable, the clues we find may prove to be invaluable."

The Thine scientist sat back on his stool. "That is, if you want to put Earth and the Moon back where they belong."

Derrota let out a breath, "I concur. It is our best option, other than the Varapin telling us directly how they did what they did."

Hardy said, "Forland 545 System isn't exactly close. Even with multiple wormhole transfers, we'd be looking at three days."

I dragged a hand down my face. *Can anything ever just be easy?*

"Okay, let's change tracks here for a minute. Let's say I needed to quansport a person down on Earth directly into our HealthBay."

"Why would that be any different than what we have been doing for years now?" Derrota said.

"Let's say that person is critically injured and hooked up to some kind of life support system."

Derrota shook his head, "Too risky."

"What do you mean too risky?"

"Who knows what kind of medical contraption the person— and I'm assuming you're referring to one, Admiral Cyprian Block—is hooked up to. We could inadvertently kill the man or injure him more gravely than he already is."

I let that tumble around in my head for a moment.

"Come, the person you really need to be talking to is Chief Knott."

I offered back a bewildered expression. "Chief Knott?"

"Come. It's right next door," Derrota said already making a

beeline toward the exit. Leaving Coogong to continue his work, I hurried after Derrota.

HEALTHBAY BORE A STRIKING RESEMBLANCE TO THE many MedBays I'd encountered during my years of service on various ships, albeit slightly more expansive. Its central hospital facility maintained the familiar semi-circular layout, featuring twenty vacant beds, each adorned with a gently rotating health avatar overhead. Soft, ambient lighting and soothing neutral bulkhead coverings imbued the space with a serene spa-like ambiance.

Adjacent to the hospital area, separated by a tinted glass partition, lay a sterile compartment housing five empty Regrow-Pods. To our left, a pair of auto-hatch double-doors beckoned, presumably leading to surgical suites, examination rooms, and doctors' offices. I half-expected Doc Viv to walk out, a vision of beauty and competency.

The auto-hatch slid open, revealing a short, plump woman making her way out. Her hair sported an oddly artificial shade of red, arranged in a meticulous 1950s-style June Cleaver bob. Her lab coat seemed two sizes too snug, while her sensible white shoes emitted a faint squeak with each step. Despite the quirks in her appearance, her smile exuded warmth and hospitality, though a hint of bright red lipstick clung to her two front teeth.

"Captain Quintos!" she boomed, her overbearing voice in direct conflict with our serene surroundings. "I was hoping you'd find your way down here. Come on. Bring it in, I'm a hugger." Her outstretched arms engulfed me, her hug akin to the embrace of a hydraulic press. I found myself sandwiched, her generous bosom making itself known against my abdomen, and the unmistakable scent of lavender enveloping my senses like a visit to a grandmother's linen closet.

She stepped back while clasping my hands in hers,

appraising me. "You are one handsome hombre. Bet the ladies onboard swoon when you pass them by."

Swoon? Is that word even in the dictionary anymore?

"I am Medical Chief Knott, but please call me Agnes. Can I call you Galvin? I so like a casual work environment." She shot Derrota a friendly wink.

"Uh... well, maybe we keep things more formal for now," I said, exchanging a quick glance with Derrota who seemed to be reveling in my discomfort.

Knott eyed Hardy, an uneasy expression crossing her features.

"In addition to making your acquaintance, Chief, I'm also here on a fact-finding mission."

"What can I do to help?" She boomed again.

"With a little luck, soon, I'll be quansporting a patient, a VIP patient, right into your HealthBay."

"Oh my... this is sounding quite clandestine. What may I ask, is this VIP suffering from? What ailment?"

"All I know is that he is critical and on life support."

Derrota added, "We can remove whatever life support he is on prior—"

"Oh no. Bad idea, Stephan. You want to kill the poor man even before I can get my mitts on him?"

"I was thinking we could quansport him directly into one of your RegrowPods," I said.

She appeared momentarily taken aback. "The advancements in technology these days are astounding. Indeed, that should be feasible. Here's what I need you to do, Galvin. Once you reach the location of this VIP individual, presumably a hospital on Earth, record a TAC-Band video of his life support apparatus. If it's possible, I'd also like access to his digital medical chart, so I can configure the pod accordingly."

.   .   .

BACK OUT IN THE CORRIDOR, I SAID, "STEPHAN, head back to your lab, you and Coogong keep going with your experiments. Hardy, I need you to make a visit to Deck 34, Blue Sector, the Marine's barracks. Fill Sergeant Max in on what we're doing. Tell him to have his team ready within the next few hours."

"To grab the Admiral?"

"Nope, they'll have a far more, uh, tenuous mission. They'll be quansporting over to a particular Varapin ship. There, they'll be snatching up another, very different, VIP. One Fleet Commander Sorlen Op, AKA, Slop."

Chapter 18

I emerged from the DeckPort into the combined Decks 98/99/100, known as the Symbio section of the ship. It dawned on me that, thus far, I hadn't encountered a single Symbio Poth crewmember, a common sight on my previous journeys aboard other ships.

I stood within a vestibule-like area, where a central ticket-window-style booth and a lone auto-hatch were located nearby. A slightly tilted handwritten sign, with evident signs of hurried taping, dangled off-center at the booth's window.

The Quest will be open to the crew... soon. So, for now, GO AWAY!

The tone of the writing bore a distinct resemblance to my niece, Sonya Winters. Approaching the auto-hatch, I was caught off guard when it didn't slide to the side as expected.

Resorting to old fashioned methods, I pounded a fist onto the metal surface as if desperate to sell Encyclopedias or vacuum cleaners.

It took a while but finally the auto-hatch slid open several inches. I saw an eye, part of a nose, and part of a mouth.

"Hi. It's not ready."

"I know that, Sonya. I read your sign."

She nodded. "So, what do you want?"

"Open the damn door."

Pursing her lips, she looked to be considering her options.

I glanced up and said, "SARAH, open this door."

The auto-hatch slid open the rest of the way, revealing Sonya standing rigid on the other side.

I took in what she was wearing. "That's beyond inappropriate."

"It's not what you think," she said, cheeks turning pink. "I'm trying on a few of the costumes. This one is new."

Her ensemble consisted of a low-cut bodice, a tightly laced corset accentuating her curves, and a flirtatious silk petticoat. Her high-top sneakers were the only aspect I liked.

"Take it off. You look like a hook—"

"Hey! I'm dressed as an 18th century bar maid. Get your old man mind out of the gutter! And if you think I like dressing like this, you don't know me very well."

"Fine. Let me in."

"Okay, but you can't go into the park."

"I'm not here to play pirate or chase dinosaurs. I need to talk to Ensign Plorinne."

"Oh. Well why didn't you say so. I think he's back in the SSC."

"SSC?"

"Symbio Slumber Chamber. I'll take you. Try not to look around on the way. The lights are out, but we're keeping things on the downlow until opening night."

I followed my niece through a darkened passageway, aware of an expansive *something* off to my right. I could almost make out buildings and a few rooftop spires.

"Hey, stop that!" Sonya scolded. "SSC is through this auto-hatch."

We entered into an enormous open section of the ship which took me by surprise. The overhead was high, easily sixty or seventy feet above the deck. I recognized the space though from the backstage Symbio areas on previous ships. This particular area was where the already formed Symbio Pods were being kept, inert, put into a deep sleep until their presence was needed. Each one was cocooned within their own custom charging stations. To me, it was creepy as hell. Many of the figures, weren't even clothed and their all too human, um, attributes were right there in the open.

"Gawking much?" Sonya said, making a disgusted face.

"Just take me to Plorinne."

We moved on from the SSC to a more factory-like area. The smell hit me first, the scent of sour milk made me cringe. It was here that Symbio Poths were fabricated. I counted ten workers moving about, all looked to be Pleidian Weonan or maybe Symbios. It was almost impossible to tell, especially with the newer 2.0 models.

Large vats filled the floorspace, while a high drying assembly with Symbio's in various stages of completion moved along a winding overhead track. It reminded me of a garment conveyor from old fashioned dry cleaner facilities. I stepped out of the way as a Symbio Poth's upside-down naked torso whizzed past.

Sonya pointed, "Plorinne's over there by the heads. I'm gonna go change."

Sure enough, Plorinne was standing in front of a waist-high crate.... a crate full of very human-looking heads. I watched as he picked one up and turned it this way and that, as if inspecting an oversized cantaloupe for physical defects.

Catching my approach, the young Ensign's face lit up. "Captain Quintos. Hey, catch!"

Suddenly, there was a man's head spiraling toward me. I caught it, surprised by its heft.

"Feels like, well, a real head," I commented.

"You've held a real severed head in your hands?" Plorinne asked, looking honestly interested.

"I'm here for a reason, Ensign, and I'm counting on you to work a miracle." I tossed the head back to him.

"Sure. If I can. What did you have in mind?"

"I want you to fabricate a Symbio Poth of a specific person for me. And it has to be real looking enough that it'll pass close up scrutiny."

"Sounds easy enough. How long do I have to design and put it into the queue."

"How long does something like that typically take?"

He shrugged, "Depends, it's not another T-Rex or fire breathing dragon, is it?"

"No, just an elderly man."

"Two weeks should do it, then."

"You have two hours."

The Ensign's eyes went wide. "That's... "

I gestured to a nearby worker. "Whatever all these guys are working on, they're now working on this project. Nothing is more important."

"But still, Sir—"

I held up my palms, "Look, the Symbio doesn't have to talk. Hell, he doesn't have to do anything but lay there. Be nice if he could breathe and have human-like biometrics."

"Most of our Symbios have human-like biometrics. And if that's all you need, a comatose body. Yeah, maybe we could pull that off."

"Not maybe. Get it done."

"Who, exactly will this Symbio-Poth be impersonating?"

"Executive Five-Star Admiral, Cyprian Block."

Again, came the blank stare. "We're about to break a whole bunch of rules, aren't we?"

Before I could answer, I received a TAC-Band message from Sergeant Max.

Sir, there's been an accident. Can you meet me in HealthBay?

Entering HealthBay, I noticed that three of the previously empty beds were now occupied, and I immediately recognized the injured crewmembers lying there. To my left, over by the admissions counter, I saw Max engaged in a hushed conversation with Chief Knott. Their gazes lifted as I drew near. Chief Knott's face lit up with a warm smile, while extending her ample chest a little too provocatively. Max, on the other hand, wore an expression that resembled a condemned man taking his final steps towards the gallows.

"What the hell happened?" I asked.

Knott said, "Now Captain. Rest assured; their injuries are quite treatable. The RegrowPods are being prepped as we speak."

I peered past the glass partition and observed two MediBots efficiently operating the controls to open RegrowPods. My focus then shifted to the three idiots lying on the beds: Ham, Hock, and Grip. Why was I not surprised. Each of them was missing an appendage—a left arm for Ham, a right arm for Hock, and the lower part of a left leg for Grip.

"Cap, I can explain," Max said. "We were readying for our mission. The team was conducting routine ADEM's..."

I held up a palm, "ADEM's?"

"Attack Droid Evasive Maneuvers. It's where a flying attack

droid tries to kill you before you kill it. But, not sure how, the Sting Pulse setting got switched to the *Kill Pulse* setting. It's never happened before."

The three patients nodded their heads in unison.

"Cap, I can bring in replacements from the Army barracks. They're trained and I'm sure itching to—"

"That's not an option, Sergeant. And you know perfectly well, why."

He closed his eyes and nodded. "Because this was to be an off-books operation."

I didn't need to answer.

"We can still make this happen, quans over to that Varapin ship, grab your ghoul friend, and quans right back. In and out. And hey, we'll have Hardy with us."

"Sorry, Hardy will have his hands full with another, um, off-the-books mission."

Chief Knott's gaze darted back and forth between us, resembling a spectator at a fast-paced table tennis match.

Max nodded, "Okay, okay... look, Aubrey's more than ready, and certainly willing for any challenge. Girl's got passion."

Don't I know it, I thought.

"We're still coming up short with combat personnel," I said.

From the middle bed, Grip volunteered, "Heard Gail's badass. All that shit she did with that time traveling General Resnick."

"I need her on Tactical..." but even as I spoke the words, I saw the logic. I'd bring Akari James back over from flight bay, as well as Captain Ryder, who'd be sitting at the Captain's Mount. Freeing, Aubrey, Pristy, and now, myself up for the away teams.

"How far had you gotten with prep for the snatch and grab of Slop?"

"With Hardy's help, we located the Varapin ship. . . uh, however the hell you pronounce it—translates to something like

The Reckoning. Hardy also helped find Fleet Commander Sorlen Op onboard his ship. But we're running out of time, Cap. The Grish are really pounding that ship. It's on its last legs."

I glanced over to Grip and his stump, the big man shrugged apologetically.

"Get your team together and suit up. Aubrey, too. I'll have a conversation with XO Pristy, although I'm not certain what her reaction will be."

I'd NEEDED TO MAKE A FEW STOPS PRIOR TO heading to the bridge. By the time I got there, Lieutenant Akari James as well as Captain Ryder were already there. Pristy was going over some of the finer nuances to the Tactical board, while Ryder was talking to Grimes and some old friends at the Helm station.

Pristy eyed me the second I came into view. "What have you gotten me into?"

"You mean, what have you gotten me into, Sir," I replied with a smile. "Just a little field trip. The perfect antidote for deep space monotony and boredom."

"That's rarely been an issue under your command," she said with a roll of her eyes.

Ryder was now seated within the Captain's Mount, spinning it clockwise, then counterclockwise. "I like the new chair. It's got extra cushioning." He looked down to the left armrest, "What do all these little tap buttons do?"

"Terrific," I said, "I'm leaving my new omninought with a five-year-old."

I pivoted to Pristy, and the others. "XO, we have to go. Akari, Wallace... you have one job to do. Keep *Franklin* hidden. And stationary."

"That's two things, Captain, "Ryder said. "Go. This isn't our first stint on a bridge. We've got your back."

. . .

PRISTY AND I RUSHED TO THE SHIP'S ARMORY, where we swiftly acquainted ourselves with Gunny Rooney, a man in his early seventies, who had a snow-white crewcut and close-cropped beard. Given the extended lifespans of the 22nd century, it was clear that this grizzled and somewhat cantankerous veteran of the U.S. Space Navy still possessed a remarkable degree of vitality and sharpness.

IT TOOK US TWENTY-MINUTES TO GET KITTED OUT with the very latest combat suits and roll-back helmets. Gunny issued both of us plasma weapons—tagger sidearms and shredder long-guns—while demanding everything come back to him in the same condition it was issued.

By the time we arrived at the Quansporter compartment, the others were already there and waiting for us. Sergeant Max, Wanda, and Petty Officer Aubrey Laramie in one team, while Hardy stood alone... he, Pristy, and I would be making up the other team.

Pristy said, "So, this is how we're divvying up the teams?" She looked from Aubrey to me, "I'm fine if you want to swap things around."

Hardy mumbled something to the effect, "This isn't awkward."

"The teams are fine as is," I said tuning to Max, "Sergeant, you're to get in and out with the least amount of conflict. Hell, he may be asleep within his Ebom-Pod."

"Ebom-Pod?" Aubrey repeated.

Wanda smirked, "The Varapin go nighty-night within a crypt-like thing. As if the ghouls weren't already creepy enough."

"What fun would that be?" Aubrey said. "I mean, here we are all kitted out for battle and what, we're going to grab the guy snoring in his PJ's?"

I was reminded, once more, of the Petty Officer's prior life as an Olympian archer. That as a teen, she'd had big-game hunted in the wilderness with her father and brothers.

Max's stern tone cut through, "Petty Officer, as I've discussed with you before, keep your thoughts to yourself."

"Copy that, Sarge," she responded, lowering her head, "Sorry."

Coogong hurried into the compartment, "Apologies. Got caught up with... uh, never mind. You're not here to listen to my excuses." He moved into position at the control console and got to work. Taking in the two teams, he said, "Hardy, the coordinates you've provided... have they changed?"

"Not to any degree it makes a difference."

That gave the Thine scientist pause. "Even the slightest..."

"As we've been conversing, Coogong, I've double-, then triple-checked the coordinates. All's good."

Coogong nodded, "Are we not missing someone, Captain?"

I looked to Hardy, then Pristy.

Hardy said, "Yeah, where's your sleeping beauty?"

As if on cue, Ensign Plorinne entered the compartment, walking backwards while fighting to maneuver a hovercart in through the open auto-hatch. From out of view came a familiar voice, "Just stop pulling for a second, Plor! The cart's at a wonky angle."

Then I saw her—Sonya, the person fighting with the other end of the hovercart. With some back-and-forth jockeying, they managed to get the hovercart into the Quansporter compartment. But my attention was on what—or who—was lying atop the cart. If I hadn't known in advance that it was a Symbio Poth, I'd swear the real Admiral Block was lying there, skinny and vulnerable, with unusually hairy legs protruding from its ill-fitting hospital gown, an odd contrast to this döppelganger's high command.

Coogong shook his helmeted head. "The, um, subject will need to be vertical. He'll need to stand upon an open transport pedestal."

Ensign Plorinne, already looking frazzled, stammered, "No one said he needed to stand. He can't stand. He can't do anything like that!"

Aubrey laughed out loud, then covered her mouth. "Sorry."

"I got this," Hardy said striding closer, sliding a metallic hand in beneath the Admiral's neck, then, unceremoniously lifting the Symbio Poth up to eye level. The Admiral hung there, head drooping down, arms and legs dangling.

"Oh my God," Pristy said looking appalled.

"What?" Hardy retorted. "It's not like he's going to wake up and complain."

"Enough," I barked. "Can you just get yourself, and the Admiral there, up onto a pedestal? Can you do that, Hardy?" All this was taking far too long. I was starting to feel like I was and extra in a Keystone Cops movie.

Sonya said, "This isn't going to work... trying to make the Symbio Poth stand up there. Hardy, you're going to have to hold him. Like, hug it around the waist."

Pristy and I stepped up onto our own respective pedestals, while Hardy awkwardly embraced the Admiral.

"Oh, God," Pristy said for the second time. "Somebody fix his open gown. Just what I needed to see, a sagging old-man-ass staring back at me."

Again, Aubrey laughed, this time unapologetically. Then Wanda. Then... well, everyone laughed.

I said, "We all know our jobs. Let's get back here in one piece. Coogong, Team One is ready to quansport."

Chapter 19

The Reckoning
High orbit over Earth
HIP 938134 Star System

Petty Officer Aubrey Laramie

We had quansported deep into the bowels of the Varapin ship. Max, fist raised, signaled for everyone to freeze.

Aubrey couldn't be any more excited. This was what she'd signed up for. A real mission. And not just any ol' mission, but one that could impact all humanity. She'd had enough inaction, enough training. Ever since her return from Stratham Hold on Genoma, starship life had become unbearably routine. Maybe that's why I kissed the Captain. Well, he'd get over it. *Maybe*, she thought, smiling to herself. Her philosophy: better to do something wrong than do nothing at all. She had to admit, that motto had led her astray a few times. More than a few times.

Sarge had moved off, stealthily advancing down the dreary

passageway, while she and Wanda stayed put. Aubrey saw the alternate channel message icon pop into view on her HUD.

Utilizing the eye prompt, Wanda opened the main channel.

Okay then. The imposing female Marine had obviously wanted to communicate through the open channel.

"What's up?" Wanda said, glancing her way.

Aubrey saw her reflection on her teammate's amber faceplate.

"I see the way you look at him."

Aubrey shook her head. Of course, she knew exactly what Wanda was referring to. "Come again?"

"Knock it off. The Captain's off limits. And anyway, you don't want to start creeping into that minefield."

Wanda's eyes were really on her now, boring into her. So, she'd heard about the kiss. *Shit.* "It was a one-time thing. And it wasn't just me... it takes two—"

Max's voice suddenly broke into their channel, "We need to move. Now!"

Wanda was off, shredder raised to the ready, running down the same passageway the Sergeant had gone. Aubrey followed, her senses suddenly heightened to the world around her, a stark reminder the Varapin could appear at any time. Any one of them could close in on her within moments, materialize behind her like a phantom, seize her helmet, wrench her head backward, and... Ghan-Tshot. Her life would be extinguished with ruthless efficiency.

I really need to get my head in the game, she inwardly chastised.

Both Wanda and the Sergeant were kneeling up ahead. Wanda turned, signaled for Aubrey to go low. She joined them crouching to Wanda's left, eyeing the intersecting passageway up ahead. Aubrey leaned in closer to her teammates, almost missing the cross-traffic—a blur of black robes streaming by in both directions. *How do they fly like that?*

Wanda tapped her leg, hitched a thumb over one shoulder. The three of them, keeping low, moved back the way they'd come.

Max said, "I saw an access to a service conduit, twenty feet back. Laramie, you take point."

Music to my ears. Keeping close to the bulkhead, she could feel the metal brushing against her left arm. Sure enough, she soon came to an inset niche. She looked up, saw an overhead access tube.

Max's hand was on her shoulder, "What do you see?"

"I see the service access, just no ladder to get up there."

He smiled, "Yeah, the fuckers wouldn't need a ladder. That's okay, we'll do a body-boost."

"A what?" Aubrey said.

"Watch and learn kid," Wanda said, handing her the shredder she was carrying. Then she started climbing up Max's body like a chimpanzee skittering up a tree. Once her boots were on his shoulders, she—somehow—pulled herself up and out of sight.

Max took Wanda's weapon, Aubrey's, then his own, and passed them up to the now out-of-sight Wanda.

"Okay, you're next Laramie. Up you go," Max said.

She did pretty much what Wanda had done, only with a little more finesse... in her opinion. Wanda reached a hand down and pulled her farther up within the tube to another horizontally running tube.

Wanda said, "Okay, here's the fun part. You're going to flip around. I'm going to take hold of your legs and drop you back down headfirst."

"I'm not liking the sound of this."

"Shut up. All you have to do is dangle there. Max will do the rest."

Aubrey did as she was told. Within seconds, she was being lowered back down, blood rushing into her head. She extended her arms down, an upside-down superman pose. What she didn't see below her was Max. A moment later, she did. He'd stepped back, gotten a running start and leapt up. They grasped each other's wrists at the perfect moment. From there, Max did exactly what Wanda said he'd do. He pulled himself up, hand over hand, grabbing onto parts of her body like ladder rungs.

A MINUTE LATER THE THREE OF THEM WERE crawling, single file, along the horizontal service conduit. It was pitch dark and claustrophobic. Now, bringing up the rear, she had the unnerving feeling she was being trailed by a hovering, hungry ghoul. *I won't look back.*

That's when she felt it—something had just brushed against her backside.

Chapter 20

Earth
EUNF U.S. Space Navy Plaza
Subterranean Bunker Facility

Captain Galvin Quintos

We quansported into a darkened boiler room with a low ceiling and cinderblock walls. Three feedwater storage tanks loomed tall, dark, and foreboding, like sleeping sentinels that could awaken at any moment. Heavy-looking black iron pipes were everywhere, resembling a tangled web of shadowy arteries in the dimly lit space.

"Watch your noggin, Hardy," Pristy said eyeing the meager one-inch clearance he had above his head.

With one arm extended out in front of him, Hardy continued to hold the Admiral Block Symbio Poth firmly by the neck. Like a scene from a scary movie—Frankenstein lumbering about with his victim clutched tight in his grasp.

I moved to the substantial metal door and tried the knob. "Locked."

Glancing around, "Because there's so much in here someone would want to steal," Pristy commented with more than a little snark.

I stood back to let Hardy do his magic, as the ChronoBot took a shot at turning the knob. And turn it, he did —so forcefully that it came off in his metallic grip. He held it up, looking at the thing as if he'd never seen a doorknob before.

"A foreboding start to things," Pristy said.

I let the comment go. I was well aware my XO was being flippant. Again. I'll be the first to admit it—I don't fully understand women. Seeing me and Aubrey, um... together, had ruffled my XO's feathers for some reason that was beyond me. Pristy had always been more of a purist for professional decorum. I suppose I was, in a roundabout way, Aubrey's superior officer, and yeah, I'd never been a stickler for military regulations... but it was natural for her to be concerned about fraternization and the potential repercussions of a relationship within the chain of command. And if you're thinking I'm an obtuse, clueless, ass right about now, well, I never claimed to be an expert in matters of the heart.

Hardy abruptly thrust a gleaming chrome finger into the indentation left by the previous knob, creating a sharp clang as the metal met the concrete floor on the other side. The door swung open, its rusty hinges squealing in protest.

Pristy grimaced, "Perhaps we should have considered bringing along a marching band, really crank up the racket."

I moved through the partially opened door, took in the block wall hallway with harsh overhead florescent lighting. I'd studied the EUNF Plaza's below-ground floorplan in advance. I knew we were approximately fifty feet from the small medical bay where Admiral Block would be situated. However, between us and that area were several of the bunker's compartments, including storage rooms, a kitchen and eating area, personnel quarters, and such forth. We'd have to navigate past all these areas to reach our destination.

Pristy brushed past me, taking the lead. I followed close on her heels, Hardy—and his hanging-marionette-like friend—bringing up the rear.

As my XO came to an abrupt halt, I collided with her back, causing both of us to nearly tumble to the floor. Catching her in my arms, we found ourselves faceplate to faceplate, eye to eye, separated by mere inches.

"Let me go," she said in a hushed voice as if our comms channel could be overheard by anyone else.

I did as told. "Why'd you just stop like that?"

"There's someone up ahead. That's the kitchen, right?" She gestured to an opening in the hallway, clearly it was an entrance to somewhere.

I nodded, "Let me take a peek inside." *Geez, now she has me whispering, too.* I crept up to the opening and stole a quick look. Sure enough, an armed serviceman wearing U.S. Space Navy fatigues was sitting at a small table. Most likely military police. At that moment, I realized that if we were discovered, I could never bring myself to open fire on fellow U.S. Space Navy personnel. While this was a mission of utmost importance, there were boundaries I couldn't cross in terms of what I was willing to do.

I tiptoed back to Pristy and Hardy. "Nighttime security."

"Okay. What's he doing?" Pristy asked.

"Eating a bagel. His back is facing the entrance. Looks to have a full cup of coffee. Doesn't look to be leaving anytime soon."

Pristy nodded and turned back to Hardy... which put her

face-to-face with the hanging Admiral Block Symbio Poth. "Dammit, Hardy!"

The ChronoBot pivoted its arm like an old-fashioned city crane repositioning cargo.

"You'll have to be extra quiet," she said to the ChronoBot. "We'll move past first; you hold back for me to signal you on."

"Roger that, Cyprian and I will wait for your signal," Hardy said deadpan.

Turning back to me, Pristy made a shooing motion, waving her hands to signal urgency. "What are you waiting for? Let's go."

After a quick look, I hurried to the other side of the entrance. Seeing the coast was still clear, I motioned her forward. She hurried across.

I left Pristy to guide Hardy while proceeding down the hallway. I passed by three closed doors on the left and four on the right. An overhead light fixture started to flicker. Up ahead, if my memory of the layout stayed true, the medical bay should be next. From what SARAH's deep penetrating sensor scans had provided, there were several injured being tended to... looked to be as many as five or six, all probably officer-level or political VIP status.

I slowed, hearing murmured voices. As with the kitchen, I hugged the wall and peered inside. My olfactory senses were struck by a cocktail of medicinal smells... ammonia, iodine, and chloroform. No doubt about it, this was the facility's hospital. I counted six beds, all occupied. Two nurses were making their rounds, both holding old-fashioned clipboards, monitoring readouts on devices that appeared to belong to the 21st century era.

It occurred to me that this underground labyrinth could have been left unchanged for the last hundred years. No one thought the worst could possibly happen. That the world as we knew it could be decimated, set back in time where there were no hovering medical avatars or RegrowPods. Mechanical airflow noises were coming from the farthest two beds, both patients must be on a ventilator.

I sensed more than saw... Pristy and Hardy were approaching behind me.

"What's the status?" Pristy said.

"We'll have to wait for the nurses to finish up. Right now, they're checking on the patients."

"Did you see the Admiral in there?"

"No, but—"

"He's in there," Hardy interjected. "Quick DNA scan confirms it."

Off in the distance we heard the distinct sound of chair legs scraping upon concrete.

"Seems our kitchen friend finished his bagel," Hardy said.

A moment later, the MP stepped out into the hallway, adjusted his holster belt, cracked his neck—first left, then right—burped, and finally, turned to the left and moved away.

I let out a relieved breath, "He could come back this way any minute." I stole another look into the hospital room. I couldn't see either of the nurses. "Let's move!" I said, slinking into the room. I moved fast, past the first couple of beds. The figure in the third bed, initially mistaken for a man, turned out to be a woman. On closer inspection, she looked like a mummy, her body wrapped entirely in bandages. She had only stumps for legs, the ends of which were stained with oozing blood. Two dark eye holes offered no clue as to whether she was awake or asleep.

Reaching the last of the patients, I found Admiral Block. As indicated by earlier sensor scans, the man was indeed hooked up to a ventilator device. I moved to his bedside and gave the vent machine a once over. I had no idea how this thing worked, or what would happen the second I disconnected it.

Looking around, I saw just how tight the space around the Admiral's bed was. "Hardy, I'm assuming you know how to remove the ventilator?"

"Uh, more from a practical knowledge kind of thing. I've never actually performed an *extubation*."

I shrugged; blank-faced.

"That's the procedure for removing an endotracheal tube or tracheostomy tube."

I looked to Pristy who merely shrugged. "No clue how to do any of that."

"Okay, let's shift positions. Hardy, you'll have to put the Symbio down, and then come over here close to Admiral Block."

"Where's he supposed to put the Symbio?" Pristy asked, sounding irritated.

"Good question. How about he sits him down on that next bed over. The guy laying there looks pretty much comatose, hooked to a ventilator like Block."

I watched as Hardy maneuvered the dangling Symbio Admiral around and set him down on the edge of the bed. The Symbio immediately flopped backward atop the other patient's legs.

"Uh... XO, you'll have to sit next to it. You know, prop it up."

The thought-to-be-comatose patient stirred, reflexively clutching the folds of his blanket. He opened his eyes and looked down at the recumbent Symbio Poth. Eyes widening to the size of softballs, muffled screams emanated from his own ventilator tube. He was attempting to withdraw his legs, as if someone had emptied a jar of spiders onto his bed sheets.

"Shit!" I looked to the nurse's station door, silently praying they hadn't heard anything. Seeing a metal stand and hanging IV bag, one labeled MORPHINE, I followed the plastic feeder tube down to the flow adjuster. I gave it five clicks, hoping I wasn't overdosing the man. Suddenly, his eyelids went heavy, and within seconds, he was asleep.

I turned just in time to see Hardy, deftly removing the endotracheal tube from the Admiral's mouth. Several swinging tendrils of mucus came out with it.

Immediately, Admiral Block started to struggle for breath; Derrota had said this would happen, it was something called dyspnea.

I'd already opened another channel to *Franklin*—specifically to Coogong. "Patient's ready for quansport."

"Yes, Captain," Coogong said. "We have a lock on him. quansporting now."

I looked Cyprian lying there. He looked old... thin, his coloring sallow. Vulnerable. His thinning gray hair was disheveled, and he sported several days' worth of stubble on his chin—features our Symbio imposter lacked. I wondered if anyone would discern the difference, but it was too late to dwell on that now.

In rapidly progressing segment blocks, starting with his feet, Executive Five-Star Admiral Cyprian Block vanished.

Hardy already had the Symbio Poth up and ready to be positioned within the vacant, still-warm contours left behind by the previous occupant.

"You do know the hospital gowns don't match, right?" Pristy said, sliding her eyes over to the line of other patients. "They're all wearing blue gowns; the Symbio's wearing green."

"I'm sure we can find where they keep their supply of gowns," I said.

"Fine. I'll let you change him. That's not in my job description."

It was at that moment the door to the nurse's station opened.

I looked up, panicked. "Coogong, quansport us out of here, NOW!"

Chapter 21

The Reckoning
High orbit over Earth
HIP 938134 Star System

Petty Officer Aubrey Laramie

Even before embarking on their slog through the dark service conduit, the trio had swiftly slung their shredders and tightened their straps. As they crawled further, a blood-curdling scream involuntarily erupted from Aubrey's lips. Unseen hands suddenly seized her around the waist.

Despite her combat suit, she recognized the unmistakable grip of knobby, bony Varapin hands. Adrenaline coursed through her veins and panic surged as she desperately twisted and flailed, attempting to confront her assailant. But her shredder weapon had become ensnared, drowning out the urgent voices of Wanda and Max crackling over their comms amid the deafening chaos.

Impossibly, the ghoul was as light as a feather, but also incredibly strong. She felt her helmet being wrenched violently left and right; it was as if her head had been captured within the jaws of a great white shark and she was its toy. In an instant, her shredder strap broke free, granting her some mobility.

She was able to twist her body... wriggle and squirm just enough to reorient herself. Now facing upwards, she screamed again. She was staring directly into the grim visage of death itself. Glowing ruby-red eyes bored into her very soul from within the blackened skull of her Varapin attacker. As if that wasn't enough, gaping white jaws were now pressing menacingly against her faceplate.

She knew what this was, Ghan-Tshot, the motherfucker is trying to suck the lifeforce from me, right through my helmet. *Oh God, where's Wanda—and where the fuck is Max!* Her energy was being drained like water vanishing down a drain. Beyond lethargic, the will to fight was almost gone now. The very substance that made Aubrey, Aubrey, was being stolen from her. All movements decelerated—hampered—like an insect ensnared in a splotch of tree sap. A deep sadness befell her.

If only I could get to my shredder, but she was too weak to move. Too tired. *Wait... don't I have another weapon?* The momentary spike of adrenalin was enough to prompt her right hand to fall onto her holstered tagger, down at her hip. It took every ounce of remaining willpower to pull the gun free and even more, to point it. *Am I even holding the thing right. Am I pointing it toward the ghoul, or myself? Does it matter?* She pulled the trigger.

She lay there, eyes closed, for a full minute before having the energy to move. She opened her eyes. The Varapin's face was looking back at her. But no longer were those hideous eyes glowing red. No longer was the ghoul moving.

Rallying—fueled by rage—she swept the black-robed attacker off of her as easily as one would brush cookie crumbs from one's shirt. As if a dam had broken, thoughts roared back into her mind. *Oh my God. Wanda. Max.* She arched her back and craned her neck enough to see if they were still in front of her... there within the service conduit. At first all she could see was darkness, then she saw them. Two human forms splayed out, one Varapin upon each of them. So, there had been three of the ghouls, one for each of them.

Clutching her tagger, she raised it, taking careful aim before unleashing a shot at the nearest beast—the one perched atop Wanda. The creature dropped, flopping lifeless onto the motionless female Marine. Further down the conduit, the Varapin, positioned atop Max, abruptly turned to face her, its eyes blazing red like twin volcanoes on the brink of eruption. Without hesitation, Aubrey fired her weapon once more.

She listened. She let the quiet surroundings inform her of any potential danger still lurking behind or in front of her. *Why aren't there more of them? Why aren't a whole shipload of the fuckers climbing all over me?* An ironic smile pulled at her lips. Simple, three had come to investigate, and being the horrific selfish ghouls they were, they wanted their Ghan-Tshot meals all for themselves. There was a good chance that nobody else was the wiser.

But now she was alone. Should she attempt completing the mission herself, or call to be quansported back to *Franklin?*

Movement.

One of the ghouls she'd shot was moving, rising up like an aberration of the undead. She raised her weapon once more, took aim, and... audibly gasped. It had been Max's arm that had raised the lifeless Varapin. He flung the Varapin corpse off himself and sat up.

"Laramie? That you?"

"Roger that, Sergeant."

He crawled back to where Wanda was lying, flung the dead Varapin off of her and peered down through her helmet's softly illuminated faceplate. Over the open channel, he said, "She's alive."

Aubrey chastised herself for not checking on her teammates as soon as possible. She'd taken it for granted both Wanda and Max were dead. She should have known, neither of them would have been that easy to kill.

"She's regaining consciousness," Max relayed, Wanda's head cradled in his lap.

Aubrey made her way forward, feeling bones crack and crunch as she crawled over a dead Varapin. When she reached Wanda, Aubrey joined Max, both now staring down at her.

Wanda's voice was weak, "If you two think I'm sleeping beauty here, and you're going to offer up a kiss to wake me, I think I'll pass."

It was another few minutes before Wanda recuperated enough for them all to get moving forward. Aubrey recounted how she had managed to kill her attacker, and shared her theory that the selfish three ghouls were hoping to grab a Ghan-Tshot meal, one they wouldn't have to share with anyone else.

"In any event, thanks for having our six, Petty Officer," Max said, taking point on hands and knees within the service conduit.

"Yeah, thanks, Aubrey, that was a close one," Wanda said, falling in behind Max.

Looking beyond Wanda, she saw that Max had stopped and was checking his TAC-Band. "We should be close to Fleet Commander Sorlen Op's quarters."

"Or, just as likely, he could be on the bridge," Wanda said.

. . .

THEY'D ALREADY PASSED BY THREE OF THE vertical access chutes, but then Max stopped. Apparently, this is where we would descend. With his back up against one side, his feet propped up on the other, he let gravity and friction guide his descent. Next, Wanda repeated the same maneuver. They both had made it look easy—no doubt something they'd practiced ad nauseam—Max, she'd discovered, was a stickler for combat drills.

She peered down the access chute, saw both Max and Wanda waiting for her down below. It was easily a twenty-foot fall. Wanda made a *hurry-up* wave of her hand. Without hesitation, Aubrey got herself into position, just as the other two had done. She knew the trick would be to release pressure from the soles of her boots in coordination with the pressure on her back. "Here goes," she said louder than she had intended.

Immediately, her back was slipping far faster than her boots; she was now falling headfirst with no way to stop herself, a bullet headed for its target. With her heart practically beating out of her chest, all she could think to do was yell, "Incoming!"

The natural response to acknowledging that you're about to be hit—in this case, by a falling, flailing person—is... well, to move the hell out of the way. But Max and Wanda, of course, did not do that. They didn't so much as catch her, as break her fall, lessening her impact onto the hard metal deck.

Dazed and slightly nauseous, she took a moment to determine if anything was broken. In her peripheral vision, she could see her two team members stealing looks down the corridor.

"All clear," Max said turning back to Aubrey, who was attempting to get herself vertical. She was relieved that neither Max nor Wanda offered to help her up. Already feeling like a spaz, she sure didn't need to feel like an invalid as well.

"Fleet Commander Sorlen Op's quarters is directly across from us," Max said. "The hatch will, undoubtedly, be locked." He held up a small device no larger than a deck of cards. "Coogong assured me this will act like a master key and open any hatch within the ship. That is, if the Varapin haven't altered their electronic access codes." He held up a palm, "Hold back for my signal."

With that, he darted across the corridor to the door on the other side. Using his magic key device, he began waving it in front of the hatch door. Over the open channel, Max had started to curse. He tried waving it higher up, then lower. The cursing intensified. He then waved the little box more toward the middle of the hatch door. That seemed to do the trick; the hatch slid sideways disappearing into the bulkhead. Checking that the coast was clear, both Aubrey and "The Varapin's quarters are kept at a perfect minus 80 degrees Fahrenheit."

A blue mist gathered several feet off the deck, dispersing as they moved about the confined space.

A MINUTE EARLIER, BEFORE THE HATCH CLOSED—before her team was completely in the dark—Aubrey had caught a glimpse of a stone coffin-like object at the center of the compartment.

NOW, SEEING THE THING ILLUMINATED VIA THEIR three light beams, it looked even more ominous.

"The Commander's Cantonment of Ire," Wanda said. "Good. We caught a break, he's in there."

Skeptical, Aubrey looked at her. "So, these helmets come with X-Ray vision?"

"No. But some of us come with a brain. "The ghouls leave

their crypts open when they're out and about. This one is, obviously, closed up tighter than a pickle jar in a hurricane."

Aubrey nodded; it made sense. "So, the big question, Sergeant, is: Does that little device open crypts as well as hatch doors?"

Max and Wanda exchanged a quick glance. He said, "I hadn't thought to ask."

Aubrey knelt next to the crypt, ran her fingers along what looked to have a row of small indentations.

"Maybe best to not just go pressing buttons—" Wanda's words were cut short.

The sound of rock scraping against rock interrupted her verbal reprimand. The Cantonment of Ire's stone lid had begun to slide open.

All three of them took a hesitant step backward.

It wasn't lost on Aubrey—even though they'd survived—that the Varapin they'd previously encountered, pretty much had handed them a thorough beat-down. Confronting these ghouls was anything but a walk in the park... more like navigating a minefield.

As Aubrey pulled her sidearm, Max said, "We need him. So, killing him isn't an option here."

"Then maybe we should have brought a big butterfly net."

"Good one, Petty Officer," Wanda said with smirk.

In a blur, something black shot out from the dark recesses of the crypt.

"Shit!" Max yelled.

"Grab him!" Wanda yelled.

Aubrey caught a glimpse of dark robes and arms outstretched. She dove. Although she missed, her left hand caught hold of fabric... and she didn't let go. As Aubrey slammed down onto the deck, her visuals became clouded by the now-disturbed, swirling mist.

It was like trying to keep hold of a crazed cat's tail. Varapin fingers tore at her suit like daggers, her faceplate quickly becoming a spiderweb of scratches and fissures. Fleeting glimpses of the fleet commander's grotesque features flickered across the beam of her helmet lamp, reminiscent of an old stop-motion movie.

"Don't let go, Aubrey!" Wanda yelled into the open channel.

Max leapt onto the black bundle of terror, wrapping his arms around the hellish creature's writhing form, determined to bring it under control.

Wanda, sounding far calmer than Aubrey felt, spoke into the open channel, "Coogong, four to Quansport."

Chapter 22

HIP 938134 Star System
High orbit over Earth
USS Franklin

Captain Galvin Quintos

I t had been two hours since Admiral Block had been quansported directly into an open RegrowPod, here in HealthBay. I'd pulled up a chair next to his pod, where I'd taken advantage of the first respite of inaction since I'd come aboard myself. With a tablet in hand, I was astounded by the volumes of paperwork that came with being a captain... which had only multiplied during my much-needed furlough.

At least I was getting more familiar with my ship and her crew. I'd also reviewed new protocols from top brass, yet still hadn't taken the time to listen to my backlog of communique messages. That, and I'd yet to visit Slop, who was currently a guest onboard *USS Franklin*—-languishing within one of the ship's high-security brig cells.

My TAC-Band vibrated. I saw that it was Akari James. "Lieutenant? You're still on the bridge?"

"Yes, Captain, Lieutenant, I mean XO, Pristy is on her way. I wanted to update you on the tactical situation."

"Go ahead."

"Three Grish warships are making their way toward us. It seems as though they know we're in the general area, but not exactly sure where. Cap, I think our time being invisible is coming to an end."

"How much time do we have?"

"My guess... one hour. Sensor scans are coming way to close."

I didn't like the sound of that—she was right, our hide and seek game was definitely coming to an end.

"Oh, and Chen wanted me to pass along that EUNF's U.S. Space Navy Admiral Sloan has left a total of thirteen increasingly angry and threatening comms messages."

"Copy that," I said. "I'll be back on the bridge as soon as I can. Captain out." I cut the connection.

It seemed as though, until USS Franklin was pinpointed— and deemed no longer a threat to the Grish—that no conditional surrender would be accepted. Just my guess, that 'conditional' meant the Admiral Perry Sloan would be spared in the process.

Chief Knott entered the RegrowPod area of HealthBay, checked the readouts then peered inside the pod's see-through clamshell top. "Captain," she started in a compassionate tone, "When Admiral Block was quansported here, he was in bad shape. Very bad shape. I would go so far as to say, if he was still back on Earth, he certainly would have passed on."

"And now?"

"He's received a full dose of regenerating nanobots, and the pod is assisting with his internal injuries—those incurred from the attack on DC."

"I'm sensing there's a 'but' coming."

She placed a comforting hand on my shoulder. "Well, he's still not breathing on his own, due to diminished auto-motor responses. And his EKG readings... they're still in the basement."

"Tell it to me straight, is he going to die, Chief?" I asked, not so sure I wanted to hear her answer.

"Let's give it a few more days. I haven't given up completely. I just want you to be prepared for what might be an inevitable situation. But the man's lived a long and fruitful life. Everyone, at some point, comes to the end of the road."

"Chief, America's governing body, legislative, judicial, and executive branches have been wiped out. All dead. The same is true for most other world powers. Rioting has erupted world-wide. Forget the Grish, the masses seem hell-bent on killing themselves. Martial law has been implemented, putting what's left of the military in charge. At this moment, the highest-ranking officer within US forces is Admiral Sloan. He's negoti-ating for Earth's total surrender to the enemy. What he doesn't understand is that the Grish cannot be trusted. In time, they will systematically exterminate humanity without a second thought."

Knott blinked away the brimming moisture in her eyes. "None of us knows who—family, friends, loved ones—has been spared. We're all living in a kind of emotional limbo."

I shook my head, "And this *Admiral Sloan*... well, the fate of our world is literally in his hands, the hands of a coward."

She straightened, composing herself. "And your Admiral Block here, he outranks him?" the Chief asked looking back down to the man lying within the RegrowPod.

"That, and he's not a coward. The man would never surrender."

"Then I suppose we can't let anything happen to your old

friend here," she said. "Go. You have a ship to skipper; people counting on you. I'll contact you the moment anything changes."

TEN MINUTES LATER, I ENTERED THE SHIP's highly secure Prisoner Holding Facility—PHF—a lower deck region of the ship exclusively operated and controlled by the U.S. Army. This area, not coincidentally, also housed nearly one thousand Army troops, complete with their barracks and essential facilities.

At the DeckPort, I was greeted by an Army Colonel, his rank evident by his silver eagle insignias pinned on his chest. Next to him was a similarly dressed lower-ranked underling. I knew it was typical for a Colonel to have a Command Sergeant Major as a principal NCO assistant.

No saluting here. Besides for being officers within different branches of the military, we were also both officer paygrade O-6. "Colonel, I'm Captain Quintos." I held out a hand for him to shake, which he ignored.

"How about you explain to me, Captain..." he said, through gritted teeth, "... why you've been ducking my request for a meeting for two days now."

I withdrew my hand. "Nice to meet you, *too*, Colonel." I knew who he was. For the past hour, I was sitting next to Admiral Block's ReGrowPod reviewing many of the Official Military Personnel Files—OMPFs—of those onboard.

While his Sergeant Major *lackey* was short, stout, and unimpressive-looking, Colonel Sanderson was a tall and imposing figure, easily six-feet-three-inches. He had a rugged, weathered look that spoke of years of military service. His short-cropped, salt-and-pepper hair, and piercing blue eyes gave him a seasoned, no-nonsense appearance. The Colonel's square jaw and broad shoulders only added to his commanding presence.

Sanderson's mouth formed a rigid line as he looked me up and down with thinly veiled disdain. One hand rested casually on the butt of his tagger. *Interesting. Who comes armed to a meet-and-greet?* His other hand was curled into a loose fist held down at his side.

"I've had my hands full, Colonel. I'm sure you can understand that."

The man took a step closer to me, his raised forefinger now pressing into my chest. "What I understand is that you've chosen to disregard the orders of your superior officer..." The man was now jabbing that same finger to coincide with each point he was making. "... which is a serious offense punishable by court martial, and in times of war, it often carries a death sentence."

A long established maritime and space-faring rule states: a ship's Captain, that being me, remains the commanding officer of a given ship. The hierarchy on a U.S. Space Navy vessel is based on the ship's chain of command. The captain of the ship holds the highest authority and is responsible for the vessel's operations, even if there are army personnel or troops onboard. Colonel Sanderson would be responsible for leading and overseeing the army personnel and troops under his command but would not assume command of the ship itself. I knew the Colonel already knew this, and it probably had become more than an annoying, festering burr under his saddle.

I locked eyes with the man, feeling my own ire growing by the moment. "I'm going to give you three seconds to take that finger away from my chest, and for you to step the fuck back."

You wouldn't think so, but a lot can happen in three seconds. The mind can process an almost inconceivable amount of information. Data collection, situational awareness, the making of strategic calculations, assess threats and contrive variable responses... all that can happened within the count of three.

The man was three inches taller than me, bigger, and more muscular—probably a real powerhouse in the gym when it came to lifting kettlebells or dumbbells. Hell, maybe he was a real champ when it came to hand-to-hand fighting, too. But I can assure you he's never experienced the same advantage I had a few years ago—the neon green Gorvian plasma injections courtesy of Doc Viv. Throughout the years, I've rarely found myself resorting to the kind of violence that elixir enables. I can count those instances on one hand... well, maybe both hands. The point is, I don't actively seek brawls. Nor do I engage in arm-wrestling matches with those possessing the strength of the Incredible Hulk to prove myself.

His three seconds were up.

Two things happened at once. First, his lackey's left hand twitched, moving toward his sidearm. Second, Sanderson was no longer jabbing at my chest, he had now taken a fistful of my uniform and brought himself even closer to me. His broad chest continued to rise and fall like a human accordion.

In the heat of the moment, Colonel Sanderson's lackey tensed, preparing to draw his sidearm, while the Colonel's grip on my uniform only tightened. I felt an adrenaline surge through my veins. Pulling the colonel along with me, I executed a quick Judo-style sidestep—Yoko Aruki—redirecting the lackey's momentum and causing him to stumble, his hand no longer anywhere near his holstered sidearm.

I was only peripherally aware of the fact that no less than ten green fatigue-wearing soldiers had crowded in around us. Nice of them to make this a real *welcome-to-the-neighborhood* shindig.

Meanwhile, Colonel Sanderson's one-handed grip was now a rough and unambiguous two-handed grip—apparently the

Army officer was attempting to regain control, to manhandle me into submission. Pulling from past trainings with Wanda—which often left me bruised, battered, and beaten—I administered a Brazilian Jiu-Jitsu, Ude-Hishigi-Tekubitori leverage maneuver, using his hold against him and executing a perfectly timed shoulder throw—one I'm sure Wanda would have been proud of. The Colonel went down hard onto his back, the wind knocked out of him. I turned to his principal NCO assistant who had regained his balance and looked ready to try for that sidearm again. The riled-up Army personnel had simultaneously moved in closer, ready to defend the honor of their fallen, dare I say, *humiliated* Commander.

"I wouldn't do that if I were you," came a familiar, Boston-accented voice from behind. Towering over everyone, Hardy, subtle as a bull in a china shop, was now barreling through the throng, toppling several grunts in the process.

Few were unaware of a ChronoBot's devastating capabilities. Besides their unimaginable brute strength, they possessed five concealed plasma cannons, each poised for deployment at a moment's notice.

Needless to say, the Colonel's Army squad backup, all took several tentative steps backward.

I knelt down next to the Colonel, who was attempting to sit up. I let him do just that, so we could be at eye level to one another.

"That superior officer you referred to earlier, one Admiral Sloan... well, he is currently in the process of surrendering all military resistance to the Grish Empire. I'm not okay with that, Colonel. And even if there was a Navy's Judge Advocate General's Corps still in existence to conduct a court martial, which I'm pretty sure there isn't, I'd still disobey that order to surrender. Especially knowing what I know."

His chin rose just enough to inflect his interest.

"First, the only superior officer I recognize in this situation, is still very much alive and will soon regain consciousness."

Sure, that may be a bit of an exaggeration, but hey, I was on a roll.

"Second..." I continued, "... there may be a means to put Earth back where it belongs, back to where our Space Navy fleets—all our assets—can find us again, so we're able to ward off these Grish bastards. Send them packing."

Sanderson stared back at me stone-faced. "Captain, do you take me for a complete imbecile?"

Before I could answer, he continued, "Admiral Block is lying in a RegrowPod wearing a diaper, and incapable of rational cognitive thought. As for any possibility of returning Earth to the Solar System, from what SARAH tells me, that's highly speculative, at best."

I involuntarily glowered up towards the overhead; I'd be dealing with SARAH's loose lips later. "Colonel, there's no reason for you and I to be at odds. You, me, our respective personnel... we're Earth's—humanity's—best and last hope for survival. You need to forget about chains of command back on Earth. All that... it's been fractured, and now led by a scared little man whose primary concern is self-preservation."

I glanced at my TAC-Band. "We have mere minutes to leave this star system—"

"Hold up there," the Colonel said. "So now you're abandoning Earth?"

"No, I'm trying to save Earth, dammit! As much as our onboard scientists have figured out the science, the physics, to return Earth to our own solar System, there's actual, real alien hardware we don't have access to. Tech that we need to get our hands on, examine, figure out, for us to even the playing field."

The Colonel seemed to be weighing my words. "And that Varapin prisoner you have in my brig?"

I was tempted to correct him, that it was *my* brig, but I let it go. "Fleet Commander Sorlen Op, has additional crucial information we'll need."

We both got to our feet. Sanderson pulled on his shirt tails, straightened his shoulders. "Why would you trust what this ghoul says any more than you would a piglet?"

"I wouldn't. But we have a bargaining chip."

"And what is that?"

"I know the Varapin, as a race, are dying. And it's happening relatively fast."

"I know about that, it's a kind of genetic catastrophe that is beyond the Varapin, or I suppose any of us within the Alliance, have the ability to thwart."

"That's right," I said. "But the Ilion, can do something about it."

Sanderson furrowed his brow. "Go on."

"I have limited knowledge about them, but what I do know is that they are an incredibly advanced society with scientific capabilities, including with genomics, that surpass those available to both allies and adversaries."

"I still don't get why we want to dip our toes into that mess. Let the damn Varapin die off? Period. Good riddance to all of them."

Murmurs of agreement emanated from the still-encircling Army personnel.

"You're not getting the crux of things, Colonel. First, the Varapin will probably be around long enough to destroy Earth. Second, it should be no great revelation that the alliance has been faltering this past year or so. Engaging both the Grish and Varapin simultaneously has turned into a battle of attrition, and as you're aware, we're running low on two crucial essentials: warships and troops."

"We're holding our own, Captain. Wars are a nasty business. Giving up is..." the Colonel's words drifted, their meaning evident. Giving up was exactly what Admiral Sloan was doing.

"Look, Colonel, I don't have all the answers. But if there's a one-in-ten chance we can get the Varapin to stand down, to drop out of this war, we should take it. The Varapin used a diabolical, ungodly means to pressure humanity. To get us to build a relationship with these Ilion. To share their advanced genetics technology. So, yeah, we're going to do that for the Varapin, but we'll have iron-clad conditions of our own."

"That they stop fighting us," he said.

I shook my head, "No. That the Varapin surrender, unconditionally, to the Alliance."

The corners of the colonel's lips curled up.

Suddenly SARAH's voice echoed down from above:

Battle stations! Incoming!
Brace for impact! Battle stations!
Incoming! Brace for impact!

XO Pristy appeared on my TAC-Band, "You're needed on the bridge, Captain. The Grish have a lock on us."

"On my way. Take countermeasures, return fire!"

Chapter 23

Responding to Pristy's TAC-Band request, I quansported directly onto the bridge. "SitRep!" I said, hurrying to the Captain's Mount.

"The Grish are on us like fleas on a dog," Pristy said from the Tactical 2 station.

Lieutenant James, at Tactical 1, said, "We're taking heavy fire, Cap. Shields are falling fast, and it seems our cloaking capabilities have outgrown their usefulness."

The ship shook. The familiar sounds of distant rumbles signified a possible hull breach.

"Helm! Jump us out of here!" I commanded.

Fingers moving across his board, Grimes, a look of determination on his face, glanced over to me. "Tried that first thing, Sir. No can do."

I spun around to Jorkins at the Engineering Station, "Lieutenant, status on our drives!"

"Stellar Rift Engine for wormhole manufacturing, fully operational, Nova Fusion Propulsor Drives for FTL, operational, and our four Quantum Transposer Orbs, for quick jumps, all good. This isn't a propulsion issue, Sir."

"We're being held in a kind of tractor beam, Captain," Ensign Lira said from the Sensors and Reconnaissance Station.

"She's right, Captain," Pristy said. "It's a capability we didn't think the Grish had mastered yet."

"Evidently, they did—they do," I remarked, my gaze fixed on the newly displayed asset logistics projection that Pristy had just unveiled on the primary halo display. Glancing at the information key, I swiftly deciphered the meaning behind the various icons. There were eight red, which denoted Grish ships—Varapin ships were symbolized with blue icons, though there were none in sight—and green denoted Alliance ships, with USS Franklin being the sole representative. The icons shifted in real time, providing a dynamic snapshot of the players and their positions on this intricate battlefield chessboard.

Hardy, accompanied by Derrota, took up their standard positions on either side of me.

SARAH announced:

Hull breach, Deck 5, Deck 9, Deck 33. Vac-Gates being deployed now...

Vac-Gates served as quickly-sliding-into-place, reinforced emergency bulkheads. Strategically placed throughout the ship, they partitioned breached sections to minimize the loss of precious atmosphere into the vacuum of space. An unfortunate result, though, were those poor souls trapped within those isolated areas. There were emergency EVA stations, but reaching one in time was a race against the clock, and not everyone would make it in time.

A Grish warship exploded off Franklin's starboard side. Then another off the portside. Pristy and Akari stood, high-fived each other, then quickly got back to work.

"Someone tell me where's that tractor beam emanating from," I said.

"It's not the Grish!" Ensign Lira proclaimed with excitement, a prospector striking a vein of precious gold for the first time.

"It's coming from the sixth exoplanet. Originating from an underground Varapin outpost. One that's extremely well hidden," Pristy said.

"Can we destroy it? I know we have penetrating munitions... bunker buster missiles."

"We do," Pristy said, "but they'd be useless for this application. That bunker is miles below the surface."

The ship suddenly shuddered, as if caught in a violent maelstrom, a cacophony of groans and creaks echoing through the corridors. The very bones of *Franklin* were being pushed to their limits, as if the ship itself were engaged in a relentless battle for survival.

Hull breach, Deck 2, Deck 15, Deck 85...
Vac-Gates being deployed now.
Shipwide Maintenance being dispatched.

I looked to Hardy, his faceplate black; he had nothing for me.

Turning to Derrota, I recognized a glimmer of hope there. "What? Talk to me, Stephan."

"We're not going to survive this... predicament, Galvin. At least not shooting it out with the Grish."

"That's not helpful."

Derrota smiled, "Do we not still have a Varapin Fleet Commander being held within *Franklin's* Prisoner Holding Facility?"

I jumped to my feet. "Yes!" I took Derrota by the shoulders and looked at him, "You're a genius!"

"SARAH, quansport me down to PHF, do it now!"

There were strict regulations pertaining to onboard quansporting. Something I had now done twice within the last few hours. Leave it to say, it wasn't allowed. And for good reason—it was too easy to quansport right on top of another person. One would think that that would result in a horrific commingling of body parts, a freakish amalgamation of dual heads, arms, and legs. But the technology has been perfected to the point that that doesn't happen. What does happen, is this...

Security Officer Gomer Bruster was conducting his late afternoon rounds within the ship's sparsely populated prisoner holding facility. No doubt bored out of his mind due to the solitary prisoner check each hour, he experienced what any person would consider to be an otherworldly moment: Bruster was abruptly hurled off his feet and sent headfirst into a nearby bulkhead.

Seeing that I'd quansported right onto the man's previous position, I rushed to the security officer's crumpled, unconscious form. I grimaced as I felt for a pulse at his neck. *Thank God.* It was there.

"SARAH, contact HealthBay; tell them that we have a man down here."

Yes, Captain. Please note that Inter-Deck quansporting is against ship regulations...

I disregarded the AI's admonition and hastened down the corridor, which was flanked by vacant, diamond-glass holding cells on either side. I found Slop floating within the farthest cell on the right. I stopped, took in the prisoner, who appeared to be sleeping.

Red glowing eyes came open. "Ah, Captain Quintos... so kind of you to drop by for a visit."

"Knock it off, Slop. We need to have a serious talk."

The ship shook and trembled. *Franklin* was being pummeled again.

I stood in an at-ease position in front of the ghoul's cell. "Before I waste even a moment of my time, I need to know something."

"I'm listening, but I imagine I already know what you're going to ask."

"Can you instruct that underground bunker of yours to release *Franklin* from the tractor field?"

Slop was now slowly circling his holding cell. His movements were lackadaisical and effortless. As if he was floating upon a cloud, without a trouble in the world. He had yet to answer me. Then he said, "You've gotten yourself... what is that human idiom? Ah yes, you've gotten yourself into quite a pickle, haven't you, Captain?"

Overhead, SARAH was listing more Deck breaches, and the deployment of more Vac-Gates.

I continued to watch the floating ghoul, envisioning myself tearing him limb from limb. *Why do they all wear the same stupid robes? Have I ever seen one of them without them?* The thought disgusted me. Like seeing the underbelly of an insect, best to not go there. Still... you do what you gotta do. "Remove your robe."

That caught the Fleet Commander's attention. Coming to a slow stop, the Varapin looked back at me. "I will not."

I said, "SARAH, have Hardy join me down here in the PHF."

A few moments later, the AI responded:

The ChronoBot is on his way, Captain.

I'm not exactly the president of the *Torture Your Enemies Club...* that whole process tends to drag on forever, serving up a delightful mix of half-truths, tall tales, and a side of *OUCH*. Me? I'm more of a fan of the gentle art of persuasion, like offering up a little bribery, making some well-placed threats, or maybe a friendly game of truth-or-dare. You'd be surprised how much quicker and more dependable it is to get the scoop that way. Efficiency is king, right?

I could hear Hardy's heavy footfalls approaching; I was sure Slop could as well.

"You will find no success with harming me. In fact, you will only make your perilous situation worse, Captain."

I shrugged. "You hear that, Slop? The loud cadence of Hardy's approach? Like the drumbeat of your impending fate."

Slop's leisurely meandering circles had evolved into rapid revolutions, akin to the frenzied movements of an agitated bee.

Hardy arrived and took in the circling ghoul with a tilted head. "Dizzying."

"If you would be so kind, I'd like you to do me a favor."

"Snap his neck?"

"No, nothing so dramatic as that. I'd like you to go in there and... disrobe that Varapin."

"That's an interesting request. Especially considering what is going on around us. The battle and such."

"Indulge me."

Hardy approached the holding cell's door and entered a complex multi-digit code on a waist-high access pad. Mechanical clicks and clanks heralded the door's unlocking, allowing it to swing open slightly. Hardy hesitated, looked back at me. "You sure about this?"

I made a two-handed shooing gesture, "Go on."

Slop had timed his attempted escape at the perfect moment —right as Hardy swung the door open and was stepping inside.

But as quick and agile as a flying Varapin could be, the ChronoBot was faster. Like the Karate master catching a fly in his chopsticks, Hardy's mechanical appendage shot up, taking hold of Slop around his neck. Now inside the holding cell, the door securely closed, I could see Hardy was having a difficult time keeping his grasp on the unwieldy Varapin.

"Be much easier if you just let me snap his neck," he said.

"You have your orders, Hardy," I said.

Thrashing about like a captured, wild banshee, Slop was now screaming... what I guessed were Varapin obscenities.

Hardy appeared to be growing increasingly frustrated. Several times, Slop slipped from his grasp and darted away, eluding his attempts to recapture the elusive alien.

At one point, the ChronoBot's shoulder canon emerged from its hidden compartment, where the weapon tracked and locked onto Slop, ready to eviscerate him with plasma fire.

"Hardy, we talked about this," I said, thoroughly enjoying the consternation being thrust upon the unwieldy fleet commander.

Suddenly, Hardy managed to grab hold of Slop's robe, yanking the Varapin closer and securing him with his other hand. Even through the diamond glass, I could hear the fabric ripping and tearing away.

What I saw next, just might give me nightmares for weeks to come, maybe months.

Chapter 24

Y ou might be wondering why I've gone through such considerable effort to investigate such a seemingly trivial question: What lies beneath a Varapin's robes? However, my true aim was to unravel the mystery of whether it's the Varapin's inherent biology or the robes themselves that grant them their gravity-defying abilities, considering the ghoul's never seem to be without them.

Well, with Hardy's help, the question has been answered.

With the now-shredded black robe lying upon the holding cell's deck plates, Fleet Commander Sorlen Op was making a failed attempt to hide. And to be honest, he was making a valiant attempt by wedging himself up high into the far-right corner.

Hardy said, "Do you want me to catch him again?"

"No, you can leave him be."

I waited for Hardy to exit and join me at the glass partition. We both stared up at the atrocious sight.

Slop's form was gaunt, with thin—almost transparent—skin, tightly clinging to bony structures. His limbs were spindly, like withered sun-bleached branches. And his skin, it seemed to be slick with some kind of viscous ooze, mirroring the sheen of rot upon a fetid marsh.

Strip away the robes, and the Varapin's anatomy hits you like a prank gone wrong. Imagine a creature buoyant with... I don't know... helium, hydrogen, or maybe some alien gas they're hoarding from the far corners of the cosmos. So light they'd make a feather seem like lead. We stood there, mouths agape—me, not so much Hardy, as Slop's inner workings—gooey little gas sacs—pulsed and gurgled like a chorus of queasy stomachs. They inflated and deflated with the grace of a novice bagpipe player, a bizarre, squishy cacophony of the grotesque.

"I think I'll pass on dinner tonight," Hardy said.

I tore my eyes away from the freak show and glanced up to Hardy. I was rewarded with something I hadn't seen in quite some time—a faceplate animation. On a continuous loop, it was a digital doodle of a guy doubled over, relentlessly losing his lunch into a pail.

I brought my attention back to Slop and spoke loud enough for him to hear me. "How about I bring you a replacement for your, um, ruined attire?"

"This affront, Captain, will not stand. Mark my words, the retribution I bring will echo in your bones, suffering beyond the wildest reaches of your nightmares."

"Now-now, Slop. I'm not in the business of critiquing physical appearance," I said, then casting a glance at Hardy. "Is that the correct contemporary term?"

"I believe the proper term would be body-shaming."

"Slop, it's important we all accept ourselves as we are. Learn to love our—"

"Mark my words, Captain, you will die a thousand excruciating deaths!"

"You know that phrase never made much sense to me,"

Hardy interjected. "If you're dead, how do you go on to have nine hundred and ninety-nine more deaths?"

I looked up. "SARAH, do our guest a favor and have someone bring him proper replacement attire."

Perhaps a generic uniform, Captain?

I shook my head, "That won't work. Maybe something like a bathrobe. Needs to be on the smaller side. Yes, like a woman's bathrobe. Oh, and something in a darker shade. Black, preferably."

We only had to wait five minutes, but it was five *tense* minutes because *Franklin* was still being pounded hard. This was evident by the continued, near constant, overhead announcements pertaining to Deck breaches and the summoning of shipwide maintenance crews.

A form was fast-approaching. I tensed, not immediately knowing if it was friend or foe. As the form got closer, I was surprised to see it was none other than Petty Officer Second-Class Aubrey Laramie. She was running, her long, agile legs taking her down the Prisoner Holding Facility's main corridor.

Slightly out of breath, she tossed me the garment. "Sorry, no one had anything in black. And all of the onboard clothes replicators are in use... something to do with the Symbio Deck."

I looked at the garment. It was probably the right size, but... "It's what? Satin?"

"Silk," she said with a shrug.

"And that color? Pink?"

"Fuchsia. And before you ask, yes, it's mine."

I wobbled my head, "It's perfect. Hardy get in there and present our guest with his new robe."

It was only at this moment that Aubrey's eyes landed on the

alien cowering at the cell's apex, its form as repulsive as it was ashamed.

Aubrey raised an eyebrow, "Who would have thought, huh?" she mused. She turned to leave, then looked back over one shoulder, "Needless to say, I don't want that robe back."

My TAC-Band was practically vibrating off my wrist. And yes, I knew things were becoming dire while I stood here making idle conversation with the prisoner. But without the help of the Varapin—all would be lost anyway. And we'd just uncovered the bargaining chip of all bargaining chips.

"Hardy, hold up. Let's not give Slop his special gift just yet."

The ChronoBot, who had been waving the fuchsia silk robe high in the air, quickly withdrew it.

"Slop, did you know that each of our holding cells comes equipped with all-seeing cameras? 24/7 security."

The fleet commander now appeared to be trying to burrow even tighter into the high-up corner.

"Was that a whimper I just heard?" Hardy queried.

"What that means, Fleet Commander, is that I could broadcast your, um, nakedness, out to the farthest reaches of the cosmos if I wanted to. Hell, even back to your own ship where each of your subordinates, your shipmates as it were, can point their boney fingers and gawk at your hideous nudity."

I waited.

AFTER A TENSE, DRAWN-OUT MINUTE—A minute that seemed like an eternity, given that I did not possess the luxury of time—the ghoul finally spoke. "What do you want, Captain?"

≈

I decided to screw regulations once more and quansported back onto the bridge. Both XO Pristy and Akari James were too busy to even look at me.

"SitRep," I said.

"Other than being a target for..." Pristy glanced up to the logistics display, "... thirteen Grish warships, we're still in one piece. Shields are stable at twenty percent, and we've taken out eleven enemy vessels."

Akari added, "Captain Wallace is chafing at the bit to deploy Arrows."

"That won't be necessary," I said, turning to the Comm Station. "Mr. Chen, you should have received a coded frequency matrix from Hardy."

Chen looked down and leaned forward, "Uh, yes Sir. Just arrived."

"You're to open a feed from that specific PHF holding cell provided."

"Done, Captain."

"Now, with luck, you should be able to connect Fleet Commander Sorlen Op with that below-ground Varapin stronghold."

Two halo display projections popped into view, one with Fleet Commander Sorlen Op, the other with another Varapin, undoubtedly miles below that 6th world's surface.

"Is that a bathrobe?" Pristy asked.

Now Slop and the other Varapin were talking back and forth. Slop, getting louder and angrier by the moment, practically apoplectic with fury. Finally, the subordinate, perhaps being adequately threatened, nodded, seemed to have complied with his superior's demands.

For some reason the auto-translation protocols hadn't been enabled. Perhaps it had something to do with the quickly kluged-together hook-up.

"SARAH, tell me if there's any, um, treachery, going on between the two."

At some point, Chen added himself into the communications mix. "I'm on it, Cap. So far Fleet Commander Sorlen Op's doing what we wanted him to do. That doesn't mean he's being nice about it."

"Captain!" Pristy exclaimed, "Tractor beam's been disabled. We're free—"

I cut her off, "Helm! Jump us the hell out of here!"

Chapter 25

Manufactured Wormhole Transit...
USS Franklin

Captain Galvin Quintos

W e were four days into the first of four manufactured wormhole jaunts. All four days would be needed to take us where we needed to be—the extreme far side of the galaxy. Estimated time of arrival into Forland 545 System was three weeks. *Franklin* would need every minute of that—and more—to address the dozens of deck breaches.

Currently, the loss of life was holding steady at thirty-five, with over one hundred injured seriously enough to require medical attention. HealthBay was a madhouse. In order to tend to the wounded, eight MediBots were activated, and they moved about the facility with more urgency than finesse. More beds were needed than were available, so the bots were forced to find more cots next door, encroaching into Coogong's and

Derrota's R&D space... much to the chagrin of the two scientists.

Inside the manufactured wormhole, the novelty of bending space had long since worn off. The ship's interior hummed with a monotonous drone, the constant vibration a reminder of the vast emptiness outside. Days stretched into each other, marked only by the ritualistic cycle of synthetic meals and sleep shifts. The crew moved through the vessel with a languid predictability, their tasks automated to the point of redundancy.

Screens blinked with data, the same sequences repeating, while outside the viewports, the Universe itself seeming to yawn, the stars blurred into indistinct streaks. Conversations had been whittled down to essential exchanges; the silence engulfing words before they could fully form. Even the air, recycled and stale, seemed to hang motionless. The journey, once a marvel of scientific achievement, had settled into a tedious waiting game, a test of endurance against the void's unyielding monotony.

As I made my customary rounds in HealthBay, attending to each of the wounded, their stories unraveled before me—tales of loved ones, ambitions, and visions of futures uncertain. The weight of our conversations compounded, leaving me not just tired, but soul-weary. Each day merged into the next, a mirrored sequence of care and distress.

Yet amidst their personal afflictions, their gravest concern lay elsewhere—in the silence from Earth after the Tidal Basin Massacre. No news could penetrate our confines in the cosmos, no reassurances could be given or received. The injured, grappling with their own serious wounds, were haunted more by the unknown—unaware of which familiar faces had survived, which family members we could see again. The void between us and home grew deeper, laden not just with distance, but with the aching unknown.

Exiting HealthBay, my TAC-Band came alive with Sonya's projection. Long ago, she had figured out how to hack communications so her calls wouldn't have to be accepted first, enabling her to just *pop* into view, sometimes at the most inopportune times—like when I'm asleep, or eating, or when seeing a man about a dog. And if you don't know what that means, I can't help you.

Fortunately, in this case, I was simply making my way toward the closest DeckPort.

"It's ready!" she said with far too much enthusiasm for my mood.

"That's good news, Sonya," I said with a pasted-on smile. I didn't have a clue as to what she was referring to. "Let's talk about that a little later." I cut the connection.

Two strides later, Sonya was back. Her earlier exuberance replaced by a scowl. "No. You're not going to do that, Galvin."

"Maybe you should call me Captain, or even Uncle Galvin."

"Did you hear me? Independence Quest is officially online. Ready for its maiden test run."

"Wait, are you wearing that inappropriate outfit again?"

"Barmaid costume and get over it. I want you, and several of your besties, to get up here to the Symbio Deck. Come on. It'll be fun. Empress Shawlee made me swear I'd get you off the bridge once in a while. Get your mind off of Doc Viv."

"You know, I don't appreciate my personal life being bantered about behind my back."

"You mean like your trysts with one long legged, hard-bodied Petty Officer?"

"There are no trysts going on. Who's saying there are trysts?"

Smiling, she made the *zipping-her-lips-closed* gesture.

What I needed to do was get off this subject. "When shall I, and my... um, besties, get up there?"

Sonya looked away for a moment where I heard Ensign Plorinne off in the background say, "In an hour would be good."

"In an hour. Oh, and you're to leave your TAC-Bands behind." She abruptly cut the connection.

I didn't like the sound of that, but, there again, SARAH was always close by in case of any kind of emergency.

Pristy, Derrota and I entered the drawing room. Baby-blue silk wallcoverings, a domed, mosaic-patterned ceiling, and Baroque-style furniture of mahogany and rosewood decorated the lavish space.

We were within the combined Decks 98/99/100, but it felt like we had been transported to an opulent colonial estate somewhere in the mid-1700s. Our team assembled in the middle of the room around an intricately carved foyer table with scalloped edges. Some kind of alien scrolling was etched into the wooden tabletop.

"What do you think it says?" Pristy asked with forced enthusiasm.

While Derrota had eagerly agreed to this mid-morning request to join me for a full day of Symbio Deck R&R, Pristy had been far less enthused. In fact, she had listed a multitude of chores that needed to be done ASAP. Of course, her excuses were—for the most—as insignificant as organizing her sock drawer or alphabetizing food packets in the galley.

"No idea," Derrota answered, examining the scrolling etched into the tabletop. He arched his brows, "Perhaps, some kind of clue?"

I was about to add my own two cents when another person

entered the room. I use the word person loosely because I was certain this was a Symbio Poth. He was solidly built with a rounded, rather than angular physique. The man wore a maroon, coarse, home-spun suit straight out of colonial times. At about five-foot ten-inches, he had a larger-than-average-sized head, balding on top like a bullseye... centered on a crown of longish, messy, light-brown hair. Featuring a humorous mouth and sporting a pointed upper lip, he steadied smiling grey eyes at us through silver spectacles.

"Benjamin Franklin," I said.

"A gold star for you, Captain Galvin Quintos." Franklin brought his hands together in a faux clapping gesture. Stopping suddenly, he raised his bushy brows. "The quest you are about to embark upon will require much more of you than stale text-book facts."

"What do you mean by that?" Pristy asked.

"XO Gail Pristy. So pleased you've decided to join the conversation." Franklin fixed a warm gaze on her. "You see the script here on this foyer table." He pointed to the foreign-looking scribblings.

Pristy glanced down, let out an audible sigh.

"Very soon, you will be able to translate that message."

"Really? That would be some trick." She looked up to Franklin then to me, then to Derrota.

"All who enter Independence Quest must first pass through this indoctrination room." Franklin made a dramatic hand gesture to their surroundings. "Here, each of you are already being inured with special... um, shall we say *powers*, of sorts. Powers that come with specific talents attached. Captain Galvin Quintos will be a decorated Starfleet officer known for his analytical abilities and courage under fire. His role is to lead the mission and develop strategies to fulfill the objective of the quest."

"Doesn't sound so different than the real self-obsessed character," Pristy interjected.

"Perhaps, but some traits will be enhanced, may even take you by surprise," Franklin countered. "Now, for you XO Gail Pristy, you will be a brave and accomplished undercover agent as well as a xenoanthropologist."

"So, I'm a spy, as well as an expert in alien behavior, cultures, and societies," Pristy chimed in.

"Very good, XO. Subcategories of xenoanthropology include linguistics and biology." Franklin shifted his attention to Derrota. "Science Officer Stephan Derrota will be a loyal and sensitive crewmember... an expert cryptographer, precise in his ability to decode and decipher. One who also relies on his sixth sense to avoid sticky situations."

"But what is the purpose of this quest?" Pristy asked, not even trying to disguise her impatience.

"To find my diary, of course. Once you find it, read it. The words will reveal how to end the war, and perhaps... future wars."

"The war?" Derrota asked.

"Yes, my intelligent friend," Franklin said, his gaze softening. "The American Revolution, the very struggle that forged the Declaration of Independence and birthed the United States."

Derrota, looking dubious, started to say "But we—"

Franklin lifted his hand, a gesture that commanded attention, "This journey, this piece of living history, has been intricately crafted just for you. The conflict you'll engage with, this depiction of the American Revolution, is laced with subtleties that may diverge from the recorded events of the 1700s. Yet, the essence, the very spirit of that tumultuous era, will be undeniable, inescapable. Within the pages of the diary, you seek lie designs—blueprints of clandestine innovations, the kind that could pivot the trajectory of human progress. You and your team, Captain Quintos, bear the responsibility of uncovering this tome amidst the perils and deceptions of both human and, shall I say, automata adversaries."

"Symbios," Pristy said.

"Threats, nonetheless," he corrected. "No more questions." Franklin said with a tone that belied his amiable appearance. "I will see you soon. Off you go—learn, stay vigilant. But first, you must be dressed appropriately." He gestured toward a set of tall, fifteen-foot-high French doors. "Your respective ladies' maid and gentlemen's gentlemen, are awaiting your arrival."

Pristy made a face, "I'll have a maid?"

"What Old Ben is referring to..." Derrota said, "... are individuals specialized in helping their patrons with clothing choices, properly dressing, that sort of thing."

Pristy grimaced.

I opened the doors for the other two. Empress Shawlee had gone to extraordinary lengths to produce this elaborate game for me—for us. So, I figured I may as well play along, no matter how difficult it was leaving the real world behind.

We had entered into a rustic space, one far less frilly than the drawing room. Here was the very epitome of a colonial log cabin—a humble home of the period: stained, roughly hewn timber walls, modest furniture, and a stone fireplace with several cords of wood, fully ablaze. A hefty chain swung from a rudimentary metal swivel from which a cast iron pot simmered. Wafts of a tart and pungent scent, reminiscent of spoiled meat, filled the air.

"Yummm... mutton stew." Derrota raised his chin, a hound sniffing for treats.

"Yum wouldn't be my first reaction," Pristy said. "But, to each his own."

Three closed doors flanked the interior walls, each with a sign above the threshold. They read:

Derrota... Pristy... Quintos...

Standing before one door was a modestly dressed ladies' maid, while two gentlemen's gentlemen wearing equally nondescript valets' attire, stood in front of the other two doors.

"Alright, everybody, let's get to it," I said, getting into the mood. The three of us disappeared behind our respective doors.

Chapter 26

Pristy's expression was etched with stark misery. A twinge of guilt crept up on me, finding some perverse pleasure in her discontent. "That's quite the gown, XO," I commented, my voice tinged with surprise. "A significant switch from your regular... um, choices."

She looked at me with narrowed eyes. "I didn't choose this," she snapped back. "I'd forgotten the sexist nature of these times. Where men wear sensible clothes, but nooo—women are forced into corsets, petticoats, and poofy, linen hats. I feel ridiculous."

I swallowed hard, momentarily captivated. I'd forgotten just how lovely Pristy was, and more so when out of her somewhat unisex uniform. Standing there, her dress was a vision of the 1700s femininity, tailored to accentuate her slender frame. The fabric clung delicately to her form, a corset cinching at the waist to emphasize her petite silhouette. The gown cascaded in layers, the outermost, a rich brocade. Perhaps it was the deep navy that made the blue of her eyes seem even more vivid. Embroidery, subtle but intricate, traced the hem and bodice, catching the light with every disgruntled shift she made.

Underneath, the whisper of petticoats rustled, their volume

a stark contrast to the practicality of men's attire. And atop her head sat a linen hat, its exaggerated puffiness casting a shadow over her features—a final touch to the era's complex standard of beauty. Blonde, side-swept bangs were the pièce de resistance that had me forcing myself to look away.

And then I saw it, her lips quirked upwards in a faint, enigmatic arc, hinting at amusement tucked away just beneath the surface. Was she, in fact, starting to enjoy herself?

She was giving me the once-over... seemingly, taking in my own period attire.

I was wearing a long shirt... made of linen, I presumed. Whatever the material, it was itchy as hell. Pristy covered her mouth, now out and out laughing at the rest: stockings, garters, doublet, knee-length breeches, a waistcoat, and neckcloth. Derrota's clothing was nearly identical. But overall, Pristy was right, the men's clothes would be far easier to get around in.

"I think you look lovely, Gail," Derrota offered with a genuine smile.

Pristy waved away the compliment, then stopped short, as if suddenly remembering something important. "I know what that alien message is... the one inscribed on that foyer table."

"Well?" I asked.

Her gaze drifted, flickering with the effort of summoning a memory. It said: "Unleash your talents with care, throughout your quest they're always there. As the finale draws near, their strength may veer. From Main to Market, let instinct flow, a gift to guide, a power to show."

"How would you know all that?" I asked, skeptically. "I mean, that's not something anyone would just, out of the blue, be able to decipher, let alone remember."

Irritation flashed across her features. "Is it because I'm not smart enough to decipher a message?" she asked, her voice carrying a mix of challenge and vulnerability.

Derrota stepped in closer to her, studying her face, as if examining her every freckle.

"What are you doing?" she said, taking a step back.

Ignoring her question as well as her indignant attitude, he looked at me. "I know how they're doing it."

"Doing what?"

Derrota held up a *wait-a-second* finger—as if still mentally putting pieces of a puzzle together in his head.

We moved outside while I was trying to figure out what Derrota was getting at. Now, looking about our surroundings, we were in front of that same modest, log cabin, which was surrounded by an abundance of staghorn sumac, spicebush, and other overgrown scrub. An emaciated dog, some kind of underfed hound, scurried across our path.

"We must consider everything we see as a possible clue," Derrota said, taking a keen interest in the dog.

While Pristy lifted the hem of her dress, we followed a pathway into a nearby tree line, one that was little more than a game trail, but soon became more substantial. I marveled at the seemingly real deciduous forest around us. I stopped, gaped up at the assortment of American Chestnuts, Eastern White Pine, and American Sycamore. I reached out a hand and felt the rough bark of a nearby pine. Was it real or perhaps a Symbio Poth re-creation?

Eventually, the path transitioned into a cobblestone walkway, and then we were walking single file between timber structures—an alleyway of sorts.

We arrived at what looked to be an 18th-century main street in a port town bustling with merchants, sailors, and townspeople. Stray hogs and chickens roamed cobble streets lined with wooden buildings, shops, and brick homes with candles in the windows. Wagons loaded with goods creaked down cobblestone lanes. Gulls circled above the tall ships docked in the not-too-distant harbor. The smell of tobacco and sea battled with the stink of animal excrement. Symbio Redcoats marched in formation, on guard for signs of rebellion.

Derrota's eyes went wide with astonishment, taking in the stunning intricacy around us. I shared in the disbelief, the realism of it all challenging the knowledge that it was all a facade, despite the convincing evidence of our senses.

"What now?" Pristy asked.

Derrota continued with his earlier train of thought, "Ben Franklin had said something to the effect of... here, each of you are already being inured with special... um, shall we say, *powers* that come with specific talents attached."

"That made little sense to me, figured it was just part of the silly game," Pristy said.

"No," Derrota said dismissively. "You being able to decipher a seemingly indecipherable clue has to be science, not magic."

"What then?" I asked.

"What do all U.S. Space Navy personnel have in common? Something that occurs day one after taking the oath."

"Does this really matter, Stephan?" Pristy said, "Let's just play the silly game and move on."

My curiosity piqued, I urged, "Hold on, continue... what do you suppose—"

"Not suppose, Galvin... I'm sure of it." Derrota touched at an area behind his left ear, "Nobody uses them much anymore these days. Our ocular implants."

I'd almost forgotten about those. Like TAC-Band auditory communications facilitated right into our brains. Most don't use them these days, opting to deactivate the technology in favor of just using their far more richly featured TAC-Bands. But sure enough, we have all had ocular implants.

Smiling, Pristy nodded, "And your niece is like a hacker

extraordinaire. The little trickster, she's found a way to hack our damn brains!"

I thought about that, and I had to give it to the teenager, the girl was smart.

Pristy looked at me, shook her head. "You're proud of her. I can see it written all over your face."

I shrugged, "You're right, how about we just play the silly game. Let's head in that direction." I gestured towards an array of shops; their identities proclaimed by vibrant, hand-painted signs with elaborate script. "The Pennsylvania Gazette," I announced, my eyebrows arching in a gesture of intrigue. "That's old Ben's newspaper printer shop!"

ONCE INSIDE THE PRINTING SHOP, I WAS enveloped by the aroma of ink and paper. The wooden floors creaked underfoot, polished by years of traffic. Shelves bursting with stacks of paper and leather-bound books lined the walls. At the center stood a massive oak and iron printing press, its polished lever glinting from streaming in sunlight from nearby windows.

Compositors worked with ink-stained fingers, setting type precisely as apprentices mixed vivid red and black inks. Journeymen operated the presses rhythmically, the heavy thuds resounding. Sheets of paper hung overhead like flags of progress. I pictured the real Ben Franklin hunched in the cluttered corner, quill dancing across some unfinished manuscript.

"Well, looks like we're at the correct location," Pristy said, staring up at a portrait of a much-younger-looking Ben Franklin, while simultaneously trying, unsuccessfully, to loosen her snug bodice.

I strode over to the now open printing press, as if I knew what I was looking for. The machine was setup for the printing of the day's newspaper. But lying beside the press lay a tattered, sepia-colored scroll. Examining the elegant cursive prose, I felt like I was glimpsing history itself, holding something memorializing the past.

It was a poem composed in flowing English script; the kind used to write the Declaration of Independence. I could tell it was penned by a master calligrapher. I recognized it, immediately. The Rhyme of the Ancient Mariner by, Samuel Taylor Coleridge.

Day after day, day after day,
We stuck, nor breath nor motion;
As idle as a painted ship
Upon a painted ocean.

Water, water, everywhere,
And all the boards did shrink;
Water, water, everywhere,
Nor any drop to drink ...

"The apothecary shop across the street," Derrota said, tapping a thoughtful finger upon his chin. "Remember the sign? It stood out like neon on a dark night—painted a bright venetian blue: Elixirs and Tonics. People drank that stuff thinking it would cure their ills."

"Seems like a stretch," I said.

"I think he's right, Quintos," Pristy said. "A lot of those tonics had a water base with extracts of poisonous plants like belladonna and stramonium."

I shrugged. "I'll take your word for it. But come on, are you listening to yourselves?"

"What?" Pristy said rolling her eyes, like a teenager called out for a curfew violation.

"We're being fed where to find these clues..." I pointed to my own ocular implant.

"Yeah, so what? I thought we were past that. Are we going to analyze every little thing, or just play the game?" Pristy admonished, now making a beeline for the door.

As soon as we walked in, the stench hit me with the force of a sledgehammer—sickly-sweet herbs, pungent musk, and spoiled fruit. This was definitely an apothecary. Like an old-fashioned drugstore—a place where they made and sold medicines, herbs, and potions back in the day. Derrota had explained on the way over, it's where you'd go if you were sick and needed medicine or advice on what to take.

"Why does everything reek in this town?" Pristy said wrinkling her nose in disgust.

The place was packed with chattering townswomen, mostly women. Their old-fashioned dresses came in all styles - some plain linen gowns, others boasting stripes and flower patterns, swishing over quilted petticoats. Their hats showed who's who in society—made of materials from everyday twill to fancy silks. In my mind, as I was watching the ladies, they were swapping gossip and long tales. I heard laughter and the occasional burst of a gasp. Conversations blended into a steady hum as this mix of plain and elegant socialites circulated around the room.

Derrota beamed, "I must say, these Symbio Poths are on a whole other level. Incredibly real."

Pristy and I smirked at his child-like enthusiasm.

The square footage of the shop was meager and made all the more so because of copious amounts of product and furniture crammed into the space. Shelving, tables and counters, each displaying various herbal merchandise cluttering the small room. A weathered rosewood display table in the middle of the shop was brimming with books and pamphlets about tinctures and remedies, tins of dried tea leaves and mystery powders.

As Derrota, Pristy, and I surveyed the shop, all the while dodging patrons, an older man of about 65, harried-looking with sad eyes and slight of build, approached us. "Good afternoon. My name is Daniel—Daniel Waterson. May I help you find something?"

My breath caught. As if not believing what I was seeing. "Dad?"

Bewildered, the proprietor said, "I'm sorry young man... but, uh, I don't believe we have met. As I said, I'm Daniel Waterson, a simple shopkeeper."

I stared at him, feeling exposed and off-guard. My father was long dead. But I had seen another Symbio Poth version of the man, back within my hometown of Clairmont upon *USS Hamilton's* Symbio Deck. Another Symbio Deck created by Empress Shawlee.

My emotions towards my father were a tangled web of fondness and complexity. Shawlee, what's your angle in dredging up my father now? I shook it off. No. This wasn't some kind of subterfuge or misguided ruse aimed specifically toward me, I knew that Symbio Poths were endlessly repurposed, their forms reused while their digital essences refashioned into fresh personas. It was entirely possible that my mother, too, who I've stumbled across within other Symbio Decks on other ships, was part of this charade, perhaps even nearby within the crowd.

I shook off my discomfort and embarrassment. Of course, this wasn't my real father. I said, "Yes, Sir, we're looking for a particular water-based tonic. Something strong. My job takes me out to sea. And I'm prone to seasickness."

"Oh my, that is quite a predicament, isn't it?" The merchant gave me a sly smile. "I know just the thing, Galvin." Waterson pointed to two glass jars that were sitting by themselves. "Actually, either of these would do the trick."

"Which is better?" I asked. But realized, the Symbio had called me Galvin. *How did he know my name...*

"I'm afraid, that is as far as I am able to help. I can only say, choose wisely." The man stepped away, shuffled toward a woman who had hailed him near the unguents.

Pristy approached the pair of solitary jars, scrutinizing them closely. Derrota and I, my mind still reeling, edged in beside her, curious for a better view. The fronts were bare, but turning them revealed labels on the back, scripted by hand in what seemed to be Latin.

The XO translated as if Latin was her second language. "Okay, this one says it's made from ingredients found at the stables in rural Massachusetts. There's some kind of emblem next to the script." She set down the almost-empty jar and picked up the other one. Pinkish liquid swayed about a quarter of the way up from the bottom. "This one says it was created, originally stored, and cultivated at the shipyards that built the USS *Constitution*."

"The USS *Constitution*? It's gotta be that one, right?" Derrota said, eyebrows raised.

"Wait. What was that emblem on the first one?" I asked.

Pristy picked up the jar. "It's a Continental Army insignia. See this flowing red banner and the blue numerals? They translate to the specific time period of 1775."

"So, what do you think?" I asked, since clearly, she was the one receiving the clues here.

"It's a known historical fact that the shipyards where the USS *Constitution* was built is in Charleston, South Carolina... and that ship wasn't built until after the American Revolution ended. But the clue leading to the stables... well, it is common knowledge that Benjamin Franklin specifically bought horses to give to George Washington's Army to help them in the war effort."

Loud voices outside.

Startled, I turned in time to see the front door being kicked in with a resounding *CRACK!*—wooden splinters catapulted into the room like shrapnel from a burst grenade. A multitude of musket-armed intruders were storming into the establishment. I didn't need any ocular hints to guess who they were. I took in their crimson-red uniforms trimmed in black and garnished with silver buttons. White, fitted undercoats peaked out through their military garb. White knee-length breeches completed the ensemble.

A man, obviously an officer, moved to the forefront. He was adorned in a redcoat with gold braid, gold buttons, and gold-fringed epaulets. At his waist, a spontoon hung, secured and dangling at his right. Broad-shouldered and rugged, his wild beard framed a face topped with oily brown hair pulled back into a ponytail.

"Hold your positions! No one move without command," he ordered, his voice carrying the unmistakable tones of an English accent.

The members of the regiment raised their muskets as if to emphasize his orders, practically daring anyone to step out of place. The patrons, huddled together, some gripping onto strangers standing next to them, others held handkerchiefs to their mouths.

That's when my gaze met the shopkeeper's across the room; his eyes held a hint of forewarning, as though he had foreseen this rude invasion. The officer's gaze snapped to mine, steely and direct.

I moved towards him with deliberate calmness, "Why this disruption? This is a place of business, not a battleground."

The officer narrowed his gaze as he too advanced, his demeanor radiating authority. "Address me with due respect—as General. General Jarvis Graves," he demanded.

"Coming across a little over the top, General?" Pristy murmured with a snarky tone, and loud enough for the general to hear.

In an instant, everything turned for the worse. Rooted to the spot, I could only watch as a soldier under the General's command made a sudden thrust, ramming the stock of his musket against Pristy's cheek. The impact was so fierce that Pristy was hurled backwards, her feet swept from under her as she toppled into the display behind her.

Pandemonium reigned as the room erupted with shrieks and desperate calls. Patrons scrambled, some colliding with the stationed soldiers in a frantic bid for freedom. It was amidst this chaos that I glimpsed the scene unfolding outside. Redcoats were everywhere, detaining captives—men and women alike, shackled and blood-streaked. Their faces etched with panic and fear. Recognizing some of their faces—Oh no—these were not the native Symbio Poths; they were crewmembers, fellow players, each seized in the midst of their own *Independence Quest*. My heart missed a beat, Oh God... there among them was Sonya, her barmaid attire ripped, shredded, her arms desperately trying to cover her exposed chest.

Chapter 27

At that moment, I faced an impossible decision. Should I rush to aid my visibly battered and terrified niece, or should I attend to Pristy, who was just steps away with what could be a severe head injury and possibly in need of life-saving care?

I shouted, "Derrota, see to Gail!" I lunged into action; muskets boomed in unison. A searing pain lanced through my upper right arm, yet I propelled forward, bulldozing into the mass of redcoats with the unstoppable force of a charging full-back at the goal line. The soldiers toppled beneath my surge, arms and legs entwining in disarray.

Out of the corner of my eye, I spotted General Graves. His gaze was fixed, intense; his sword drawn and poised high for a downward strike at my head. With no route back and the front door compromised, I leaned into my momentum, teeth clenched against the impending blow and hurled myself through the shop's front bay window, glass shattering around me as I made my desperate exit.

I landed hard onto the cobblestone street, feeling the sting of glass shards embedding in my legs and back. Another volley of musket fire thundered behind me, its sound ringing in my ears. I shook my head, struggling to regain my senses amidst the swirling white smoke and the pungent, sulfurous scent of gunpowder that hung heavy in the air.

"Help me!"

Sonya! I staggered to my feet, aware that one of the redcoats was already clambering out through the broken window. Knowing the odds were against me outrunning him, or a musket ball, I grabbed for his weapon, tearing it free from his grasp. Hands gripping the end of the long barrel, I swung it Babe-Ruth-style, clocking the Symbio hard across his chin, before spinning away and running in the direction of Sonya's recent cries for help.

I spotted the fleeing regiment of redcoats, along with five or six bound prisoners some fifty yards away. While the soldiers were being hampered by unwieldy hostages, I was not. Ignoring the pain in my shoulder, and the multiple cuts to my legs and back, nothing was life-threatening. I sprinted after them.

My mind flooded with questions. This, unfortunately, was not the first time a group of Symbios had gone rogue, had turned on their human overseers. The incident within Convoke Wyvern, with its mounted nights, tall castles, and fire breathing dragons, came to mind. Maybe it was time to put these Symbio Deck experiences to bed.

Periodically, one or two of the redcoats had turned around, caught site of me advancing on them.

There was something about that General Graves that had seemed... familiar. Where had I seen him before? Was it a situation like with my father, General Graves being just another repurposed Symbio from some past Symbio Deck?

Up ahead, three of the redcoats had turned and were now taking aim at me. I stopped in my tracks; I was out in the open with no place to take cover. Strange, but only now did I remember the ship's AI, that I could put a stop to all this right now. "SARAH! end this game! Deactivate the Symbio Poths!"

Nothing.

I dove to the ground, just as the redcoats discharged their weapons, a trio of booming reports filled the air. One musket ball whistled past my right ear.

It was then that I caught the faint, distorted sounds filtering through my ocular implant—a voice struggling to emerge amid a haze of static, reminiscent of a distant broadcast trying to find its frequency.

I was up and running again, more determined than ever to reach Sonya and the other hostages. And then what? I was unarmed and bleeding. In fact, I was bleeding like a stuck pig. What the hell? The sleeve of my injured arm was sopping with blood. Can't stop, have to keep going... need to save Sonya.

I stumbled, feeling weak, feeling dizzy. No longer was I closing in on the redcoats. My fingers and toes had gone cold, my heartrate pounding in my chest like a jackhammer. Yeah, I knew the signs, the effects of too much blood loss. And there was that damn crackling voice in my head!

I staggered forward; the hostages, the redcoats, were no longer individuals, more like a blur, a smudge of color against an indistinct backdrop. And then I was down, staring up at the sky which I knew, wasn't really a sky.

"Change... settings...ocula... implant... Capta..."

I lay there trying to make sense of the garbled voice in my head. Gail? Is that Gail?

"What settings? What the hell does she want me to do?" And then it came to me. Perhaps no longer exerting myself, no longer trying to run, I had found a moment of clarity. I needed to change the settings of my ocular implant back to being two-way communications.

I concentrated through the growing fog, brought up the

mental imagery of my ocular implant's *primary settings menu*, something that typically would have taken me a split second, now, it was like swimming through a pool of tree sap. The virtual menu hovered into view. Taking a ridiculous amount of effort, I scrolled through what seemed like and endless list of choices. Then I found what I was looking for. It occurred to me that this is what Sonya must have hacked within my—everyone's —head. I changed the settings from **Input Nudges** to **Full Duplex Communications.**

"Captain! Galvin!" Gail's voice rang out in my mind, clear and crisp. "Can you hear me?"

A surge of relief flooded over me as I responded, "I hear you," I said, in a voice that sounded like it belonged to someone else.

"We're on our way to you. Sit tight."

"Sonya... where's Sonya?"

"We're coming—"

That was all I heard before blacking out.

Chapter 28

Manufactured Wormhole Transit…
USS Franklin

XO Gail Pristy

P risty, Derrota, Ensign Plorinne, and Hardy rushed towards the spot where Quintos lay sprawled upon the dusty road up ahead. Earlier, Derrota had crudely wrapped a rag around Pristy's forehead. Hardy, wearing a 1700's era redcoat, had, miraculously quansported into the frantic melee, plasma weapons deployed with bright-red plasma bolts tearing through all those in the vicinity.

Twenty minutes earlier, Derrota had Pristy laid out on the apothecary's display table.

Hardy, weapons already snapping back into their respective hideaway compartments, hurried to her side.

Looking down at Pristy, Derrota said, "The bone above your right eye—the frontal bone—is broken."

She swallowed. The pain was dull, throbbing, and constant, but bearable. "I feel like I've been hit by a truck," she managed to say, trying to sit up. She spotted Ensign Plorinne bursting through the front door, stepping over the bodies of fallen soldiers. The horde of earlier patrons, long gone... having run for their lives.

Derrota, hovering over her like a worried momma bear, said, "You need to lay back, Gail. You have a serious injury—"

She swatted his hands away, sitting all the way up, then getting to her feet upon shaky legs. "We need to find the Captain."

"He went after Sonya... she was taken by the soldiers," Derrota said almost apologetically, as if he should have found a way to stop her abduction.

Pristy looked to Plorinne with her one good eye. "What the hell happened? What's with the attacking Symbios?"

The young Ensign, flustered and momentarily tongue-tied, looked as though he might just pee his pants.

"Spit it out, Ensign!" Hardy said, his typical cool calm demeanor gone by the wayside.

"There's been a major assault upon the ship's network," Plorinne stuttered. "*Franklin's* AI has been reduced to bare minimal ship functions... not what you want happening while rocketing through a wormhole."

"How is the ship even functioning?" Derrota said looking incredulous.

Hardy pointed to his own head, "LuMan is trying to pick up the slack. But it's not a long-term solution. The hack is sophisticated and dynamic, elusive. Coogong is in his lab working on it as we speak."

Ensign Plorinne standing ramrod still, suddenly inhaled. "I should have anticipated..."

"What?" Pristy coaxed.

"There was one Symbio Poth in particular that had... problems. Constant build checksum errors." He looked to Pristy, "All of our Symbios are digitally stored, their physical, mental, personalities—all of it is stored code. That way, when they get injured, destroyed, such forth, during a game, we can simply initiate a new hardware build. That's why people are starting to remember seeing some of the Symbio's from other Symbio Decks."

"Get to the point, Plorinne!" Pristy said.

"I don't think we've ever built this one. Don't remember it being among the hundreds of build options."

"Was it the General?" Pristy blurted out. She looked to Derrota questioningly.

"General Jarvis Graves," Derrota said. "It all started with him barging in here. I remember something odd about him."

"Other than being a diabolical killer?" She spat back.

Derrota looked lost in thought; suddenly all the color had drained from his face. He murmured, "Oh no..." he looked to Pristy, then Hardy. "Sentience."

"What's he talking about, Hardy?" she asked suspecting she already knew the answer.

"Self-realization," the ChronoBot said. "What makes you suspect—"

Derrota gestured toward the spot where the General had previously been positioned. "There are signs, often quite subtle, that indicate when an AI—an automaton like yourself, Hardy—is in the process of becoming self-aware," he explained. "One observable manifestation is unnecessary movements... illogical, wasted gestures, such as absentmindedly scratching one's beard, nervously twitching a finger near a musket trigger, or even the act of sniffling. These seemingly human traits symbolize a growing self-awareness."

Pristy looked to the floor, scanned the faces of fallen British regiment soldiers. "He's not here."

"He ran off," Derrota said. "I saw him flee, just prior to Hardy's quansporting arrival."

Pristy waved away the comment. "Fine. Right now, we need to find the Captain. Find Sonya and the others." She looked to Hardy, "Isn't that one of your trademark superpowers, finding people, DNA scans and such?"

Hardy shook his head, "Those sub-systems are unavailable. Shut down while LuMan manages innumerable critical operations for an in-flight omninought."

"So, there's no way to contact him? The Captain?"

Derrota suddenly clapped his hands together, almost giving Pristy a heart attack. "Christ, Stephan!"

"Our ocular implants. They're probably not under SARAH's control, but under the hacker's control."

Pristy, Derrota, Ensign Plorinne, and Hardy slowed and paused, as if not believing what they were seeing.

The XO knelt on the dirt road, beside Quintos' seemingly lifeless body. Splotches of blood stained the surroundings.

Then she stopped; a chilling realization gripped her chest, causing her heart to skip a beat. "Oh God, he's gone. We've arrived too late," she whispered.

Hardy's voice, now taking on LuMan's more digitized tone, affirmed, "I am detecting no signs of life from this body."

Chapter 29

Manufactured Wormhole Transit...
USS Franklin

Sergeant Max Dryer

Sergeant Max Dryer, Wanda, Grip, Ham and Hock all quansported onto the combined Symbio Decks in fully kitted out combat suits and shredder weapons. Just ten minutes earlier, while Max was showering, he had been inundated by desperate voices—more like pleas—abruptly echoing in his mind. It was XO Pristy, and she needed him and his team, his Marines, RIGHT NOW!

What he knew, which wasn't much, was that the Symbio Poths—either some of them or all of them—had gone rogue. For sure, the ones dressed as revolutionary redcoats were probably hostiles. Their mission: find and free Sonya and the other human hostages.

The five of them moved off in the direction the redcoats had taken according to the XO. The team was quiet... gone was the typical adolescent ribbing and kibitzing.

Max slowed, now seeing the exact spot where the Captain had taken his last breaths. Copious amounts of rust-colored, still-drying blood marked the fateful spot.

The team gathered around, forming a somber circle, each member silently pledging retribution—a pursuit of Marine justice in response to the unthinkable—a ship's captain unexpected demise.

Wanda was the first to break ranks and set off ahead. Max empathized with her; she had been the closest among them to Captain Quintos, sharing a kind of brotherly/sisterly bond. They had dedicated countless hours in the gym over the years... training, sparring, and working to get the man in peak fighting condition.

"Let's do what we came here to do," Max said, his voice transmitting via their respective ocular implants.

Max caught up to Wanda; she appeared to be studying the ground in front of her.

"If you look closely, you can see where they left tracks in the dirt. One of the hostages might be limping, see there? Looks like a foot being dragged."

"Let's pick up our pace," Max said. "They can't be all that far ahead of us."

They set off at a dead run. Their physical prowess hadn't regressed since completing Basic Training a decade past. Every morning, they incorporated HIIT, High-Intensity Interval Training, into their regimen, enhancing their anaerobic endurance and replicating the rigors of real combat scenarios. But now, they had a different level of motivation driving their pursuit.

One would think... the twins, Ham, and Hock—who at first glance looked a bit on the pudgy side of beefy—would be laboring for breaths by now, but looks were often deceiving. The two brothers were not only keeping up but starting to stride ahead of the pack.

From what Max knew of this latest iteration of a Symbio Deck, it was among the largest, most ambitious yet. Five miles in length and a mile wide... 3,200 acres of mostly wilderness.

"There's the XO, Derrota, and Ensign Plorinne," Max announced, pointing off to the left.

"Why isn't Hardy with them?" Wanda asked.

"He's in pursuit of another of the redcoats," Max said. "A General someone or another."

"General Jarvis Graves," Grip interjected. "The Symbio MoFo that's currently jacking the ship."

Wanda appeared frustrated. "So, how many Symbios are actually involved in this... uprising? Is it solely the redcoats, or do the Symbio townsfolk have a role in this as well?"

Max shrugged; he didn't have an answer for that.

"Maybe we just mow down the lot of them," Hock offered up in his Arkansas drawl. "Put down all the Symbios, you know, just in case. It's not like they're human... or even alive."

"Let's knock off the chitchat," Max said. He didn't like the direction this conversation was going. He'd interacted with enough Symbios over the years to have his doubts, especially the latest versions, like the 2.0 Symbios that had originally crewed USS Adams; they certainly seemed, well... if not alive, on their way to being self-aware.

They reached XO Pristy, Officer Derrota, and Ensign Plorinne. The XO was sitting upon a tree stump while Derrota seemed to be adjusting a bandage wrapped around her head which covered one of her eyes.

Pristy said, "Glad you're here. Unarmed, all we've been able to do is follow them."

Max chinned toward her bandage, "You doing okay, XO?"

"Fine. Look, they seem to be taking cover near that cluster

of trees. There're no more than nine or ten redcoats keeping half that many hostages."

Moments earlier, Max and his team had raised their faceplates... all their HUDs seemingly on the fritz. The five of them now squinted toward the distant cluster of hostiles and hostages.

Pristy thanked Derrota and abruptly stood, "Max, the hostages' safety is what's most important here. The Captain's niece is amongst them."

Max inwardly acknowledged Pristy's overly matter-of-fact demeanor. It was common knowledge the XO and Captain had had a close relationship. No one really knew if it was more than that. But still, the recent realization that he'd been killed must be taking a heavy toll on her.

"Okay, let's divide our forces," Max said breaking the awkward silence. "Ham, Hock, and Grip, you move out and position yourselves to approach from the far flank. Wanda and I will engage them from this direction."

He watched as the three of them headed off.

"This doesn't seem all that well thought out on their part," Wanda commented gesturing toward the regiment of soldiers.

"I've been thinking the same thing," Pristy said, her voice tense with concern. "It appears to me like a feeble attempt at a stall tactic, as if we're being deliberately diverted or... she hesitated, searching for the right words."

"Or distracted from what's most important?" Max offered up. "It makes sense, here we are chasing after this bunch, while Hardy, who's apparently barely operating at 20%, is the only one chasing after General Graves—the apparent mastermind and probably our most pressing concern."

Max's ocular implant crackled with Grip's voice. "Sarge, we're in position for a well-executed crossfire attack."

"Copy that, Grip," Max replied thoughtfully. "Considering

the circumstances, a sniper approach might be the most effective. Can each of you target a redcoat?"

He noticed that Wanda was already lying prone, her eye firmly fixed on her shredder's eyepiece. Her ability to anticipate his directives was uncanny.

She said, "I'll take down any that the boys fail to neutralize."

Max looked to Pristy.

She pursed her lips, "Whatever you do, don't miss." Then she nodded.

Bright plasma bolts found their respective targets and within moments, it was done. Not a single redcoated Symbio Poth remained on his feet.

Pristy was already running toward the hostages. Over one shoulder she yelled, "Leave me Wanda, the rest of you check the perimeter. We don't want any surprises. And Max, contact Colonel Sanderson, ask him to put his Army on standby."

WHILE THE DESPONDENT ENSIGN PLORINNE had sprinted ahead of everyone, Pristy's pace dwindled, her head spinning, dizziness overwhelming her. She was acutely aware of the concussion she'd sustained and the urgent need for treatment within a HealthBay RegrowPod. However, her singular focus was on Sonya. That's what Galvin would have wanted. Ensuring Sonya's safety and well-being was her sole mission now, even if it meant risking her own life.

She sensed Derrota and Wanda approaching from behind, and then Wanda's reassuring grip on her arm. "I've got you, XO," Wanda declared with determination.

Except for one, the hostages were all on their feet, looking down at the fallen soldiers around them. It was clear they were indeed all human... *Franklin* crewmembers. All were bloodied and looked to have been savagely beaten. Pristy quickly dropped to her knees next to Plorinne, who had his arms wrapped around Sonya. The teenager was curled into the fetal position. Her hair was matted and streaked with blood. There were several deep cuts on her cheeks and chin. Plorinne had removed his own shirt and wrapped it around her, covering her exposed chest.

Pristy watched as Sonya mindlessly rocked back and forth, back and forth—and now heard her mournful sobs. Oh God... she knows—Sonya knows about her uncle.

While Derrota and Wanda attended to the others as best they could, Ham, Hock, and Grip arrived ready to help.

Pristy looked up to Derrota, "What's the status of the Quansporter?"

"Like most of the ship's subsystems, inoperable. We'll need to walk out of here."

She nodded, "Ham, Hock, and Grip, carry the injured out of here—those who require assistance. We've got the girl."

Sitting up now, Sonya sniffed and gently pushed Plorinne away. "I'm okay. I can walk." She suddenly grabbed at Pristy sleeve," I know what he's after."

"Who?"

"The General... I know who he is and what he wants!"

Chapter 30

Admiral Cyprian Block

HealthBay was a hive of activity, with nurses, doctors, and a few MediBots scurrying about, tending to the dozen or so patients. Medical Avatars revolved slowly, suspended on invisible axes over their prone proxies.

EUNF U.S. Space-Navy's Executive Five Star Fleet Admiral Cyprian Block was sitting upright in bed, emerging from the RegrowPod just two hours prior. Sadness weighed heavy, like a lead blanket upon his frail shoulders. *Should have just let me be... should have let me wither away back on Earth.*

Chief Knott had been there when he was roused back to consciousness. And she had been the bearer of the awful-awful news about the Captain.

Block had been an eager military man since the age of 18, starting out as a young cadet prepared to confront the challenges of a thousand distant star systems. His journey within the U.S. Space Navy had been nothing less than remarkable. So, he had encountered death and coped with his fair share of losses. But this... this was an exceptionally tough one.

"You need to eat something, Admiral."

He looked up to see Chief Knott, short, stout, and freckle-faced—younger than him by at least a decade, she was the one bright spot in all of this... whatever this was.

He had lost his wife, Briar, after thirty years of marriage, two years ago. Since that time, the Admiral had immersed himself in his work and embraced solitude, awaiting the day he would eventually reunite with her. However, life had a way of surprising him. Strangely, he now found himself searching for this woman—his dear departed wife—his eyes instinctively turning toward the auto-hatch doors with each opening, hoping to catch a glimpse of her being busily engaged, holding her tablet, and giving orders to her staff.

"I'm sorry. Must have been lost in thought, what did you say?" The Admiral replied.

"You need to eat, look at you... you're a rack of bones."

Ouch, that stung. *She's right, I must be a sight.*

Knott smiled, and it was as if the Sun had emerged from a stormy sky.

He said, "You know, I think I could eat something. Maybe you could join me..." *Christ, did I just say that? What, I'm now hitting on my doctor? Have I gone totally fucking daft? The woman's busy—beyond busy.* "Um, I need to be brought up to speed on, well, everything. Prior to today, the last thing I remembered was the ceiling of my DC office falling in on me." He looked to her; bushy brows raised. "... an excellent recovery, if I do say so myself."

She sat down on the edge of his bed and took his hand in hers. "Admiral, at this very moment you are the most important person on this ship, back on Earth—hell, anywhere. So, I would be honored to have a bite to eat with you." She gave his hand a gentle squeeze and stood back up. "Admiral—"

"Please call me Cy; Admiral is so, I don't know, formal sounding. Cy is what my..." Flustered, he allowed the words to trail off.

"Cy, I would love to have a bite with you, but I'm sorry to say, your dance card is all filled up." She gestured toward HealthBay's entrance where several uniformed crewmembers were standing, impatiently waiting.

Perhaps picking up on his disappointment, the Chief said, "But dinner would work. That is, if you're free from the pressing demands of being a VIP Fleet Admiral by then?"

She gave his hand another pat and was off before he could answer her.

Captain Wallace Ryder approached, who he recognized, flanked by another officer wearing Army fatigues.

"Greetings Admiral, I'm glad to see you're feeling better," Ryder said. "Uh, this is Colonel Sanderson, the CO for the Army battalion here onboard *Franklin.*"

"And you two are the current ranking officers?" Block said, getting right down to business.

Ryder and Sanderson exchanged a quick glance.

Ryder nodded. "With XO Pristy held over within a Regrow-Pod... that and with Captain Quintos..."

"Captain Quintos what?" Block said, looking irritated, not liking how the two were pussyfooting about, walking on eggs.

"Well, with his untimely death—"

"Captain Ryder," Block spat, feeling his ire rising. "I need to stop you right there. Captain Quintos is not dead."

Both men grimaced, looked down at him with expressions of pity, or was that embarrassment? Perhaps thinking he was a pathetic old man who wasn't quite dealing with reality... that maybe he had lost a few too many marbles in the course of his injuries. "Yes, the Captain has succumbed to extensive blood loss, but this is the 22nd Century for shit's sake. The man was rushed into HealthBay, dropped into a RegrowPod, and now he's recovering."

Sanderson looked confused. "It's just that, uh, XO Pristy, prior to going into a pod, had confirmed—"

Block reached for his call button, pressed it and continued to press it until three nurses, a doctor, and a MediBot all came running.

"Yes, Admiral," the young male doctor responded, slightly out of breath as he assessed the situation. The nurses were occupied with monitoring the readouts and data from his various medical devices, while a MediBot stood nearby, holding a bedpan.

Block remarked, "Could one or all of you kindly inform these two officers that reports of Captain Quintos' demise have been greatly exaggerated."

The medical staff appeared momentarily taken aback by the unusual request. Dr. Cramer, as indicated by his brass name-plate, spoke up, saying, "Captain Quintos is most certainly alive. We acknowledge that shipwide announcements are affected with SARAH being partially offline, so please, do feel free to spread the good news."

Ryder, angered, said, "His niece... I just stopped by to see her in the overflow section of HealthBay. Dammit, she thinks he's dead. She's devastated. As I'm sure, XO Pristy thought prior to being placed in a RegrowPod."

The nurses all stopped what they were doing, Dr. Cramer stiffened, clearly feeling the not-so-subtle rebuke. "I apologize; I will inform her immediately," he said with a sense of urgency.

"Like hell you will," Block declared, flinging his bedcovers aside and swinging his boney, naked legs over the edge of the bed. "Someone get me a damn bathrobe; the last thing the poor girl needs is to see my bare, hairy ass hanging out of this gown."

SONYA HAD SENT PLORINNE AWAY, HIS HOVERING— constantly asking her how she was doing—had made her want to scream. Sonya lay curled up on the harder-than-concrete hospital bed, the covers pulled up all the way over her head. She was half-asleep, half-awake, drifting within her dark little sanctuary, away from the rest of the world. Her injuries had been minor, but emotionally, she was devastated. She now knew what the term heartbroken *really-really-really* meant. Her fists clenched for the hundredth time. She was so mad at him for dying. Hell, the whole reason she was here on this ship—had been on any of these stupid fucking ships, was Uncle Galvin. He was her only surviving family member. Now what?

"Excuse me, Miss Winters?"

"Go away, I'm not hungry, and no, I don't need anything—"

"I'm Admiral Block. Please come out of there so I can speak with you."

Her muffled voice was stern, "I don't need any more condolences from people. Good God, I just want to be left alone!"

"You may be interested in what I have to say, Miss Winters. Your uncle is not dead. I am so very sorry you were not told."

Her eyes widened, brimming with tears. Did she hear him correctly? She cautiously lowered the blanket and blinked against the harsh, intrusive lighting. An elderly man in a bathrobe stood before her. "Who are you, exactly?" She couldn't shake the feeling that this might be some sort of cruel prank. Father Time here needed a shave and a comb, and he seemed like he might be a bit unhinged. Perhaps he derived pleasure from messing with people's heads.

"There you are, Sonya. I am Admiral Block, but my friends

call me Cy, which I hope you and I can be. May I?" he asked, gesturing to the end of her bed.

Sonya hesitated, then nodded, pulling her blankets up closer around her neck.

The older man sat, looking tentative at where to start. "Your uncle is very much alive. I promise you that."

"Well then, I want to see him!" she said, stirring. She was so relieved, she felt giddy, like she wanted to laugh, or cry, or both at the same time. Was that even possible?

"He's not conscious just yet. You can go to him in a few minutes. But first, it's been brought to my attention you may know, more than anyone, who is responsible for the Symbio-Poths malfunctions—the subsequent issues with major ship systems."

The memories rushed back in a flash, her heart nearly jumping from her chest. "Yes! Oh God, I almost forgot. Admiral, I help up on the Symbio Deck. Mostly on the programming side of things. They're like my, um, I don't know, pets seem like a demeaning word—"

"Please, Sonya, just go on."

"You have to understand, they all start out as QuansScript code. Zettabytes of physical information that are the equivalent of our human DNA."

"Okay, I follow that..."

"Well, I thought I knew all the Symbio characters. Their code comes with metatag flags so they're easy to distinguish. A lot of them are reused, reprogrammed to play different parts in the various Symbio Deck games."

The Admiral nodded.

"But I'd come across a new code set for a particular Symbio. One that we had never introduced into any of the previous games. And there were some anomalies, nothing major, with the exception that this Symbio code was for a higher level 2.0B model. This Symbio code was once utilized on *USS Adams*. 2.0B's were the original crewmembers when that ship was still a repurposed starliner, a cruise ship."

"And you know specifically who this particular Symbio crewmember—"

Impatient, Sonya said, "It's his metaflag. It meant nothing at the time, but it came to me up on the Symbio Deck, it was designated as Com/Stan2.0B."

The Admiral shook his head, "I'm not following."

"It stood for Commander F. Stanley who was a real prick, excuse my language. He was the Symbio Captain's second in command on *Adams*, and he hated my uncle. And later, when the 2.0's were pretty much forced off the ship, maybe even marooned somewhere..." She shrugged. "... it makes sense when I cross-referenced the QuansScript code, that the General Jarvis Graves was, in fact, Symbio Commander F. Stanley. That he's here onboard, somehow, perhaps to make us all pay."

Block stared at her for a long moment. "You are a very intelligent young woman, Sonya."

She nodded.

"But there is a good bit of conjecture, leaping to conclusions with your assumptions, young lady."

"I know I'm right."

"And there's no connection to what's going on with the attack on Earth, the Varapin Fleet Commander we have onboard, all that?"

"No, I don't believe so. Now can I go? I want to be there when my uncle wakes up."

"Yes, of course. And thank you, Sonya."

Chapter 31

Manufactured Wormhole Transit...
USS Franklin

Captain Galvin Quintos

I awoke in a deep, luxurious fog, like a young boy having slept in for twelve hours on a blissful Saturday morning. It felt as if I could almost hear my mother bustling around in the kitchen, the aroma of freshly made pancakes wafting through the air as they sizzled on the griddle. But amid this peacefulness, the first of abstract thoughts began to sneak into my perfect morning.

A gentle, familiar hum continued to draw me away from my idyllic moment in time. I knew that sound, and right now, I hated it. *Stop... just let me be. Let me stay here, where life is simple, where I can pretend to be anyone but myself.*

Cool, fresh air was now billowing into the confined space; the intrusion of way too bright light hit me like the business end of a sledgehammer.

I groaned.

"Rise and shine, Captain," came a somewhat familiar voice.

I opened one eye. A blurry, fuzzy shape came into focus. A red-haired middle-aged woman peered down at me. But it was her white doctor's coat that brought her name into the forefront of my mind. "Chief Knott," I croaked.

"Good, brain processes are indeed functioning."

Why wouldn't they be functioning? "Um... Doc, can you close up this pod? I need just a few more centuries of sleep."

Several more shapes took form behind the doctor. A grizzled looking old man in a bathrobe came into focus first. Admiral Block? And... oh... Sonya's there too.

"Get up so I can give you a good punch in the face," Sonya grumbled, her voice raspy and filled with both irritation and relief.

I winced. "You need to work on that *respecting-your-elders* thing, kid," I said attempting to sit up.

The Admiral leaned in; surprisingly strong hands helped me do the same. "So good to see you back from the brink, Galvin. You had us all quite worried."

It was at that very moment that memories, like a dam breaking loose, surged into my consciousness.

Having been pulled up onto my feet, I teetered.

"He'll need a moment to get his sea legs," the Chief said.

Suddenly, arms wrapped around me like a boa constrictor, making it nearly impossible to breathe. Sonya's tears soaked through my thin hospital gown. "Hey, Sonya, it's okay. I'm alright." I hugged her back, kissed her head. Looking beyond her to the Chief, I mouthed the words, "What's all this about?"

"Captain, you died up there on the Symbio Deck. You were legally dead for close to an hour. That might be some kind of record."

I considered that. Perhaps it was Doc Viv's administered Gorvian plasma shit that had saved me.

"Everyone thought you were dead," came the teenager's muffled voice. "You're such an asshole!"

Sonya finally released her vise-like grip and stepped back, self-consciously wiping her eyes. "I have things to do. Someone has to save this stupid ship." She spun away, seemingly back to her typical obstinate self.

Suddenly, my mind was racing with an influx of questions. "Gail! Is Gail... still alive? And what's the situation with General Graves?" I exclaimed. My thoughts turned to the Symbio Deck, the other hostages. "Damn it, and what's happening with my ship?"

The Admiral placed a hand on my shoulder, "Son, we have a lot to talk about. The good news, XO Pristy is alive and recovering." He gestured to the adjacent RegrowPod where I could just make out Pristy's bandaged face through the clamshell's blue tinted lid. "The hostages have been freed and your robot is fast on the trail of General Graves."

"And the bad news?"

"*USS Franklin* is in trouble, Galvin, big trouble..."

Showered, dressed in a crisp clean uniform, I strode onto the bridge to heads turning, eyes widening in surprise, jaws dropping in unison. Approaching the Captain's Mount, I said, "Captain Ryder, permission to take back command of my ship."

Startled, both Ryder and Akari abruptly turned and jumped to their feet. Akari, with a burst of emotion, closed the distance for an embrace, which I wholeheartedly accepted.

Lieutenant Hargreaves from the Flight Control Station announced, "Captain on the bridge."

Ryder, smiling, said, "The Captain's Mount is yours, Sir." And then he stepped aside.

"Captain Ryder, bring me up to speed."

TEN MINUTES LATER, RYDER WAS GONE, needed back in flight bay—Akari James seated at the Tactical station. Ryder's overview had been brief but thorough. *Franklin* was one hour from coming out of her final wormhole leg, where we would be arriving .5 light-years from Forland 545 System. There was no way of knowing what or who would be there to greet us.

Hardy was on the move. A dedicated halo display projected his slow, methodical, progress through the ship in search of the elusive Symbio Poth General Graves. Currently, Hardy was on Deck 11 on all fours crawling through a service access chute. The ChronoBot was still doing double and triple duty taking on much of what the incapacitated SARAH typically would have been tasked with, while also keeping in close contact with Coogong and Derrota, who were tackling the formidable physics challenges posed by moving worlds through interstellar space.

Crewmember Chen said, "Captain, I have SWM Chief LaSalle for you."

"On display, Mr. Chen."

The Shipwide Maintenance Chief appeared within what looked to be a darkened section of Engineering and Propulsion. Behind him was a backdrop of looming tall reactor cisterns and bundled conduit runs.

"Apologies, Captain, for the delayed update."

"It's understandable, I know you're busy. Talk to me about battle damage incurred."

"We've made excellent progress as far as internal repairs. Most of the deck Vac-Gates have been re-opened. External blast damage is still being attended to by a virtual army of little hull-bots. Unfortunately, until SARAH is fully back online, our ability to test primary ship systems and sub-systems will be hindered. The big issue will be coming out of this wormhole without SARAH being 100%. It's far more than what the robot can handle."

"What's the worst-case scenario?" I asked.

LaSalle just looked at me as if I was an idiot. Finally, he said, "Worst-case scenario... according to Science Officer Derrota, USS *Franklin* would be reduced to her most basic elemental, molecular state."

"Understood. I'll keep you abreast of our progress, Chief LaSalle."

"Lieutenant James, put in a request... request Colonel Sanderson to—"

"Army has already been dispatched, Captain. Same with Sergeant Max and crew," she said. "A grid search has been set up. If he's still onboard, they'll find him."

"If he's still onboard? We're traveling within a wormhole construct—there's no means for getting off the ship."

Akari turned to look at me, "I know that, but we have to remember, the General got onboard by nonphysical means, terabytes of QuansScript code. Even if we find his Symbio form, who knows where he is beyond that?"

I dragged my palms down my face. *Fuck, she was right.*

Chen said, "Sir, Admiral Block is requesting your presence within the Prisoner Holding Facility."

I looked blank-faced to the Comms Station. "No-no-no. Please tell me the Admiral hasn't taken it upon himself to meet with Slop."

Chen shrugged uncomfortably.

I got to my feet, "Lieutenant James, you have the Captain's Mount."

"Aye, Captain," she replied.

· · ·

Minutes later, I arrived within the PHF. I was starting to really love the quick accessibility that the DeckPorts offered. Two anxious looking security guards were keeping their distance from Slop's holding cell down the corridor. They turned at my approach.

"I was told the Admiral wished to see me. He's not here?"

"Oh, he's here all right, Captain," the guard sporting a trimmed beard said, looking disgruntled. His brass name tag read, *L.B. Crenshaw.*

The other one, short and stout, gestured toward Slop's cell. "Admiral ordered us to stand down."

Irritated, I raised my brows, "So, where's the damn Admiral?"

The bearded guard said, "He's... in there with the, um, prisoner, Sir."

My breath caught, I felt the blood drain from my face, "No. Tell me you didn't leave the Admiral alone with that ghoul, that damn killer!"

I didn't wait for an answer, already sprinting down the corridor saying a silent prayer that at this very moment, the Admiral wasn't on his back, his mouth open in a silent scream, his essence being drained away.

Halting before the transparent diamond-glass partition, I gazed, utterly captivated by the sight. There was my friend and mentor, Admiral Cy Block, seated upon the integrated molded bench, mere feet from Varapin Fleet Commander Sorlen Op. The Admiral was animated, talking... gesturing with his hands, as if seated upon a park bench within Manhattan's Central Park. Slop, on the other hand, was simply listening, every so often nodding his ugly skull of a head.

I caught the Admiral's attention mid-sentence—a crooked smile crossed the man's lips.

I tried the door, it wasn't locked. Just terrific. They both turned their full attention to me. "Sorry to interrupt your little tea party here, Admiral, but what, may I ask, do you think you're doing?" My mind flashed back to the Tidal Basin Massacre in DC, buildings being decimated, so many lives lost—I fought to tamper down my growing rage.

A flicker of annoyance passed through the Admiral's gaze. "Captain Quintos, it seems you've overlooked the chain of command. Remember, I am your superior officer. It's important you don't forget that. As for my presence here... I'm assessing the possibility of any mutual understanding that might exist between Varapins and Humans."

I looked to Slop; the ghoul's expression unreadable. "And may I ask, what have you two determined?"

Slop raised a bony claw, "It is understood that occasions arise for adversaries to engage in conflict, to go to war... and likewise... moments arise for conflict to cease. Though friendship is unlikely, it is conceivable that a reciprocal respect might be achievable."

I shook my head, "Please tell me you're not buying this load of horseshit, Admiral."

"The Varapin have no sense of honor, no moral compass to guide their actions. They're driven only by a cold calculus of gain and advantage. As we speak, our world has been decimated, I couldn't even calculate the death toll."

Slop said, "Allow me to pose the question once more, Captain. And I seek your candid response. To what extent would you venture to safeguard the survival of your species? Would you not annihilate the entire Varapin race if it meant the preservation of humanity?"

My hand shot forward, taking Slop by the neck and pulling him up to eye level. "You chose the wrong way to make your damn point!" I stared into Slop's glowing orbs for a long moment.

"Galvin, please... release the Fleet Commander," Block said. "We're at a point in time where revenge serves little purpose."

I felt his hand on my arm, gently pulling it down. I released my grip and stepped back.

"I have agreed to assist the Fleet Commander. To approach the Ilion—to offer myself as a third-party emissary."

My TAC-Band suddenly began vibrating, which was unexpected since no one's TAC-Bands were supposedly working. I saw it was Hardy. Turning away, I opened the channel. "Go for Captain."

"We have a problem, Cap," the ChronoBot said.

"Tell me where you are, I'll come to you."

Chapter 32

Charging into Environmental Systems, I was ambushed by a gust of heat that could fry an egg on a sidewalk, and the humidity? Like a sauna in Miami cranked up to a level that even the air was sweating.

In an instant, I took in the space; a Klaxon was shrieking, amber warning lights strobing. Five school-bus-sized air recirculating generators loomed, along with five massive overhead fans, each ominously motionless. Beyond, were multiple twelve-foot-high rows of filtration array banks, like walls of interwoven fabric. Typically maintained so that they were white and pristine, now they were a dark gray, a slurry of black goo pooling below them upon the deck.

Hardy was there, as was a shirtless SWM Chief LaSalle, his muscular coffee-colored skin glistening with sweat. Also, there was Petty Officer Second-Class Aubrey Laramie. Not shirtless, but she may as well have been, her sopping, tight, cotton T-shirt revealing every well-toned inch of her upper torso.

General Graves had evidently ensconced himself in the Environmental Systems' command pod, a booth encased in circular diamond glass. Within, a ring of panels and control units hemmed in the area. Clad still in his crimson coat, missing one shoulder epaulet, his once-white trousers were now marred with streaks of soot and dirt.

While Hardy, his arsenal of cannons deployed, was taking turns firing bright plasma bolts at the enclosure, both LaSalle and Aubrey were taking turns swinging sledgehammers. The loud concussive thwacks had me wincing with each strike.

"Stop!" I yelled above the cacophony.

LaSalle and Aubrey took one ineffective swing before turning their attention to me. Hardy held his fire.

"He's shutting down the ship's atmosphere... our air supply!" Aubrey shouted over the still screaming Klaxon, her eyes wide with frustration.

"We have to stop him," LaSalle said, his chest heaving.

"And you think you're going to get through tempered diamond glass?" I yelled back. I looked to Hardy. "What's wrong with you?"

The ChronoBot looked beaten and defeated. Slumped and sluggish, Hardy managed a nod. "Sorry. This old boy's not firing on all cylinders right now, Cap."

But my attention was on General Graves, who didn't seem to be affected by the scorching heat, humidity, and noise. His fingers were a blur of movement across the control board. His face showed frustration—whatever the Symbio Poth was attempting, he was not having total success.

Suddenly, Derrota was brushing past me, tablet in hand. For every keystroke command the General was making within the booth, it looked as though Derrota was countermanding those same commands. Like back-and-forth dueling banjos, the general and Derrota maintained their relentless tempo.

I saw her starting to teeter, then caught Aubrey around the waist midfall.

"It's the heat, get her out of here, Captain, I got this!"

Derrota shouted—A warrior who's found the one battle he was born to fight.

Limp and unresponsive, I hauled her into the hallway where the air was notably cooler. Stretching her out on the deck, I searched for a pulse. Her wrist yielded nothing; similarly, her carotid offered no telltale throb. Immediately I started CPR, thirty chest compressions followed by two mouth to mouth breaths. I repeated the cycle three times starting to feel light-headed and out of breath. "Don't you dare die on me, Petty Officer!" I yelled down at her. Her lips had turned blue, her half-opened eyes unfocussed and lifeless.

"Out of the way!" came a voice from behind. Chief Knott shouldered me out of the way. She wasted no time, tearing open her shirt, and getting defibrillator pads onto her exposed flesh. The Chief yelled CLEAR and tapped at her tablet. Aubrey's body went rigid, arching as a 200-volt jolt coursed through her body.

Knott checked her vitals once more and shook her head. She tapped at her tablet, bringing the next jolt up to 500 volts. CLEAR!

I watched Aubrey's body go rigid and arch once more. But there were still no signs of life. I tried to blink away the tears but found it impossible. I wanted to reach out to her, to cradle her in my arms, to whisper desperate pleas into her ear—Come back to us, Aubrey, this isn't your time to go.

I looked away. Unaware I'd been biting my lip; the taste of my own blood made me want to retch.

Chief Knott smiled. "There you go, deep breaths... that's it. Slow, deep breaths."

I glanced back to Aubrey, and my own heart missed a beat. She was breathing, her eyes were open and looking about. The Chief took off her lab coat and covered her with it.

Aubrey, full consciousness now returning, looked up at me. "What... Captain. What... what's happening?"

"What happened is... the Captain just saved your life," Knott said. "You're extremely dehydrated and far from out of the woods yet."

Aubrey seemed to be taking that in when two MediBots arrived with a GravGurney.

I watched as they hurried her off.

"Go, Captain. We've got this," Chief Knott said, giving my arm a quick squeeze.

Shit! I spun and hurried back to the Environmental Systems.

The Klaxon had been muted, the incessant hazard lights no longer strobing. A 3D projection emanated from Derrota's tablet. Sonya was arguing with the Science Officer, "You're not listening to me, Stephan! It's not just a hack, it's a full-scale infiltration. More than commandeering our central AI, Graves has unleashed a swarm of botnets. They're autonomous, executing orders from shadow servers embedded in our infrastructure."

General Graves was no longer tapping at the control board. But he was glowering at me from within his Diamond Glass shelter.

Derrota nodded patiently at Sonya. "Can we sever the uplink to the command servers? Stop the directives at the source?"

Exasperated, Sonya made a face. "They're mirroring through multiple nodes. I need to deploy an AI sentinel to hunt them down, initiate a neural net scrub. We're talking synaptic firewall rewrites in real-time."

"What about the AI core? Can't you just flush the rogue data streams?"

"It's not just data streams; it's a synaptic siege. I'll have to induce a recursive logic bomb, but it's got to be pinpointed—any collateral damage to our AI's heuristic pathways, and we could lose critical functions."

Derrota slowly shook his head. "A logic bomb? If you miscalculate, the AI could flatline, leave the ship brain-dead within the wormhole."

"We fly blind for a bit, then. I'll set up an emergency neural bypass to keep life support and essentials running. But I'll have to code the bypass live—no net, no autopilot."

LaSalle and I exchanged befuddled looks. It was as if they were talking a different language. Which, I suppose, they were.

Derrota said, "And if the bypass fails? We're talking about the neural spine of the ship!"

"Without it..." Sonya said, already tapping at her board, "... we're just a floating hunk of metal, Stephan. I'll reroute core functions through sublight processors and manually reboot the AI from the quantum up. It's risky, but it'll cut Graves' puppet strings."

Derrota looked to me. "What do you think Galvin?"

I looked to the General, who raised his chin several millimeters as if taunting me to take my best shot.

"Do you have a better option?" I asked.

Derrota thought about that, his brow furrowed. "Not really."

"The ship, the crew are in your hands," I said.

Derrota turned back to Sonya's projection "Get it done. And Sonya... make sure we come out of this with our quantum cores intact, or when we come out of this wormhole, we'll be navigating by the stars like ancient mariners."

Chapter 33

W
e had mere minutes before *Franklin* would be extricating itself from the manufactured wormhole. But there was nothing I could do—what would come next, the very fate of the ship... it was out of my hands.

Throughout the years, it had escaped my notice that Hardy had fashioned his own hidden-away personal quarters on each of the multitude of ships where we had been stationed. He was revealing that to me now, his voice a faint whisper. The long pauses between sentences emphasized the physical and mental pain he must be experiencing.

It struck me that I should have known that. Shouldn't a true friend know the whereabouts of the other's home? Having taken his mechanical arm, as if guiding an elderly feeble relative, I slowly walked with him down the passageway, turning left, heading down another corridor. I had no clue where, precisely, within the ship, we were... other than mid-ship, Deck 1.

Hardy came to a stop and wavered, the ChronoBot was still bearing the weight of many millions-per-nanosecond AI processes. He was the one keeping this massive vessel steady, navigating the tumultuous tides of a wormhole sea.

"We're here, Cap." Hardy said attempting to raise a chrome digit to a closed auto-hatch.

"What can I do to help?" I asked feeling useless.

"Knock three times, then two times, then five times."

"Are you serious?"

"Do I look like I'm in the mood for silly pranks?"

"No. Sorry."

Fully cognizant that our time—thanks to Symbio Poth General Graves—each precious second that slipped away felt like an assault. Will awareness grace us, in that final instant, the knowledge that our joined existences have been reduced to nothing but cosmic dust?

I did as directed by Hardy, knocking three times, then two, then five. The auto-hatch slid open. I wasn't sure what I'd expected, but it wasn't this. The compartment was small, but... what's the word I'm looking for? Homey? It was furnished, no bed, of course, but there was a bureau... or was it a chest of drawers? There was a high-topped desk suitable for a Chrono-Bot's height with several stacks of old-fashioned hard back books —interesting, the ChronoBot was into science fiction, I perused the titles: *Boy Gone, Ship Wrecked- Stranded on an Alien World, Scrapyard Ship*. I shrugged, never heard of them.

A nearby shelf had a collection of odds and ends strewn about, tchotchkes. Someone's old TAC-Band, a small wooden hand carved statue. I leaned in taking in the intricate feminine form, the delicate wings, a familiar-looking fairy. "Is that... Iris?"

Hardy hadn't moved since entering his compartment. Head lolling to one side, he tried to raise his head. Then, seemingly thought better of it. He said, "I miss her..."

There were pictures on the bulkheads, still images of Earth —Boston to be specific. One was of a modest two-story home in suburbia, another was a snapshot of two young men, goofy grins, arms slung around each other's shoulders. I said, "You and your brother Aiden?"

"I miss him too."

I checked my TAC-Band. Two things were about to happen simultaneously. One, we would be coming out of the wormhole. Two, Sonya's and Derrota's last-ditch effort to thwart Graves' hack of USS *Franklin* would culminate. The final seconds were counting down 9, 8, 7, 6, 5, 4, 3...

I closed my eyes—2, 1...

I waited a few moments and said, "Well, we're still one piece."

"Shocking revelation," Hardy drawled. "Clearly, such astute observations are what propelled you through the ranks."

With a glance to my left, I saw Hardy was standing upright, his faceplate displaying an animated meme of a happy dog, head extended out a car's window, ears flapping joyously in the wind.

"I take it you're feeling better?" I asked.

Before Hardy could answer, SARAH was making an announcement:

Captain Quintos you are required on the bridge...

A moment later, she followed up with:

Incoming!
Incoming!
Battle Stations!
Battle Stations!

Chapter 34

Tempted to quansport, I thought better of it and sprinted for the closest DeckPort. Minutes later, I ran onto the bridge where, in that instant, several things competed to blow my mind.

XO Pristy, sans her head bandage, was hard at work at Tactical 1. Next to her was Akari James at Tactical 2. The Captain's Mount was empty... *interesting*. And a total of eight separate halo displays were active, each presenting a unique viewpoint of the ongoing battle.

Reaching the Captain's Mount, I took in the kaleidoscope of brightly colored plasma bolts crisscrossing the inky-black void. Warships of unknown origin were attacking with unbridled gusto. "SitRep. Who the hell are we fighting?"

Pristy said, "Welcome to Forland 545 System. I can tell you who we're not fighting... it's not the Grish, and not the Varapin."

Akari said, "That's a good thing. While they have us outnumbered twenty-five to one, their technology is second-rate."

"You sure about that?" I asked, thinking the alien warships certainly looked formidable enough to me.

"Let me put it this way... before you arrived, there were twenty-seven enemy warships," Pristy looked back over one shoulder, "How's Aubrey doing?"

I shrugged, "Last I checked, still alive."

Chen said, "We're being hailed, Captain."

"Ignore it," I still needed a moment to understand what the hell was going on here. "Someone find Stephan Derrota and tell him to get to the bridge. Belay that order, quansport him onto the bridge. Now!"

He materialized five feet away from me, still in the process of tapping at his tablet. Startled, he looked about the bridge until his eyes came to rest on me. The Science Officer smiled, then chuckled. "That was unexpected."

"Apologies, Stephan. We're here—Forland 545 System. So, what are we looking for?"

"Looking for?"

Exasperated, I said "That Varapin platform thing, or what's left of it?"

"Ah, yes." He hurried over to the Science Station—the only unoccupied console—and went to work. Multiple small halo displays came to life over the board, data streams, each a water-fall of symbols and characters. Derrota's eyes darted from one to another, grasping the unfathomable with each passing moment.

He grimaced and looked to me.

"Well?"

"It's here. It's in better shape than I could have even hoped."

"That's a good thing, right?" I asked.

"It's also currently being dragged into one of those enemy vessels. A tractor beam has hold of it."

I glared at Akari, "You said their technology is second-rate, hell, the U.S. Space Navy doesn't have that tech."

"Yes, it does, at least they do now. This ship has four individual tractor beam systems."

Another two enemy warships exploded—short lived fireballs that dissipated into a scattering of space debris. "Got em'!" Pristy exclaimed punching the air with a tight fist.

"Helm, get us in close to whoever is trying to steal our platform!"

Grimes looked back at me; a deer caught in the headlights.

"I've got you," Derrota said, his singsong Mumbai accent more pronounced. "Sending coordinates to you now, Mr. Grimes."

I turned and surveyed the fully manned bridge. Finding the Damage Control Station, I saw Crewmember Soto. He was in charge of deploying response teams to manage and repair damage throughout the ship, ensuring the structural integrity of *USS Franklin*. Since coming out of the wormhole —and not understanding the residual effect of whatever Sonya and Derrota had accomplished—I needed to know first-hand, how my ship was really doing. "SitRep, Crewmember Soto!"

Startled, she looked up from her board, "Um..."

"It's okay Lindsay. Just tell me how this overgrown tub of a warship is doing."

"You know my name..."

"Status of the ship, Crewmember?"

"Oh, um, she's fine. Actually, really fine. All departments reporting being fully operational."

"Captain, we're approaching the other vessel. The one that has a hold on the platform," Grimes said.

The primary halo display showed the enigmatic platform. Amid the depths of deep space, an alien warship loomed menacingly, its metallic hull shimmering with an eerie lumines-cence. The warship's pulsating green tractor beam enveloped the platform, holding it in a kind of ethereal grip.

"We're being hailed again, Captain," Chen said.

"Ignore it, Mr. Chen. XO, how about you put a couple of our new-fangled tractor beams onto that..."

I looked to Derrota, who said, "It's the genesis of what has been determined to facilitate Quantum Spatial Entanglement and Relocation... we call it a QSER platform."

"Yeah, that," I said. "XO, I want you to steal back that platform from their grubby little paws."

Akari said, "Interesting, Captain, the platform seems to still be... powered on."

Indeed. The QSER platform was certainly a sight to behold —covered in an intricate array of alien antenna dishes. These structures varied from delicate filigree to imposing spires, covering every inch of the platform's surface. They extended outward in all directions. Their purpose? That remained a profound mystery to me. Among the antennas, peculiar crystalline structures pulsed with an unsettling energy, casting strange shadows and bathing the platform in an iridescent glow. From my perspective, it was an artifact of alien ingenuity, a testament to someone's advanced technology.

The QSER platform was making quick progress toward the alien warship. An illuminated bay, like a wide-open hungry maw, poised to bite.

Pristy scratched at her head. "Captain, I've never actually deployed a tractor beam before."

She looked to Akari as if her fellow crewmember held the answer.

"Don't look at me."

"Seriously?" I said, now looking to Derrota for help.

He shook his head.

I said, probably louder than necessary, "SARAH, put two tractor beams onto that QSER platform and drag it into Flight Bay 2."

In an instant, two vivid aqua-blue beams, both brighter and

more substantial than the feeble green beam of the enemy, stretched out across the emptiness of space. The QSER platform gradually decelerated, came to a halt, and then started advancing toward *Franklin*.

I smiled and leaned back in my seat, exhaling a prolonged breath that felt like it had been waiting to be released since my arrival on the bridge. Two more green alien tractor beams suddenly took hold of the platform.

"Seems a game of tug of war is at play here," Pristy grumbled, then lifted a finger. "But I think I've got this now."

Two additional aqua beams radiated from *Franklin's* midship.

"We have four tractor beams to their three. Let's just pray they don't have any more, because we certainly don't," the XO said.

The platform was back moving toward *Franklin* and picking up speed. Appearing to have given up hope of holding onto the platform, the three alien beams disappeared. But the warship, which was larger than any of the others, now seemed to be concentrated on getting even.

Incoming!
Incoming!
Incoming!

Chapter 35

Forland 545 System
USS Franklin

Captain Galvin Quintos

"Smart nukes," Akari said. "Ten... no, fifteen. ETA to impact—two minutes."

"I can take them out," Pristy said with confidence. "Bringing Phazon Pulsars to bear—"

I watched as the QSER platform finally disappeared into *Franklin's* Flight Bay 2. "Belay that, XO. We're done here. We've got what we came for."

"Helm, jump us out of here."

Franklin jumped.

I took in the primary halo display and was relieved to see no other vessels. In fact, there wasn't much of anything around us but deep dark open space.

"Helm, where are we?"

Grimes peered down to his board, "I jumped us thirty thousand miles from Forland 545 System, Captain."

Derrota looked up, as if silently conversing with the All Mighty. But it was his *oops* expression that had me nervous.

"Talk to me Stephan."

"I think I know who they were."

"They, as in the fleet of warships trying to destroy us?" I parried.

Derrota, now in deep thought, glanced over to the Comms Station.

"Stephan?" I prompted.

"We may have just, um, blundered."

"Are you going to tell me, or do I have to—"

"Forland 545 System was—is—their territory. And that QSER platform... I believe it falls within interstellar *salvage rights* law. This is their little quadrant of space, and that platform most definitely was abandoned."

I let that information settle in. "I thought this quadrant was designated as protected sanctuary space."

"Perhaps, as per the EUNF Space Navy. But for the locals who have resided here for centuries, maybe not so much."

"So, not only did we intrude into a civilization's backyard, but we also absconded with claimed alien technology," I said, shaking my head. *I thought I'd put my pirating days behind me.*

Another voice emanated from the back of the bridge, "There's more. That alien civilization just happened to be, or at least used to be, a U.S. Space Navy strategic partner. They're called the Cadil-Hasil."

Coogong joined Derrota, climbed up on to his chair and began tapping. "Captain, perhaps not all is lost."

I stared at the Thine scientist, not knowing what to say. I'd royally fucked up. And there wasn't going to be an easy solution.

While we all waited for Coogong to offer up his words of wisdom, things went from bad to worse—EUNF Space Navy's

Five Star Admiral Cyprian Block had just sauntered onto the bridge.

Fleet Commander Block is on the bridge.

Everyone, including me, saluted.

I caught Pristy's eye; she attempted a consoling shrug and a smile.

On the positive side, the Admiral was looking much better—back in uniform, he had regained his coloring, and his posture was now ramrod straight. He came to a stop next to me. Hands on hips, he surveyed the bridge, took in the crew.

"At ease... as you were," he said, his eyes now turning to me. "Maybe we should take this conversation to your ready room, Captain."

"Yes, Sir. Very good, Sir. This way." The academy had taught me—and the Admiral—the same lesson, praise in public, criticize in private.

No sooner had the auto-hatch swooshed shut behind us, the Admiral let me have it with both barrels. "How the hell could you let this happen!" He raised an open palm. "Don't even think about answering that."

He was pacing now, head bowed, one hand cradling his jaw. "Shit!" he muttered. He looked at me, his eyes like two orbs of ice. "Recite the Celestial Diplomacy Directive."

"Seriously? Now?"

"Yes, Captain, right fucking now!"

"The EUNF Space Navy shall observe the Protocol of Celestial Respect when encountering extraterrestrial civilizations. In the uncharted territories of space, the U.S. Space Navy shall endeavor to be the embodiment of interstellar diplomacy.

Always initiate communication through universal codes of peace and diplomacy. Vigilantly respect the sovereignty and sanctity of alien realms, extending our hand in friendship while upholding the cosmic balance. Unauthorized intrusion shall be met with immediate rectification and earnest pursuit of peaceful coexistence."

The Admiral nodded. "Tell me, Captain Quintos... how well did you follow those principles when entering Forland 545 System?"

He continued to stare at me.

"Oh, apologizes... I thought that was a rhetorical question, Sir. Uh, not well. Not well, at all. I made an assumption. But there's really no excuse."

I watched him move around to the other side of my desk and sit down. "Officers have been court-martialed for less. You know that, right?"

I nodded.

He let out a weary breath. "How about we take a minute and review where things stand."

I nodded.

He held up a finger, "The Varapin utilized incredible alien tech, probably not their own, to transport Earth and her Moon to HIP 938134 system."

Raising another finger, he continued, "In this scenario, Earth, devoid of the protection once provided by its extensive space fleets and situated beyond the reach of our Thine and Pleidian Weonan allies, faces a brutal onslaught. The assault methodically obliterates all military bases and global government hubs. Earth now finds itself in an ill-fated orbit, rapidly transforming our once-beautiful world into a frigid interstellar sphere. Time is no longer in our favor."

"Yes, Sir."

He held up a third finger, "Omninought, USS Franklin,

having been in Earth's high orbit while that aforementioned shitstorm occurred, may be the one bright spot in all of this. Via a communiqué with one Varapin Fleet Commander Sorlen Op, we—you—find out the diabolical reasoning behind their attack and what, precisely they want from us. The Varapin are dying off from some kind of incurable genetic disorder, and they're demanding we, the nearly defeated humans, broker a deal with the Ilion."

He held up a fourth finger, "Also gleamed from your—and subsequently, my—discussions with Sorlen Op, it seems Earth has a rare mineral desperately needed by the Ilion... Antarcite. And thus, we have the foundation for the tripartite dynamic deal."

Apparently, the Admiral was done with raising fingers.

"Why didn't the Varapin steal the genetic technology from the Ilion themselves?"

"I asked the Fleet Commander that same question," Block said. "The Ilion are extremely advanced and have impenetrable security around their genetic research facilities. The Varapin simply could not breach their defenses to steal it directly."

"Things have changed," I said. "We have a QSER platform of our own, even if Coogong needs to fiddle with it... get it working. So, why do we still need to help the Varapin? Why not work with the Ilion directly? Fuck the Varapin. Let's establish our own relationship with the Ilion."

"Excellent point. And I've thought about that. Gone round and round in my head about that... we're in an existential predicament," I added.

Block's demeanor shifted abruptly; weariness etched deep into his countenance. The weight of relentless responsibility, accumulated over years of unyielding military dedication, had exacted its toll on him. The lines etched into his face spoke volumes of the burdens he had carried, the sacrifices he had made, and the countless sleepless nights that had become an all too familiar companion in his pursuit of duty.

"Let's say we sidestep the Varapin, Fuck em', as you eloquently mentioned."

I shrugged.

He continued, "We have no real way of knowing how long they will survive as a race. Is it years, decades, centuries? Surely, it's plenty of time to finish what they started. Reign down hell and brimstone on Mother Earth, then finish us off with a good dose of Ghan-Tshot." He shook his head. "I'm tired of facing two horrid enemies. I can deal with one enemy... fighting just the piglets."

That did sound good. "But..." I hesitated. "... I'm struggling to come to terms with the notion that the Varapin would be walking away unscathed. After all they've done to us. Admiral, the Tidal Basin Massacre cannot go unanswered."

"Accountability will come, I promise you that, Galvin. But it may be years in the making."

"So... we suck it up for now. Save Earth. Save humanity."

Chapter 36

Captain Galvin Quintos

We returned to HIP 938134 System cloaked, without notifying what was left of EUNF U.S. Space Navy command, or any of the world governments, that we were back in local space.

It felt gratifying seeing Earth once more. Although, I couldn't shake how vulnerable and out of place our home world seemed.

A scattering of both Varapin and Grish warships crisscrossed open space, perhaps in search of a possible, clandestine, return of *USS Franklin*. I wasn't planning on sticking around long enough to be detected.

Pristy pounded a fist down onto her board. "It just pisses me off! Look at them out there... as far as the ghouls and piglets are concerned, they've already won."

"Well, they haven't," I said. "For now, we just need to keep to the plan."

I stood. "Crewmember Chen, contact Mr. Derrota. Tell him it's time. Have him meet me in the Quansporter compartment."

"Aye, Captain."

It was imperative that no one on Earth, or on *Franklin* —loose lips sink ships and all that—know the details of what we were about to do. My plan was for Coogong to quansport Derrota and me down to Earth. Get in, do what we need to do, and get right back out again. Stealth would be paramount for my plan to work. Earlier, upon entering the star system, Sonya, assisted by SARAH, pinpointed the exact research location of that exceptionally rare Antarcite sample we'll be needing before we try to bargain with the Ilion.

McMurdo Station research facility is located in Antarctica. It is the largest research station on the continent and has served as a hub for scientific research for over a hundred years. While it is primarily operated by the United States Antarctic Program (USAP), it hosts researchers and scientists from various countries.

Arriving at the Quansporter compartment, I was surprised, and a little irritated, to see others waiting there.

Coogong was at the controls console, Derrota standing next to him. Two others were also there... Sonya and Petty Officer Second-Class, Aubrey Laramie.

"Before you start freaking out," Sonya began, "you're going to need my help bypassing the security measures in place." She held up a small tablet and arched her brows.

I shook my head, "Stephan can handle—"

"She may be better equipped for that job, Galvin," Derrota interjected.

I turned to Aubrey, "And you? I seem to remember you were recently... hmmm, what's the word I'm looking for? Oh yeah, dead."

"I'm fine now. Better than fine!" Aubrey said enthusiastically. "Chief Knott's given me a clean bill of health. Call her yourself."

"We don't need you for this, Petty Officer. The fewer the better—"

"You saved my life, Captain. I need to do this," she said, looking far more concerned than warranted.

I saw Sonya roll her eyes in my peripheral vision.

"And look, we have lab coats just like Stephan's," Aubrey added.

"Fine. We're burning daylight."

"Okay... um, not sure what that means," she said, making a face.

I just stared at her. How could she not know that epic phrase? I said, "The movie, *McLintock*. The 1963 Western... John Wayne..."

Derrota said, "The younger generation don't watch the oldies anymore, Galvin. Uh, we should probably go."

We all took our places upon our respective Quansport pedestals. I looked to the others as I donned my own lab coat. Derrota, the least acclimated to away missions, was looking nervous.

"Talk to me about this McMurdo Station, Stephan." I said, getting his mind onto something else.

He swallowed, "Well, it provides infrastructure and support for a wide range of research activities, including geology, biology, climate science, and other specialized areas. But with the recent presence of Antarcite, added security measures will undoubtedly have been added."

I nodded to Coogong, "We're ready."

· · ·

WE QUANSPORTED. RELEASED FROM ITS HOLD, I stumbled, barely catching my balance as my boots sank into deep snow. Icy wind whipped against my exposed face, and I shuddered violently, the bitter cold piercing through my flimsy lab coat as if I was wearing nothing at all.

"Coogong!" I shouted through chattering teeth. "You quansported us outside?!" Of course, he wasn't there to hear me, but screaming at him at least made me feel better.

Sonya, tablet in hand, with Aubrey at her side, huddled against a nearby building's stark exterior wall. The teenager furiously tapped and swiped at her device, striving to crack the security panel that stood between us and our entry.

Derrota wrapped his arms around himself, quivering. "H-hurry! I am extremely s-susceptible to the c-cold."

My limbs were already growing numb and my thoughts sluggish. With a glance, I saw Aubrey's lips were turning blue, her cheeks turning white, a thin coating of ice developing over her entire face.

Derrota looked on the verge of collapse.

"Keep moving, Stephan," I said, as I paced vigorously in place, trying to get my blood pumping. I cast another angry glare up to the sky, to Coogong, who was, no doubt, sitting somewhere comfy and warm. We were two minutes in, and I was already contemplating abandoning the mission. My TAC-Band started to vibrate, I glanced at the projected message:

WARNING! Extreme Low Temperature of -38F.

"Dammit!" Sonya barked.

"What's taking so long?" I said through chattering teeth.

"Hey, you want to try? The keypad is iced fucking over!" Her breath came out in thick white puffs.

I could see the Sonya's hands were shaking. She was struggling to input commands on her tablet with, fingers that were, no doubt, numb... on the verge of frostbite. "It keeps locking m-me out!"

I shuffled over. "Seriously, how much longer? We're all risking h-hypothermia or w-worse."

I was in close behind Aubrey, peering over her shoulder. She glanced back at me and whispered, "Stay right there, you're blocking the wind."

I then felt her, ever so slightly, push her derriere in closer to me. Into my, um, loins. While her attention looked to be concentrated upon Sonya's efforts, a bemused smile crossed her lips.

Damn, this woman was trouble.

A frozen-looking Derrota stepped forward looking like death incarnate. "J-just fucking knock on the door!"

Sonya stopped mid-tap then looked back at him.

"He's right, knock on the door, screw this sneaking around bullshit," I said.

Both Sonya and Aubrey began pounding fists on the icy, metal door. "Hello! Let us in!"

Within seconds we heard the muffled voice of a man, "Who's out there!"

I said, "Open t-the d-door, w-were the good guys."

The door creaked open exposing a large, bearded man, wearing a heavy coat and a fur-lined hat.

Sonya plowed past him, followed by Aubrey, Derrota, and finally me. I heard the door clank shut behind us.

The big bear of a man looked at us, clearly astonished.

"Don't just stand there," Aubrey commanded, "We need coats, blankets—whatever you have! Move it, man!"

I would have laughed if I wasn't half frozen.

Others were now coming into the confined hallway. All were dressed similarly to the bear man. Heavy coats, sweaters, hats...

A woman, perhaps mid-thirties, was already removing her own coat and putting it around Sonya.

Sonya said, "Who's bright idea was it to come dressed in cotton lab coats? Look at them, nobody wears lab coats here in the Artic!"

"Antarctica," Derrota corrected, now receiving a heavy blanket around his own shoulders.

The big bear of a man said, "I am Dr. Jeroen van der Berg, the lead scientist of this facility. I insist you tell me what you are doing here." He had a Dutch accent, featuring a crisp, staccato-like cadences with flat vowel sounds and sentences having a lilting, questioning intonation.

He took off his coat and handed it to me—which I most appreciatively accepted.

I said, "I am Captain Quintos of USS Franklin."

"I knew it!" the thirty-something woman said. "You're famous. I recognized you the moment I saw you." She looked to her three coworkers. "He's the dashing warship captain that saved Earth from the Grish years back."

Dashing? I mused.

"You know, USS Hamilton... all his heroics in space, and he has a robot friend, Howard..."

"Close enough," I said.

The scientists were looking at me as if I was one of their petri dish experiments.

"Oh, ya... now I see the resemblance," Dr. Jeroen van der Berg said.

Sonya was visibly annoyed. "It's not a resemblance, it's him, he's Captain Quintos."

One of the other scientists spoke up. He was an older, slender man, with white wisps of hair on top. "I am Dr. John Lux, how about you tell us what you want of us."

"American?" I asked.

He nodded.

"How familiar are you with what's going on... you know the attack, the transposition of Earth to HIP 938134 System—"

"The what?!" Lux said with disbelief. "Attack? HIP 938134 System? Are you out of your mind? Granted, our comms have been down for the last week or so, but that's typical this time of year."

Aubrey pursed her lips. "Looks like you've got some 'splainin' to do Cap."

For a full hour, we recounted the cascade of recent events. Questions abounded, some beyond our grasp. Given the scientific minds at play, it fell to Derrota to delve into the intricate physics that had flung Earth and the Moon across the galaxy to an almost unfathomable distance. Soon came the frantic realization that family and friends, dear ones, may have been killed, and that there was no means to reach out to anyone. Subsequently, tears started to stream down their ruddy cheeks.

Dr. Jeroen van der Berg said, "We have three samples of the mineral you seek. All I ask is you leave us one so we can continue our experiments. It will keep us occupied. Allow us to not dwell on things."

I looked to Derrota, "What do you think Stephan? Will that work?"

"First of all, can I ask how you were able to excavate these samples?"

A woman, whose name we learned was Dr. Lilian Bowman, said, "Oh, we didn't excavate it. We discovered it. Eons ago, probably thousands of years ago, a meteorite struck this area of Earth. We discovered the impact crater years ago, but only uncovered the Antarcite this past year."

We exchanged glances.

"How large of a sample are we talking," Derrota asked.

"Pretty big," Bowman said. "One is the size of a small AirCar, the other two are the size of a small house. I hadn't mentioned this, but we're talking about a very large meteorite, one that hit Earth's surface at incredible speeds of over 70,000 mph. It had penetrated Earth's crust to about 15 to 20 kilometers... 9 to 12 miles. So yes, it created quite the impact crater, dislodged the samples from way down."

Looking at me, Sonya smirked, "What were you thinking... that you'd be able to put the sample in your little lab coat pocket?"

Chapter 37

So much for keeping our sample extraction mission a secret. Once back on *Franklin*, the process of moving a ninety-ton—the smallest of the three massive Antarcite samples—up and into the omninought's Flight Bay 3 had proved to be an extraordinary feat of engineering prowess.

As explained to me by Coogong, the exact value of the gravitational pull in Antarctica, or any other specific location on Earth, is not typically stated as a single figure because, well, it varies depending on several factors, like the precise location (latitude and altitude), mass distribution in the crust, and changes due to factors like ice melt.

Generally, Earth's average gravitational acceleration is approximately nine point eight one meters per second squared, but it can be slightly more or less depending on the factors mentioned. On the other hand, in deep space, the average gravitational acceleration is pretty close to zero.

There was one nagging issue. While *Franklin* remained cloaked, the AirCar-sized sample of Antarcite, would not be. So, if by chance any of the Varapin or Grish warships in the vicinity spotted the anomaly, one that would seem to be defying the laws of physics—floating away from Earth vs. the other way around—our position could be dangerously compromised. But it was a risk we had to take.

Coogong, stationed at the controls of the Quansporter, was tasked with a delicate operation: to disentangle the sample. This first step required finesse to shake it loose, initiating a precarious dance that set the sample wobbling. The Quansporter's limits were tested, the system groaning under the strain, circuits sizzling to the brink of overload.

Then it was Pristy's turn... with the help of SARAH, displaying impeccable precision. With a deft hand, Pristy synchronized the activation of the ship's four tractor beams, each one locking onto the sample with the precision of a seasoned marksman. The beams had to work in concert, ensuring the sample was secured without a hitch. This operation was as much about timing as it was about technology—a single misstep could mean failure. But Pristy had been up to the task, her efforts pivotal, eventually getting the big rock into *Franklin's* Bay 3, and doing so without so much as a scratch upon the ship's hull.

LEAVING EARTH BEHIND, A STAR SYSTEM WITH ITS strange, cold, white star, and unfamiliar exoplanet neighbors, I had the awful feeling that we might not return... that our trajectory through the stars would be a one-way ticket.

After a restful eight hours of sleep, a blistering hot shower, and a breakfast befitting a hungry lumberjack, I was ready to tackle the next phase of the plan. But first, I needed to make a quick stop at the Prisoner Holding Facility.

$\approx$

One of the same security guards was on duty as the last time I was here. The bearded one, LB Crenshaw. He was standing at the PHF's admittance counter... greeted me but seemed a tad jumpy.

"Captain, oh good, you got my message."

"Message?" I said not slowing, heading down the corridor to the holding cells.

Fast on my heels, Crenshaw said, "Uh, Sir... there's a problem with the prisoner—"

I arrived at Slop's cell and looked in. "Where's the prisoner," I said, doing my best to stay calm.

"That's what I wanted to tell you, Sir. He's not here."

"Really, thank you for that. I wouldn't have noticed the completely empty cell without those words of profound wisdom. So, where the hell is Slop?"

"The Admiral, uh, called it a field trip."

"Admiral Block took Slop on a... field trip?"

Shrug. "That's what he called it."

I glanced up. "SARAH, tell me the exact location of prisoner Sorlen Op."

Prisoner Sorlen Op is with Admiral Block.

"I already know that. Where are they?"

That information is classified.

"From the captain of this ship?"

Admiral Block is the ranking officer onboard *USS Franklin*.

I thought about that while taking several deep breaths. Losing it here wasn't going to improve the situation. "Quansport Hardy to my location."

Per your own directives, quansporting of crewmembers within—

"SARAH! Just do it!"

Four seconds later, Hardy was standing in front of me there within the PHF corridor.

"Good thing I wasn't sitting on the potty, Cap. That could have been embarrassing for the both of us."

"Hardy, use your people finding skills to locate Admiral Block and Slop."

"There's a shipwide directive from the Admiral under penalty of public flogging: that information remains classified."

"Uh huh, so are you going to tell me?"

"Of course. I've been flogged before... wasn't so bad."

I let that go. "Where are they?"

"Deck 49, White Sector, Hold 22C."

I shook my head. It made no sense.

"I'd hurry it up, though Cap. Just a suggestion," the ChronoBot said, his faceplate now animated with a cartoonish figure walking toward a giant cliff.

"SARAH, quansport Hardy and I to Deck 49, White Sector, Hold 22C."

That ship location has been designated off limits to the crew...

"Fine," I said with a snippy tone. "Quansport us to Deck 49, White Sector's main corridor."

. . .

We arrived within the White Sector corridor, finding it devoid of any other crewmembers.

Hardy said, "Welcome to the Siberia of USS *Franklin*."

It was a place forgotten by the bustle of daily operations, a ghostly stretch within the vessel where one's solitary footsteps might be the only indication of humanity's presence.

I said, "I suspect that's the whole point. Just the place, isolated and desolate, a neglected expanse where one would not be observed."

Now arriving at Hold 22C, Hardy and I moved a few steps inside, taking in the compartment. The massive deck to overhead height auto-hatch doors were secured—a nearby access panel glowing red with a single word: **RESTRICTED.**

I tapped at my TAC-Band in an attempt to reach out to the Admiral. I was prompted to leave a message. No big surprise there. He'd made it perfectly clear he didn't want to be disturbed.

I stared at the massive metal doors.

Hardy said, "If you're done practicing your mind-control magic, you might want me to give it a try."

I hesitated. I was already walking a tightrope with the Admiral with the whole big-footing into Forland 545 System fiasco. "In for a dollar..."

Hardy moved closer to the auto-hatch, looked it up and down, side to side. Then as if coming to a decision, he raised his mechanical hands, wedged chrome plated digits into the vertical-running seam between the two halves. The sounds of grinding gears and straining motors filled the corridor. Inch by straining inch, the auto-hatch doors pulled apart. As soon as the opening was wide enough, I ducked below Hardy's arms and squeezed through sideways.

I'd been pretty sure of what to expect... unfortunately, I'd been right. I took in the grisly sight—unconsciously wincing, perhaps for the condition of the Varapin prisoner, perhaps for myself, having to witness this other side of Admiral Block.

Now don't get me wrong, when it comes to the Varapin no punishment would be harsh enough for the crimes against humanity having previously been inflicted. But this, it was too much.

Hardy, having extricated himself from the hold doors, joined me at my side, speechless.

The Admiral, his back to us, said "You don't want to be here, Galvin."

Hardy mumbled, "I'd guess Fleet Commander Sorlen Op would rather not be here as well."

I shot the ChronoBot a look then said, "Admiral, I thought you and the prisoner were, um, getting along. Talking treaties and tripartite dynamic agreements."

Knife in hand, Admiral Block turned to face us—in the process, providing a clear view of Slop in his confines—restrained and manacled. Offering me one more unwelcome opportunity to witness the freakish alien sans robe.

The Admiral's uniform was a mess, stained, gunked-up with Varapin bodily secretions.

"Is he still alive?" I asked.

Hardy answered before Block could, "He's alive. Not sure, at this point... that would be his choice."

"Let's just say the Fleet Commander had a dramatic about-face, a change of heart," Block said. "He no longer wishes to work with us."

I chinned toward the prisoner. "What, exactly, are you doing to him?"

"Those little gooey gas sacs—the way they pulse and

gurgle... you ever wonder how many are actually needed for a Varapin to achieve positive buoyancy?"

"No, Admiral, can't say that was of much interest to me."

He pointed to where three bloodied gas sacs lay oozing upon the deck. "Varapin warriors have an amazing tolerance for pain. That's a known fact." Again, he looked at the removed organs. "But you take away a Varapin's ability to slice through the air, to float and fly... well it's enough to drive them out of their mind."

"Killing the Fleet Commander serves no purpose, Sir."

"Who said anything about killing him? No, our Varapin friend here will live a long, healthy life within a U.S. Space Navy cell. Of course, if I remove just one more gas sack, he'll be doing that sitting down or maybe lying on his back. Flight, that will be out of the question."

"Why don't you take a break? Let me talk to him, see if I can talk some sense into him."

He shook his head, "Best if I finish what I started."

"The problem is, you want to remove that last huffing and puffing gas sack. You want revenge, not compliance. As despicable as Slop is, he's still our best hope for the future."

Block stared at the prisoner, his expression—pure hatred. "You have five minutes, Galvin. Then I finish what I've started."

I waited for the Admiral to leave the hold before approaching the prisoner. I found his bathrobe crumpled on the deck and carefully draped it over his tortured form. I said, "Why'd you change your mind? I thought you wanted, needed, help with the Ilion? To save your populous from a genetic catastrophe?"

His orbs momentarily flared orange then subsided to mere diminished cinders. His voice was a bare whisper, "I... didn't... change... my... mind."

I stared back at him not comprehending.
"He changed his..."

Chapter 38

While we waited for Chief Knott to arrive, Hardy and I got Slop released from his shackles, his manacles, and got him lying down. She would be needed for two separate diagnoses. One, to evaluate Admiral Block's mental faculties. His actions today had put everything at risk—the fate of Earth and the very existence of humanity hung in the balance. Second, to evaluate Slop, see if his removed organs could, possibly, be reattached.

She arrived within the hold fifteen minutes later looking flustered.

"Did you get the opportunity to speak with Admiral Block?" I inquired, though the answer was something I already suspected.

She nodded, "Left him with Hardy." She caught sight of the Varapin Fleet Commander lying on the deck. "Good God..."

"Yeah, pretty grisly, huh?"

Putting on latex gloves, she knelt next to Slop, taking in the extent of his injuries.

"I put his... displaced organs there next to him."

"I can see that, Captain" she said curtly. She leaned in

closer. "Oh, for shit's sake. He sure made of mess of this creature's anatomy."

"Can you repair what Block's done to him?"

"I don't know. Is it really that important? He and his ilk killed thousands, maybe millions of our kind."

The question took me by surprise.

She looked up at me. "I'm sorry. That came out more heartless than intended. The thing is, I am not familiar with Varapin anatomy enough to bring this creature into a surgical bay."

"We have MediBots—"

"Already checked before coming here. The bots don't have the necessary Varapin Anatomy software packets. And before you ask, the RegrowPods wouldn't be up to the task either."

"So, we're powerless to help him? Doc, just for your information, keeping him alive—and preferably content—is crucial. So much hinges on that—for all of us."

"I just don't have the expertise. I'm sorry." Knott stood; her expression dire. "Now, if my predecessor was here, things might be different."

"You're referring to Doc Viv."

"Yeah, I've been reviewing her past surgical notes. Watched several of her more recent surgery vids. That doctor was in a class by herself."

"Yeah well, she's not here and it's not an option anyway."

"Okay, that's fine," Knott said. "You seem fairly definitive about that. There again, we are still here in Earth's space. Maybe I could try to contact—"

"No!" I said, "Just drop it."

Taken aback by my outburst, Chief Knott stared at me for several moments. "Doth he protest too much?" She said with a raised brow.

"Sorry. That was unwarranted. And yes, I'm letting personal feelings get the better of me. I'll try to reach out to her.

Not easy since most of America's power and communications grids are down."

"Maybe she still checks her TAC-Band on occasion."

I thought about that, why would she?

Okay, by now you're probably wondering what the hell happened between us. Why the sudden breakup? Why had I needed a month away, alone, deep in the Colorado wilderness to mend my broken heart? The easy answer could have been my close working relationships with other crew members, had sparked jealousy and trust issues, but that wasn't it. Or it could have been the necessity of keeping our relationship a secret due to military fraternization rules taking a heavy emotional toll, but no, that wasn't it either.

The truth of the matter was much, much more serious. Doctor Vivian Leigh had been married to another man for years and somehow, she had neglected to mention that to me. Sure, she had thought the man, Army Colonel Raymond Clark, was long dead—killed light-years away in an interplanetary battle of some sort.

Then, a month and a half ago, the news arrived. The Colonel was discovered very much alive upon an adrift shuttle, miraculously having escaped from a Grish deep-space penal colony. Last I heard, she was in Florida, attending to his physical and psychological recovery, helping him readjust after such a horrendous ordeal.

It had come to me in an eloquently written, ink-penned, correspondence—yes one of those old-fashioned *Dear John* letters that absolutely nobody wants to receive. Clearly, she had spent some time writing it—almost poetic, she had used all the right words. To paraphrase, she had requested time, a pause in our narrative, urging patience as she navigated the tumultuous waters of her revived past.

It was about granting her the breadth to grapple with the

resurgence of a spouse once lost to the stars, to reconcile the resurrection of a relationship she believed had ended. Space, she implored, to heal and perhaps to weave together the frayed ends of what life had unexpectedly unraveled. Yada-yada-yada... so yeah, I gave her the space wanted. That's when I disappeared alone into the back country. Well, alone except for my trail horse and Climbo, my robot pack mule.

BACK TO THE HERE AND NOW, I WAS PACING BACK and forth within the confines of my captain's ready room, trying to rally the nerve to tap out a simple TAC-Band message. I stopped, frustrated, and glared down at my wrist, whereby my TAC-Band blatantly stared back at me—mocking my inaction.

Keep it simple, I told myself. This wasn't about her and me, it was about the survival of the human race. It was business— yes, this was business. We were both professionals, there was no need to get personal feelings involved.

CAPTAIN GALVIN QUINTOS:

Viv, we need your help. *I* need your help.

I sent it and felt pretty good about the message. Short and sweet. Nothing personal, just the facts. I let out a breath. Now I'd need to wait for her to check her TAC-Band which she'd probably left buried deep in a coat pocket or tossed into a kitchen junk drawer. Shit, she may never check the thing.

My TAC-Band vibrated:

MAJOR VIVIAN LEIGH:

What kind of help?

At least she didn't tell me to go screw myself.

CAPTAIN GALVIN QUINTOS:

Surgery on a Varapin fleet commander.

MAJOR VIVIAN LEIGH:

I'm no longer a member of your crew. Or had you forgotten that?

True enough. About to parry that, she hit me with a follow up.

MAJOR VIVIAN LEIGH:

Oh, and BTW, thanks for checking on my wellbeing. Since it's an everyday occurrence that Earth is 1) brutally attacked by the Varapin and 2) flung into another star system! Oh, and thanks for blocking my messages. What are you, twelve? A real dick move, Quintos.

I guess I should have mentioned that I had, in fact, put a TAC-Band block on any incoming messages from her. But in my own defense, did I mention she had a fricking husband she never told me about!?

CAPTAIN GALVIN QUINTOS:

I'm sorry, Viv. Truly. Will you help? You know I wouldn't ask if it wasn't a life-or-death situation.

MAJOR VIVIAN LEIGH:

Can I think about it? Things are not good here. Where are you, anyway?

CAPTAIN GALVIN QUINTOS:

In high orbit. Sorry, need to know now. Please...

MAJOR VIVIAN LEIGH:

Fine. Give me twenty minutes. But don't expect me to be nice to you. Do I need to bring anything?

CAPTAIN GALVIN QUINTOS:

Nope. Just be ready for quansport.

Chapter 39

F ifteen minutes later, I was holding vigil within the Quansporter compartment. I started to pace while Coogong stood at the controls... apparently, busying himself, sensing my nervousness.

He said, "It has been twenty-two minutes, Captain."

I came to an abrupt halt, straightened my shoulders, and practiced my best impression of nonchalance, as if her arrival was as mundane and unremarkable as a janitorial robot trundling by to empty the trash—just another routine occurrence in this spaceship's daily life.

Viv quansported into view. As she stepped down from the quansport pedestal, it was as if she had undergone a transformation. Her blonde hair, typically worn in a no-nonsense style, now fell in casual, sun-kissed waves, echoing a laid-back Florida vibe.

Adorned in a sunny yellow tank top and crisp white shorts, complemented by the casual slap of flip-flops, she presented a vision of relaxed, tan, sun-soaked ease. And that fragrance—was it the quintessential scent of Coppertone sunscreen? It wasn't until that moment that I noticed the delicate red straps peeking out from under her tank top, hints of a bikini... waiting for the beach.

How had she phrased it? Can I think about it? Things are not good here.

Really? Was the beach sand too hot for your little tootsies? Or maybe your husband had missed a spot rubbing sunscreen on your perfectly tanned shoulders.

"Okay, Quintos, I'm here. Let's get this over with."

No smile, no peck-on-the-cheek hello.

I gestured to the exit, letting her go first. "Thank you again, Viv. This means a lot to me."

"I'm not doing this for you," she said, taking in her surroundings. "They keep making these behemoths bigger and bigger. Maybe someday they'll realize bigger isn't always better."

Her words left me in a maze of conjecture, hinting at a layered subtext, possibly a double entendre. It stirred up a silent rivalry within me—a contest between me and her long-lost spouse? She'd been here all of thirty seconds, and already she was making me wish I'd opted to do the surgery on Slop myself.

Reaching the DeckPort, I showed her how it was used, before going through first.

"Oh, you mean, you just say where you want to go and just walk through? I'm so glad, Quintos, I have you here to mansplain such a complicated device for me."

Arriving on Deck 18, I led the way to HealthBay, where Chief Knott greeted her as if they were old friends.

"Everything's set for your arrival, Doctor. Your patient is prepped in Surgery 1. Down the corridor, you'll find the scrub room stocked with all the necessities for your procedure," Chief Knott informed her.

"Thank you, Chief Knott," Viv said turning away, then, turning back to face me. "Your services, Captain Quintos, will no longer be needed. You can go."

Chief Knott looked between us as the uncomfortable moment lingered.

"Thank you again, Doctor," I said. "Good luck in there."

"Uh-huh, it's skill, not luck." She turned and disappeared through the auto-hatch doors.

The Chief eyed me, "Is... everything all right, Captain?"

Fuming, I said, "Peachy. Do me a favor, let me know how the surgery progresses."

"Will do."

Glad I'd shown her how to use the DeckPorts, later, she could show her own way back to the Quansporter compartment.

I MADE MY WAY TO DECK 68 WHERE FLIGHT BAY 3—one of the smallest bays on the ship—was located. I found Derrota and Coogong there, along with Sonya, who brightened when seeing me. At least someone appreciates me.

But the real star of the flight bay was the Quantum Spatial Entanglement and Relocation platform. Suspended from the overhead by no less than a dozen thick fabric straps, the device swayed back and forth ever so slightly as Derrota fiddled with something toward the far side of the thing. Up close, the QSER platform looked alien and unconventional.

Spires resembling antennas of various heights jutted out at odd angles, similar to needles randomly inserted into a pin cushion. Circular devices that bore resemblance to dishes rotated in erratic patterns, as if scanning for a signal. Scattered among them were crystal structures that seemed organic in nature—some emitting a soft glow while others remained dark. The sharply cleaved structures towered like buildings, adding to the landscape of otherworldly technology.

Sonya said, "Before you ask—no, it's not functional."

Both Derrota and Coogong nodded in unison.

She moved to the far end of the hanging structure, gestured for me to follow her. "Take a look up at that section." She made a *this-is-what-I'm-talking-about* face and pointed upward.

Sure enough, there was a blackened, scorched section, four or five feet in diameter, where clearly something had fried. "That section's needed for the rest of the thing to work?" I asked.

She rolled her eyes. "As much as you'd need your cerebral cortex to tie your shoes."

"Can you use the ship's replicators to replace the bad components?" I asked.

"Yes and no, Captain," Derrota said. "The crystals are the problem. Yes, they can be replicated, but each has unique characteristics. We just don't know enough about this device to accurately replicate the necessary properties. It's like trying to recreate a vintage wine from scratch; you can get something close, but without the original vineyard's environment and the exact process, it won't be the same."

I LEFT THE THREE OF THEM TO CONTINUE THEIR work, deciding to make one more stop before heading to the bridge.

Admiral Block admitted me without fanfare; his quarters were nearly identical to my own. Block was wearing a clean uniform and was seated at his small desk, apparently, working on a tablet.

"Just wanted to check in on you, Sir."

"I'm alright, Galvin, or as close to it as one can be after what I've done," he admitted. He settled back into his chair and motioned for me to join him in the nearby seat.

A pregnant pause... then, I asked, "What the hell happened, Admiral?"

The man didn't answer for a long while. "What the hell happened is... I snapped. I began thinking about all the men, women, and children killed at the hands of this monster and his ilk. I began replaying the destruction of Washington DC, the very bedrock of our Republic. I began remembering awakening after being buried in all that rubble, seeing my executive assistant, Donna, dead—her head flattened like a pancake by a fallen I-beam." He shook his head. "I wanted revenge. I wanted to make this one Varapin pay a price for the misery he'd caused."

"I've been there. More than once."

"What I've done is unconscionable. I've jeopardized... everything. Captain, I will be resigning, effective immediately." He gestured to his tablet.

"How about you put that on hold for now. Some good news: we tracked down Doc Viv, she's currently working on Fleet Commander Sorlen Op as we speak."

"It's too late. What I've done—"

"Come on. A brilliant, resourceful Admiral once told me, every setback is a setup for a comeback."

He shook his head. "I think we're well past catchy platitudes, Galvin."

It was clear, I needed to take a different track. "Did Commander Sorlen Op give you anything. Anything that would help?"

"I wasn't really looking for answers."

"That's not what I asked."

The Admiral shook his head then stopped. "He did mention Aquilori Prime System."

"I don't understand. What is that?"

He shrugged. "Slop was trying to tell me that that's where the Ilion were based. But he could have just as easily been lying."

Excited, I shot out of my seat and headed for the exit. Over my shoulder I said, "Stop beating yourself up Admiral, you just gave me exactly what I needed to know. As for Slop, fuck em', he got what he deserved."

I ARRIVED ON THE BRIDGE HAVING ALREADY notified Grimes to set a course for the Aquilori Prime System. I'd remembered Hardy once telling me he'd been deployed there a century back when he was a mere killer ChronoBot.

Hardy was standing next to the Captain's Mount, Pristy was at Tactical 1, Akari James, now gone—probably back among her fellow pilots, within Flight Bay 1.

The primary halo display showed the emergence of a manufactured wormhole.

"Coordinates charted and locked, Captain," Grimes said.

The mouth of the wormhole glistened with a rainbow of cosmic hues indicating it had reached formation. "Take us in, Helm."

It was only then, at that moment, I remembered we had a not-so-willing passenger still onboard. First, I grimaced. And then I smiled.

Chapter 40

Wormhole travel is about as exciting as listening to a lecture on lint removal. For that reason, it's a good time to bring in the second bridge shift—get some needed rack time.

Strange... I knew I was dreaming, where I found myself seated on a moss-covered rock, surrounded, once more, by the lush Colorado wilderness. A gentle breeze rustled through the tall pines, carrying the scent of pine needles through the air. I looked down and noticed I was dressed in rugged 22nd-century camping gear, with the deployable scouting drone by my side.

The drone came to life, projecting 3D holographic images of Native Americans moving stealthily through the woods. They had bows raised, arrows nocked, and faces painted with fierce determination. In the distance, a majestic herd of elk appeared, their hooves pounding the earth as they fled into the dense woodlands. The holographic scenes brought the past to life before my eyes, vividly recreating a bygone era.

Amid this surreal display, a young Native American boy, around twelve years old, materialized before me. His eyes held a mixture of wonder and wisdom beyond his years. I greeted him warmly, feeling a sense of connection to this wilderness, to this time period.

"Hello there," I said with a friendly smile. "My name is Galvin."

The young boy, who introduced himself as Nahele, regarded me with a mix of curiosity and caution. He wore traditional Native American attire, and his presence felt remarkably real, despite the dreamlike quality of our surroundings. We spoke for a while, the boy curious about my life, my time-period centuries into the future. He wanted to know how one travels to the stars, such vast distances. Hey, this is my dream, who cares if an Indian boy would ask such ridiculous questions. Anyway, I decided to share the remarkable technological advancements of the 22nd century with him.

"Nahele," I began, "I come from a time far beyond yours, in the year 2184. We've developed incredible technology, like *Quantum Phase Drives*, which power our ships for space travel. These drives allow us to go faster than light, exploring the cosmos in ways you can't even imagine."

Nahele's eyes widened with intrigue as he listened intently.

I continued, "We've learned to manipulate something called quantum entanglement and phase coherence. It's like tapping into alternate quantum states of spacetime, bending and folding it to our will. This technology enables us to hop across the universe. And the best part is, it helps us evade the effects of time dilation. So, while hours or days might pass for us during our journeys, we don't age like you would expect. It's like magic, Nahele, but it's all thanks to the wonders of science."

Nahele regarded me with a thoughtful expression. "Your world sounds very different from mine," he mused. "Do you hunt in space?"

"Sure. Sort of. But I'm talking about space travel, kid."

A small rabbit darted between us. "But there's something

even more intriguing, Nahele, something known as manufactured wormhole travel. It's a way to fold and twist space and time itself."

Nahele's eyes sparkled with curiosity. "Tell me more, Galvin."

I obliged. "Manufactured wormholes are like gateways through the fabric of the universe. They're created by manipulating exotic matter, energy fields, and gravity control systems. When we step into one, it feels like embarking on an incredible journey, like you're entering another realm entirely."

The holographic scenes around us began to shift, resembling swirling vortexes of light and energy.

"But here's the paradox," I continued, "as you traverse through these wormholes, Einstein's theory of relativity comes into play; we're talking the folding of spacetime. Where time itself seems to bend and stretch, making a journey that should be instantaneous feel like an extended adventure."

Nahele had picked up a small tree branch and was poking at a pinecone. "Einstein?" he asked, looking more than a little perplexed.

"Uh... that's not important," I said. "Anyway, where was I?"

Nahele's gaze was now fixed upon the swirling vortexes of light around us.

"Oh yeah," I continued, "Imagine, it's as if you're walking through a doorway in time, witnessing the wonders of the universe, but the moments stretch and twist around you. The journey becomes an experience that defies explanation, where the mysteries of advanced technology and the enigma of spacetime manipulation come together."

Nahele nodded, eyes losing focus, perhaps I'd exceeded his level of understanding. "I think I need to get back to hunting with my father," he whispered.

I smiled and nodded in agreement. "Yes, Nahele, good talk."

I opened my eyes, replaying the weird dream in my head.

SARAH's voice startled me all the way awake.

Captain Quintos, USS Franklin has emerged from the wormhole. XO Pristy has requested your presence on the bridge.

"How long was I asleep?"

Nine hours, twelve minutes.

Rushing onto the bridge, I spotted Doc Viv, hands on hips, engaged in a conversation with Grimes at the Helm station. If her expression was any gauge of her mood, she clearly wasn't pleased that we had departed Earth's orbit with her onboard.

As I discreetly made my way to the Captain's Mount, Pristy cast me an odd glance. A look that left me pondering its significance.

"SitRep, XO. I take it we're within the Aquilori Prime System?"

"Roger that, Captain," Pristy said back in a monotone. She glanced over to Viv. "Yes, indeed, we're entering uncharted territory."

I caught Chen's eye over at Comms. He gave me a wary shrug.

Viv was at my side now, "May I have a word?"

"Yes, of course."

"I mean away from the bridge. Out there." She didn't wait for an answer, was already headed for the exit.

I said, "Give me a minute, XO, be right back."

"It's your ship, Captain Quintos, take as long as you want."

Doc Viv was waiting for me within the Rotunda, leaning against the railing, arms folded across her chest.

Before she could say a word, I raised my hands in mock surrender. "I am so sorry. I totally forgot you were still onboard. That was inconsiderate of me. I promise to get you back home to your... back home as soon as possible."

"Are you done?"

"Yes."

"First of all, nothing is more important than what you're doing, or trying to do. Getting Earth back to the Solar System and fending off the Grish and Varapin. My personal life takes a backseat to all that. Second, I wanted to give you an update on the patient."

"Thank you. How'd Slop come out of the surgery?"

"Slop?"

"Sorry, that's what I call Fleet Commander Sorlen Op."

"He's stable, I've reattached his organs. We're still waiting to see if they can function normally."

"You mean like inflate and such? Pass gas?"

She looked at me, "Are you making a joke?"

I was, kind of. "No, sorry, it just came out that way. So... he'll be okay? Be up and flying around HealthBay like a witch on a broomstick in no time?"

A line had formed between her perfect brows. "Now I know you're just being juvenile. But yes, he should be back to normal within a week or so. It was a tricky operation. Chief Knott assisted. She's a good doctor. Glad you found someone competent to replace me."

I had nothing to do with her deployment, but let the comment go.

"I need to get back to the bridge. Feel free to make yourself at home onboard *USS Franklin.*"

"Chief Knott has granted me temporary medical credentials while I'm onboard, I'll be helping out with patients and such till you get me back to Earth." She spun away, heading for the DeckPort.

I yelled after her, "Let me know if you need help figuring out that DeckPort!"

She kept walking but did offer up a single finger reply.

Pristy came out of the bridge and headed directly for one of the Rotunda podiums. She made a few taps, bringing up the Gravity Well's real-time 3D interstellar cartography projecting the Aquilori Prime System on an immense scale. From my vantage point, I gazed out at the breathtaking expanse. The primary star, Aquilori, bathed the orbiting planets in a warm, golden glow, illuminating the celestial bodies. Rings of brilliant turquoise encircled one of the gas giants, casting shimmering reflections across the vastness of space, while the vivid hues of distant nebulae painted a surreal canvas beyond.

Others from the bridge filed out into the Rotunda. Then Hardy emerged from the DeckPort with Derrota fast on his heels.

And while everyone oohed and aahed at the visually spectacular star system before them, my eyes had settled upon XO Pristy at the podium. The glow of the Gravity Well's projection was illuminating her fine, some would say perfect, features. Unaware she was being so closely observed, she smiled at the crew's reaction to the visuals. With a child-like expression, she stifled a laugh.

I don't know if she felt my stare, or her eyes flicking toward me was just happenstance, but as XO Pristy's gaze met mine across the Rotunda, the din around us faded, the world narrowing to just the two of us. In that electrifying moment, her professional facade seemed to fall away, revealing something more intimate and vulnerable beneath the surface. We regarded one another openly, our connection unguarded, each seeing past long-held barriers for the first time.

How long we lingered there I cannot say, years of unvoiced affection passing between us in a single look. For those fleeting heartbeats, possibility shimmered in the air—a sense of undiscovered country suddenly, perhaps, within reach. But then the spell passed, the demands of duty reasserting themselves as she offered me the subtlest of affectionate smiles. Her expression settled back into one of disciplined composure as she resumed surveying the crew, our moment once more concealed from view.

So here I was, ostensibly *Franklin's* steadfast leader, secretly torn between three complex women. It was a puzzle—did I pursue Viv's substance and unavailability? Explore Aubrey's affectionate interest? Or dare I test these newly awakened feelings with my poised yet perhaps longing First Officer?

Christ. When had my love life turned into *The Young and the Spaceless* - a bad sci-fi soap opera?

What I really needed was a trip to the airlock to clear my head—maybe exposure to a frigid vacuum would help me get a grip. Or maybe I just needed Aubrey to stop looking at me like I was the last open docking bay on *Prom Night*... or for Doc Viv to cure my lovesickness along with the Tasparian flu. As for the XO... well actually, I wasn't sure what to do with that. I needed to stop acting like a pimple-faced teenager whose voice just changed octaves. You're the Captain damnit, act like it!

Captain Quintos, *USS Franklin* has an incoming hail from the Ilion...

Taking my seat at the Captain's Mount, I regarded the lone Ilion representative within the halo display. His tall, slender form was covered in scales that shimmered with rainbow-like iridescence. Faintly glowing veins pulsed under translucent skin, radiating a soft bioluminescent light across an elongated, faceless head. Most striking were four luminous eyes set in a diamond pattern – the alien's appearance was both mesmerizing and disconcerting.

The Ilion began in a voice that was neither male nor female, "I understand you are the ranking officer of this vessel?"

"Yes, I am Captain Quintos, of USS *Franklin*... we are from Earth, a planet—"

"I know who you are and where you come from. You have entered a closed star system, Captain. This is a society that discourages uninvited visitors, more so, intentional trespassers."

"Captain, seven vessels have just uncloaked around us," Pristy said.

Another halo display offered an aerial perspective of *Franklin,* dwarfing the seven Ilion ships encircling it. These vessels bore an organic, avian quality, their wings arching gracefully, in stark contrast to the rigid metallic form of the omninought.

Hardy, at some point, had arrived at my side. "What a prick," he murmured.

I couldn't disagree. Playing nice was not going to work with these creatures.

"To whom am I addressing here?" I barked.

The Ilion, taken aback by the sudden sharpness in my voice, said, "You can address me as Losthen. I am the interstellar liaison for this sector."

I just stared at the alien figure until the silence became uncomfortable for him.

He finally said, "If there is nothing more—"

"So, this is how the Ilion treat their potential trading partners? With rudeness and disrespect?"

Losthen hesitated, wavered, "Uh... trading partner..."

"Why am I speaking with, what did you say you were? An interstellar liaison? What the hell is that? Some kind of switchboard operator? A low-level lackey with zero authority? Someone incapable of making a real decision?"

Near apoplectic, the alien's head pivoted left then right, as if searching for someone, anyone, to come to his rescue. "How dare you! I am a level 4 highly respected interstellar liaison—"

"Lackey. Lackey, lackey, lackey. Now get me someone who is interested in talking about the twenty-five tons of incredibly rare and priceless Antarcite taking up space in my flight bay."

"Antarcite?"

"Did I stutter? Maybe you're right. Maybe I should just turn this ship around and find a more appreciative trading partner—"

"No! Wait! Please, Captain Quintos... I am transmitting the docking coordinates now for our closest outpost, Caspern Station."

I glanced to Chen. "Cut the connection."

Hardy said, "I almost feel bad for the beanpole. Was close to peeing his proverbial pants."

"Just received the docking coordinates for that Caspern Station, Captain," Grimes said.

"Let's make them wait. Let them think we're rethinking our decision to trade with them."

Chapter 41

Aquilori Prime System
USS Franklin

Captain Galvin Quintos

Facilitating a docking berth for a ship the size of *Franklin* would pose a challenge to most deep space outposts. Caspern Station, in particular, would be a no-go. Chen re-established communication with Interstellar Liaison Losthen to convey that, instead, our boarding group would be employing Quansportation to materialize directly aboard the station.

Upon arrival, three looming tall Ilion representatives were there to greet us. For the occasion, they'd donned fancy outfits, long, stiff looking robes that shimmered with even the slightest of movements.

My own landing party included Hardy, Derrota, and Petty

Officer Second-Class Aubrey Laramie. I can already hear you asking, why bring along the beautiful, hard bodied, often troublesome, Petty Officer? Hmm, I'll have to get back to you on that.

Introductions dragged on for a while. Apparently, the Ilion believed—once you have been deemed worthy—an initial meet-and-greet was an important first step preceding getting down to any real business. With the exception that male and female Ilions are distinctly different in size, they all looked pretty much alike to me.

The ranking dignitary here was High Negotiator T'vren, the Chief, in charge of trade and interstellar commerce; he was draped in a robe of deep indigo. Next, Master Scholar Elira, a scientist renowned for her expertise in mineralogy; her garment sparkled with the intricate patterns of crystalline formations. And finally, Diplomat Soren, liaison for intercultural relations; he wore a robe with a tapestry of the worlds within their star system.

Quickly ushered into a large conference chamber, they all took measure of Hardy who had taken up a position in the corner. Nervously, each had one or two of their four eyes locked upon the big ChronoBot at all times.

High Negotiator T'vren regarded me with thinly veiled skepticism. "You claim to possess Antarcite in substantial quantities? An audacious assertion, yet you offer no evidence beyond words. We do not appreciate our time being wasted."

"Hey, you're being disrespectful," Aubrey fired back. "If you're not interested—"

I placed a *let's-bring-it-down-a-notch* hand upon her arm.

I met T'vren's intense gaze with one of my own. "I make no empty claims here. Twenty-five tons of unrefined Antarcite ore resides within our flight bay as we speak. Look, I've anticipated your need to verify the product. I'm fine with that. Why not have your expert accompany Science Officer Derrota back to my ship?"

THE THREE ILION SPOKE AMONGST THEMSELVES for what seemed like an eternity, T'vren's back to me.

Then, T'vren turned, and said, "Master Scholar Elira, our mineralogy expert, will accompany your Science Officer. We will wait for their return before any further negotiations continue."

I reached out to Coogong, who was waiting for my signal, prompting him to initiate the quansport sequence. Instantly, Derrota and Elira were quansported back to *Franklin*, materializing in Flight Bay 3. A hush fell over us, broken only by an endless series of Tic-Tac-Toe games cycling on Hardy's faceplate display.

Aubrey, sitting to my left, leaned in close and whispered. Her lips tickled my ear, sending a jolt of electricity down my spine. "I don't like these superior-acting fuckers. We shouldn't be taking their shit." She sat back and stared at the three Ilion defiantly.

Ignoring her, I said, "Hardy, if you're not too busy, how about you show us what's happening within the flight bay."

A swath of light emerged from Hardy, a projected image taking center stage upon the conference table. We watched as Master Scholar Elira moved nearer to the giant sample, her features alight with fascination. "Remarkable... its crystalline matrix displays the unmistakable conductive latticework unique to Antarcite." She extended a slender digit to graze the ore's surface, visibly awed. "And such clarity and density of crystals... simply exquisite."

Derrota leaned in, a self-assured smirk etching his lips as he —as we had—caught the glint of desire in the scholar's eyes.

"Master Scholar Elira," he asked, his tone laced with vindication, "does this sample meet your exacting standards?"

"Oh... most definitely," she said. "And to be honest, I have never witnessed such a substantial quantity of this mineral, not ever."

High Negotiator T'vren squirmed in his seat, his earlier skepticism fading. "It appears you speak accurately, Captain."

"Yeah, just like we told you," Aubrey said.

Both Derrota and Elira quansported back into the chamber, Master Scholar Elira still seeming somewhat breathless from what she had witnessed.

T'vren said, "Let us reconvene discussions. I look forward to making an equitable exchange for this... seemingly adequate mineral."

I placed a preemptive hand on Aubrey's arm. She nodded but narrowed her eyes toward T'vren.

While Hardy still lingered in the corner, Derrota and Elira took their places around the table. The air had grown charged as the negotiations commenced, with T'vren's sonorous tone reverberating through the austere, domed chamber. "State your terms, Captain Quintos. What do you seek in exchange for this Antarcite?"

I leaned forward. "We have need of your expertise in two specific realms—quantum engineering and genetics. First, I take it you are aware of Earth's recent, vicious attacks, the translocation from our own Solar System to another star system many light years away?"

T'vren raised his chin, acknowledging he was aware.

"And how the Varapin utilized what we refer to as a QSER platform? A Quantum Spatial Entanglement and Relocation device to facilitate this horrific act?"

The High Negotiator nodded.

"And perhaps, the origin of this device is in fact, Ilion?" I asked.

There was a pause as the three Ilion's exchanged looks. "I can neither confirm nor deny that assumption," T'vren said.

I nodded in acknowledgement. "That answers my question," I began. "Look, we urgently need your expertise for the repair and reactivation of our QSER platform. The fate of our world is hanging by a thread, and we're racing against time—a concept I'm certain isn't lost on you."

T'vren maintained his composure, replying, "The extent of repair will heavily depend on the damage to the device itself. You must understand, such technology can be incredibly intricate, perhaps overly so for civilizations less advanced in such matters." He shook his elongated head. "I'm sorry but the answer is *no*. You must understand, the Ilion have stringent policies against divulging the intricacies of our technology."

Aubrey interjected sharply, "The Varapin didn't come up with that tech on their own. They must've taken it from someone—my money's on you guys. By that logic, you share in the responsibility for this shitshow."

I caught Derrota's eye, a silent exchange of wariness passing between us. Aubrey's candor was as blunt as it was untimely. The Ilion representatives visibly bristled at the mention of their adversaries. "Any begotten Varapin contraption we shall gleefully dismantle, not reconstruct!" Diplomat Soren declared, his harmonious voice momentarily discordant.

"With respect, that device's unique capabilities make it invaluable for resolving Earth's present... predicament," Derrota persisted. "Lend us your expertise not to aid the Varapin, but to restore Earth's rightful place—and in return, receive sufficient Antarcite for your long-term needs."

Elira wavered, clearly torn by temptation, but T'vren

remained unmoved. "Your first request shall require greater deliberation. Now name your second condition."

Here, I hesitated, choosing my next words with care. "The Varapin, as a race, faces a genotypic collapse. I'm sure you are well aware of this, too. We ask only that you provide us, Earth, with the scientific expertise to reverse their condition. The technology, materials, all the knowledge, so we can be the custodian of the Varapin's survival."

"Out of the question!" Diplomat Soren objected.

"Again, Earth wouldn't be sharing that technology with the Varapin, only providing them a limited medical allocation," Derrota added.

A charged silence followed. T'vren's multiple eyes now locked onto me. Flashing with anger, he said, "You ask us to rescue those vile creatures? They who sought to steal our genetic secrets by force?" His voice rose in indignation. "I should put you in irons just for the suggestion!"

"Yeah, I'd like to see you try," Aubrey said, readying to stand.

"Sit down and be quiet, Petty Officer!" I commanded, shooting her a quick wink to let her know I wasn't really reprimanding her.

"Hear me out!" I pressed. "The Varapin offense against your people cannot be forgiven. But their looming, decades—or centuries—long, slow extinction may be worse for all of us. Avoiding galactic chaos requires stabilizing the balance of power." My tone turned grave, "And there are larger threats encroaching—the Grish grow ever bolder, hungering to dominate the galaxy. Without Earth and our alliance with the Thine and Pleidian Weonan, it wouldn't be long before you'll be stuck fending them off alone."

The Ilion exchanged uneasy looks, clearly my warning striking a chord. After a taut pause, Elira leaned forward, her bio-luminescence pulsating. "Your arguments echo truth, Captain Quintos. To withhold aid risks grave consequences." She turned her gaze to T'vren, imploring him. "The Antarcite could secure our technological prowess for generations. Can we ignore this opportunity for open-mindedness and potential conciliation?"

The Negotiator remained silent, weighing her appeal. Finally, he emitted a resigned chime—an oddly musical tone conveying, I hoped, capitulation.

"You have petitioned us to transcend old divisions for the greater galactic harmony. Can the Ilion turn away from such a plea?" T'vren shifted in his seat, back erect and proud. "Very well. We shall render what scientific assistance we ethically can... in return for your twenty-five tons of Antarcite ore."

I gave a clipped nod. "Good. Then we have an agreement." I extended my hand, aware the human custom was likely unfamiliar, yet T'vren grasped it without hesitation—we shook.

Chapter 42

After entering the bridge, I made my way to the Captain's Mount. I noticed my XO wasn't at her station—probably on a break.

"Captain, we'll be emerging from the manufactured wormhole in less than three minutes," Grimes updated from the Helm station.

I sat back, relieved to be far away from the Aquilori Prime System and the pretentious Ilion.

We had endured four excruciatingly slow days of QSER platform repairs, followed by an additional two days of painstaking tutoring by a team of Ilion Gene Therapy Specialists. Their task was to provide a comprehensive knowledge-base in molecular genetics that Derrota and Coogong could recreate within *Franklin's* laboratory. Together, they were now on a mission reminiscent of the old saying, *Why buy the cow when you can get the milk for free?*

Their objective was to develop an annually administered vaccine that would be extremely difficult, if not impossible, for the Varapin to reverse-engineer. This would ensure their continued existence, even as they remained indefinitely reliant on Earth for all future treatments. It would be a delicate balancing act but a crucial one for the survival of humanity.

My TAC-Band suddenly came alive with an all too familiar projection. "We have a problem," the teenager said.

I took in her appearance. "What's that in your hair?" I said taking in the preponderance of white suds."

She made a face. "It's shampoo."

I just stared at her.

"I was in the shower which is irrelevant to why I'm talking to you now. Plorinne just messaged me. Frantic. He told me Graves is on the loose."

"Graves?"

"Are you like on... sedatives? You need to keep up. General Graves... you know, the Redcoat Symbio who tried to take over the ship... the Symbio that—"

"No." I cut her off. "I gave explicit orders for him to be dismantled," I said, feeling my blood pressure skyrocketing.

"His head was removed and taken to the SSC, put into deep slumber. I didn't think a fricken decapitated head could be of much danger."

"So, he's just a head?"

"You're really getting on my nerves. No, he's not just a head anymore. He found a body."

"You should have destroyed that head, Sonya."

"Really? Gee, Captain Obvious, I'm so glad you're here to enlighten me to that fact. Look, I'd figured, as soon as things calm down, I could do a little retro-engineering—find out how that Graves Symbio had been hacked. I was being proactive, you know, by ensuring this type of thing doesn't happen again."

"So where is the Symbio now, Sonya?"

The entire bridgecrew was now looking at me.

Grimes said, "Thirty seconds till emergence from the wormhole."

"Uh, that's the thing," Sonya continued, "No one has a clue. As you know, he's a slippery devil. What we do know... and please don't yell at me again, is that someone on the ship has been dispatching highly encrypted messages. And it's probably that Symbio. It started back when we were within the Aquilori Prime System."

I looked to Chen at Comms who shrugged and nervously shook his head while frantically tapping at his board.

"What did the messages say?" I asked Sonya, who was now using a towel to wipe soap suds from her eyes.

"They were all encrypted. Didn't I just say that? Hardy's working the code with me. But I think I know to whom they were sent." She grimaced.

Chen interjected, "I see it. Crap! They were sent to Grish High Command, Captain."

"Yeah, that," Sonya added in a barely audible voice.

The *all-too-familiar stomach-elevator-drop-feeling* hit as we emerged from the wormhole into HIP 938134 System.

INCOMING!
INCOMING!
INCOMING!
BATTLE STATIONS!
PREPARE FOR IMPACT!

Pristy practically flew into her seat at Tactical 1. "Dammit! I should have had us cloaked. Deploying observation drones!" Pristy yelled.

Overhead, a Klaxon blared. SARAH continued to spout warnings.

"We're being hailed, Captain." Chen announced. "It's Captain Darren Hawke of *HMS Queen Elizabeth*."

All eight halo displays came alive with observation drone feeds—various perspectives of the emerging spacial battlefield caused my jaw to drop. *Oh my God.* "He'll have to wait. XO, what are you doing about those incoming missiles?"

"Working on it..."

"Someone give me a damn situation report!" I barked.

"We're taking fire. Cloaking is offline. They're the Grish, Sir," Ensign Lira said from the Sensors and Reconnaissance Station. "I'm counting..."

I spun to look at her.

The blood had drained from her face. "Close to two hundred Grish warships, Sir. We dropped into an ambush."

"Took out the incoming missiles, for now. Engaging all rail cannons and pulsars," Pristy said, her voice remarkably cool and calm considering what we were up against. She shot a glance back to me. "We're being swarmed, Varapin-supplied Cyclone Death Fighters."

"Deploy our Arrows," I said. "I want every pilot we have suited up and wheels up, within two minutes. XO, I want our broadsides taking out some of those larger warships. Grimes, get us into a better firing position."

"Aye, Captain."

I took in the sheer number of enemy warships—tried to swallow, but my throat was as dry as the Mojave.

"Broadsides are down till further notice," Pristy said.

"Shields are taking a beating, Captain," Crewmember Davit said. "Already down to 70%."

"We need to jump out of here!" Pristy shouted.

I watched as one after another bright red Arrows streamed out from multiple *Franklin* flight bays. "Not till our Arrows are clear."

Chen said," I still have Captain Darren Hawke—"

I stood. "Someone tell me what's happening on Earth. See if

you can put together a surface damage report. And yes, Mr. Chen, you can put Captain Hawke through."

The ship shook so hard I needed to reach for something to grab onto. Sparks fountained up from one console then another.

SARAH announced the closure of Deck 15 Vac-Gates.

The primary halo display was pixelated and staticky with the feed from *HMS Queen Elizabeth*.

Captain Darren Hawke said, "Captain... they jumped in just minutes before your arrival in system." Hawke's British accent lent an air of refinement to the man. A tall and imposing figure, his sharp features were accentuated by a well-groomed beard. His piercing blue eyes bore the weight of command, and his pristine uniform contrasted starkly with the chaos surrounding him.

"What's happening on Earth?" I asked, getting straight to the point. Our ships and this situation paled in comparison to the survival of our home world.

"As of now, the enemy has had little time to attack Earth," Hawke said. "We may be a much smaller contingent, but not a one of us has jumped from this system to save ourselves. No, we'll continue to protect Earth until the very end, Captain."

Pristy, somehow, had found time to project another display with what warships and their respective Captains were still in play and those taken off the battlefield:

IN SERVICE: *USS Franklin...*

Captain Galvin Quintos

IN SERVICE: *RFS* - Admiral Gorshkov (Russian dreadnought)...

Captain Ivan Kuznetsov

DAMAGED: *HMS Queen Elizabeth* (British battlecruiser)...

Captain Darren Hawke

HEAVILY DAMAGED: *CNS Liaoning* (Chinese destroyer)...

Commander Li Wei

DESTROYED: *USS Trident* (U.S. battle cruiser)...

Captain Leo Braxton

DESTROYED: *FS Charles de Gaulle* (French battle frigate)...

Capitaine Marie Dubois

The British Captain was talking again, "Please tell me you've returned with help or perhaps something, a means to thwart this Grish armada."

"Maybe, Captain. But what I'm going to require from all of our remaining Captains is to continue the good fight. I'll be in touch."

The connection ended.

INCOMING!
INCOMING!
INCOMING!
BATTLE STATIONS!
PREPARE FOR IMPACT!

Chapter 43

HIP 938134 Star System
USS Franklin

Captain Galvin Quintos

The void flickered with dozens of simultaneous explosions as our railguns and pulsar cannons exchanged relentless volleys with the encroaching Grish armada. Despite our defenses, their overwhelming numbers soon closed the divide.

BRACE FOR IMPACT!

Came again from above.

I grabbed the armrests of my chair. A shudder resonated through *Franklin's* expansive frame as the latest salvo of enemy missiles careened into our shields.

"Portside shields down to 89%," Crewmember Davit

updated from Defensive Systems Station. Her fingers danced across the console with practiced efficiency.

On the display, a brilliant ball of flame marked the violent end of a Grish destroyer. I watched as our Arrows wove between pulsars and missiles with daring precision, their superior maneuverability balanced against the Grish's brute Cyclone Death Fighter's firepower. For now, the dogfight seemed to be at a stalemate—but the enemy armada... clearly, we were getting our asses handed to us.

"Broadsides are finally online, Cap," Pristy announced.

"It's about time," I murmured. "Helm, bring us forty degrees to starboard," I ordered. "And Mr. Chen, Get the *RFS Admiral Gorshkov* on comms. Tell them to stand down and back off while we introduce that Grish battle cruiser to our bowler ordnances."

"Aye, Cap. On it."

I said, "Target their aft portside, XO."

"Copy. Unleashing broadsides now."

Franklin shook as a concussive *Boom! Boom! Boom!* resounded through the ship. The Grish battle cruiser went up like a Fourth of July fireworks display. Fragments of its hull, like shrapnel, swiftly demolished two nearby Grish frigates caught in the explosive aftermath.

I eyed the logistical display, a frenzy of multi-colored icons. Five enemy warships were inbound, undoubtedly looking for a little payback for taking out one of their largest assets.

"Minimize our profile, Helm!" I yelled. "We're a big ass five-mile-long target."

"Aye Captain, coming about now." Grimes said as *Franklin* was already lumbering into a new situational attitude.

Off our portside, the massive Russian dreadnought loomed, unleashing salvo after salvo from its big guns. I had to give Captain Kuznetsov his due. He was giving the Grish hell, but flashes of missile impacts marked fresh glowing craters along the vessel's hull. She wouldn't withstand that pounding for long.

"Captain Kuznetsov is signaling they've lost aft shields," Chen relayed from Comms. "Their drives took a bad hit; they're solely relying on docking thrusters."

I knew if Gorshkov's maneuverability was compromised, it would only be a matter of time before the Grish would surround and overwhelm her. "Tell them we'll cover her retreat."

Pristy cut in, "Too late - their starboard side just took a direct impact. Heavy damage... wait." She leaned forward taking in her readings. Her eyes went wide. "Their reactor casing's been breached. Shit, they're venting plasma."

Sure enough, glowing hot gases spewed into space from the dreadnought's portside. The ship's fate was already sealed. Without containment, an overload was imminent. "Helm, get us clear!"

But our own lumbering ship couldn't outrun the explosion. The primary halo display, as visually accurate as any diamond glass window, went white—a brilliant-blinding flash leaving white spots in my vision. The resulting shockwave slamming into *Franklin's* shields a moment later. More Klaxon alarms blared overhead as the ship groaned under the strain.

"Damage report!" I sputtered, blinking away the glare.

"Starboard shields holding at 68%," Davit relayed. "Minor damage across Decks 5 through 12, Vac-Gates deployed. No casualties."

We were lucky this time. I watched shattered fragments and a lone remaining torn and jagged segment of Admiral Gorshkov's ship drift past our bow, a gut-wrenching reminder of the battle's continuing cost.

"Over seventeen hundred souls were just lost to the void," Pristy said, taking a moment to observe the heavy cost of battle.

I took in the myriad of halo displays as the battle raged. My eyes came to rest, once again, upon the logistical display. The remaining allied ships were all in dire straits. "Get me a better view of that Chinese destroyer."

Zooming into view, the box-like silhouette of the Liaoning was being relentlessly battered. Gaping wounds marked where armor plating had been blasted away, venting clouds of crystallizing gases fountained into the void. Return fire sputtered weakly from her few operational guns.

Pristy swore under her breath. "Liaoning's lost main power... their comms are down. No way to know how many are left alive onboard."

Prior to all this chaos, Captain Li Wei had been the lone Earth Captain wanting to go his own way. But I had to admit, he'd shown courage and unwavering resolve. Now, he and his crew faced a slow and merciless suffocation.

"Grimes, pursue vector seven-three-six to Liaoning's position," I said. "I want options people, how to shelter them via docking or emergency crew quansport." I knew we were likely their last hope for survival.

"No clear vector, Cap," Grimes said. "It'll be a minute." His voice faded behind the thunderous crack of *Franklin's* railguns.

On the tactical feed, a shower of sparks marked where rail spikes had torn through an approaching Grish frigate. Seconds later, Pristy wielded *Franklin's* phazon pulsar batteries to silence the vessel forever. She punched the air. "Got you, you son of a bitch."

I smiled. But the moment of triumph was short-lived. New hostiles were flooding the area, coming into view from the far side of Earth—a reinforcement wing, dropping in to ruin my day. I counted thirty more gleaming attack ships to replace the recent losses we'd inflicted.

"Christ... where are they all coming from?" Pristy muttered.

Franklin shuddered again under a renewed barrage.

The deck tilted precariously as multiple impacts staggered our momentum. Such an occurrence shouldn't have happened. The integrated subsystems of Centrifugal Force, Linear Acceleration, and Magnetic Stabilizing Fields work in unison to provide the crew with a consistent sense of orientation, simulating the feeling of being on Earth.

Suddenly, a sense of vertigo had me reeling, nausea had me swallowing bile at the back of my throat.

Crewmember Soto suddenly retched then threw up, then threw up again. The stink of it quickly wafted throughout the bridge like a toxic cloud.

"Keep it together people," I said.

Damage alerts flared across multiple consoles—it was getting harder to track the blows we were weathering.

Chen said, "Being hailed, Cap."

A garbled transmission filtered through bursts of static—Captain Hawke's voice from the crippled *HMS Queen Elizabeth*. "*Franklin*... we cannot... maneuver... drives... down..."

The channel went dead.

"Get them back on comms!" I barked.

Suddenly, sparks erupted from Chen's console, an arc of electricity shot upward. He recoiled with a pained shout, clutching a blackened hand. An acrid tang permeated the air as smoke whisked from his fried panel.

"Comms array just overloaded," he gasped. "For now, we're done hailing, broadcasting or receiving."

Grimes, at the helm, glanced to his friend. "Just reroute your station to an auxiliary console."

"I know that. Not so easy with one hand though," he said, holding up his blackened digits.

I took in the hellscape before me. We were cut off from half of our allies, all of our ships were crippled, some were quickly dying. An icy ball of dread settled in my gut. Whatever our next move, *Franklin* and her crew would be facing it alone.

Crewmember Soto at Damage Control Station, her retching having momentarily relented, reeled off another damage report, her tone clinical despite the graveness of our circumstances. She chronicled the Decks having been breached, sections exposed to a vacuum, casualties steadily mounting as the Grish tightened their noose. And still the relentless pounding continued, our shields now struggling below 45%.

"Captain Ryder reports heavy losses out there," Hargreaves added grimly. "Barely a third of our Arrows still in fighting condition."

"Order Captain Ryder to bring his birds home," I said.

"Comms are down," Chen reminded me.

"Then find a way, dammit!"

"Copy that, Captain," Chen said.

THE NEXT FEW MINUTES CRAWLED BY, EACH precious second marked by *Franklin's* death throes—the groan of bulkheads strained beyond limits, hissing pipes ruptured by plasma burns, panicked SWM and damage control teams infused with Army personnel rushing to futilely patch the worst breaches. All while the Grish pressed their advantage, like pack hunters toying with wounded prey.

"Comms coming back online, Cap."

"Excellent, Mr. Chen. Now get me the status on Liaoning" I demanded, clinging to that sole glimmer of hope.

He didn't look up. "Their reactor's dangerously unstable, but I've accessed pod logs - at least three hundred crew jettisoned so far." His expression shifted between despair and desperation.

Pristy said, "Trying to calibrate our tertiary array... just need their comm frequency..."

I took in the constant crisscrossing of red and blue plasma bolts. "Work fast. And let's get Coogong ready at the Quansporter. Those escape pods won't survive long." I shook my head. "They're like ducks in a barrel."

Pristy gestured to a halo display, highlighting a familiar silhouette—the sleek arrowhead form of a Grish Phantom Class Destroyer. Magnification revealed gaping holes blown through its hull, atmosphere spewing through twisted corridors exposed to space. Yet still it turned ponderously towards us, weapons charged for one final act of vengeance.

"Taking her out with Hellfires," Pristy declared.

Moments later, flaming streaks marked a volley of antimatter missiles crossing the void—burning as bright as small captive suns. Then their nuclear payload consumed the target in a singular cataclysmic detonation.

When the flare subsided, only scattered debris remained. This one small victory, I knew would be too little too late. The logistical feed showed fifty Grish capital ships still hungry for blood, and twice that many lighter craft harrying our retreating battered Arrows.

Then Crewmember Davit's strained voice called out, "Got them! Locked onto three hundred twenty-seven Liaoning escape pods..." But his expression suddenly collapsed into despair. "No! The signals... they disappeared. Just like that, they're gone. Some kind of wide-spectrum jamming..." he said, his voice faltering.

He didn't need to finish that sentence. Unarmed and adrift, those capsules were little more than death traps. It would be just a matter of time before the Grish would be using them for target practice.

Grimes suddenly yelled out from his console, "Captain - *Franklin's* been ensnared in multiple tractor beams!" His hands flew over his board to no effect. "Thrusters at full, but we're locked in place!"

"Source?" I barked, though the answer was obvious.

He swallowed hard. "Five Grish battle cruisers have a target lock, engines full reverse."

I watched feeling useless. They had us trapped like a caged animal awaiting a singular fate. In a matter of minutes, the enemy would breach our hull and invade these very decks. Then the piglets would swarm onboard. A mix of anger and despair consumed me as our demise loomed.

Around me, the bridgecrew exchanged wordless looks of dread. So close to grasping victory, now we were staring down the gun barrel of defeat. Had our journey really come to this? This couldn't be how it all ends, for my crew, for Earth...

"Captain..." Pristy said softly, "Galvin..." breaking the spell of despair that had fallen over me like a heavy shroud. I looked up to see her kneeling before me, her hand gently clasped over mine, blue eyes glistening with emotion. "We're done, there's nothing more we can do..." Her words cut off as she lowered her head.

I heard several of my bridgecrew start to sob behind us.

But in Pristy's tender touch, I found renewed resolve. Our hopes might lie in ruins, but I wasn't quite ready to throw in the towel.

I squeezed her hand, "XO... Gail, can you do me a favor?"

She raised her head, her eyes moist, searching mine. "Anything."

"Keep this ship afloat just a little longer. Do whatever you have to do. If we're boarded, ensure the Colonel and his army earn their paychecks."

"You're acting like you're leaving... leaving the ship, leaving me?"

"I am."

Chapter 44

There was no one I trusted more to skipper *Franklin* than my XO. But was I leaving her to a certain death? God, I hope not.

Sprinting toward the DeckPort on the far side of the Rotunda, I tried reaching out to Hardy but, like much of the ship, my TAC-Band wasn't functional. I yelled over the din of Klaxon alarms, "SARAH, if you can hear me, I need you to find Hardy for me. Also, have Sargent Max and team meet me in Flight Bay 1."

Hardy... Deck... Breach...

I couldn't make heads or tails out of that. Could only hope the AI understood me enough to follow my orders.

Reaching the DeckPort I was suddenly tongue-tied, not remembering the Deck number I needed to get to. "Damn!" I slapped my forehead. Then it came to me. "Deck 18, Violet Sector."

. . .

I RUSHED IN AND CAME OUT ON DECK 18. UP ahead was HealthBay and the Science and R&D Departments. But what I saw there in the middle of the wide corridor brought me to an abrupt standstill.

I've seen a lot of crazy things in my time as a U.S. Space Navy Captain. Nothing should surprise me at this point, but I would be wrong. A group of lookie-loos had encircled them—including Chief Knott, and next to her, Doc Viv. Her pink scrubs were splattered with blood—undoubtedly, there had been back-to-back surgeries since the battle had begun.

I joined them, my eyes locked onto the raging battle at the center of the crowd. There stood Hardy, all of his plasma cannons deployed, but not firing. There were a handful of scorched craters upon his chrome plating. Hardy's opponent... it was Climbo, or, should I say, a monsterized version of Climbo. The mechanical pack mule was standing upright on back legs. His hoofs, replaced by human-looking hands—one of which was holding a tagger. Climbo's original mule-like head was gone and replaced by, yup, you guessed it—none other than the elusive General Jarvis Graves.

Breaking through the onlookers across from us, Sonya arrived. Looking out of breath, she took in the bazaar scene. As Hardy and Climbo continued to circle one another, I gestured for Sonya to make her way over to us.

Climbo, or should I say, General Graves, fired off another two plasma bolts from his tagger, adding two more smoldering, glowing hot, craters to Hardy visage.

Viv said, "As vain as the ChronoBot is about his appearance, he must be furious. Why the hell doesn't he just shoot the damn thing?" she said, exasperated.

"From what I can surmise... he doesn't want to hurt the mule. They've developed... a relationship," I said.

She made a face. "I don't have time for any of this crap.

Have an arm that needs amputating." She turned and headed back toward HealthBay.

Chief Knott said, "I also have patients." She headed off after Viv.

Sonya was now at my side, eyes like saucers, her hands covering her mouth. "This is all my fault."

I couldn't argue with that. So instead, I said, "Hardy, I order you to put an end to this nonsense!"

Hardy raised a metallic forefinger, "I just need to get through to Climbo."

"Don't be ridiculous. I'll buy you a new pack mule."

"Why does he get so attached to non-biological beings like this?" Sonya asked.

I didn't have an answer. And I didn't have a spare second to waste here. I said, "This is your mess, Sonya. You deal with it. I have to go."

"Go where? What am I supposed to do here, with... these two?"

I was already heading toward the R&D Departments and yelled over one shoulder, "Put that Symbio Mule monstrosity down. Do it now, Sonya."

I found the R&D lab empty—both Coogong and Derrota nowhere in sight. "Of course, they're not here," I chided. I looked up, gritting my teeth. *Should I chance it?*

"SARAH, quansport me into Flight Bay 3." I closed my eyes, winced, envisioning this reckless act could very well be my last.

I successfully quansported into Flight Bay 3.

Both Derrota and Coogong were there, along with a handful of others lab-coated scientists. The platform loomed tall, still supported by hanging straps, but now, more of the contraption was aglow with hundreds of illuminated crystals.

Franklin shook with a thunderous *BOOM*... a dire reminder that moments counted. Derrota looked up as I approached. "Talk to me Stephan. Tell me this thing is operational."

He tilted his head slightly, saying, "I wish I could, Galvin. There's an issue with the QSER's capability to sync with the local star, HIP 938134."

I wanted to emphasize to Derrota that the fate of Earth and humanity itself hinges on this device performing its intended function. But I could see the strain and pressure on my friend's face now. His complexion had turned pallid, his eyes were bloodshot, and dark circles had formed beneath them. I was tempted to ask when was the last time he'd eaten, or slept, for that matter. Instead, I said, "You have one hour—two at the most, to deploy the platform. After that, there won't be a need for it. It'll be too late."

That caught Coogong's attention as he came around the far end of the QSER platform. "We will have it working, Captain—one way or another."

"Good. One more thing... I won't be here to remind you. So, get it done."

Derrota, brow furrowed, opened his mouth to speak, then seemed to think better of it. He nodded and got back to whatever he was doing with the device.

I ARRIVED AT FLIGHT BAY 1, MY SENSES accosted by the noise of a hundred Arrows winding down, the ever-present Klaxon overhead, and the strident smell of ozone exhausts.

Akari James was headed for the same DeckPort I'd emerged from. She was still dressed in her flight suit, her helmet clutched in one hand. Her hair was matted with sweat, and I could see the exhaustion—battle fatigue, from too many hours within the cockpit of an Arrow fighter craft.

"Captain! Why'd you pull us from the fight?"

"I had my reasons. Where's Captain Ryder?"

"You didn't hear?" she said, her expression dire. It was no secret she and Ryder had been an *on-again-off-again* item for years now. Eyes welling, she blinked away tears. "He got hit. It's bad, Captain. Plasma blast took most of one arm, then hypothermia..."

I remembered Viv's comment about having an arm to amputate. Was it Ryder's?

"If you don't mind, I'd like to see how he's doing?" She readied to skirt by me, but I caught her arm. "Ryder will be fine. I promise. You, on the other hand, have more piloting to do."

She looked at me questioningly. "Back to my Arrow?"

"Nope, you'll be piloting that." I pointed off to the back of the bay where the military Craven-Class 550 *Off Worlder* sat. Nearby, a small team of combat-suited individuals looked back at us.

Akari looked from the *Off Worlder* to the DeckPort and back again.

"We need you, Lieutenant. More depends on what we'll be doing than you could possibly imagine."

She nodded. "Wallace will be okay?"

"Doc Viv's seeing to it personally."

That seemed to make all the difference. Smiling, she said, "Then what are we waiting for?"

WHILE AKARI GOT HERSELF SITUATED AT THE *Off Worlder's* controls, I took the spare combat suit Wanda had brought along for me and headed aft. The team consisted of Sergeant Max, Wanda, Grip, Ham and Hock, and, surprisingly, Petty Officer first Class, Aubrey Laramie.

Now, standing nearly naked, with only my boxers on, I attempted to get dressed in my combat suit. These new suits were so snug, conforming to one's body, that wearing clothes underneath was discouraged. As the craft's lift thrusters engaged, causing it to rise somewhat unsteadily, I struggled with the task of putting on my combat suit trousers.

If you've never tried to pull on a pair of these unwieldy nanomaterial breeches, constructed with advanced ballistic-resistant Kevlar, let me assure you, it's no walk in the park. I was taken aback when Aubrey stepped close, offering her support as I hopped around on one foot. I felt her eyes on me.

"Relax, Captain, you're not the first man I've helped to get dressed in a hurry."

I didn't have a quick comeback for that, so I said nothing. By the time I was fully dressed, she was there to hand me my helmet. "Uh, thanks."

"Anytime," she said, heading away to join the rest of the team.

The only one who knew specifically where we were going, was Akari James.

THE OFF WORLDER WAS STILL HOVERING, POISED at the open bay. All of us were seated and strapped in. The timing had to be just right. The last thing we wanted to do was bring undue attention to ourselves with countless enemy warships, support vessels, and pesky Cyclone Death Fighters all about.

"Here it comes," Akari said over our helmet's open channel. "You're right Captain, that should work just fine."

What she was referring to, was the same jagged warship segment of the Admiral Gorshkov—I'd seen earlier—and still adrift in local space. Akari, coordinating with Grimes up on *Franklin's* bridge, he'd repositioned the omninought so the destroyed ship segment would pass by the bay extremely close—not an easy task while a raging battle ensued, and the ship's propulsion system was barely operational. I'd have to remember to give the helmsman an accommodation... that is if we live long enough for that to happen.

A dark shadow eclipsed our view out the craft's forward window.

"Hold on!" Akari announced, as the *Off Worlder* suddenly shot forward, G-forces pinning us to our seats.

Max, seated to my right said, "Spill the beans, Cap. Where're we going? If it's Earth, there's not a lot this lone shuttle can do."

Chapter 45

HIP 938134 Star System
USS Franklin

XO Gail Pristy

Pristy gripped the edges of her console, knuckles white. The overwhelming battle raged on as *Franklin* shuddered under yet another devastating salvo. She barked orders, guiding her outmatched but resolute bridgecrew —a fight that they all knew, would be a battle to the death. Missiles and phazon pulsar bolts crisscrossed the void as they took out two more Grish destroyers in quick succession—but at a cost.

"Starboard shields at 37%," Crewman Davit called out, shouting over the din. Blood trickled from a gash on her blue glowing Pleidian Weonan cheek, but her fingers never slowed on the controls. "That's their fifth coordinated strike on the same section. If they keep hammering us like that, shield grid's gonna fail."

Pristy swallowed back growing despair. Their situation was dire. Quintos was gone—making some last desperate gamble, and, of course, she had no clue what that meant... what exactly he was doing. The man was infuriating. There again, what else is new?

I need to get a grip, she inwardly scolded. The defense of the ship had fallen to her, and her alone. She toggled views between tactical readouts and status feeds from across the five-mile leviathan. One halo display showed a full company of Army troops fighting a savage close-quarters battle on Deck 34, while struggling to contain the breach point. Other halo displays showed diminishing Army grunts, all being forced into retreat on three separate decks. The piecemeal defense was barely slowing the relentless tide of Grish invaders.

"Helm, get us out of here!" she commanded. *Franklin* was in the thick of battle, so many enemy ships pounding their shields at once, their only hope was to flee the onslaught, even if disabled and venting atmosphere.

Grimes shook his head, panic tightening his youthful features. "Main drives took a direct hit in that last exchange. We're dead in space, XO."

Pristy swore under her breath, slamming a fist onto the console. Now they were little more than a bullseye pinned in place.

She looked to see which warships and their respective Captains were still in play upon the battlefield:

DAMAGED: USS *Franklin...*
Captain Galvin Quintos
DAMAGED: HMS *Queen Elizabeth* (British battlecruiser)...

Captain Darren Hawke

DESTROYED: *RFS Admiral Gorshkov* (Russian dreadnought)...

Captain Ivan Kuznetsov

DESTROYED: *CNS Liaoning* (Chinese destroyer)...

Commander Li Wei

DESTROYED: *USS Trident* (U.S. battle cruiser)...

Captain Leo Braxton

DESTROYED: *FS Charles de Gaulle* (French battle frigate)...

Capitaine Marie Dubois

She let out an audible moan. And I thought I was depressed before...

MOMENTS LATER, THE HARSH SCREECH OF metal signaled more breaching ships—others cutting into *Franklin's* massive hide. She stood, eyes moving from one halo display to another. The nightmarish sight of a dozen lamprey-like boarding craft clamped to the hull, burning through layers of ablation armor.

Squat pig-like forms poured from troop carriers in waves, heavily armed Grish infantry infesting the omninought by the hundreds. She took in the views of the lower decks, where Colonel Sanderson's regiments mustered rapidly into tight fire-teams, steeling themselves at choke points to repel the onslaught. But being so outnumbered, she knew their efforts would, ultimately, be in vain.

She looked to Chen at comms, "Get me an open channel to the Colonel."

"Channel's open, XO."

"Colonel Sanderson, it's time to earn your paycheck," Pristy said, now patching coordinates directly to his heads-up display. "Grish boarders incoming on Decks 7 through 31 in force. You need to redistribute your forces, we're being overrun."

"Don't tell me how to do my job, missy. I've been doing this before you had your first training bra."

She almost laughed at his chauvinistic ranting. "Just get it done," she ordered.

Sanderson offered a terse acknowledgement, "Yeah well, I'll deploy what I can... implement security protocols... that'll maybe slow them down. But were losing this battle, best you come to terms with that young lady."

Again, with the fucking condescending, belittling, not to mention patronizing bullshit. If I ever get out of this mess, I'm going to throttle that son of a bitch.

On another display, she glimpsed Derrota and Coogong still barricaded within Flight Bay 3. Earlier she'd insisted Sanderson provide them with a protective squad of soldiers. The scientists were working feverishly to activate the QSER platform—perhaps the only hope of reversing Earth's spatial exile. She chewed at the inside of her lip; time was running out. A quick glance to the chronometer up on the bulkhead ticked down as *Franklin* shuddered under fresh blows.

Her attention snapped back to Sanderson's regiments as screeching alerts announced Vac-Gates on Decks 17 and 33 were failing. The *rolled-into-place* hard-sealed bulkheads were designed to partition breached areas, slowing the loss of atmosphere—but too many localized system failures had taken their toll. Instantly the grid overlays on her tactical feed updated with a damage projection report from SARAH:

At current rates of deterioration, lethal vacuum exposure will propagate to over 60% of the ship's interior space— happening within eighteen minutes.

Terrific.

She watched as pandemonium engulfed the corridors; Army regiments engaged the invaders in savage close-quarters combat. The harsh crack of energy fire, with searing streaks of plasma, crisscrossed the passageways. Bodies, Army and Grish alike, were splayed out—lifeless, upon the deck. She toggled rapidly between feeds, from two dozen hotspots, monitoring the chaotic scene.

Soldiers in their combat suits advanced relentlessly down, once previously clear corridors, were now being stormed by the Grish. Despite the optimal firing conditions for Sanderson's troops, the Grish continued to advance, and their numbers never seemed to decrease, even though they had suffered significant casualties.

In main junctions and choke points, the battle stalled into tense standoffs. From behind, crisscrossed barricades of cargo crates were positioned—a makeshift cover. The two sides traded blistering torrents of weapons fire across the divides.

Here the training and advanced weaponry of the allied troops took its toll on the piglets, as precision shredder bursts and frag grenades tore through ranks of Grish infantry. But at each hard-fought breach, five more pig-like aliens clambered over the heaped corpses of their comrades, screaming blood-curdling war cries, muffled by their helmets, as they surged into the fight.

Pristy's gut twisted as feed after feed, revealed the horrific mounting toll. Soldiers cut down by scorching Grish plasma fire, some dragged off by squealing aliens to suffer brutal fates. The battle still hung on a knife's edge, with over two dozen major clashes raging across a quarter of the ship's decks—but inch by bloody inch, the Grish were gaining ground through their sheer numbers alone.

A proximity alert snapped her gaze back to the closed bridge entrance, just as an explosion rocked the compartment. "That sounded way too close..." Davit warned over the groaning protest of bulkheads. "I don't think the Colonel's men can hold the main junction much longer."

Then, Pristy saw smoke coming from above, filling the bridgecrew's nostrils and lungs. The XO turned and saw movement through the glass viewport of the auto-hatch. Shadows appeared, soon revealing enemy Grish warriors approaching with loud battle cries echoing in the Rotunda beyond.

She spotted Hardy out there, battle ravaged and not looking his best. Pristy suddenly sat forward, her eyes going wide. "Is that... Admiral Block out there... leading the charge?"

Davit said, "Been monitoring that. Looks like the Admiral and Hardy had hastily assembled a fire-team of Army and ship security personnel."

Pristy watched as they traded panicked fire with a line of pig-like forms who were now starting to fall back—step by step.

She silently thanked the Admiral and the ChronoBot, even if this was a temporary reprieve. But she knew this was, indeed, the end. A chill ran down her spine. She moved to take a seat within the Captain's Mount. There was little more she could do at this point.

Chen said, "Wait! The Grish ships—they're moving off... retreating!"

Pristy froze, daring to hope the comms crewman was right.

Sure enough, blinking icons on her tactical feed showed the enemy attack ships withdrawing en-masse from their prize —USS *Franklin*. "I don't understand. We're helpless here... what the hell are they playing at?"

Then she glimpsed something on the display— a familiar silhouette slicing rapidly into the fray. "Is that...?"

Chapter 46

HIP 938134 Star System
Craven-Class 550 *Off Worlder*
Captain Galvin Quintos

One hour earlier...

T he *Off Worlder* hung in the shadow of what was left of the RFS *Admiral Gorshkov*. Now seated next to Akari at the controls, I could feel her restlessness at being forced to move along at such a snail's pace.

"There!" I shouted.

"Yeah, I see it... the big white sphere called the Moon," she retorted with ample snark in her voice. "Sorry, Cap. Didn't mean to talk to you like that. Stress must be getting to me."

"No problem, but I wasn't talking about the big white sphere, I was talking about that reflective mass of metal, Halibart Station, off to the right of the Moon."

She nodded, checked her readouts, double-checked her display. "Okay, we're away from the bulk of Grish warships, the fighting. I think we can mosey on over to the station without being noticed."

"Do any throttling up here behind the *Admiral Gorshkov*. The last thing we want is the *Off Worlder's* fiery exhaust catching any of the piglet's eyes."

"Cap," she said, clearly losing patience with me, "not my first rodeo."

The *Off Worlder* raced toward Halibart Station, dodging debris and damaged ships as Akari deftly maneuvered the nimble craft. Up ahead, the massive station loomed. A metallic leviathan bristling with scaffolding and skeletal warships, it stood eerily silent.

WE TOUCHED DOWN IN A REMOTE LANDING bay, finding the area deserted. With our plasma weapons primed, senses sharp, the team of Marines and I disembarked.

Moving through a winding accordion-like space-way, we made it to an actual enclosed and atmosphere-maintained section of Halibart Station. Long diamond glass view ports provided panoramic views out to the shipyard; farther off, there was *Franklin* caught within the ensuing battle.

Snuffling grunts echoed through gloomy corridors as we spotted a company of Grish soldiers patrolling nearby. We hurried through twisting passageways on high alert, their own heavy hoof-falls masking our footsteps.

"There's our girl," Grip whispered, spotting the familiar broad-winged silhouette of *USS Lincoln*, nestled within her repair dock. But my heart sank as we drew nearer. Gaping wounds still marred her hull; whole sections disassembled into a metallic ribcage; her smooth exterior left scarred by jagged gashes. Once the embodiment of human ingenuity, now she was a shadow of her former glory. Despite the damage, I knew this old warhorse still had some fight in her—she just needed the right coaxing.

Max said, "We'll hang back, do what you have to do to buy you some time."

Aubrey and I hastened aboard, taking in our surroundings. Corridors had been left stripped of paneling with exposed beams and wiring. With main power offline, emergency lights cast an eerie, red pall across her ravaged interiors. I swallowed rising doubts. "Get to the Bridge; I'm off to Engineering and Propulsion," I told Aubrey.

"Wait! I don't know anything about getting a ship up and running."

Of course, she wouldn't know that. I needed to think but had little time to do so. I crossed my fingers behind my back and glanced up, "Sir Calvin... are you online?"

Nothing. And then the familiar British-accented voice boomed down from above:

Yes, Captain Quintos. I am very much online. How may I be of service?

"Ask and you shall receive," I said, looking to Aubrey. "Sir Calvin will help you every step of the way. With his help, you'll want to initiate getting all the main systems back online: Environmental, Helm control, Navigation, Tactical, Weapons... all of it. Ask for help. I'll be up there as soon as I can."

"Got it—access the bridge, initiate start up." She raced off to rouse the beast's dormant systems.

LINCOLN'S ENGINEERING AND PROPULSION section, once the throbbing pulse of the ship, was now dark and cold—tomb-like. Grimacing against the gloom, I began the process of throwing mechanical breakers and flipping manual switches that would trigger the ignition sequence—sequences that couldn't be initiated from the bridge. Circuits slowly flickered back to life as electronics seemed to groan under the sudden strain. "That's it, girl... time to wake up," I urged.

A sharp clatter spun me around. But it was only Max hustling in, steel in his eyes. "We got trouble brewing outside, Captain," Max warned, his tone urgent. "Looks like we've been detected. Got close to a hundred piglets incoming from every corner of the station."

I checked my TAC-Band—it was still twenty minutes until main drives would spin up to anything close to being operational. Usually hours were needed, but I'd implemented an emergency Fast-Start process. I looked to Max. "You need to buy us more time."

He offered up a crooked smile. "No problem, do what you have to do, Cap. Guess it's time for me and my team to start having some fun." And with that, he headed out, disappearing back into the same darkened corridor he'd arrived from.

AFTER FINISHING OFF AFT, I FOUND AUBREY ON the bridge arguing with Sir Calvin, as the two, seemingly, were struggling to kickstart the ship's dormant nervous system. Suddenly, the dim emergency lights gave way to the standard, and somewhat blinding, brightness of the bridge lights. Console boards flickered to life, and a multitude of projected displays sprouted upward like swiftly growing plant life.

Taking the Captain's Mount, my left hand went to the controls on the armrest. Years of training melded with muscle memory as I brought up the central halo display. Around me I heard more rudimentary sensors and readouts sputtering to life above consoles.

"Sir Calvin, get me optics and sound of *Lincoln's* outside perimeter."

The halo display segmented into four quadrants, each providing a different perspective of the raging battle between the Marines and Grish security forces. While Max and crew had the advantage of good shelter positions, they were ridiculously outnumbered. Their open comm's back-and-forth battle-smack blared. Max's voice rang out above the cacophony, "Stay down, Ham, I can see your fat ass from here!"

I watched as the squad scrambled, Wanda and Grip sprinting for new positions, shredder weapons spitting plasma bolts at the onrushing horde.

"Fried two more piggies!" Hock whooped. "Makin' bacon over here!" He lobbed a frag grenade, the explosion sending severed Grish limbs spiraling.

I watched as Wanda sighted down her plasma rifle, picking off piglets with ruthless efficiency. "Headshot!" She bellowed, as another piglet's skull erupted. "And scratch one more snout-face."

More Grish reinforcements stormed from an adjacent catwalk, nearly overwhelming Ham's position. His shredder blazed for what seemed an eternity before overheating. He tossed it away and grabbed his tagger pistol. "Shit, they're rushing in like rats on a sinking ship!" he yelled. The Marine continued firing into their midst, downing two piglets at point-blank range... two that had gotten past his earlier onslaught.

"Ham, fall the hell back!" Max ordered. But his severed scream over comms... was too late.

I took in Ham's slumped, unmoving shape behind one of the makeshift barricades.

"Ham!" Hock yelled in anguish. With a savage roar he broke from cover, shredder raging on full auto taking out a half dozen before the piglets' return-fire peppered his combat suit.

"Hock is down!" Wanda reported grimly.

But... I saw he wasn't. Shot, yes, but he was limping away, taking cover behind an outcropping of *Lincoln's* hull.

Max said, "Relax, Wanda. Check your HUD... he's still sucking oxygen... as is Ham, but he's not in good shape."

Wanda was already sighting down on her next target. "Still... I want these bastards to pay!"

Plasma fire blazed.

Grip tossed another frag grenade. "Fried pork belly, anyone?" He raised his shredder and fired; a relentless onslaught that brought the Grish security forces to a standstill. "You piglets goin' chicken?"

Overhead within the bridge, Sir Calvin's sudden announcement made me jump:

Ship primary systems are functional, Captain. Main propulsion drives on-line.

"Sergeant, pull back! Pull back. Collect your injured and get back on the ship—we're clearing out of here in one minute."

"Copy that, Cap," Max said.

"Music to my ears," Wanda added. "Took you long enough."

I leaned back and released a long breath.

Aubrey retracted her helmet and shook out her lustrous auburn hair. Christ, does every little action the woman makes have to be so enticing?

Captain, the Marines are onboard. All ship entry points secured.

Distant-sounding explosions suddenly rocked the ship.

"Piglets are attempting to breach!" Aubrey yelled.

I moved over to the Helm station, got myself situated behind the controls. It had been a while since I'd piloted a warship of this size.

Aubrey must have observed my hesitancy, and said, "Just like riding a bike, right? You never forget... why don't you show me how it's done."

Her sly smile kindled renewed confidence. My fingers moved over the board with purpose as the ship's massive drives ramped up—deckplates rattled under the abrupt strain.

Up on the halo display we watched as *USS Lincoln* tore free from her moorings, sparks and small explosions erupted the whole length of the station's superstructure.

I winced, "Guess I should have released those grappling clamps beforehand, huh?"

"There again, you just took out a shitload of little Grish fuckers," Aubrey said with a laugh.

I maneuvered the dreadnought away from Halibart Station and out into the void. "Hey, what do you say we go make some noise?" I said with a smirk.

Aubrey raised a provocative brow.

"Get your mind out of the gutter, Petty Officer. I meant, as in blazing railguns and phazon pulsars."

She took a seat at the Captain's Mount, gripped the armrests. "I could get used to sitting here." She sat up straight, and said, "Helm, how about you show me what this warship is capable of."

Chapter 47

HIP 938134 Star System
USS Lincoln
Captain Galvin Quintos

Present time...

I followed the Petty Officer's lead and retracted my own helmet, breathed in *Lincoln's* stuffy recirculating air. A series of small lights started to blink over on the Comms Station.

"I'm on it," Aubrey said. "Comms are the one thing I know how to work on this bridge." Plopping down into the seat, she made a few quick taps. "We're being hailed, Captain."

"Franklin?"

"Uh, no." she grimaced, "It's Akari James."

I slapped my head for the second time that day. "On display."

Lips pursed and making a spiteful face that almost made me

laugh, Akari stared back at me. "So... what? You just leave me here? Hit the road, forget about the date that brought you to the dance?"

"My bad, Lieutenant. Best you hightail it away from that station. Whatever piglets are still snorting... they'll be looking for blood."

"Already fast on your tail. Just wanted to give you a little shit."

Aubrey cut the connection.

Up ahead the battle raged. Dozens of Grish warships were pounding what seemed now a totally adrift *USS Franklin*. What return fire the once magnificent omninought was making, was sporadic and limited. What we were witnessing were the last death throes of a ship.

"Give me a second." Aubrey had moved over to the Tactical. "It looks like we have all phazon pulsars and several minimally functional railgun cannons. Targeting that closest battle cruiser." She glanced over to me. "And yeah, I'm about to make some real noise."

The halo display flashed with multiple streaks of *Lincoln's* vivid plasma fire. A row of fiery explosions dotted the flank of the distant battle cruiser.

Wanda hurried onto the bridge out of breath. "How can I help?"

"Get on Comms," I said. "How's Ham and Hock?"

Wanda took her seat. "In HealthBay being attended to by a MediBot." She worked the board. "Reaching out to *Franklin*."

XO Pristy's stunned, dismayed face stared back at me from the halo display. "Captain?"

"Yeah, sorry for the delay," I said. "Situation Report, XO."

"There is no situation, the ship is overrun with Grish piglets, all ship systems have either failed, or will within minutes, including propulsion. The handful of weapons still operational are pathetically inefficient."

"And how are the boys doing in Bay 3?"

"Stephan says it's as ready as it can be. But there's a problem. A big problem."

"Tell me."

"Derrota and Coogong aren't 100% sure how to operate it. Sure, the Ilion gave them the basics, but according to Stephan... they're not so sure how to proceed."

"Christ, are you kidding me?" I snapped back.

"We're being swarmed," Aubrey interjected sounding in over her head.

With a glance to the tactical display, I saw way too many approaching Cyclone Death fighters to count.

I put my attention back to Pristy, my mind spinning. "Okay, here's what I want you to do..." It took me several minutes to lay out the details.

Afterward, she looked at me as if I had two heads. She scanned *Franklin's* bridge still taking in what I had proposed. "Fine, but we'd have to do it in stages."

"Yeah, and stage one... you and I swap places. Like right now."

"No, phase one, we quansport every Grish invader off *Franklin* out into the void."

I nodded; I should have thought of that myself.

She glanced upward. "You got all that SARAH? You're on quansporting duty until further notice."

Yes, XO Pristy. Got it.

Pristy closed her eyes for several beats, then looked back at me. "Okay, let's do this." She cut the connection.

· · ·

PRISTY'S ASSESSMENT WAS ACCURATE; *USS Franklin* had become little more than a derelict husk drifting through the void. However, the omninought possessed one significant advantage—a still intact and fully operational SARAH. The AI would maintain what few remaining shipwide systems that were still operational, including that crucial quansporting capability.

I stood and readied myself.

Before Wanda and Aubrey could even look up, I was gone from *Lincoln's* bridge.

I now stood on the bridge of *Franklin*, and if all had unfolded according to our plan, XO Pristy would be on the bridge of *Lincoln*, prepared to assume command of the only fully operational allied warship in the star system.

"Uh... welcome aboard, Captain," Grimes said from Helms.

I took in the harried-looking bridgecrew. The space still smelled like barf and rancid smoke.

"Everyone, prepare for immediate quansport over to *Lincoln*. You'll be the first group to head on over."

Blank faces stared back at me.

"That ship...it's pretty old technology," Davitt said. "Not sure I'll know how to work the board—"

"You'll adapt," I interrupted, my tone firm. "That ship is now Earth's last hope. When you reach the bridge, take your positions and start your tasks. But remember, your mission is no longer about engaging Grish assets; it's about keeping the enemy occupied and diverted while the few of us remaining on *Franklin* work to restore Earth to its rightful place."

I looked to Grimes, was about to tell him he'd be the first to go, but he'd already quansported away in a series of quick segmenting flashes—leaving his seat suddenly empty. I looked to the gobsmacked others. "Good luck, everybody." I spun around and headed for the still-closed exit. With a quick look through the diamond glass window, I saw that the Rotunda was quiet, only the dead from a hard-fought battle remained. "SARAH, open the bridge auto-hatch."

As the hatch swooshed open to one side, behind me, I heard the telltale sounds of quansporting taking place within the bridge.

I BURST OUT OF DECK 18'S DECKPORT IN A FULL sprint, making a beeline for HealthBay. The corridor was a chaotic scene, with unsuspecting crewmembers abruptly vanishing mid-stride, whisked away like apparitions. The eerie, blue flashes of quansport energy adding to the confusion and casting ghostly reflections on the nearby bulkheads.

Hurrying into HealthBay, I found it was in the midst of the same I'd recently witnessed on the bridge... bed-ridden patients suddenly disappearing while bedcovers deflated. Overhead rotating medical avatars seemingly disoriented, their movements faltering at their patient's sudden disappearance.

"Captain!"

It was the voice of Admiral Block; he must have been injured during the Grish invasion. He tried to sit up, raising a hand to signal me, only to disappear in a series of rapid, compartmentalized flares.

I turned to see Wallace Ryder coming out of the RegrowPod compartment. A partially regrown stump of an arm hung useless at his side. "What the hell's going on?" He gestured back to the RegrowPods.

All the clamshells were open, several other patients attempting to crawl out.

"We're swapping ships, Wallace. Trust me, it'll be okay." I smiled just in time for him to quansport away.

I wasn't here to make small talk. I rushed through the auto-hatch doors leading to the back offices, exam rooms, and surgical bays. Three strides in, I ran headlong into Doc Viv, catching her around the hips just as she was about to topple over.

"Dammit Quintos, what the hell is happening! Why are my patients energizing out of my HealthBay?"

I thought about reminding her it wasn't her HealthBay any longer, but instead, asked, "Where's Slop?"

"Slop?"

"Um, Fleet Commander Sorlen Op?"

Befuddled, she pointed to the nearest exam room. "The little shit's in there. Did you know he tried to bite me?"

I was already heading for auto-hatch, but it didn't open.

"Let me," Viv barked. "He needed to be secured." She tapped at a nearby key-pad—the auto-hatch slid open. Darting inside, I found the bed empty. Fists clenched I wanted to punch something. The empty bed, the bulkhead—anything.

"Calm down, Quintos, he's up there!" Viv said pointing an accusing finger toward the overhead.

Sure enough, the Varapin Fleet Commander was watching us from the high ceiling. Clearly, Viv's surgical prowess had proved to be unmatched. He was as boyant as he ever was.

"Get down here, Slop. We have to go."

"No."

"What do you mean, no?"

"I'm convalescing."

"You can convalesce later. For right now, you're keeping your end of the bargain." I leaped, tried to grab hold of the Varapin's bathrobe but he was too high. I turned to ask Viv if she had a ladder but saw that she was gone. Undoubtedly, she was already now within *Lincoln's* HealthBay.

I said, "Let me ask you, Fleet Commander Sorlen Op. Do you want to live?"

"A stupid question."

"How about this... Do you want your vile species to survive? To endure that genetic curse that is plaguing your kind?"

His glowing eyes stared down at me.

"We've done it. We met with the Ilion, with their scientist and we have the cure."

"You lie. Humans are devious and treacherous."

"Why in God's name would I be in here wasting precious minutes while the Grish eviscerates this ship?"

I saw indecision flash upon the alien's face.

"I need your help with the QSER platform. You do know how to operate the thing, right?"

I took his hesitation as a *maybe*. "Come on, let's get out of here before the ship implodes around us." I reached out a hand, "Come on, dammit, I'm giving you what you wanted."

Slowly, far too slowly, Slop descended while keeping a wary eye on me. "This better not be a trick."

As soon as the ghoul was within arm's reach, I thrust out a hand and grabbed him around his boney neck. The Varapin instantly thrashed, sharp clawed digits tearing into my forearm. I gritted my molars and tightened my grip. He went rigid, struggling to breath.

"I'll loosen my grip if you promise to behave."

We stared at each other for several seconds.

"I will behave," the Varapin's voice little more than a croak.

A heavy shadow fell across the two of us from behind. I turned, ready to face whatever had come to make my shitty day just a little shittier... but was happy to see it was Hardy. Or what was left of Hardy.

His chrome-plating was a mass of charred and pitted craters. A horizontal crack segmented his face display. His shoulder mounted plasma canon, now limp and drooping.

"I guess you've had better days," I said. "Can I take it you took care of Climbo?"

"Climbo is fine. General Graves... not so much."

"Good to hear." I held out Slop's dangling form to Hardy. Take him. He's turning my forearm into ground beef. Don't let go of him."

Chapter 48

The three of us arrived at Flight Bay 3 in time to see four of the Army security team suddenly disappear in simultaneous blocky, blue bursts of light.

Both Derrota and Coogong looked exhausted, seated with their backs up against a bulkhead.

I stepped closer to the open bay where an aqua-hued energy field was holding the extreme conditions of deep space outside.

I looked back at Derrota who was slowly getting to his feet. "Please tell me this thing is fully operational."

Derrota and Coogong exchanged a look. "Yes, Galvin," Derrota said. "It is at least as operational as we can make it." He looked to the Varapin, wincing at Hardy's tight grip around his neck.

Coogong now approached the prisoner, peered up at Hardy. "Please, let the Fleet Commander go. It is not in his interest to escape."

Hardy looked to me for approval. Reluctantly, I nodded.

Unencumbered, the Varapin rose high enough he would be out of reach, even for Hardy.

"Coogong, please explain what we are doing. Tell the Fleet

Commander how his ilk no longer needs to fear a slow and steady extinction," I urged.

It took far longer than I felt we had time for. But an hour later Coogong with his endless patience and kindness, had gone through every aspect of the complex science involved in creating a viable vaccine. He'd divulged enough molecular genetic specifics that the Varapin would have little doubt as to its authenticity.

Now, as Slop floated above us, taking in all the work that had been done to the platform, he turned his gaze back to me. "What you want in return, Captain... that is a very big ask."

"We're offering to save your entire worthless species! Are you kidding me?"

"And in return, we'll be saving yours, as well, no?"

I waved away his comment. "Look, I need two things from you, or I'm going to toss you right through that bay opening and watch you die. One, right now, you're going to assure me the war between Varapin, and humans is over. Forever. Secondly, you will assist us in restoring Earth, the Moon, and all the space in between, to its previous state before your ruthless assault on my world."

The flight bay went quiet while we waited. No one moved, no one so much as took a breath.

"Agreed," Slop finally croaked.

It was another full hour before Derrota, Coogong, and Slop had made the necessary alterations to the QSER platform. A control panel had been exposed in the process that neither Coogong nor Derrota had known even existed. I silently cursed the Ilion. What else had they failed to mention?

Did I have absolute certainty that Slop was truly aiding us? No, but if he wasn't, it would undoubtedly lead to a mutual demise.

And then it was time. With Hardy helping to release the supporting straps, we found that the platform floated, anti-grav generators having kicked in.

Local space was relatively clear. Far off in the distance, I saw USS *Lincoln* out there causing mayhem for the dwindling, but still substantial, fleet of Grish warships. I had to smile. My eyes fell upon Earth... bright blue and heart-stoppingly beautiful. Am I about to deliver her into oblivion? Maybe I should just let things be...

I looked to Derrota, Coogong, and then Hardy. "I guess we're ready."

"It's about time," Hardy said.

"What do you say we send this thing out of here together," I suggested.

Derrota, at the control panel, entered one last set of commands before stepping back.

The four of us each placed our hands upon the QSER platform, getting ready to shove it out through the open bay. Slop descended from above, joining the effort, even if it was only symbolically.

I said, "On three. One... two... Push!"

MINUTES LATER, STANDING SHOULDER-TO-shoulder, we observed the platform in the distance, its multiple softly glowing crystals flickering and diminishing in size. It brought to mind a Viking farewell for the departed—a raft constructed from branches, set ablaze to eventually merge with the sea.

We waited as the final seconds wound down to either a

rebirth or a final catastrophe. Either way, I was good with it. *What will be will be...*

HIP 938134, the system's cold and utterly impersonal star, suddenly brightened, its blinding glare enough to cause each of us to shield our eyes and look away.

The ensuing flash was brilliant, penetrating even through my closed eyelids, casting the silhouette of my finger-bones upon them. They say that no sounds can pierce the oppressive stillness of space, but there was a thunderous *CRACK!* as deafening as any shotgun blast.

When I opened my eyes, I blinked away the lingering flash bulb effects. And then I saw it... nothing had changed. Earth was right where it had been. As was the Moon. As was the graveyard of broken and fractured warships still lingering like carcasses of the dead. My heart feeling heavy, I let out the breath I'd been holding and looked to Derrota. So why was he smiling? Has the man gone mad?

"Look Galvin... the Sun. That's our Sun. We're home!"

Thank you for reading USS Franklin — When Worlds Collide. If you enjoyed this book, PLEASE leave a review on Amazon.com—it really helps! Want more? GOOD NEWS! The sequel, USS Washington - The Black Ship, Book 9 and USS IKE - Quansport Ops, Book 10 in the series are available NOW on Amazon.com

To be notified the moment all future books are released, please join my mailing list. I hate spam and will never ever share your information. Jump to this link to sign up:

http://eepurl.com/bs7M9r

Acknowledgments

Acknowledgments

First and foremost, I am grateful to the fans of my writing and their ongoing support for all my books. I'd like to thank my wife, Kim—she's my rock and is a crucial, loving component of my publishing business. I'd like to thank my mother, Lura Genz, for her tireless work as my first-phase creative editor and a staunch cheerleader of my writing. Others who provided fantastic support include Lura & James Fischer, Sue Parr, Charles Duell, and Stuart Church.

Check out my other available titles on the page that follows About the Author.

About the Author

Mark grew up on both coasts, first in Westchester County, New York, and then in Westlake Village, California. Mark and his wife, Kim, now live in Castle Rock, Colorado, with their two dogs, Sammi, and Lilly.

Mark started as a corporate marketing manager and then fell into indie-filmmaking—Producing/Directing the popular Gaia docudrama, 'Openings — The Search for Harry'.

For the last nine years, he's been writing full-time, and with over 40 top-selling novels under his belt, he has no plans on slowing down. Thanks for being part of his community!

Also by
Mark Wayne McGinnis

The Simpleton Series

The Simpleton (Book 1)

The Simpleton Quest (Book 2)

Galaxy Man

Ship Wrecked Series

Ship Wrecked (Book 1)

Ship Wrecked II (Book 2)

Ship Wrecked III (Book 3)

<u>Boy Gone</u>

Boy Gone / the expanded Anniversary Edition

Cloudwalkers

The Hidden Ship

Guardian Ship

Gun Ship

HOVER

Heroes and Zombies

The Test Pilot's Wife

Junket: Untamed Alien Worlds

The Fallen Ship Series

The Fallen Ship: Rise of the Gia Rebellion (Book 1)

The Fallen Ship II (Book 2)

-

USS Hamilton Series

USS Hamilton: Ironhold Station (Book 1)

USS Hamilton: Miasma Burn (Book 2)

USS Hamilton: Broadsides (Book 3)

USS Hamilton: USS Jefferson –

Charge of the Symbios (Book 4)

USS Hamilton: Starship Oblivion –

Sanctuary Outpost (Book 5)

USS Hamilton: USS Adams – No Escape (Book 6)

USS Hamilton: USS Lincoln – Mercy Kill (Book 7)

USS Hamilton: USS Franklin - When Worlds Collide (Book 8)

USS Hamilton: USS Washington - The Black Ship (Book 9)

USS Hamilton: USS IKE – Quansport Ops (Book 10)

ChronoBot Chronicles

Printed in Great Britain
by Amazon